CHRIS̲ ... ue,
Sha̲ Shet̲ ... rse
infl̲ ... she ̲ .014
an̲ .u̲7. Her poetry collections have won several awards over
the years and her poems, much anthologised, have been translated
into many other languages. She enjoys creative collaborations, most
recently with artists Victoria Crowe (*Another Time, Another Place,*
Scottish Gallery, 2021) and Brigid Collins, and with musicians
Tommy Smith and Catriona Macdonald. *The Trials of Mary
Johnsdaughter* is her second novel.

By the same author

Poetry Collections
Veeve, Mariscat Press, Edinburgh, 2021
The Art of Poetry & Other Poems, (Translations), Hansel Co-operative Press, Orkney, 2021
Edinburgh: Singing the City, Saltire Society, Edinburgh, 2017
Dat Trickster Sun, Mariscat Press, Edinburgh (pamphlet), 2014
North End of Eden, Luath Press, Edinburgh, 2010
Parallel Worlds, Luath Press, Edinburgh, 2005
Drops in Time's Ocean, Hansel Co-operative Press, Orkney (pamphlet), 2004
Plain Song, The Shetland Library, Lerwick, 2002
Wast Wi Da Valkyries, The Shetland Library, Lerwick, 1997
Voes and Sounds, The Shetland Library, Lerwick, 1994

Bilingual volumes of poetry
Northern Alchemy, Shetlandic poems with English versions, Patrician Press, Essex – Selected, 2020
Glimt av opphav – Glims o Origin (with Odd Goksøyr), Ura Forlag, Norway – New & Selected, 2017
Heimferðir – Haemfarins (with Aðalsteinn Ásberg Sigurðsson), Dimma, Reykjavik, Iceland – Selected, 2017
Questo sole furfante (with Francesca Romana Paci), Nuova Trauben, Turin, Italy – translated collection, 2015
Mondes Parallèles (with Jean-Paul Blot), éditions fédérop (France), 2007

Fiction
And then forever, Shetland Times, Lerwick, 2011

Children's storybooks
Grotti-Buckie an Tirli-Wirli, Shetland Times, Lerwick, 2021
Smootie an da Toon Hall Clock, Hansel Co-operative Press, Orkney, 2010
Smootie comes ta Lerrick, Hansel Co-operative Press, Orkney, 2005

Translations of storybooks for children
Da Trow, Itchy Coo with Black & White Publishing, Edinburgh, 2016
The Shetland Gruffalo's Bairn, Itchy Coo with Black & White Publishing, Edinburgh, 2016
Dodie's Phenomenal Pheesic, Hansel Co-operative Press, Orkney, 2008

The Trials of Mary Johnsdaughter

CHRISTINE DE LUCA

Luath Press Limited

EDINBURGH

www.luath.co.uk

Falkirk Council	
30124 03167022 9	
Askews & Holts	
AF	£9.99
MK	

First published 2022

ISBN: 978-1-910022-56-6

The author's right to be identified as author of this book
under the Copyright, Designs and Patents Act 1988 has been asserted.

The paper used in this book is recyclable. It is made
from low chlorine pulps produced in a low energy,
low emissions manner from renewable forests.

Printed and bound by
Severnprint Ltd., Gloucestershire

Typeset in 10.5 point Sabon LT Pro by
Main Point Books, Edinburgh

Maps by Robert Wishart

This novel is dedicated to all the pupils, past and present, who have attended Happyhansel School, Waas, Shetland, and to their teachers.

It is also dedicated to the memory of our parents, Alexander & Jemima Pearson, who both loved teaching at Happyhansel.

Contents

Characters   8

Dear Reader...   12

Foretochts   13

Prologue   15

The Trials of Mary Johnsdaughter   17

Postscript   249

Glossary of Shetland dialect words and phrases   253

Sources   264

Acknowledgements   271

MAPS

Waas and environs   10–11

Shetland parishes   18

Journey of the *Batchelor of Leith*   121

Mary Johnsdaughter's Journey from Waas to
Lerwick and return   192–3

Characters

The Johnson family of Brunatwatt (real characters but some of the storyline is necessarily fictionalised)
Joannie Johnson – crofter and Far Haaf fisherman
Baabie Johnson (fictional name) – crofter and knitter, his wife
John Johnson – son
Jerome (Jaerm) Johnson (fictional) – son
Jean Johnsdaughter – daughter
Mary Johnsdaughter – daughter
Christian Johnsdaughter – daughter

Waas notables
Rev James Buchan, Voe House (recent widower) – parish minister and heritor
Jane Scott, née Henry – widow of previous laird, lives in Vaila Hall
John Scott (b1760) – boy laird, son of Jane Scott
John T Henry of Forratwatt and Bayhaa – local heritor and merchant-trader, owns a sloop, the *Hawk*
Margaret Henry, née Scott – his wife, (aunt of boy laird)
Thomas Henry of Scord and Burrastow – local heritor and merchant

Happyhansel schoolhouse
George Greig – headmaster and session clerk (recent widower)
Archibald (Erchie) Greig – son of George, helps as assistant teacher
John Jeems – neighbouring crofter who assists Greigs (fictional)
Leebie – his wife, neighbouring crofter who assists Greigs (fictional)

Friends of Mary
Jaanie Jeromson, Stove – local howdie (midwife) (fictional)
Walter Jeromson, widowed son of Jaanie, Stove – merchant seaman (fictional)
Willm Jeromson, Stove – young son of Walter (fictional)

Friends of Jean
Sophia Henderson from Delting; also friendly with David Bain
Margaret and Christian Morison from Stove
Margaret Irvineson from Stennestwatt
Agnes Sletter from Stove
Bess Sletter from Forratwatt

Ann Johnsdaughter from Whitesness
Helen Fullertown from Whitesness

The *Batchelor of Leith*
Mr Inglis – *Leith* owner
Captain Ramage
Thomas Liddle – Mate
Alexander Ross – ship's carpenter
John Shanks
James Bennet
Alexander Shaw
David Currie
Philip Stephenson
Charles Jolly
David Watters

**Other incomers, mainly emigrants on the *Batchelor of Leith*, from Caithness and Sutherland
(real people, but some detail fictionalised)**
David Bain – labourer, working in Shetland, originally from Caithness
James Hogg – emigrant, organiser of the emigration to North Carolina, billeted at Haa of Saand
Eliza McDonald – emigrant, servant, billeted with the Johnsons at Brunatwatt
Willie McLeod – emigrant, tenant farmer, from Sutherland, billeted with Jaanie Jeromson at Stove
Katie McLeod – emigrant, his wife
Alexander MacKay – emigrant, tenant farmer, billeted at Mid-Waas
Patrick Ross – emigrant, schoolteacher, billeted at Happyhansel schoolhouse

Other locals
Mr & Mrs Hughson (fictional) – Alex Ross is billeted with them at Stove
William Deyell – from the neighbouring croft, Gröntö, near Brunatwatt
James Ollason – church officer
Miss Agatha Cumming

Other Shetland gentry or notables
William Balfour – Deputy Vice-Admiral of Shetland
Sir John Mitchell of Westshore, Scalloway and Sand Haa
Arthur Nicolson of Lochend, Northmavine

WAAS AND ENVIRONS

STOORBURGH HILL

To Dale o Waas

Uphoose

Finnigart

Mid Waas

Trölligart

VOE O FOOTABROUGH

Scarvister

Breck

Scord

Burrastow

0	1000	2000	3000	4000	5000	5280 Feet

0	1/4	1/2	3/4	1 Mile

Scale: Two Inches to 1 Mile

WASTER S

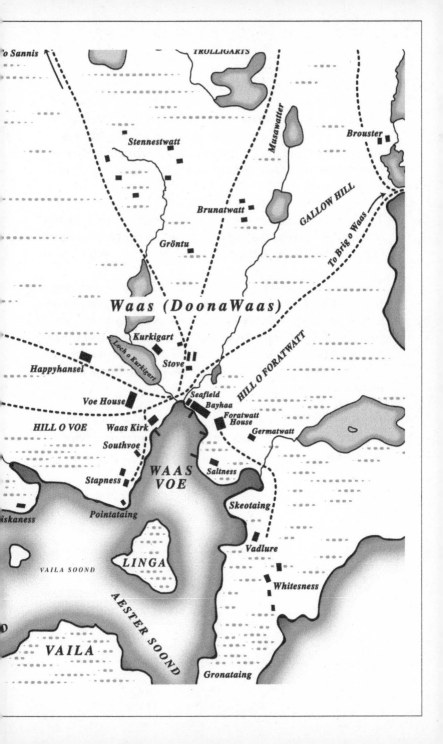

Dear Reader...

This story is set a quarter of a millennium ago in a small Shetland township local people called Waas. Yes, life was different then, but are we not made of the same stuff, with similar sentiments to our forebears? We even speak in much the same way.

The broad narrative of this tale is documented in parish and other records. Almost all of the characters existed; but much is imagined and the dialogue is fictional.

Your patience is sought with the Shetland way of speaking. It is impossible to impose a foreign tongue on speakers talking with their families and neighbours. In those days, they would have faced derision for knapping! However, they will speak English where they must. Even shoe-horning the narration – let alone their private thoughts – into English feels like sacrilege.

But first, perhaps a mild indulgence by way of a prologue? Skip it if you must; there is an English translation a little further on...

Foretochts

DEY WIR BÖN ten parteeclarly grim years in Shetland: gales an caald wadder, an crops no ripenin. Fock said hit cam eftir da 'black snaa'. Fishermen said dat cam fae Iceland. Dey wir spaek o emigration.

Da parish o Waas wisna muckle different fae idder places in Shetland in da 1770s, wi maist fock livin affa da laand an da sea, maistlins fae haand ta mooth. Hit wis haem ta twartree hunder fock, but a bit o a backwatter wi a undertow o secrets an scandals. Hit wis hard ta say whedder da laird an heritors hüld da ropps, or da kirk, fur dey wir dat weel spliced tagidder.

As you cam wast, wan peerie clim owre da Gallow Hill an Waas wid come inta view wi da isles o Linga an Vaila keepin da Atlantic at bay. Mony a ship fan shalter dere i da bosie o da parish, atween da Aester an da Waster Soond, atween da Hill o Foratwatt an da Hill o Voe.

Da croft-hooses aroond da voe wis maistlins low an taekit, wi a byre-end an maybe a barn forbye. Alang baith da aest side an da wast side o da voe – wi Germatwatt an Skeotaing luikin across da watter ta Stapness an Pointataing – dey wir strippit rigs: some years you got da staney rig or da steep een or da rig fardest fae da ebb wi hits arles o tang, but hit wis aa fairly pairtit. Some crofts wis peerier as idders but aye a coo or twa dat dey could pit tae da hill i da simmer time. Maist crofters fished tae da laird as pairt o der tenancy – der boats wid a bön lyin aff if hit wis fair wadder, or poo'd up abön da ebb if hit wis coorse.

An dey wir idder biggins dat wid a catcht da eye. Bayhaa for wan, staandin prood ithin a huddle o cotters' hooses at Seafield, near da head o da voe. Hit wis a sombre haa wi tree storeys an eicht windows tae da front. Luikin oot ony o dat windows da Mistress o Bayhaa could see da isle o Vaila, da saet o her ain fock, da Scotts, da local laird. But Mistress Margaret wis a Scott nae langer; shö wis mairried wi John Thomas Henry o Foratwatt. He wis a laand-owner or heritor, an hed a tradin sloop caa'd da *Hawk*. Ivery voe he slippit inta, boats wid bring him whit he wis oardered: barrels o fish oil or butter; bales o oo or dried fish.

An wha could a missed Happyhansel, da brand new scöl an scölhoose, sittin prunk apö da Hill o Voe? Or, alang da hill, set in hits ain toons sweepin doon da brae tae a pier, da terrace o hooses an da braa gairden belangin ta da Reverend James Buchan? Da widower Buchan wis bön mairried inta da land-ownin Foratwatt Henrys an aa. He wis da second husband o Margaret Bruce. Shö wis come wi a lang pedigree fae Muness Castle in Unst whaar her faider was Vice-Steward o Shetland. Laandit faemlies hed a wye o keepin a hadd o da money: nae doot shö wis hed a braa coarn.

But James Buchan wis brunt oot wi years o wark ta establish da new scöl in Waas an tryin ta keep da fock on da straicht an nairrow whin hit wis clear dat da gaet ta perdition wis a lock aesier ta traivel. Lately, since he had nae direct heir, he wis bön trang wi da legal transfer o his property ta someen at wid accept, as a burden in perpetuity, dat pairt o hit – includin da scöl an scölhoose – wid be fur da use o whaaivver wis appointit as scölmester.

Da boannie daals o Mid Waas an Dale o Waas lay wast-owre. Sannis an da farder isles o Papa an Foula wis aa pairt o Buchan's parish, quieter dan Waas maybe at a first glance, but nae doot jöst as foo o stories an intrigue. Dey wir hardly a week at gud by ithoot a meetin o da kirk session ta hear o some pre-nuptial relations or fornicatin. Hit wis rife. An noo dey wir a rumour o adultery ta deal wi; a capital offence.

But dis isna jöst a story aboot da lairds or da merchants an idder heritors, nor aboot da meenisters or da scöl-mesters... although nae doot dey will aa play der pairt.

Prologue

THERE HAD BEEN ten particularly grim years in Shetland: gales and cold weather and crops not ripening. Folk said it came after the 'black snow'. Fishermen said that came from Iceland. There was much talk of emigration.

The parish of Waas (Walls) wasn't very different from other places in Shetland in the 1770s, with most folk living off the land and the sea, mainly from hand to mouth. It was home to a few hundred folk, but something of a backwater with an undertow of secrets and scandals. It was hard to say whether the laird and heritors held the ropes, or the church, for they were so well spliced together.

As you came west, one gentle climb over the Gallow Hill would slowly reveal Waas, with the isles of Linga and Vaila keeping the Atlantic at bay. Many a ship found shelter there in the bosom of the parish, between the Eastern and the Western Sound, between the Hill of Foratwatt and the Hill of Voe.

The croft-houses were mainly low and thatched, with a byre-end and maybe a barn as well. Along both the east side and the west side of the inlet, the voe – with Germatwatt and Skeotaing looking across the water to Stapness and Pointataing – there were narrow strips of fields: some years you got the stony strip or the steep one or the strip furthest from the shoreline with its timely gifts of seaweed, but it was all fairly shared out. Some crofts were smaller than others, but there was always a cow or two which they could graze on the common hill pasture in the summer time. Most crofters fished for the laird as part of their tenancy – their boats could be seen anchored in the inlet if it was fair weather, or pulled up above the shore if it was stormy.

And there were other buildings that would have caught your eye. Bayhall for one, standing tall among a huddle of cotters' houses at Seafield, near the head of the inlet. It was a sombre hall of three storeys with eight windows at the front. Looking out through any of those windows, the Mistress of Bayhall could see the isle of Vaila, the seat of her own Scott family, the local laird. But Mistress Margaret was no longer a Scott; she was married to John Thomas Henry of Foratwatt. He was a land-owner or heritor, and had a trading sloop called the *Hawk*. Every inlet he slipped into, boats would bring him what he had ordered: barrels of fish oil or butter; bales of wool or dried fish.

And who could have missed Happyhansel, the brand new school and schoolhouse sitting proud on the Hill of Voe? Or, along the hill, set in its own fields sweeping down the slope to a pier, the terrace of houses and the fine walled garden belonging to the Reverend James Buchan? The widower Buchan had been married into the land-owning Foratwatt Henrys too. He was the second husband of Margaret Bruce. She had come with a long pedigree from Muness Castle in Unst where her father was Vice-Steward of Shetland. Landed families had a way of keeping a hold of the money: no doubt hers was a goodly share.

But James Buchan was burned out with years of work to establish the new school in Waas and trying to keep his parishioners on the straight and narrow when it was clear that the path to perdition was much easier to walk. Lately, since he had no direct heir, he had been occupied with the legal transfer of his property to someone who would accept, as a burden in perpetuity, that part of it – including the school and schoolhouse – would be for the use of whoever was appointed as schoolmaster.

The lovely valleys of Mid Waas and Dale o Waas lay further west. Sandness and the more remote isles of Papa and Foula were all part of Buchan's parish; quieter than Waas, maybe, at a first glance, but no doubt just as full of stories and intrigue. Hardly a week went past without a meeting of the kirk session to hear of some pre-nuptial relations or fornicating. It was rife. And now there was a rumour of adultery to deal with; a capital offence.

But this isn't just a story about the lairds or the merchants and other heritors, nor about the ministers or the school-masters... although no doubt they will all play their part.

The Trials of Mary Johnsdaughter

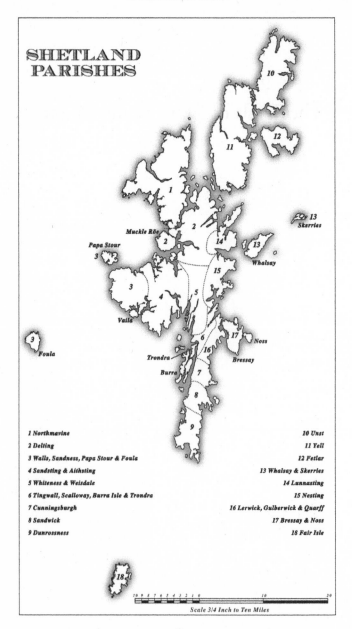

SHETLAND PARISHES

1 Northmavine
2 Delting
3 Walls, Sandness, Papa Stour & Foula
4 Sandsting & Aithsting
5 Whiteness & Weisdale
6 Tingwall, Scalloway, Burra Isle & Trondra
7 Cunningsburgh
8 Sandwick
9 Dunrossness

10 Unst
11 Yell
12 Fetlar
13 Whalsay & Skerries
14 Lunnasting
15 Nesting
16 Lerwick, Gulberwick & Quarff
17 Bressay & Noss
18 Fair Isle

Scale 3/4 Inch to Ten Miles

Monday 13th September 1773
Happyhansel

George Greig, teacher and session clerk in the parish of Waas, had his head in his hands. A hairst sun was dipping in the west, casting a final evening glow through the schoolhouse at Happyhansel, high on the slope above the Loch o Kurkigart. He was exhausted after a day of drilling pupils and then attending the unexpected kirk session meeting. Now he had the minutes to write up. He had found from years of experience that it was best to tackle it sooner rather than later, while still fresh in the memory.

His son Erchie had attended to all his chores, mostly related to the six boys – the school-boarders – now safely in their beds upstairs. He was a blessing to the old man, especially after the loss of Maggie, his wife of nearly twenty years. The two men, despite the years separating them, had grown closer in their mutual loss and now in their shared endeavour with the new school.

So how could he write this up? It was the usual agenda – fornication. Or perhaps worse. Would folk never learn continence and propriety? It seemed to him that this particular case, this David Bain, was an arrogant young man. He had come to the session meeting to admit fathering the child newly born to Sophia Henderson, currently lodging with Jaanie Jeromson at Stove, and to seek infant baptism. He seemed to lack any sense of wrong-doing or remorse.

When asked, Bain had said he was a quarryman from Caithness by way of Orkney, and had worked for many of the Shetland lairds and merchants: Bruce of Sumburgh, Scott of Scalloway, James Hay of Nesting, Sir John Nicolson of Sandsting, Gifford of Bustae; and yes, that he had indeed brought testimonies of his good character from the minister and session clerk of the parish of Bower in his home County. He promised to submit the testimonies as soon as possible. Currently, the papers were in Delting, in the north of Shetland, where last he lodged. Or so he had said.

George had felt an unease among the elders as Bain had confirmed that his wife had died two years previously, soon after he had left Caithness to find work in Shetland; and no, he didn't have their only child with him. He had agreed that he would also submit to session the relevant letter from his brother; the one which told him of her death. He shamelessly admitted to fathering Sophia's child, and to fornication with another Delting lass before her, but stated all this was after his wife had passed away.

George was left wondering why he had not married Sophia if he was free to do so. There was something untrustworthy, sleekit, about this man; something disrespectful to women. But, given the lack of evidence, the elders couldn't determine whether Bain was an adulterer or a fornicator and, since the act had been committed in Delting, they had decided to pass the decision to the higher authority of the presbytery. George had thought he saw Bain flinch at this decision, as if suddenly trapped. Perhaps he was wondering how he would get to the island of Bressa, near Lerwick, for the hearing in eleven days' time. And he would have to find lodgings for the night. More likely, Bain was wondering if the Delting minister would be there; and how he might get out of the situation. But at least the child would be baptised now that old Joannie Johnson of Brunatwatt had agreed, before the session meeting, to be sponsor. George had also noticed what might have been a measure of relief in Bain's expression: perhaps Sophia would have less reason to nag him, given there would be less shame on the child.

The Reverend James Buchan had conducted the proceedings with his usual firmness and grace. His final closing prayer was for the child. George knew that the minister depended on him to make an accurate and timely minute. They had both been recently widowed and seemed to find a kind of solace in each other's company. Margaret Buchan, who was older than Maggie Greig and socially superior by birth, connections and marriage, had been her mentor and friend. All four of them had been focused these last few years in getting Happyhansel school built and established as the first legal school in Shetland. Happyhansel – happy gift; happy inauguration. Only the huge goodwill and hard work of local people had made it possible.

George had to stir himself from these thoughts: it was as if his wife would walk into the room at any minute. He took up his quill, dipped it in the inkwell and, in his perfect copperplate, wrote:

Voe in Walls Sept 13th 1773 – After Prayer and Sederunt the Moderator and Elders of Walls.

This day the Mod.r reported that David Bain whom Sophia Henderson had given up in the time of her Pregnancy as guilty of uncleanefs with her and the Father of the Child she was then with, had come to him this day and acknowledged himself Guilty, as the woman had Declared and same; offering to give in his Judicial Confefsion before the Sefsion, and to satisfy Discipline as the proper Judicatory should appoint...

Erchie brought him tea and a thick oatmeal scone spread with a little fresh butter and added a peat to the open fire which otherwise was in danger of collapsing into ash.

'A'm aff ta bed, Faider. Da boys is aa settled for da nicht. Dunna sit owre lang noo.'

'Wan o Mary Johnsdaughter's brönnies – dat'll keep me gyaain! Tanks, Erchie. Gödnicht, mi boy... oh, if only aa young men hed dy göd sense.'

Erchie guessed at the implication of his father's final remark.

Tuesday 14th September 1773
Brunatwatt and Happyhansel

The sun had gone past its zenith when Baabie Johnson stepped on to the briggisteyns in front of the Brunatwatt croft house to wave a white cloth to her daughters, Jean and Christian, who were working in the far rig. On the table, she had set out some fresh beremeal bannocks and a jug of well water. She was stirring a pot of broth hanging from the crook above the fire when her husband, Joannie, hirpled through to the but-end from the byre. She didn't look up, but encouraged him to take the worst of the dirt from his boots. The two girls dipped their heads as they came through the doorway, then washed their hands in the basin of burn water which sat at a tilt on the simple washstand nearby. They slid along the resting-chair placed against the window wall. 'A'm fantin, Midder,' said Jean, the older sister. 'Settin up stooks o coarn is tristy wark.'

'Weel, hae du a plate o dis broth an a bit o da hen he's med apön.'

'Dat aald hen 'll be as tyoch as ledder, lass, so mind dy teeth! If shö'd tried harder to lay, she'd still be rinnin aboot.' Their father, Joannie, was given to sarcasm and skyimp.

'Foo got you on wi da coarn, lasses? Is hit nearly aa liftit noo?'

'Ya, Midder, we got twa trave set up.'

'Weel dön, Jean. Aet you up noo. You man be needin hit.'

'Whin can I geng back ta scöl, Faider?' Christian, at thirteen, found croft-work irksome and would much rather be at the local school.

'Whin aa da tatties is taen up an da coarn skrews biggit. An da hidmist paets taen haem fae da hill. An da hairst-kill feenished an sheep's puddins med...'

'An nae doot kale set, da girnal filled wi aetmel... an da ram slippit...' Christian added, sounding downcast.

'Dy bridders med sure dey wir some pennies laid by sae dat you younger eens gyet whit you need ta geng ta da scöl, Christian. An noo wi Mary wirkin ta Greig, an helpin wis aa wi da money, du'll be back at da scöl da meenit da hairst wark is feenished. Sae aet up!'

'Waste o göd money, wumman. I could fine do wi a young mare.'

'Hadd dy sheeks, Joannie Johnson! John an Jaerm is workit hard at da whalin an want ta help der sisters. Hit'll no be lang afore dey hae der ain faemlies ta luik til, an canna spare onythin fur wis.'

'Weel, John 'll hae ta tak my place fishin at da Far Haaf, fur mi aald banes couldna tak anidder year o hit. An onywye, da factor wis axin me aboot da boys.'

'Hit'll shurly no be lang noo afore dey win haem, Midder?' said Christian.

'Ya, mi jewel, dey sood be back shön fur dy hidmist term, as lang as da Press Gang dusna catch dem! I hoop da captain 'll drap dem aff somewye quiet afore dey win ta da Bressa Soond.'

Jean looked truculent. 'I nivver wan ta da scöl, Midder. Hit wis aye Mary an Christian!'

'We didna hae ony spare penga dan, lass, or du wid a gien. Da boys nivver wan ta da scöl doon at Stove mair as twartree year. Du sood be blyde Mary is laerned dee ta read an write. Hit's mair as I ivver learned. I can only sign mi name.'

'A'll teach you, Midder.'

Baabie smiled at Christian, her youngest.

Silence fell as the family finished their meal. The girls rose first to make way for their father on the resting-chair. He would have a cup of tea and a pipe, and then would stretch out for his customary afternoon nap, his cap over his eyes. They went outside to sit on the yard dyke for a breather before returning to the rig to finish stooking the oats to dry.

'Jean, does du ken why Faider hed to geng tae da kirk meetin dastreen? He rarely darkens da door o da place.'

'Weel, mi freend Sophia – du kens da lass at cam fae Delting twartree mont ago an hed da bairn owre da helly – shö axed me a week ago if I wid persuade Faider ta staand as sponsor fur da baptism. Shö's in trouble wi her fock back in Delting – der no plaesed wi her ava.'

'Why wid Faider agree ta dat? He hardly kens her.'

'Dat's true, but he kens Davie Bain somewye. I tink dey maybe wrocht tagidder at a quarry last year.'

'Sae Davie Bain is da bairn's faider? I dunna laek him. He aye luiks me up an doon.'

'Du sood be sae lucky! I laek him fine. He's da best-luikin man aroond here.'

'Jean Johnsdochter, dunna be sae silly! He's gotten dy freend inta trouble. Whit wye is he no mairryin Sophia?'

'Shö's taen-til! Is du seen da erse apön her?'

'Foo can du say dat aboot dy new freend? Come on, lat's win back ta wark an gyet dis dwined coarn feenished.'

'Mary Morison said dat Davie Bain telt her dat he wis fed up wi Sophia naggin him aboot gettin da bairn registered an baptised! An shö said shö tocht Sophia sood a bidden in her ain parish an no come here giein Waas a ill name!'

Meanwhile Baabie was busy flitting their tethered cows to fresh grazing – Bessie, still suckling her young heifer and Bella, still in milk. She had a churning to do, having gathered milk over a few days. She loved her kye and also the peaceful task of making the butter. And Joannie was snoring away.

***

Brunatwatt was a mile and a half from the new school and schoolhouse at Happyhansel, but to Mary Johnsdaughter it felt like a world apart. She had been working for the Greigs for more than a year now. She left home early every morning and didn't get back till well after tea-time. Her brother Jaerm had let her take his pocket-watch, his prized possession, into the closet where she slept so that she could check the time. He had brought it back from the whaling. It had a picture of a sailing ship on the face.

Mr Greig was a kind employer who treated Mary more like a daughter than a servant. She had been a good pupil. He seemed grateful for all the housewifely tasks she undertook and trusted her to work out what needed to be done. Unlike at Brunatwatt, she knew that if she needed flour or oatmeal or tea or sugar, there was always enough money for it, and a pony to use, if necessary, to fetch it from the shop. It was a busy household, with the two schoolrooms buzzing during the day and, in the evening, a meal to make, not just for Mr Greig and Erchie, but also for the boarders. Erchie, still only sixteen and a year younger than her, looked after the boys, lighting fires and getting them to keep their two attic rooms clean and tidy. He was now a pupil-teacher, helping his father.

Mary was in charge of the kitchen, the cooking and baking, the cleaning and any mending required. Mr Greig employed John Jeems and Leebie – whose land adjoined theirs – to take the washing away to be done, to deal with the peats and, with the help of their family, to look after the schoolhouse croft. There were crops of oats, bere, turnips, potatoes, kale and hay as well as grazing in the park and on the common hill land. And with hens, cows, sheep and two pigs, there was always some work to attend to. While Mary was glad not to have to undertake croft work, she liked taking a basinful of kitchen waste to the pigs. Her other big relief was not having to deal with the school or schoolhouse dry-closets. The old man emptied them regularly.

Generally, the division of labour worked amicably. Erchie helped her with grinding the oats and bere in the barn, while Mary preferred churning and making butter and soft cheese. Fetching water from the well was another of her daily chores. There was a good spring nearby which rarely let them down. She was grateful for the work and knew that, although just seventeen, her wages helped keep the Brunatwatt family. Sunday was a day off, but she had to make sure there was enough water and food ready for the Greigs and the boarders. They all had good appetites.

Mary's day had been good. The fires in both school and schoolhouse were already glowing by the time she arrived in the morning. She had soaked the oatmeal overnight, so porridge was quick to cook. She was careful not to make too much as, although there was plenty oats stooked in the yard, it had to last the year now that oatmeal was a shilling a peck at the Bayhaa shop. There was bread from yesterday's baking, plenty fresh milk and butter, some rhubarb and ginger jam and a big pot of steaming tea waiting for the boys when they came downstairs from their rooms. After grace was said, she took her food in the scullery to get a bit of peace and left the men to it. The boarders were expected to help with tidying up after breakfast before moving through to the schoolrooms.

Soon the day-school children arrived, the older ones carrying a peat. They were glad of a warm fire. After some initial jostling, the classes soon settled into their familiar rhythm. At this time of year, with the hairst still underway on some crofts, older children could only be spared when the weather was too poor for outside work.

After the Lord's Prayer, the morning was spent on reading, spelling, writing, and religious knowledge. Erchie had shown Mary the books he used with the younger pupils: *Directions for Spelling* with its rhymes and illustrations helping them learn the alphabet; and *Tommy Thumb's Pretty Song Book* with its simple nursery rhymes which were easy to memorise. She remembered, as an older pupil, having Bunyan and the bible as readers. Then, in the afternoon, while Mr Greig took the senior boys for navigation and book-keeping, Erchie had to try to keep the remainder of the pupils engaged on arithmetic. She knew that he could depend on the senior girls to help the youngest children with their numbers and simple sums and with cleaning their slates. Occasionally, Reverend James Buchan would come along and help with a class. They all respected the minister, knowing how fortunate they were, and that schooling in Waas would have remained rudimentary had it not been for his tireless pressure for financial support on the local heritors and on the Society in Scotland for Propagating Christian Knowledge (SSPCK), which paid a basic wage to the schoolmaster.

The schoolhouse had been a peaceful place for most of the day. Mary had fetched water from the well and baked. She had set out sweet milk, bread, and soft cheese – her kirn-mylk – for several of the pupils who had not been able to bring food with them. Dinner was on the table for the two men when they had their break at noon and she had helped Erchie clear up the two schoolrooms before she started making the tea. The boarders were served separately and, once they were fed, Mr Greig always insisted she ate with the family, an arrangement she found most agreeable.

Sometimes Mr Greig would go quiet and she suspected he was still grieving. His young life had been hard too: she knew from hearsay that his first wife had died in childbed and their baby girl hadn't survived for long. Through his part-time teaching role on the nearby island of Papa Stour, he had become well known to the Reverend George Duncan, then the minister and teacher in Waas; and mixing with that family had brought him into contact with Maggie, the only daughter. Mary knew the marriage had been happy and that their only child, Erchie, who seemed to be following in his father's footsteps, meant everything to his father. It looked like he would take over as school-master when the old man finally gave up.

Mr Buchan came along the schoolhouse after tea to take the boarders aside for their Latin class. He was also instructing George in Latin, but they had forgone that pleasure lately as both men had been busy. The boys' Latin classes were a good source of additional income for the school.

Mary was then able to slip away home to Brunatwatt. Often the wind dropped in the evening and she enjoyed that short time walking on her own. If the weather was fair, she would stop to pass the time of day with folk out in the rigs. At the head of the voe, she turned north up the gaet to Stove where there was usually someone working outside around the cluster of cotters' houses. She hadn't seen Jaanie there for some days. No doubt she would be very occupied looking after Sophia, her lodger, and the new baby. Mary always felt the better of a blether with Jaanie Jeromson.

When she got home, her father was at the peat-stack and her mother and sisters knitting. She made an eight-o-clocks for them all – tea and a buttered oatcake – and then, as she was tired and wanted a quiet read before bedtime, disappeared to the closet between the but and the ben-ends. She was glad that, when their granny had died and the closet became available, her older sister Jean had still preferred to share the ben-end with Christian, their two short beds separated by a thin partition. Their parents had the box-bed in the but-end and the boys, when at home, had the partly floored attic which they accessed by a ladder. They intended to build up the gables and create two proper attic bedrooms with skylights and to raise da aeshins, but had never had enough time when the weather was conducive to opening a roof to the elements.

Mary had borrowed *Robinson Crusoe* from Mr Greig's bookshelf. He always encouraged her to have a book to read and had recommended it. She was enjoying the narrative. It took her mind off the irritations of family life and gave her an excuse to extricate herself. The closet was stuffy and there was hardly enough room to turn around. She wedged the window open a little. There was just enough light to read by. The air was still, and had a braeth o hairst about it. Her mind wandered as she undressed and hung her clothes on the door-peg: the carry-on about Sophia and her infant, and Bain... why on earth had her father become involved... and how had Sophia fallen under Bain's spell? With his swarthy complexion and dark eyes, yes he was good-looking... but there was something... something deceitful about him, untrustworthy. And what did the kirk session and Mr Buchan make of him? And Jean... with her sonsie ways and her habit of teetering on the edge of trouble, the boys fell for her easily... no wonder... with her brown hair and olive skin that darkened in summer, making her blue eyes look even bluer. Thank goodness, Christian has some sense... just thirteen, but more level-headed than Jean at nearly twenty... Being the middle sister can be tricky...

But she got back into the story of shipwreck and survival before drifting off to sleep.

Sunday 3rd October 1773
Brunatwatt and Voe Pier

The Johnson family had all been to the kirk service as a thanksgiving, not just for a reasonable harvest at last after two bad years, but also for the safe return of John and Jaerm from the Greenland whaling. The new kirk had been full and decorated with sheaves of grain and kishies of vegetables which the crofters had carried there on their backs. Joannie was pleased with the sheaf of oats he had brought: it was as heavy with puckles of corn as any of the others propped up in the kirk. Baabie was proud of their fine-looking family, especially now that the boys were home safely. The only stain on the family name had come the previous year: Jean had been in trouble for fornication. Mercifully, the pregnancy had ended in a miscarriage. Even so, she had to admit her guilt before the whole congregation. But Jean could carry it off. Baabie was sure such a thing would have killed Mary. It had just about killed her.

John and Jaerm had been back home in time to round up a few lambs and castrated rams for the harvest kill. Jean and Christian had lifted the potatoes and turnips and stored them under faels, thick squares of mossy turf. They had all helped cart the corn and bere back to the yard near the house and had built the big skrews, covering the tops with old sailcloth, secured by ropes made of rushes. These flossy ropes were looped round large flat stones to keep the hard-won harvest from the predations of winter weather. The previous winter had been particularly stormy. It was fortunate that the last of the peats had been brought home from the hill before the recent severe and sudden gales. Some folk had not been so lucky with their timing.

At least the day was fair and bright, a merciful release from the unrelenting wind and rain. On the way home by Stove, Jean wanted to see Sophia, so the others walked on ahead, eager to sit down to their dinner. Baabie had cooked a bit of new hill lamb the day before and the potatoes were ready to boil. It was always a treat to have fresh meat after all the reestit mutton or salt pork.

But soon Jean came running to catch them up. No, there was no sign of Sophia, or the infant or Bain. Out of breath, she threw aside their questions and merely pointed to the voe. Seeing three tall masts far out at the eastern entrance to the inlet, they quickly doubled back to Stove where they had a better view. The ship was limping through the narrow Aester Soond, one poor sail held loosely in the light wind. The rigging looked in disarray. They stood for some time as if transfixed. Was it a ghost ship?

Then they saw a small boat, away out at the entrance to the voe, with its oars catching the sunlight. She seemed to be towing the barque into Vaila Sound.

'Yun'll be da Gronataing boat – dey man a seen da ship fae da point!' Jaerm was knowledgeable about boats and from having studied some navigation at school.

Eventually Baabie said she would go on ahead and get the potatoes on to boil. Almost imperceptibly, the ship edged forward, past Gronataing and on towards the Isle of Linga, the little boat now joined by men from Vadlure in their fowrareen. By now they knew their dinner would be spoiling, but it was impossible to ignore the drama unfolding before them. Gradually, they could pick out that the deck was lined with people. The three girls decided they should get home, hunger having overtaken curiosity. They urged the men to follow quickly.

It was another hour before Joannie and his sons reached Brunatwatt, full of the news that the ship had at last safely rounded the point of Saatness and anchored with her head into the wind. There were huge numbers of people on deck. They were still stunned, barely knowing which question to consider first: where were they all from and where bound at this time of year? What state were they in and whatever would become of them?

After their dinner, John, Jaerm, Jean and Mary decided they would set off for DoonaWaas to see what was astir. As they hurried down the Stove brae, they could see many people walking along the head of the voe – the Fud – and on past the kirk towards the Voe House pier. It was the biggest ship they had ever seen in the anchorage. Already, several smaller boats were out at the vessel and a rope ladder over the side. They picked out Buchan's boat and one belonging to Mrs Margaret Buchan's step-grandson, John T Henry of Bayhaa. It was known that James Buchan was a little wary of this ambitious young land-owner and merchant-trader, even if he was linked to him through marriage. And everyone knew that through John Henry's marriage to the boy laird's aunt – Mistress Margaret Scott of Bayhaa – he had become one of the most influential heritors in the district.

There was a strange silence as local people crowded along the shore, aware that, for the people crammed on the deck of the stricken ship, life onboard must have been unbearable and now had become completely out of their control. The number of people looked far too many for the size of the ship.

Soon two boatloads of men arrived at the Voe pier. Despite looking haggard and unkempt, it was easy to pick out the captain and mate from their clothes and bearing. Besides crew members, there was one man, taller than the others and ruddy in complexion, who stepped ashore. He seemed of some importance. No one could hear what was being said, but it was clear that they were being welcomed by the local worthies. A look of relief spread over the faces of the crew. Gradually the voices of the local folk started to rise, higher and higher, as they crowded ever closer to the shore.

Jean and the boys were pushing forward to hear what they could. Mary caught sight of Erchie standing a little way from his father. She edged towards him. He was eager to share what he had heard: that the ship was full of emigrants from Caithness and Sutherland on their way to North Carolina. They had been at sea for almost three weeks, struck by all the recent storms. Erchie had overheard that they had many sick and frightened men, women and children on board.

'What 'll happen tae dem, tinks-du, Erchie?'

'Hit soonds as if dey'll need ta be taen ashore while da ship is repaired. But Göd kens whaar dey'll aa geng, hit's…'

'A'm sure aaboady 'll try der best. Hit's a mercy he's bön a moaderate hairst da year or dey wid be naethin ta spare ava.'

'Dey seeminly hae ample proveesions dey could use, so dat's a blisseen.'

The crowd gradually started to peel away, moving slowly in groups, heads down. Memories of terrible drownings and loss of life were not far below the surface. Mary was keen to get home, to think through what she had just witnessed.

'We'll see dee damoarn's moarn, Mary. An I daar say dey'll be mair uncans ta tell dee. Dat is – whin we get a meenit! Faider is ta meet wi Mr Buchan danicht an twartree idders ta see whit can be dön.'

'Apö da Sabbath?'

'Ya, hit'll mak a change fae da usual business!'

With that, Mary had to push back through the crowd till she found her brothers and Jean. They were all full of the bits of information they had gleaned: the tall, red-faced man with the thick moustache was James Hogg, the Caithness factor who had chartered the ship, the *Batchelor of Leith*; that there were bodies on board for burial; that the emigrants were in despair having been locked between decks with no light and little air for many days; and that many were sick. There were rumours of smallpox.

Jean wondered why Bain was nowhere to be seen. He must have known his countrymen were set on a journey of emigration.

Monday 4th October 1773
Happyhansel

As she hurried down the morning brae, Mary could see the *Batchelor* lying at anchor. Climbing the Kloss of Voe to Happyhansel, she felt a knot in her stomach at the thought of what would, before very long, meet her face to face: a flood of people – men, women and children – probably as poor as herself, but with no home to go to. And no doubt some would be ill or distressed. The ship looked forlorn. She could barely imagine what such a loss of hope might feel like.

The school day had a surface normality about it, but there was a strange quietness with the children – almost a sense of fear. Their little world had suddenly been invaded and no one seemed to know what would happen next. At teatime, George Greig looked tired as he sat down to a plate of spicy sausage-meat and eggs.

'Bliss dee, Mary. Dis sassermaet smells most horrid fine.'

'Der no dat mony jars o hit left noo, Mr Grieg. Pör aald grice – een o dem 'll be for da chop afore lang I doot!'

Erchie was keen to hear how the previous evening's meeting had gone. He had been in bed by the time his father had got back from Mr Buchan's and during the school day there had been few chances to chat. Mary never felt excluded from these family conversations, though no doubt there would be many things her employers talked about privately when she wasn't around. Thankfully the boarders had been set a writing task, so all was quiet upstairs.

'Foo got you on wi da meeting? Wha wis aa dere, Faider?'

'Hit wis a lang nicht, I can tell dee! Hit cam tae da point we wir datn tired, we couldna tink straicht; but we got a lock dön I wid say. Dey wir fowr affa da *Batchelor*: Captain Ramage an da Mate, a Thomas Liddell bi name. Da ship's carpenter, Alexander Ross, wis dere; an James Hogg an aa – mind dat muckle man wi da ruddy face an whiskers – weel, he's da factor fae Caithness dat's agent fur da trip ta Nort Carolina an collectit aa da fares affa da fock. I doot he's a hard man an we could see der a braa argie-bargie atween him an da Captain as ta whit's whit; an maybe atween him an da ship-owner an aa, a man caa'd Inglis, fae Leith. Hogg seemingly paid him near enyoch aa da passage money fur da trip, an fur da proveesions. An Captain Ramage is in charge o dat. An dan, besides me an da meenister, dey wir John Henry o Bayhaa an Tammie Henry o Burrastow. Or sood I say Thomas Henry? I doot we'll need der influence among da tidder heritors at dis time, fur der dat muckle help needit, an richt awa. I man say A'm relieved hit wisna a kirk session meeting an I dunna hae ta write da meenits fur dey wir datn a lock ta spaek aboot. But Mr Buchan wis axed me ta come an tak notts sae we dunna forget whit we hae ta dö.'

'I hoop we can aa help.'

'Dat we can, Mary. We'll aa hae ta dö dat! Noo lat me see – da main thing is dat der owre twa hunder an fifty emigrants dat need ta be billeted fur a peerie while till da boat is repaired. But we'll hae ta gyet on wi dat while da wadder hadds. Der still hoopin ta cross da Atlantic da year! Der mainly faemlies, wi bairns, pör tings. An dat's no coontin da crew or James Hogg an his party o fifteen. Seeminly his midder-in-laa deed on da wye here. Da ship has proveesions for eicht weeks or mair, but Captain Ramage said dey wir only fur whin dey wir aboard ship! Wid you believe hit? I canna tink he wid lat dem starve. Mr Buchan 'll be writin tae Balfour, dat's da Deputy Vice-Admiral, ta come oot ta Waas an help.'

'Sae whaar dey aa gyaain ta bide, Faider?'

'Weel, da meenister 'll tak a Gordon faemily – a tenant fairmer fae Sutherland. He's gyettin on a bit an his twa sons is already settled in Nort Carolina an wantin da hael faemly ta come oot. Sae dat's him an his wife, six grown bairns an twa dochters-in-law.'

'Ten? Dat's a ontak!' said Mary.

'Dat hit is. But he feels becaas he haes a muckle hoose an servants, he sood dö his best. An John Henry o Bayhaa 'll tak in een o a faemlies dat has servants wi dem, an he'll set aboot writin ta some o da idder kinda graand Shetland faemlies laek Mitchell o Saand an Henderson o Gairdie axin if dey micht tak in some faemlies an aa. Thomas Henry o Burrastow 'll tak in some wi servants tö, an he'll spaek wi da idder heritors i da parish here ta help an aa. Twartree elders ir gyaain ta be axed ta pass wird aroond DoonaWaas, Mid Waas, Dale o Waas, Brig o Waas, Sannis an maybe even Papa Stour dat onyboady dat can manage ta tak in a faemly – even sleepin i da barn fur noo – sood pit der name apö da list wi foo mony dey tink dey could manage. Da emigrants hae der ain beddin wi dem, but whit state hit's in I canna imagine.'

'Weel, if dey come wi der ain proveesions an beddin maybe fock 'll be mair laekly ta add der names tae da list. I man ax wir fock at Brunatwatt, an maybe Jaanie an aa, if hit's jöst fur a week or sae.'

'Dat wid be a help, Mary. An we man offer wir closet, Erchie. I tink der wan or twa on der ain. Noo, dat wis da main business. But der a börial ta organise fur a MacKay faemly; der ting o bairn. I tink dey wir some börials at sea, but we didna ax owre muckle aboot dat. Nae doot, dey'll be grievin faemlies among dem. Alexander Ross, da ship's carpenter, is already med a peerie coffin fur da bairn. He seemed a fine sowl, an helpful. He wis ta row owre daday wi da coffin, an een o Mr Buchan's servants 'll arrange wi da grave-digger ta prepare aathin an ta meet Ross at da pier an tak him tae da mortuary wi da boady. We hae a mort cloth dey can use an dey'll be nae charge.'

'Jöst as weel da collections is bön braaly göd lately an da Poor Box no empty.'

'Ya, Erchie, dat hit is. We still hae twartree pound in it. Eence wir gotten da fock billeted, an da maet affa da boat – John Henry said dey could lock hit up in his store eenoo – dan da crew can get on wi da repairs. Ross is keen ta get hadd o a blacksmith ta mak him a new baand fur da tap o da rudder. Mr Buchan said dat his pier can be used whinivver dey need hit, an his böd, if dey need ta stowe onythin.'

Mary looked up as she spoke. 'I widna tink dey'd set aff again dis saeson fur America. Surely dey'll geng back haem.'

'I dunna ken whit der plannin, but besides da rudder, da bilge pumps need ta be sortit. An der langboat is braaly damaged and twartree oars missin. Dey canna geng onywhaar till aa dat is fixed. An da riggin an sails – der braaly hattered an need a braa bit o wark.'

'Foo mony o a crew ir dey?' asked Erchie.

'Noo, lat me see. Besides da captain, da mate, da carpenter, an da bosun an... da cook, I tink der anidder six or sae, maistlins fae Leith. I tink dat Ross is da only een fae Caithness – but he bides in Leith noo.'

'We hae ta hoop dat wir waal-watter 'll hadd oot,' Mary commented, looking at Mr Greig.

'Wir braaly lucky here fur watter. Last time I coontit up da waals jöst aroond da voe here, I got ta twenty-seeven afore I lost coont, sae I tink dat'll no be a problem. Noo, if hit wis simmer... hit micht be a different story.'

Over their cup of tea and a bit of Mary's baking, Erchie asked his father about Hogg, the agent for the trip and factor for the estate on which many of the emigrants had been tenant farmers.

George took his time replying. 'Tae be honest, I fin him a strange mixter. Laek dem aa, he's suffered aafil. Der nae doot he's a capable man but he's a tough een. I widna laek ta wirk tae him. I canna say dat I took tae Captain Ramage edder: he didna seem ta grasp dat he wis responsible fur dis poor fock. But he'll hae ta bide on da richt side o da laa an inform da Admiralty an da Customs.'

Mary refilled their cups. 'A'll need to be clearin up an winnin haem. You twa 'll be tired danicht I warn!'

Mr Greig nodded. 'Dy fock 'll be luikin fur dee, hinny.'

On her way home, Mary decided to see how Jaanie was getting on and to exchange news. Her mother and Jaanie Jeromson had been girls together and, when Jaanie's husband had died when their son was still a child, Baabie had helped. The two families had remained on friendly terms and, when Mary was born, Jaanie seemed to find in her a surrogate daughter. She was a laundress and the local howdie, often helping new mothers in those first critical days after birth. Mary pushed the door a little, announcing her arrival gently. The heat met her at the door. In the shadow, Jaanie was bent over a table busily pressing the frilly edge of a cap across her goffering iron.

She looked up. 'Bliss dee, Mary, set dee in. A'll be dön wi dis dwined bonnet in a meenit. Da licht is fadin an I manna scorch hit.'

'Hit's haet wark fur you, Jaanie. But lovely ta see da boannie aedge aa prunkit up.'

'Ya, dat hit is. Dis is Mistress Henry's bonnet; an I hae a lace collar an cuffs ta dö fur her as weel. An a sark an collars fur her man. But dat can wait till damoarn.' With that she quickly removed the heated rod from the tube and hung it safely on the raep above the fire. Before she set the iron aside to cool, she took a cloth dabbed in beeswax and laid it nearby so as not to forget to clean it.

'Whit news dan, lass? Isna dis jöst solemn? I hear der hunders o dem apö yun ship!'

Mary was keen to recount what she had learned from Mr Greig, and Jaanie responded with 'Is dat so?' or 'My, my!' or an occasional shake of her head. It seemed that she had heard a fair bit of gossip from the Bayhaa maid, not all of it true. Mary tentatively mentioned the idea of perhaps taking in a couple. Jaanie seemed open to the suggestion, as long as it would just be for a short while till the repairs were done.

At that point in the conversation, Willm, Jaanie's grandson, came through from the ben-room. He was rubbing his eyes.

'I canna win ta sleep, granny.' Mary reached out to the little boy.

'Come du here, Willm, an A'll gie dee a cuddle.' He knew Mary well as she was often called upon to stay over with him when Jaanie was delayed with a difficult birth or with a delivery some miles from Stove. Willm edged on to Mary's knee and looked up at her. She amused him with a finger game for a bit till he was ready to go back to bed.

Mary asked, 'Nae wird o Walter winnin haem?'

'Na, naethin, Mary. A'm no lippenin him fur a while yet. He'll be keen ta keep on sailin as Mate, noo he's won dat far. But… A'm sure he'll want ta come haem afore settin aff on anidder trip. He kens Willm misses him.'

'I doot dat, Jaanie. But you're bön baith midder an faider tae Willm since his midder deed.'

'Weel, whit can you dö idder as your best? Hit's bön a herd twartree year fur Walter, an fur me an aa, whit wi him mairryin sooth, in Liverpool, an me no able ta be dere fur him an his wife whin Willm wis boarn. Shö wis caa'd Etta, but I nivver met her. I tink I could a helpit save her life. An dan he hed ta luik tae her aald midder fur twartree year. I wis jöst blyde he browt Willm haem.'

'Ya, I mind mi midder spaekin aboot hit at da time. You're dön a göd job wi him, Jaanie. He's sic a happy ting.'

'Dat he is. Noo, du'll tak a aer o tae, lass?'

'Na Jaanie, no danicht, tanks. A'll need ta be gyettin haem. I wis gyaain ta ax if maybe you wid laek Willm ta geng tae da scöl, noo dat he's six. You widna hae ta pay, an hit wid gie you a chance ta gyet your wark dön ithoot wirryin aboot him burnin himself apön a iron.'

'Does du ken, I wis winderin dat mysel da idder day. I tink dat wid be da fine...'

'He could tag alang wi da idder Stove bairns... an I wid luik oot fur him.'

'I ken du wid, jewel. A'll tink hit owre an speak wi Willm. I ken Walter wid be keen.'

Mary rose to leave for Brunatwatt. 'Der nae wird o Sophia, is der, Jaanie?'

'Na lass, her an yun Bain man set aff twartree days ago wi da infant. I tocht shö wid wait fur da baptism, but he seemed ta be on a amp ta get awa. I tink dey wir makkin fur Sandsting, but shö wisna gyaain ta be tellin me. I nivver raelly took ta her, but wis blyde ta help her whin shö needit it. I doot shö'll no hae her soarrows ta seek[1], du mark my wirds!'

Mary smiled and waved as she set off the short mile to Brunatwatt where she knew her arrival would be eagerly awaited for news of the *Batchelor*. She'd be lucky if she got to her bed before midnight. There was no doubt in her mind that this was going to be an almighty undertaking for the whole community. Maybe she could persuade her folk to take in just one person.

Monday 18th October 1773
Happyhansel

Mary knew that this was Willm's first day at school, so she looked out for him at breaktime and lunchtime. He was with some other little children from Stove and looked happy enough. He waved to her. She slipped him a buttered bannock with some kirn-mylk on it. At teatime she mentioned to Mr Greig that the turnout at the morning service the previous day had been good, remarking that, not only had the sailors from the *Batchelor* attended the service, but they had been invited to attend the kirk session meeting afterwards.

---

1 Will find things get difficult (expressed in negative); to have trouble on one's hands.

The offer had taken everyone by surprise: the kirk session was not given to issuing invitations. She had thought Mr Buchan had preached an uplifting sermon, exhorting them all to be of goodwill at this time of trial and, as she had left the kirk, it seemed that folk were willing to be hospitable as best they could, even if resources were strained. She knew Mr Greig would have already written up the minutes...

But she said little of the speculation among neighbours as they had walked back from the kirk. There had been talk about the billeting at Saatness, at Stapness, at Vadlure and Riskaness; of families taken all the way to Finnigart, to Dale o Waas and to Sannis; of families crammed into attics and closets and barns. And about the fact that no provisions had yet been forthcoming. And she had overheard mutterings about smallpox, and pilfering; of feeling their homes invaded. She wondered if the minister was going to demand that the ship's provisions be shared out. She knew, as did everyone else by now, that Captain Ramage wanted them stored for use when they set sail, while James Hogg wanted them available now for the emigrant families as was their due since they had paid in advance for the food. He, however, was thought to be comfortably settled with his family and servants at the Haa o Saand, in a neighbouring parish. There would be no lack of food on the table there.

Over his salt beef and vegetables, Mr Greig was willing to divulge that the billeting arrangements were all but complete, with families dispersed as far as Bressa and Saand, and that there was to be a day of public fasting, humiliation and prayer on Wednesday 27th October, which would be announced from all the pulpits in the parish next Sunday. And the parishioners were exhorted to bring money for a special collection. The money would be set apart for the relief and assistance of the emigrants – especially the poorest among them – unless relief arrived from other districts. He was, however, tight-lipped about the on-going row about provisions, session business being confidential.

Mary knew from Eliza McDonald, the young Caithness woman

now billeted with them, that many of the emigrants were angry they could not get the food they had paid for and were thus dependent on the kindness of their hosts. Being poor people themselves, they knew the strain they were putting on local families. Eliza was a good help to some of the families struggling with small children or with illness. She had even got Jean and Christian roped in to help. Joannie was given to remark that there was plenty work around the croft needing to be done and was it not the bible that said charity begins at home?

On her way home, Mary dropped by Jaanie's to hear how she was getting on. She was keen to find out not just what Willm had thought of school, but how the couple who had recently been billeted with Jaanie were settling in. The McLeods were sitting in at the fire and Jaanie introduced them as Katie and Willie. The woman, though probably only in her middle twenties, looked pale and worn, and her husband haggard. She had heard that their only child had died on the voyage and had been buried at sea. Mary could have wept for them, but managed to remain composed. She knew they were in the best house in Waas, however small it might be: Jaanie could always judge when to speak and when to be quiet, and her quietness was like something wrapped round you. However, the McLeod's presence did make it difficult to show enthusiasm about Willm's day. He was fast asleep, but his granny could tell Mary he had enjoyed himself and had shown her how to write and sound out the letter 'a' which was for 'apple' and 'animal'. He'd never seen an apple, but the young Mr Greig had shown them pictures. And the children had done some counting with tiny cowrie shells Erchie had let them use, drawing the numbers 1, 2 and 3 on their slates. They would get another letter tomorrow, and some bigger numbers. Mary was relieved to hear that he had settled as she knew that sometimes the first day could be difficult or feel long.

When Mary reached Brunatwatt, she found there was a visitor; Alexander Ross, the ship's carpenter. She was surprised to see him by the fire: in winter time neighbours and cousins came along in the evenings, in aboot da nicht as they would say, but not strangers. He was having an eight o'clocks cup of tea with the family. Her mother eased the awkwardness of her entrance.

'Come dy wys in trowe, Mary, an say hello tae Alex affa da *Batchelor*.'

Mary hung up her coat and scarf before greeting him. He seemed shy. Afterwards, she took a cup from the hook on the shelf of the dresser and poured herself a cup of tea, offering first to the others. She pulled out a low stool from underneath the resting-chair and sat down on the other side of the small room.

Listening to the men chatting, Mary learned that her brothers, John and Jaerm, had been passing Mr Buchan's bothy where Alex was working on the ship's damaged longboat and, being seamen, had easily struck up a conversation. When Alex had mentioned that he could do with a bit more planking, John had suggested he come back with them to Brunatwatt to have a look at the wood they had stowed in the barn rafters; wood that over the years had washed ashore. Alex had gratefully settled on some pieces and the brothers had arranged that they would bring it down to the bothy the next day. They had also offered to take him, with the broken rudder band, to the smithy at Southvoe so that a replacement could be made.

Mary found herself a bit tongue-tied. Jean, however, had no such problem. She had already offered to make Alex a pair of woollen hose. Baabie lit a koli-lamp on the wall. It cast shadows across the room. Alex rose to go.

'It's gettin late an I have to row across the voe and bide weel clear o the skerries... an clim a rope ladder! It's a bit strange bein the only fowk on the ship!' With that he thanked them all for their help and hospitality and said he'd be grateful to see the brothers whenever they could manage. They followed him as far as Stove where the path became wider and easier.

'Well, dat's a fine fellow, Mary. Whit tinks du? He fairly laekit dy hufsi. He hed a extry slice wi his cup o tae.'

'Jean! White noo! He's no fur you. I warn he's a mairried man.'

Baabie continued: 'He seemed braaly interestit ta hear aboot Bain an Sophia. He said he kent Bain weel an wis relatit tae him. But he'd nae idea whaar dey micht a gien.' Mary did not divulge what Jaanie had told her about them.

After they had exchanged their news, Mary went to bed. She was glad to shut out the world. But yes, Jean was right: Alex Ross did seem likeable; there was something physically attractive about him too, in a way. And Eliza had fitted into their family well. It had been an easy exchange, despite the mayhem that was all about them.

Sunday 24th October 1773
Brunatwatt

Joannie Johnson had not accompanied his family to church as it would have required him to tidy his whiskers and clean his boots. Baabie insisted on keeping the Sabbath as best they could, and so the rest of the family were there, Eliza with them.

The morning sky had looked ominous as the local folk and a few emigrants filed into the kirk. It was almost dark despite being noon. The beadle had lit a few lamps. Mr Buchan had read the heavens as he came down the brae and, knowing that many of his parishioners had several miles to walk to reach home, kept his sermon short and cut out some verses from the longer psalms. In the intimations he announced that Wednesday should be set aside from all but the most essential of work and was to be a special day of fasting, humiliation and prayer. They were all encouraged to bring with them whatever money they could spare, all of which would be put towards the poorest among the emigrant families in their current distress, many of whom had used up what little they had left – after paying their fares – subsisting in Thurso, having given up their homes, while they waited almost two months for the promised passage.

By the time the Brunatwatt folk got home the sky was almost

black and the wind had whipped up almost to gale force. They held on to one another, unsteady, as their boots sank into the guttery path. Everyone was soaked through. The sea was like ink and already breaking in huge sprays over skerries and shores. Before coming inside for their dinner, John and Jaerm checked the yard to make sure the corn skrews and hay desses were still standing secure and any implements were safely stowed in the barn. Mercifully, the cows were already in the byre for the winter. Before retreating inside, they nailed some wood over the three tiny windows. Joannie, who had earlier lit the wick of the koli-lamp on the wall, was smoking his pipe peacefully by the fire.

He spat out the words, 'Dat'll laern you!'[2]

By tea time it was a hurricane from the south-west and they feared for the roof, despite the fact that the thatch was netted and well-weighted with stones. The wind was whipping under the door and, when a gust of wind decreed it, the fire belched a cloud of peat smoke.

John was particularly anxious about the ship and her crew. He knew they would not want to abandon her; and Alex would be bitterly disappointed just when he had managed to do enough repairs so that she was ready to sail, awaiting a fair wind. This was the week they were due to get all the emigrants back on board and load up with the provisions. They knew it would take a few days to round up and account for everyone. Balfour, the Vice-Admiral of Shetland, was with Hogg's party at Garderhouse, Sand, getting the plans underway and had also sent word to the group billeted in the grand new residence at Gairdie, Bressa.

But all that was looking ever less likely as the night wore on and the hurricane deepened and roared. Eliza was very quiet, her recently raised hopes having been dashed. The boys recounted their worst nights at the whaling, climbing masts to reef in the sails, battening down; when the hull would be creaking and groaning, and the blocks squealing; when sleep was impossible as you waited for the moment when the ship shuddered as she

---

2 You won't be doing that again! (lit, that will teach you!).

fell into a trough. They were all anxious about the crew most likely still onboard the *Batchelor*.

The storm continued unabated on the Monday and there was no chance of safely venturing forth, certainly not for the school children. The family huddled round the fire, only going through to the byre-end to milk the cows and take through some more peats from the store they had brought in. A gloom settled on them as the noises of the gale rose and fell.

Baabie was determined not to capitulate to the thrashing meted out by the elements.

'Jean, lay by dy makkin an bring trowe da saat piltocks I set ithin da press ta steep. We can hae dem wi tatties. An some fresh butter an blaand. At laest we'll no starve.' Mary too rose to help prepare their frugal meal.

'If we keep da fire up, A'll mak some bannocks apö da braand-iron eftir denner.'

By Tuesday, the weather had eased enough for John and Jaerm to remove the window boarding and investigate what damage had been done to the croft; and, later in the day, to struggle as far as Stove, to find out, if they could, how the crew had managed to weather the storm. They were away for what seemed like hours and Baabie was starting to fret when at last the family heard their voices above the wind and felt the sudden draught as they opened the door.

'Ir you fun oot whit happened tae da crew?' Mary was particularly anxious and much relieved to see her brothers back safely.

'Lass, lat dem draa der braeth an hae somethin tae aet afore we whiss dem.'

'Oh, Midder, dunna wirry. We can speak in atween moothfoos!' Jaerm knew he had to put their minds at ease. Bowls of broth were quickly dished up and once they had supped a few mouthfuls they started to recount what they had been able to find out.

The crew were all safe; that was the main news, and met with much relief. But the *Batchelor* was severely damaged. At the top of the brae they had witnessed a shocking sight. She was lying almost on her side on the far shore below Germatwatt, near the Point of

Saatness. They could not make out the extent of the damage, but had been anxious to know whether the crew had made it ashore safely. They had managed to walk down to the Fud and were about to turn towards Saatness when, much to their surprise and relief, they had caught sight of Captain Ramage and the crew battling their way down the slope towards the head of the voe, almost within hailing distance. John had tried to run, but the wind was still strong and had made it almost impossible. They could see that Buchan's man-servant was coming with them, leading a horse and cart, laden with gear. Some had packs on their backs.

Baabie was wringing her hands, almost rocking back an fore.

'Sae whit wis happened? Foo did dey win affa da ship, boys?'

'Weel, dey said dat baith her anchors brook aff wi da hurricane, an shö wis driven clos inta da shore below Germatwatt – an da boddom is dat badly damaged you can see daylicht trowe her! But da masts hüld, an didna brak.' Jaerm continued, 'Da crew wis hed tae abandon ship. Hit wis hellish. Dey aa managed ta win ashore, sokkit tae da skyin, an scramble owre da rocky beach but da gale wis laek ta lift dem. Dey wirna bön able ta rescue ony o da proveesions fae da galley.'

'Deil tak da proveesions as lang as der safe!'

'Du's richt, Mary.' John picked up the story. 'Hit wis dark, but dey could see a peerie glooral o licht i da but-end o Saatness, an dey managed somewye ta arl der wye up da broo. Dey didna want ta gluff da fock sae late at nicht, sae dey huddled i da barn. Da fock cam luikin fur dem i da moarnin fur bi dan dey wir seen da ship just aff da boddom o der rigs!'

'Whitna gluff dey man a hed whin dey got up!' Jean added.

'Ya, nae doot,' said John, nodding his thanks to his youngest sister, Christian, who was ladling in some more broth. 'Seeminly whin Buchan wis seen whit wis happened, he wis jaloused dey micht a fun shalter at Saatness, sae he wis sent his man ta fin oot if dey wir aa accountit fur, an if dey needit somewye ta bide eenoo. He wis happy for dem ta böl dem ithin his fine böd an he wid mak sure dey wir plenty strae fur beddin an paets fur a fire;

an dey could use his waal fur watter. Ramage haes ta feed dem an pay dem sae dey sood manage no sae ill. Dey wir bön able ta rescue some o der belangins an proveesions at low tide daday but da ship is in a terrible state.'

Eliza was visibly upset. Mary could see that she did not fully understand the ins and outs of the family's way of speaking. She put an arm around her shoulder: that new life she had enthusiastically chatted about – how she would never have to be a servant again – probably now seemed doomed to failure. Now she was a pauper, thrown on to the goodness of a poor family in a parish struggling to live from hand to mouth.

'I think we're here for the winter noo, whether we like it or no; an whether the fowk o Waas can face the thocht o it! It's just awful!'

'Lass, tak paes,' comforted Baabie. 'You're mair as wylcom, an a acht forbye wi aa da help you gie wis.' Eliza had no idea what an 'acht' might be, but she could sense it was something positive. Enough for her to lift her face.

John went on, 'We followed dem as far as da böd an set a fire tae dem and helpit gyet dem some maet. Dey wir dug-tired an desperate ta lie doon. Sae we left dem. Dey said dey likkly widna be at da kirk damoarn fur da fast, but dey hoopit we'd pass on der news dat dey wir aa safe.'

Thursday 28th October 1773
Happyhansel and Brunatwatt

Wednesday's penitential fasting had been well attended in Waas, and had seemed providential in its timing. Mr Buchan had read the scriptures of the old prophets, Joel and Jonah, with their stories of repentance and delivery. He had preached passionately of salvation by grace alone and of the need for true contrition. The congregation had given generously of the little money they had. They had sung the penitential psalms. No doubt the lay leaders in Sannis and Papa and Foula had done their best to lead the community in the same undertaking.

By Thursday, the storm had abated and many of the children were back at school, including the older ones now that hairst was finished. Any crop that hadn't been taken in was barely worth lifting. Christian, too, had rejoined classes and was keen to come early with Mary.

Mary had been busy making a lamb stew in the Dutch oven. She had kept an eye on the hard blue clods she'd placed on the big cast-iron lid, replacing them as necessary to sustain the simmer. Besides the boarders, there was now another big appetite to feed with the arrival of Patrick Ross, their billeted emigrant. She was anxious that she could spin out the fresh meat while it was available. Stews went that little bit further and she could make fine broth on the bones for the next day.

Ross came through from the parlour and leaned against the scullery door jamb.

'What's for tea, then, Mary?'

She paused briefly to consider how she should address him. 'Lamb stew and meallie tatties. How does that sound?'

'Sounds good to me. Though, to be honest, I'm angry that all that food we paid for before we set out is stuck in barrels, locked up, and we're not allowed to have some. Hogg seems uninterested and Ramage – well, he's useless.'

'He's the captain?'

'Yes. But not much of a captain, I would say.'

'It does seem unfair. Still, you'll not starve here.'

'I'm fortunate indeed being billeted here at Happyhansel, but I dare say some crofters must now be wondering when we'll all be back on board and on our way. I hear that some of the emigrants got turfed out and have had to be moved on to other houses.'

'That's a pity, Patrick. I suppose it's one thing looking after a family for a week or two… with a promise of provisions, and another thing having to face the winter months wondering how you can manage to share the little you have.'

Mary was busy moving between scullery and parlour, peeling potatoes and setting the table. She put a pot on the crook and filled it from the kettle. Patrick was somewhat in her way.

Erchie helped her serve the boys their meal and then the four of them came to the table. Mr Greig said grace and Mary dished up the food. He looked tired after what had been an exhausting day dealing with all the children in such a time of upheaval. A few of them had billeted families and had seemed confused by the fact that the emigrant children couldn't come to school. But others were saying, 'Hit's wir scöl, no der scöl!'

'Seeing that it looks like the emigrant families will be here over the winter now, maybe we should be thinking of opening up the old schoolroom at Stove?' Mr Greig was looking at Patrick as he spoke. 'Patrick, you could teach them and encourage the children to attend. Schooling is so important. And it would give them something to do. I dare say the old benches and desks are still there, and slates. It's becoming dilapidated, but at least it's a reasonable space. It's a pity we don't have extra room here for them all.'

'I don't think the families have any money for schooling.'

'Well, it's just a suggestion. I'm sure we could spare some books, and chalk and a wall-map. And of course you could still stay here with us. I wonder if perhaps some of the offerings from yesterday's services could be used for that purpose?'

'My dream is to make a new life in the Carolinas. I have some friends already settled and they report that living is easy there; I don't see myself as a poorly paid teacher in Caithness or, for that matter, as an unpaid teacher here! Anyway, how come you have such a fine school here in this remote place?'

Over their cup of tea, Mr Greig recounted the ten years of struggle to get the school built; the dream of Mr Buchan, the minister. How he had faced opposition from presbytery and had eventually decided to push ahead by gifting the croft – nine merks or four acres of land – for the use of the headteacher, for all time; how local heads of families, about two-thirds of them, had agreed to pay for local workmen; how those eleven men had built the school and schoolhouse – slate roof and all – in less than a month. And that Mr Buchan, Mrs Scott – mother of the boy laird – and the merchant Thomas Henry of Burrastow – all gave money, too.

'You manna forget da drams an bacca fae da young men an aa!' Erchie had lapsed into his mother tongue in his enthusiasm.

'You're right, Erchie. It all helped. And so there was a feeling that the school truly belonged to everyone. And the schoolhouse croft, like any croft adjoining the scattald – the common land – meant there were grazing rights too: one cow on the Heogan and sheep and cattle on the Hill of Voe; as well as the right to cut peats. Not only that, but Mr Buchan promised a small annuity of £24 Scots, which the teacher would receive at Martinmas from the owner of the Voe property.'

'That was quite an undertaking. The minister must be a wealthy man,' said Patrick Ross.

'Well, I think his wife had quite a bit of money. And they had no living children: their little baby only lived a day and sadly her son by a previous marriage died.'

Mary could see a look of sadness in Mr Greig's eyes. But he continued, possibly aware that his early life, though similar, had later been transformed by his own second marriage and the joy of Erchie's safe arrival.

'The nearest relative is her step-grandson, John Henry of Bayhaa, and he has plenty money of his own. I would say Mr Buchan has almost won the battle for legal school status, rather than just charitable status. He'll get there. I think he senses his time is shorter now and he wants to see this through; and he also wants SSPCK schools in all districts in the parish.'

Erchie excused himself as he had work to do with the boarders. At this time of year they got little chance of fresh air and exercise so, when there were no evening lessons for the younger boys, he often brought them down to the schoolrooms after their meal to do their homework and then play a game of draughts or chess or do a bit of drawing. Sometimes they moved the desks back and played leapfrog. The older boys who were preparing for college had been set additional lessons in literature or Latin and were no doubt glad of the peace.

Mary was relieved to be back at work after the storm. As she walked homewards, down the Kloss of Voe and across the little bridge, her eyes grew accustomed to the dark. By now she knew the gaet like the back of her hand. Somehow, Happyhansel was not quite the same for having Patrick Ross around; but she could not quite put her finger on why she felt like that... he might be a teacher, but so sure of himself; so full of himself... mid-thirties maybe... no word of a wife or family. He could surely do something to help the children and, if not, could he not offer to bring in peats or water, or grind some oatmeal for baking, or collect some eggs? So different from Erchie... in every way.

At Brunatwatt, she soon caught up with the day. There had been a lot of croft work in the morning, fixing and rescuing things after the storm. Somewhat unbelievably, there were few losses. They'd heard that a house at Skeotaing had lost its thatch and a henhouse at Stapness had landed up at Saatness, right across the voe. Where the hens were no one knew; probably drowned. Eliza had helped Jean flail oats in the barn. John and Jaerm had mucked out the byre and brought the fresh straw through. There had been talk of Davie Bain: Eliza had said that she was sure she had heard that his wife was a sister to the ship's carpenter, Alex Ross, and that she was very much still alive, perhaps with a child. They all wondered what had happened at the presbytery meeting in Bressa and whether Bain had turned up and what punishment, if any, had been meted out to him and Sophia. That case had all gone curiously quiet.

Friday 12th November 1773
Happyhansel and Stove

Patrick Ross was still not around at tea-time much to George Greig's surprise. He had gone off the day before to see his friend Alexander MacKay, one of the emigrants billeted in Mid Waas. He had said he would stay overnight as the afternoons were getting darker and he was unfamiliar with the two-mile track. He had told Mary he might stay an extra night. There was a look of relief on

Erchie's face at the thought.

The men were hungry. On Wednesday, John Jeems had killed and butchered one of the Happyhansel lambs for them and Leebie had taken the intestines down to where the burn flowed into the sea and had cleaned them thoroughly. Mary was delighted she had been spared the task, one she had helped her mother perform many times; the stink unbearable. Leebie had presented her with the big bag, the king's head and the sparl, all as clean as a whistle having been steeped overnight in salty water. Mary had stuffed the two larger skins with her mix of flour, oatmeal, mixed spice, finely chopped fresh suet, steeped currants and raisins, sewed them up and simmered them for hours in her largest pans. She was just vexed there was no bacon left to dish up with them.

'Horrid fine curny puddeens, Mary!' Mr Greig was keen to have another of the slices she had fried. 'Dat smell gengs roond mi haert laek a yard o waarm flannel!'

'Da boarders cam back fur mair an aa. Dey'll be nane left at dis rate,' Mary replied, 'but A'm blyde you enjoyed dem. Aet you up. A'll stuff da sparl for wis damoarn if you wid laek dat?'

Both the men looked delighted at the prospect.

'Sae foo got you on wi da meenister last nicht, Faider? I doot you never got doon tae your Latin. He man a bidden braaly late fur I hed ta geng tae mi bed eftir eleeven, I wis datn tired.'

'Ya, Erchie, hit wis eftir midnicht afore he left! He took a fiery-braand wi him ta licht his wye.'

'An his keetchin-maid fae Voe Hoose browt back wir tengs dis moarnin,' said Mary, 'sae he man a keepit his feet gyaain doon da Kloss o Voe!'

Mr Greig continued, 'I tink he wis owre blyde ta gyet awa ta wir fireside an no hae ta be mixin wi da Gordon faemily dat's billeted wi him. Der fine enyoch, but jöst a braa lock o dem.'

'Ya, fock is wearyin noo wi dis billetin an finnin hit herd ta feed dem. Wir lucky we jöst hae Eliza – shö's freendly an wirks herd; an doesna aet wis oot o hoose an haem!'

'Weel, dat wis whit Mr Buchan wis tellin me aboot.' George

Greig sipped his water and went on, 'Dey wir a lock o news fur he wis bön ta da Haa o Saand ta meet wi Balfour – da Deputy Vice-Admiral – an wi James Hogg. He got da chance o a trip on da *Hawk*, da Bayhaa sloop, aa da wye ta Garderhoose Voe whaar dey wir bales o oo ta pick up. Hit's no far fae dere ta Mitchell's Haa whaar Hogg an his faemily an servants is aa billeted.'

'He's da factor dat organised da emigrant passages?'

'Ya, Erchie. Da very wan. Hit's a braaly swanky billet, seeminly. Mr Buchan wis describin hit – Sir Andrew Mitchell o Wastshore built hit as a simmer hoose twenty year ago. Hit soonds kinda laek Bayhaa here in Waas but fancier, wi fine pine panellin an plester cornices. Some o da dressed steyn fae Scallowa Castle wis bön used, an der a fancy steyn panel abön da door as you geng in.'

'Weel we hae a peerie panel abön da scölhoose door, Faider!'

'Ya, maybe a chevron, but no a coat o airms, Erchie! Onywye Balfour telt wis he wis written tae da owner o da *Batchelor*, Inglis in Leith, becaas he wis sure Captain Ramage hed nae intention o gyettin da *Batchelor* mendit, laekly hoopin shö micht be declared a wreck an dan he wid hae nae responsibility fur da emigrants. Balfour tinks dat Inglis 'll want to gyet his ship repaired.'

'A'm heard dat rumour aboot Captain Ramage an aa,' said Mary, 'fur mi bridders is freends wi Alex Ross, da ship's carpenter, an he's finnin he canna gyet ony plans fae Ramage. An da pör boat still lyin apön her side below Germatwatt.'

'Noo dat's interestin, Mary. An Balfour could tell wis dat eicht heritors fae Waas wis axed him ta oarder Ramage – an Hogg an aa – edder ta dish oot da proveesions dat's still stored or hire anidder ship. Mr Buchan said dat Hogg tumpit his nev apö da table at dat suggestion! Dey wir a braa stooshie, fur hit wid seem dat Hogg – i da comfort o da Haa an wi his ain servants forbye – didna seem ta realise foo herd hit wis fur local fock facin a winter an seein der maet supply gyaain doon an doon. He argued dat da emigrants wis filt Shetland wi rumours an complaints, an set aaboady against him an ruined his göd name. An he didna seem ta accept ony responsibility fur feedin dem even though he wis da wan dat signed dem up, an took da fares affa dem. Hit seems he felt dat he wis da pör sowl expelled fae his security in Caithness; an dat he wid sue Inglis an Ramage!'

Erchie looked disbelieving. 'Whitna onkerry! Whit tink you will happen wi aa dis upheaval, Faider?'

'Weel, Mr Buchan said he tocht dat Balfour wisna supportive o da Waas heritors an hoops dat wi gifts o aetmel an tatties fae aa owre Shetland an, whaar necessary, mövin emigrants ta idder billets... an if Inglis 'll be as göd as his wird wi repairs... dat we'll gyet trowe dis winter somewye; an, come da green shoots o voar, da emigrants 'll get ta'en affa da isle, back tae Caithness, or ta Leith or maybe even tae Nort Carolina eftir aa!'

'I doot dey'll be a braa bit o mövin fock aroond. Da heritors 'll hae ta help wi dat, an da kirk nae doot.'

'Du's richt, Erchie. An da crew needs ta be billeted aroond Waas sae dey can dö da repairs an gyet der rations. Dey canna bide i da Voe böd owre da winter. Noo, dey wir somethin else da meenister telt me dat he wis haerd... yun sam nicht o da hurricane, whin da *Batchelor* was driven ashore here, dey wir a ship dat foondered apön da isle o Havera... da *Greyhound* shö wis caa'd... a English 400 tonner comin fae Norrawa seeminly, wi a cargo o saw-stock. Nae sign o da pör crew. Sae hit truly is a winder dat da *Batchelor* med hit ava.'

'Maybe some o dat fine timber 'll come ashore aroond da banks here,' Erchie added.

Mary looked at the clock on the wall. Its delicate hands showed 6.15pm. 'I doot Patrick is bidin owre at Mid Waas danicht an aa. Hit's far owre dark fur him noo.'

'He's maybe lost his gaet an is lyin ithin a stank at Trölligart!'

'Boy! Dunna speak laek dat,' remonstrated the father. 'We widna wiss ony ill ta come apön him.'

'I wis winderin if he'd ivver axed ony mair aboot da aald scölroom at Stove? I could a fun oot aboot hit fae Jaanie Jeromson.'

'Na, Mary, I dunna tink he's dat interestit in da idea.' Mr Greig's words seemed conclusive.

Mary briefly dropped along by Jaanie's on her way home to

Brunatwatt as she knew Saturday would be busy for both of them. Willm was still up. He was quite the schoolboy now and keen to test her on some sums. She played along with him, getting the occasional addition wrong, much to his hilarity. Willie and Katie joined in too and it seemed to Mary that some of their sadness had lifted. Though nothing was mentioned, Katie showed obvious signs of a pregnancy. When Jaanie offered to make Mary a cup of tea, Katie got up to do it. The conversation seemed easier. Willie had borrowed a fishing-rod, a waand, from a neighbour and whenever the weather allowed he had been catching sillocks from the rocks and also collecting whelks at low tide. Jaanie would bake the little fish in the Dutch oven until they fell apart. He had also had a bit of work labouring on a nearby croft and was paid in produce: potatoes, oatmeal, kale and milk. He was enjoying working with animals again as he had been a tenant farmer in Sutherland. Katie was helping Jaanie with the laundry and where mending or altering was required.

'Sae, foo's things at Happyhansel, mi jewel? I canna but tink dat Erchie is enjoyin hae'in dee aroond!' Jaanie gave the McLeods a wink as she said it.

'Dunna be daft, Jaanie! He treats me laek a sister, an dat's fine by me. I nivver feel laek a skivvy wi da Greigs.'

'We sal see. He's young yet.'

Soon it was time for Willm to get to bed and for Mary to be on her way. As she said her cheerios, she exchanged glances with Katie which left her hoping that they would not be re-billeted; that somehow all of them would manage through the winter.

Saturday 13th November 1773
Happyhansel

Saturday was generally an easier day for Mary as only the boarders remained and the place was quieter. Erchie enlisted the boys to clean their rooms and tidy their things. Usually he would help her fetch several pails of water from their well. Mary dropped along Leebie's to collect the freshly laundered clothes and linen. It was a time when they could plan what croft foodstuffs would be plentiful and what scarce: two hens to kill next week and a sack of oats ready for grinding which John Jeems would set down beside the quern in the schoolhouse barn. She would then take the pony, with its paniers strapped on, down the steep Kloss o Voe to the shop at Seafield to buy messages like tea, sugar, salt, dried fruit, flour, onions, candles and soap, often adding a few messages for Leebie. On the way back, she would occasionally meet emigrants she recognised. Their earlier acceptance of their situation seemed to have disappeared; they looked despondent and taciturn. Some of them would speak in Gaelic as they went by. She had not noticed that before.

At teatime, Mary had first served the boarders with the remainder of the sheep's puddeens and fresh oatmeal brönnies she had made. For their own meal, as promised, she cooked the sparl. She turned the anus inside out and stuffed it with a mix of oatmeal, finely diced onion, a little suet and seasoning. She had griddled it on a wire rack and the fat round the sparl melted and spat, soaking through the porous skin and basting it. It smelled appetising. Patrick returned just in time for his tea.

'Sparl? What piece of the animal is that?'

'Try it first, Patrick, and then I'll tell you.' Mary didn't think telling him it was the back passage of a sheep would encourage him to try. 'Or would you rather I scrambled you up some eggs?'

While the others tucked into the oatmeal pudding, Patrick ate the eggs, but seemed a bit distracted. He divulged that his friend Alexander MacKay had got a group of emigrants to agree to file a lawsuit with the Vice-Admiral's Court and that he wanted Patrick to write it and present it. They had agreed to sue Ramage for release of the food supplies, and also to sue both Ramage and Hogg on a series of broader charges: in particular that Ramage's navigation had been incompetent and that Hogg had inveigled the emigrants into selling up and booking a passage, with a view to them funding all the costs of the journey for himself, his family and his servants.

At that point, silence fell and Mary got up to clear away the dishes and wash up. She was hoping to get home a bit earlier.

'You should maybe be careful, Patrick. The law can be a two-edged sword,' was all George Greig said before leaving the table, admitting to himself that he had now lost track of who was being sued and by whom. The list was getting longer and seemed to go round in circles like a dog pointlessly snapping at its own tail.

Sunday 21st November 1773
Brunatwatt

Baabie and the family, including Eliza, had all been to the kirk. It was an unusually still, cold day allowing folk to linger a little after the service. It afforded the perfect opportunity to exchange news: in this case, which emigrants had left for Eid or Skeld or Gröting; and which families had gone to stay further afield. It had been a huge job moving them. There seemed to be a sadness as well as relief among the congregation. They had done their best, but it hadn't been enough. And seemingly there had been fury among the departing families that, yet again, the provisions their money had bought earlier in the year had not been doled out; that a chest of tea and barrels of salt beef and hard biscuit, meal and bread were still under lock and key. They had said John Henry of Bayhaa should never have agreed to that; he should never have given the key to Captain Ramage. Some had even thought of overpowering Ramage when he went for supplies for himself and for the crew. But the sailors were popular with the emigrants and so no one had dared to do it.

There was comment, too, that the crew had all been billeted in DoonaWaas so that, when the *Batchelor* was re-floated and serious repairs begun, they would be nearby. That seemed to meet with approval, especially since some of the crew had attended the service. Jaerm sought out Alex Ross, now billeted at Stove, and they walked up the brae together.

Joannie had opted to keep the fire in rather than accompany

the family to church. Baabie, with Mary's help, had made an Irish stew on the scrag end of an old yield yowe Joannie had killed a few days previously and had left the pot hung on the crook, simmering gently. It needed to stew for several hours to be edible. The head would make another meal, and the feet too. The legs were already salted and suspended from the rafters above the fire. Through a process of drying in the peat reek, they would gradually transform over the winter into reestit mutton.

Mary had remembered the rhyme her mother had taught them as children when they would dance and their father would whistle:

> *Dance, dance dizzy fit,*
> *Whistle Tammie Young,*
> *Sheep's heid's i da pot*
> *An du sall gyet da tongue.*

Over their dinner there was much discussion of which emigrants had left the parish for other places. Eliza seemed grateful to be staying on at Brunatwatt and was keener than ever to make herself useful. Jaerm mentioned that Alex Ross would come in aboot da nicht, maybe have his eight o'clocks with them. Jean noticeably brightened at the news.

About seven o'clock, the door creaked open and Alex came in. He stood at the door for a bit while a creepie was found. He wouldn't hear of anyone else giving up their seat, not Jaerm or John or any of the young women, so he perched awkwardly on the little stool offered. Despite the lack of decent clothes, in the low light of the koli-lamp on the wall he looked more than presentable. Mary and Christian had been attempting to read with the help of a candle, but they quickly laid by their books. No one knitted on a Sunday. Jean booced around energetically buttering brönnies and setting out the cups and milk, turning down all offers of help.

Conversation centred mainly on the current turmoil among the emigrants. Alex was now billeted with a Hughson family who had one of the few crofts at Stove. One or two other sailors were also settled in the vicinity. Others had been welcomed by local crofters at Whitesness, Saatness, Stapness, Kurkigart and Stennestwatt, all within relatively easy reach of the stranded vessel which daily seemed more doomed and less likely ever to cross the Atlantic. It was a depressing sight for a ship's carpenter, indeed for all the crew. Alex had been able to do odd jobs for the Hughsons and help with croft work. That made him feel more at ease. Also, as a crew member, his weekly provisions were welcome, particularly the salt beef and tea.

'Da *Batchelor* man be in a bit o a state, lyin coupit owre apö da shore fur, lat me see, fowr weeks noo?' Jaerm had boats in the blood and was keen to see the ship under sail again, safe and sound. He would miss the company of the crew he had come to know, but could see they wanted to succeed in their initial undertaking. Some of them had said that they would be pleased just to get the boat back to their home port of Leith.

Alex had some good news: word had got through via someone travelling between Leith and Lerwick that Mr Inglis, the owner of the *Batchelor,* had recently heard the news of the storm and the grounding of his ship; and that he would be sending the sloop *Mary* as soon as he got a clear picture of what was needed and could get it loaded with the appropriate repair materials. He had already placed an order for two new anchors. He was just waiting to hear from Captain Ramage the exact extent of the damage.

'I doot he'll hae ta wait a while afore Ramage jimps,' Joannie commented, 'I tink dat scunner wid redder shö wis declared a wreck, an dat wid lat him affa da heuk?'

'You're probably richt,' said Alex. 'I think he wid be happy enough billeted in Waas, eatin provisions, fur a while.'

'Is du still hae'in dy nichtmares aboot da voyage, Alex?' asked John. 'I ken I sometimes hae horrible draems o bein stuck i da sea-ice affa Greenland! A'm no gyaain back neist year. A'm gyaain ta geng ta da Far Haaf fur da laird instead, an fish fur cod an tusk.'

'Ya, I still hiv weird dreams, John. Far owre real for my likin:

o bairns delirious or spewin, crammed in a bunk wi their brithers or sisters; or coughin themselves to death; an me, hivvin to hap their bodies in a bittie o torn sail an slip them overboard inta the heavin dark; an the moans o their fowk, greetin.'

Baabie shook her head, 'Boy, yun's terrible – we'll aa be draemin aboot yun noo!'

'It was terrible, Mrs Johnson. The smell frae the hold was overpowerin: unwashed bodies, food gone rancid, pails o piss still to be emptied. Forgie me, I should no be tellin you this, especially wi Eliza here. I apologise.'

'No Alex, the story needs ta be heard. You an me ken fine there was over-crowdin; an that, was it eight bairns died wi smallpox? An there was whoopin cough too. Hogg and Ramage wanted to keep that quiet.'

Baabie kept an eye on Eliza, who was sitting with Mary. 'Whitna awful time o sufferin fur you aa. Noo Jean, I tink we could aa dö wi a grain o eicht o'clocks ta cheer wis up.'

'A'm heard Mr Greig spaek aboot someen caa'd Johnnie Notions fae Aeshaness an foo he's cured smaapox wi pus fae someen already infectit.'

'Gadge, Mary!' said Christian whose face, like everyone else's, was screwed up with disgust at the thought.

'Na, I tink he dries hit in paet reek an stores hit – böries hit I tink – fur ages afore he uses hit. An hit does wirk! He uses a peerie blade ta slip a coarn anunder da skyin apö da airm, an dan rowes da airm up wi a kale laef!'

'Mary, du shurly is makkin yun up?'

'A'm no makkin hit up, Midder! An I dunna tink Mr Greig wid lee aboot somethin sae serious.'

'Du's richt aboot dat, mi jewel,' said Baabie.

While they drank their tea there was talk about the news that Balfour, the Deputy Vice-Admiral, was yet again encouraging charitable donations especially from the gentry and local heritors. Seemingly Arthur Nicolson of Lochend had said he wanted rid of the emigrants and suggested a small ship of 200 tons would take them south for five shillings[3] a head. He had said that they were causing oppression in Shetland.

'Hit soonds as if he tinks da emigrants is jöst like kye,' Mary added, 'or slaves. Hit's a horrid wye ta speak aboot haemless fock.'

Joannie said, 'I heard dat some o da casks o bread wis bön shiftit fae Henry's store tae da kirk. Drier I suppose.'

'I canna tink why Buchan is agreed ta dat ava,' said Baabie.

'Well, if it saves the bread frae spoilin, it's maybe a good thing, Mrs Johnson.'

'You're maybe richt dere, Eliza.'

The night wore on and eventually Alex said he would need to get back to Stove before the Hughsons went to bed. And yes, he was confident he would find his way – it wasn't far.

Once he had gone there was a post-mortem.

Jean thought him good-looking.

Mary thought him good company.

Christian thought his dreams would haunt her.

Eliza said she knew that he was a steady man and a good carpenter.

Baabie warned them again that he was most likely a married man.

Joannie smeegit. John and Jaerm looked at one another and shook their heads.

And no one had asked about his family link with Davie Bain or whether Sophia's child had ever been baptised, despite Joannie's best efforts.

Monday 22nd November 1773
Happyhansel

Mary's day at the schoolhouse had been particularly busy. Winter time seemed to generate more work: the children's clothes and boots often needed to be dried out before they could set off for

---

3 1/- means 'one shilling' or, colloquially, a 'bob'. There were twelve pennies (d) in every shilling and twenty shillings (s) in a pound (£).

home again and keeping a guttery mess out of the schoolrooms was a constant chore. She had done a churning and made some fresh butter and kirn-mylk; and had ground some oats on the quern for what felt like an hour as the girnal was needing to be topped up and she hadn't had time to take a sack of oats down to the mill. Maybe John Jeems would do that for her. She had prepared a substantial dinner of chicken and was planning to serve boiled eggs to the boys at tea-time, and maybe offer the men a supper of brose instead, before she set off for Brunatwatt. On a cold night, that would keep them warm.

The scullery door was ajar and she was aware of Patrick standing at the window of the low-ceilinged parlour as the November light faded in the west. He was flicking the pages of a heavy book set on the window-sill. She decided to offer him some tea. Perhaps he would tell her about the book which seemed to engross him.

When she set down his cup, she quickly saw that it was the kirk session minute book, which she knew was confidential. She dusted it from time to time, but never looked inside. Patrick closed it and returned it to the shelf before sitting down by the fire with his cup of tea.

'I don't think we're meant to read those minutes, Patrick.'

'Too bad, I've read them now. Money for marriages and pew rents; and what a lot of fornication and pre-nuptial "congress"; and smuggling and borrowing money! And the kirk folk pay a lot to keep up this school and schoolhouse. He tugged at his waistcoat and said pompously, "Seven large nails for the Hearth of Schoolhouse – 7d." And £22 for an anker of wine and £3 /15/- for a lispund of flour for bread, and another 12 bob for baking it... communion must be a genteel affair here... 12 shillings for washing the cloths... no wonder they need so much bread to soak up eight gallons of wine!'

'I'm sure it's not all for one communion season, even if the kirk is full and there's two sittings and several kirks in the parish.'

'And it pays George Greig £12 a year. I bet your wages come

out of the collection plate too!'

'What if they do? Though people are poor there's a thirst for learning here, and for local bairns it's free now. And I would say they probably get more to eat at Happyhansel than many would get at home. There's always sweet milk and kirn-mylk and bread for those who are hungry. Sometimes a bit of left-over meat.'

'You're very sure of yourself for a servant!'

That comment stung Mary. She wanted to say something by way of retort, but knew her place well enough. And she knew the kirk's influence was far and wide, and could be harsh and open to criticism. She merely said, 'Well, I know several folk who have had poor relief from the kirk when their cow has died, or their man lost at sea. Or when they needed a little money to help give a child a decent burial.'

'I wonder how much fornication is needed to raise the relief given when a cow dies, or pay for school books? And how much adultery would be needed to pay for a grave-digger?'

Mary returned to the scullery.

Mr Greig and Erchie opted for a supper of brose. She didn't ask Patrick Ross if that would suit him. She had the boiling water ready and the sizzling roast lamb dripping she had saved. She measured out scoops of freshly ground oatmeal into a basin, added some salt and ladled in just enough boiling water to make a stiff paste. She heaped it into the largest, deepest serving plate she could find and patted it down firmly, pricking it with a fork. Then she formed a well in the middle and poured the hot dripping into the well. She set it in the middle of the table with small bowls of salt and sugar and four spoons.

Grace was perfunctory. Mr Greig had his spoon at the ready. He took a spoonful of the warm oats and dipped it in the fat, and blew on it before his first mouthful. 'I've not had brose for many a year, Mary. Boy, it's good! Now, don't break down the well, Patrick!'

Monday 17th January 1774
Brunatwatt

The winter solstice and Yöl had come and gone, and New'r Day.
The boarders had been home on holiday while the school was
closed. There had been the usual arguments between those who
preferred to keep Old Christmas and those who had moved to the
new dates. Mary had been given some time off. Unfortunately, her
father's older brother, Laurie o' Grötquoy, had died not long before
Yöl which had somewhat dampened the spirits of the immediate
family. There had been guizing and merry-making at the Laings'
house nearby. Some of the sailors from the *Batchelor* had been
there, and had slept over in local barns. The family had not felt
they could join in, much to their disappointment.

Once a decent period of mourning was over, there had been a
caerdin at the Johnsons' when a lot of the local girls had gathered
to caerd the wool kept back for the family's own use. In the days
to come there would be spencers and hose to knit, and ganseys
and keps. No end to the makkin.

As Mary walked to Happyhansel for the first day after the
Yöl break, her mind kept recalling the night of the caerdin. The
spinning-wheel and kishies had been cleared from the but-end
and an extra koli-lamp lit: the smell of the fish oil mixed with
the creeshy odour from the sacks of raw wool. Mary and Jean
had baked bannocks and cut some reestit mutton and Christian
and Eliza had swept and tidied. Their brothers had disappeared
after tea and promised to be back later with a fiddler. Before they
left, they had made sure there was fresh straw in the barn in case
some of their friends drank a bit too much and might need a
langbed for the night. The nearest Brunatwatt neighbours knew
of the caerdin and had asked Baabie and Joannie in aboot da
nicht. They were not so old that they had forgotten the winter
pleasures of guizing and caerdins. And that over the years many
a baby had unexpectedly 'come up atween da raas'[4] come hairst.

---

4 Illegitimate pregnancy (lit. like a stray plant).

Mary could still hear the skirls of Jean's friends at the yard dyke. In they had spilled: the Morison sisters and Agnes Sletter from Stove, Margaret Irvineson from Stennestwatt and Bess Sletter from Foratwatt. They were high-spirited young women, keen to get the caerdin done and on to the dancing. Daily life was drudgery, so any chance of some freedom and lightsomeness was to be grabbed in both hands. They had taken off their heavy boots and donned their soft hide rivlins. Each had brought with them a pair of caerds and, once seated round the room, had set to the task, cleaning the wool and then teasing it back and fore in a flowing motion, little by little, across the prongs of the caerds until the floor was covered in the softest rowers of wool, ready to spin. It had been like a sea-shore covered in airy froad blown in by the wind.

And then, just as they were finishing bagging up the rowers, they had heard the clatter of boots on the briggisteyns and suddenly the but-end was crammed with young men, including one or two sailors off the *Batchelor*. From pockets here and there they had pulled out jars filled with home brewed ale, brandy or gin, having already drunk enough to rid themselves of self-consciousness. The bannocks Mary and Jean had baked and filled with reesit mutton disappeared like snow off a hill dyke, and before the fiddler could tune up there were exhortations to get the reels and circle dances underway. How they had heuched and stamped and almost toppled as they bumped into one another. Jaerm and Eliza had seemed particularly at ease with one another. At one point, Mary's heart had been in her mouth as someone almost knocked over a koli-lamp. And Alex Ross had asked her to dance a reel. He was a good dancer and, although she felt shy with him, she liked it when they were inadvertently pushed closer together by the other dancers. Much to her disappointment, Jean had pulled him up to dance after that. The poor fiddler was soaked with sweat: he had called it a day at one in the morning. Margaret o' Stennestwatt had looked pleased to have an offer from the lad from the Beddins to follow her home over Corbie Hill; and Alex had offered to accompany

any of the Stove neighbours who were ready to go home.

Mary had asked no questions in the morning. She had heard Eliza climb the ladder to her little attic eyrie and John and Jaerm soon afterwards. Christian and Jean were meant to share the box-bed in the but-end, normally used by their parents who had slipped in earlier and, as arranged, gone to bed in the ben-end. That had left a few of the young folk to bed down in the barn, especially those who were the worse for wear.

But just as Mary had been drifting off to sleep, happily exhausted from all the activity of the day and evening, Christian had pushed open the closet door. She had been anxious that there was no sign of Jean. Mary had assured her that Jean would be back soon – she was probably out at the dry-closet. Christian was so reluctant to go back to bed that Mary had offered her the closet, and she had crept through and opened the door of the box bed and climbed inside. But sleep had gone from her. Sometime later she had heard Jean climbing in beside her, seemingly unaware of which of her sisters was her sleeping companion. Mary had pretended to be fast asleep. The smell of stale drink was unbearable. She was relieved when Jean turned over and seemed to fall sound asleep. She lay wakeful, her mind combing the night like a pair of caerds, a strange small gladness happing her like a rower. In Alex's company she had felt curiously more alive, almost insulated from others. He had spoken at some length to her; told her that Captain Ramage had received a letter from the owner saying that he would be sending a sloop with repair materials; and that meanwhile they were going to arrange a gang of men to help haul the *Batchelor* off the rocky beach at high tide so they could make some repairs.

Although Mary was tired after the previous night's revelry, her day went quickly. The children and boarders seemed happy to be back and the Greigs in their usual humour. Patrick Ross seemed withdrawn. She kept out of his way.

Thursday 20th January 1774
Stove

Since Tuesday, Mary had been briefly dropping by Jaanie's on her way home from school as Jaanie had told her that Katie's baby was due at any time. Though Jaanie had initially been reluctant to give them the ben-end – her son Walter's room – she had decided that now they would need the space, especially with a cradle. Willm had happily moved to the closet in which, up until then, they had managed. Mary offered to come back later in the evening and stay over to help. Willm was delighted at the prospect of sharing the closet with Mary. Jaanie remonstrated and said he should share the box bed with her, and give Mary peace, but Mary was happy to indulge the child. After all, he wouldn't see much of his granny for a few days as she attended to the birth and the tasks of the confinement.

'I wid hae ta geng tae mi wark of coorse, but wid try ta gyet back betimes. Maybe I could ax Mr Greig if Willm could come wi me on Setterday. Wi only da boarders an da men ta feed hit's aye a calmer day at da scölhoose.'

Jaanie was grateful for Mary's suggestions as she could then concentrate on applying her midwifery skills, knowing Willm was happy. Having to look after the little boy, with his mother dead and his father away at sea, had sometimes made it difficult. Laundry could wait, but not a birth. She was determined this baby would live and thrive.

Mary got back from Brunatwatt in time to share eight o'clocks with Jaanie and the McLeods. She had brought a few things she would need; some clothes, a small towel and comb; and her makkin-bag with some clews of wool she had spun.

Willm was already asleep in the closet and the evening was quiet around the fire. They were all tired. Jaanie had made a big pot of broth on a hen Willie had been given by the crofter he helped and he had brought in extra water from the well at Jaanie's request. The McLeods soon went off to bed, leaving Jaanie and Mary.

Mary fastened her makkin-belt around her waist and started

to make a cradle-band. She used the natural colours and kept the pattern simple and small. The rows were short, so it grew quickly.

'Yun's boannie, Mary. My aald cradle-baand is kinda moch-aeten.'

'Hit's a fine aesy thing ta mak. Jaanie, I wis winderin, foo cam you ta be a howdie?'

Jaanie took a deep breath. 'Weel, mi jewel, you can only laern fae someen dat's döin a göd job. I laerned fae a wife at baed at Saatness. Shö hed göd haands on her an took pride in makkin sure da midder wis safe. Hit's no aesy fur a wumman bringin a bairn inta dis wirld, especially da first een. Hit's herd wark fur dem, an you hae ta keep dem fae lossin haert or gyettin on a amp. I try ta keep a calm sough an dat helps.'

'I canna tink o onyboady dat wid be better suitit tae da job as you, Jaanie.'

'Weel, der some birts dat mak me nearly greet, especially whin a wife haes ta deliver a bairn dat's already dead. Aa dat laaberin, an dan döl. Sometimes I hae ta help haul da baby oot, laek as if hit wis a lamb.'

'I mind Faider sayin dat's whit he hed ta dö wi wan o wir kye. He said hit cam feet first an he hed ta tie a bit o towe aroond da legs an haul. Nearly med me spew ta tink on hit!'

'Lass, if we could jöst aa manage da wye a hill yowe lays a lamb.'

'Even a yowe can hae a hard time, Jaanie. I mind traivellin up da Kloss o Voe wan late voar moarnin an saa a yowe wi a lamb's head stickin oot o her. An hit wisna muckle farder on bi da time I gied tae da shop fur airrands twartree ooers later!'

Jaanie looked serious. 'Kens-du dat birth is a graet leveller. An daeth an aa of coorse. Hit's nae aesier fur da jantry ta bring a bairn inta da wirld as hit is fur da laeks o wis; even if dey hae servants ta help. I wis blyde ta help Margaret Scott, weel Mistress Henry o Bayhaa I sood caa her. I wis kinda wirried aboot hit da first time, hae'in ta bide doon at Bayhaa dat January, jöst eftir New'r Day. Shö hed her a bassel wi dat een. But we managed, an shö hed me back fur baith da idder peerie lasses – boannie peerie tings dey ir.

An John Henry paid me weel.'

'I hoop fur aaboady's sake dat dis birth 'll no be a tyoch een,' said Mary.

'Hit wisna aesy ta ax Keetie aboot her first bairn an whit laek da birth wis, but owre da hidmist weeks shö's telt me enyoch fur me ta ken dat dey wir nae complications, laek da cord gyettin wippit roond da infant's neck. An shö löt me examine her an check whit wye da bairn is lyin an whaar da head is. Sae far, aathin seems ta be gyaain fine; but things can change. I jöst want her ta hae a infant dat's weel, an fur her ta gyet apön her fit again afore lang. I dunna believe in lyin-in unless da midder is poorly.'

'We jöst hae ta hoop fur da best, Jaanie.'

They chatted on and knitted for a bit but, as they both knew they needed all the rest and sleep they could get, they were keen to turn in relatively early.

Friday 21st January 1774
Stove

By the time Mary got to Stove it was almost seven in the evening. Willie McLeod was in the but-end with Willm, a look of anxiety on his face that told Mary the baby was well on the way. Mary gave Willm a hug and assured him how fine it would be to have an infant in the house; and how grown-up that would make him feel. She would tell him a story before he went to bed. Then she knocked gently on the ben-end door. A candle was dimly lighting the room. Both women greeted her. Katie was half lying, half propped up, sweat beading her brow. She smiled as Mary came in.

'How are you, Keetie? Can I get onythin fur you?' Mary and Katie both looked at Jaanie, who seemed to have assumed a new persona in her clean white pinnie and her hair well covered.

'Wir fine, jewel. If du can jöst luik tae wir Willm an keep Willie calm, du'll be dön a göd job.'

Suddenly Katie started to hold her belly and screw up her face.

She let out an involuntary gasp. Jaanie bent her forward gently and rubbed her back and held her hand.

'Braethe noo, braethe deep inta da cramps, my dear. Da pains is comin quicker noo. Dat's göd... deep braeths noo... anidder een... dere we go...' and turning to Mary added, 'A peerie coarn o warm broth, Mary, dat wid be fine.' Mary had been holding her breath too and screwing up her face without realising it. She could see this was indeed a labour of love. She brought through two bowls of broth and went back to see to Willm and settle him for bed.

He wanted to tell her about his school day. After a story he asked, 'Foo will yun baby win oot o Keetie's belly?'

'My dear, da sam wye as yun peerie lamb we saa bein boarn in May. Can du mind?'

'Gadge! Dat's horrible. Wis dat foo I wis boarn?'

'Dat hit wis, jewel, an du's nane da waar o hit, sae A'll tuck dee in an, damaorn's moarn, du'll see da new baby!'

Willie settled to the quiet task of making simmins for the roof. He'd carried a net, a maeshie, full of straw back with him after a session of flailing sheaves of oats, and was patiently plaiting it to make the long ropes. The crofter had said Jaanie's house would need to be re-thatched come summer and she was welcome to have some of his straw.

It was a long night with Mary as the go-between, keeping Willie company and bringing whatever Jaanie asked for through to the ben-end. She also kept the fire in and the koli-lamp burning. The cramps got fiercer and faster and at times Katie let out a cry or a moan, but Jaanie kept her calm, wiping her brow, holding her hand, rubbing her back; soothing and exhorting in equal measure.

Jaanie knew the worst point was when there was no let up, no moment of recovery between the waves of pain. That was when she had to make sure the mother didn't give up.

At last, there was a brief calm before the final stage. Jaanie asked Mary to hold one of Katie's arms. The thrashing pains were gone, but the unstoppable desire to push overtook the mother.

Jaanie kept one hand on Katie's belly. 'Hadd dy breath an push *noo*, dear! Just peerie breaths noo. Peerie puffs 'll dö. Keep on pushin!'

Poor Katie's face was red and contorted with the sheer effort. Mary took a damp cloth and mopped her brow for her. She smiled weakly in response and asked how she was progressing.

'You're döin jöst fine, jewel. I can see da croon noo. Hit'll no be dat lang.'

Mary was amazed at how calm and in control Jaanie was when she herself felt this situation was more than a little scary. She lost count of the times Jaanie had said, 'Hadd dy braeth an push… *noo*!' but eventually, in a state of utter exhaustion for Katie, the baby's head came right through, followed surprisingly quickly by the shoulders. Jaanie held up the infant, announcing it was a fine peerie lass. She asked Mary for a towel and a basin. She quickly clamped the cord and cut it and immediately the baby screamed as its lungs inflated.

'Der naethin wrang wi her lungs!' She wrapped the baby in the towel and gave her to the new mother whose face was streaked with tears of relief and joy. Meanwhile Jaanie dealt with the afterbirth and a small tear.

'You're dön most horrid weel, Keetie. Noo, Mary, can du rin an gyet Willie ta come ben da hoose? He needs ta meet his dochter!'

Mary brought the good news to a much relieved father and left the little family together while Jaanie cleared up and refreshed the bedding as best she could. There would be a big washing to come and some fresh straw for the mattress. The wooden cradle and its bedding and new band were brought in and gradually a peace came over the little house. They had all weathered a storm and come through. Mary climbed into bed, shifting the sleeping Willm over slightly to give her space. She put her arm over him, hoping to doze off quickly as she would need to be up early. She had the option of bringing Willm up to Happyhansel or leaving him at home. Happily, the decision was for him and Jaanie to make.

Saturday 22nd January 1774
Stove and Happyhansel

Jaanie and Willie were up early too and could report that the baby's first night had gone well. She had taken to the breast easily and Katie, having had some experience of nursing a baby, was comfortable. The parents had decided to call the baby Jane, after Jaanie, and Jaanie was like a dog with two tails. Willm was soon up and was allowed through to the ben-end with Jaanie to see the infant. Jane was sleeping peacefully in the cradle and Willm bent down and gently rocked it.

'Dat's my cradle, Granny.'

'Dat hit is, Willm, an isna hit da fine ta hae a peerie ting ta share hit wi dee?'

'I tink hit is.' He looked a little unsure and clung to Jaanie, but Katie was quick to thank him for the use of the cradle, which brought a wide smile.

Jaanie asked him, 'Wid du laek ta bide here wi me daday or wid du redder geng ta Happyhansel wi Mary?'

'I tink... I tink... I wid laek ta geng wi Mary.'

'Dat's fine, jewel. Du'll be able ta tell wis if du tinks Jane is grown ony bi da time du wins haem!'

The morning was cold and windy with a lowering sky. Sleet or perhaps more snow was on the way. Mary walked as fast as she could and Willm had to run to keep up with her. Just where the Kloss o Voe steepened, he shouted on her to wait for him. She turned and waited then hurried on again. She realised she was lucky Mr Greig was allowing her to bring Willm with her on a day when they generally were relieved not to have little children around.

She gave Willm tasks to do, setting plates and cutlery on the breakfast table but, much to Mr Greig's disappointment, insisted she and Willm would eat their meals in the scullery. She knew that otherwise Patrick Ross would think she was taking a liberty. She tried to keep out of the way as best she could, spending a fair bit of the morning in the barn with Willm, showing him how to kirn milk and make butter. He helped her turn the handle and enjoyed mimicking the swishing sounds of the creamy milk. She gave him the wooden pats to make patterns on the glistening butter. Then he stood on a creepie and happily turned the quern for a while, dropping in the puckles of oats and gathering the oatmeal. He was proud of his achievements. Mary had made some kale soup the day before and it was even tastier for being left to stand all night. She served it up with reestit mutton and bannocks. The boarders, with their growing appetites, had wanted seconds. After dinner, Mr Greig had a nap before taking classes in navigation and literature with the boarders. Erchie had brought in water and peats. He was happy to amuse Willm in the other classroom while he tidied it up. That gave Mary time to get a baking done and plan what they would all eat the following week.

There was fresh sassermaet and eggs for their tea: it seemed that everyone was happy and replete. John Jeems, with help from another neighbour, had killed a pig just before Yöl and Mary had minced and seasoned enough pork to fill all the big lem jars, sealing them well with fat to keep them from spoiling. She had managed to cure the legs and had left instructions with Erchie about meals he could make for the holiday period with trotters, chops, head and liver. He had joked with her after Yöl about the amazing meals he had conjured up in her absence.

While she ate with Willm in the scullery, Mary could just pick out the teatime conversation in the parlour. Patrick's voice was raised. He had been away in Lerwick for a few days, but she had not enquired of Erchie the reason for his absence. She had assumed he wanted to meet up with Alexander MacKay and some of his emigrant friends now billeted there.

'Would you believe it – Balfour has ruled against us; against the emigrants! And he said that we have to pay the court expenses into the bargain!'

Mr Greig asked calmly, 'Did he rule that the provisions should be divided up and distributed among you?'

'No, he didn't even bother to rule on that. I think he expects the food will last and can be used when we eventually get on board, but when that is, heaven alone knows. He'll have to sing for the court expenses! How on earth are they to be gathered from poor emigrants with no income and no savings left; and scattered all over Shetland now? I'll be damned if I'm paying anything!'

'Maybe you could have a word with Mr Buchan, Patrick. He knows a lot of people, including Balfour; and maybe even the session would agree to a loan meantime.'

The Poor Box haes its uses, Mary thought to herself, as she came through to the warm parlour to clear away their dishes.

'Du sood gyet on dy wye afore lang, Mary. Du haes dy haands foo an we can aesy manage ta mak a pot o tae.' Mr Greig went on, 'Is du bidin on at Stove danicht?'

'Na, A'll drap Willm back haem an see foo der gyettin on afore I geng ta Brunatwatt. A'm sure dey dunna need me noo an I wid jöst be i da wye.'

Willm, who was tagging along, said, 'Can du no jöst bide wan mair nicht, Mary?'

'Na, mi jewel, du can be Granny's helper noo! Come and we'll clear da lem afore we geng haem. A'm left you some fine ham fur damoarn. An der a pan o tatties pared an some neeps.'

When they reached Stove, Willm rushed in to greet Jaanie, full of news of his busy day. He had a peep in the cradle where Jane was grizzling and then pulled a face. Jaanie lifted the baby and gave her to Mary to hold briefly while Willie moved the cradle through to the ben-end where his wife was resting and where she would have peace to feed and settle the child. The infant flopped on Mary's shoulder, snuggling like any young thing seeking warmth and comfort.

'Whitna peerie moot. Du's jöst da best peerie bundle A'm ivver shoodered.' Willm stood beside her chair, gently touching the baby's hap, and looked wide-eyed at Mary.

Jaanie seemed relaxed and, from that, Mary knew that the day had gone well. Willie lifted the boiling kettle from the crook and made them a pot of tea. He added peats to the fire. Eventually,

Katie came through to join them briefly. Jaanie had made a cushion for her so she could be comfortable.

'I cannae thank you enough, Mary, for helping me last nicht. I can tell Jaanie is a winderful howdie. I could'nae hae gotten through that without the pair o ye.'

Mary reached out to embrace her. Though Katie looked tired, much of the anxiety seemed to have lifted. Mary hoped that the grief of the voyage would no longer haunt them.

'Hit's lovely that you called her after Jaanie. Peerie Jane. Bi da time da ship is fixed up an you on your way shö'll be takkin soleeds an growin laek mad!'

Willie said, 'Weel, that's for anither day, Mary. We're just relieved this baby seems fine an Katie on her feet again. Shö was very poorly after the last birth.'

Mary excused herself, bidding them all goodnight, promising to drop along one evening on her way home the following week.

Wednesday 26th January 1774
Waas Voe

The day planned for re-floating the *Batchelor* dawned reasonably fair despite the snow. She lay grounded below Germatwatt, close to shore, tipped over almost on her side. The crew had brought off everything that could be moved to make her as light as possible, but they were going to feel the strain of her 260 tons. The plan was to re-float her in the hope that she would right herself without them having to cut off her masts.

Captain Ramage was onboard, somewhat precariously, with Ross, Shanks and Bennet. Luckily, with January being a quiet time of year for crofting and fishing, local men were around to help, gathering at the Germatwatt jetty in the morning half-light. Thomas Liddle, the mate, was there to greet them and issue instructions. There were nearly 30 of them – including John and Jaerm – with four fowrareens, their rudders unshipped. Eight of the local men were ready to man the oars of the ship's longboat, newly strengthened and sea-worthy.

The *Hawk* dropped a spare anchor and chain where it would make a useful kedge for the crew of the *Batchelor* to use. One of the fowrareens then brought the attached anchor rope from the *Hawk* back to their stricken ship where it could be wound round the windlass. This would help in the effort to get her off the shore. Several of the other local men were delegated to push some planks underneath the side of the barque to lever her up a bit to protect the hull and rudder. It was going to need sheer brute force.

By the time all was ready, the tide was at its highest point. The five boats – the four local fowrareens and the ship's longboat – were each thrown a line. Ramage was shouting about knots, but John could interpret 'mak hit fast aroond da hoarn.' As the biggest, the ship's longboat – with its new oars and crew of eight – was in the middle of the little flotilla, with two local boats on either side. They would help not just with the hauling, but also with controlling the ship as she righted herself. At least, that was the plan.

At the captain's command they all pulled on their oars and the crew attempted to turn the windlass which was still at a difficult angle. The tension in the ropes increased as did the cacophony of shouting; a crunch filled the air as the ship slowly inched offshore. It disturbed the seagulls and they added to the commotion. The men's backs bent to the task and their muscles tightened, their feet hard against the ribs of their little boats. The pliable oars bent with the pressure. Ramage tried to orchestrate the rowing while Liddle checked where more or less effort was needed to protect the hull, using gestures to separate the boats or bring them closer. One rope snapped and another one had to be attached. Almost imperceptibly, the *Batchelor* moved until it was possible to slip some planks under her.

Gradually, the men in the small boats could feel the strain on their oars becoming less as the water was rising under her until, eventually, the ropes went slack. They had done it! She was afloat. They held their breath waiting to see if she would right herself. The masts, which had held through storm and hurricane and grounding, then rose with a quiet magnificence. A huge cheer went up from all the men and a crowd now gathered along the shore. The borrowed anchor which had taken so much of the strain was lifted on to the *Batchelor*. At last, she was free, afloat and alive.

It was, by this time, past high tide and they needed to tow her, at the mate's instructions, to safe anchorage. Another shout of relief arose as the chain gave a final rattle and the anchor disappeared below the surface.

As ship's carpenter, Alexander Ross had a list of checks to make on the hull, particularly where the temporary repairs had been done to ensure there were no leaks. It had been a moment of triumph for everyone.

Thursday 27th January 1774
Stove

There were no children at Happyhansel from Mid Waas, from Stennestwatt or from the outlying homes at Riskaness or Whitesness. Snow covered all the rigs and toons and the Loch o Kurkigart was frozen almost completely. The pupils had all been well warned that they should never try to skate on it or be tempted to cross over. At breaktime, after their dinner, if the wind relented, some of them would make a slide near the school. They usually lost track of time and had to be called back in for afternoon classes.

Walking to and from work was a struggle for Mary during the worst of the winter weather. When there was snow or slush on the ground, or there was no moon visible, Erchie would see her down the Kloss just to be sure she didn't fall in the dark. He used to say to her, 'Du's as sure-fittit as a Shetland pony!' Sometimes Patrick would raise an eyebrow, but Mr Greig would hear nothing of it if Mary insisted she could manage fine without Erchie coming out in the cold night. She was glad of Erchie's company and he seemed undeterred by foul weather. Sometimes his father would give him a note to take to Mr

Buchan whose big house stretched along the slope at its steepest part.

Mary had decided she would pass by Jaanie's on her way home. Willm had made it to school despite being one of the younger children. There were plenty bairns travelling to school every day from Stove, so Jaanie did not have to worry about him. They were all delighted to see her. Katie was up and about and looking stronger. Mary could see that she was almost blooming. The baby had just had a feed and was about to be put down to sleep.

'A wee cuddle, Mary, before I put her ben?'

Mary took Jane in her arms. Her eyes were already closed and her lips pursed in contentment. She gently cradled her, looking at the pride in the eyes of her parents, wondering for herself if she would ever have a child. She could see there was life before having children and life after having children and that, especially for a woman, these lives were very different. Her mind was racing... Katie's experience on the voyage had been solemn, life-changing; but Willie... so steady, hard-working and content with his little family... and... at home... not away at sea... or the whaling or the Far Haaf.

She handed the child back to her mother, glad of the chance to see Jane up close and feel that strange warm surrender to the body of another. Now it was Willm's turn for a cuddle.

He pushed at Mary's breasts and said, 'Does du hae mylk i dy paaps, Mary?' The family collapsed laughing and the little boy looked taken aback at their response.

'Na, mi jewel, I dunna. Only midders gyet dat fur a while eftir der hed a bairn.'

'Dat's clever.'

'Dat hit is, Willm.'

'Sae will du hae a bairn?'

'I dunna ken, mi dear. Maybe wan day.'

He seemed content with that response, but Mary felt there might well be further questions at another time. It was easier to deal with Willm's questions when others weren't overhearing.

Once Katie came back through and Willm was off to bed,

Willie asked Mary whether they could get Mr Buchan to baptise Jane, and arrange to register her. She offered to write a note on their behalf. She could drop it off at Voe House on her way to or from Happyhansel. She took down the details she would need to give him: their full names as well as Jane's. And their home parish and minister's name. They had letters of recommendation from him, so they looked them out for Mary to take with her: these were proof of their legal marriage, their kirk membership and their good character.

'I'll drop this aff tomorrow, on my way. Mr Buchan's servants 'll be up. There's aye a licht in the kitchen window when I pass.'

Much as Mary now felt at ease with the McLeods, at times she found it awkward to converse, speaking in her own tongue, or English or somewhere in between. 'You' or 'du'? They were all still adjusting to each other.

Jaanie was warming Mary's coat for her. 'I winder whitivver happened aboot baptisin Sophia Henderson's bairn. A'm nivver heard hide nor hair o dat pair since dey left here in a scrit. Whit atween dem bidin in Delting, dan comin here fur a bit, an dan mövin tae Saandsting, I doot da kirk's discipline 'll be sorely challenged, shaestin eftir dem! Whitna pair!'

Just as Mary was about to head for Brunatwatt, Alex Ross knocked and entered tentatively. Willie got up immediately and welcomed him, introducing him to Jaanie who made space for him on the resting-chair. He greeted Katie warmly, congratulating her on the birth.

He was about to greet Mary, who was already on her feet, when Katie said, 'You maybe ken Mary o' Brunatwatt? Works tae Mr Greig at Happyhansel... and was a graet help to me tha ither nicht?'

'Yes, I ken Mary fine, Katie. I'm freends wi her brither, Jaerm. He's a seaman, a whaler. An John too.'

They all congratulated him on the righting of the *Batchelor*. It had looked so forlorn for months.

'Tak aff o you, Alex, an set you in tae da fire,' said Jaanie. 'Mary, du could bide a peerie meenit langer.'

From an inside pocket Alex pulled out a small bottle of whisky and, from another pocket, a package inside which was a bit of boiled salted beef.

'Part o oor ship's rations, Jaanie. Maybe a wee bit wid be tasty for yir dinner tha moarn?'

Jaanie thanked him kindly. She found a small glass, and he filled it up and passed it to Katie and Willie who each took a sip; then to Jaanie and Mary and finally he finished it off with, 'It's good tae weet tha bairnie's heid, is it no? Here's tae a healthy bairn!'

'And here's tae da *Batchelor!*' said Jaanie. 'May shö hae göd luck fae noo on!'

They all agreed and the men had another glass each before Alex set the bottle on the table.

They newsed a bit. Jaanie mentioned the various local weddings over the Yöl and New'r Day holiday; and possibilities for renewed contracts at Candlemas.

'Dey'll be nae faer o dee bein hired fur anidder year, Mary!'

'I hoop you're richt, Jaanie. I laek wirkin at Happyhansel. An da penga helps wir fock, especially eenoo whin mi bridders is at haem.'

When asked, Alex divulged that yes, the Hughson's were good folk and he liked living in Stove fine; no, there was no sign yet of the sloop *Mary* coming with the wood and gear; no, he didn't hear much from the other emigrants now spread more widely beyond Waas; and no, he hadn't heard, nor did he want to hear, from Davie Bain, his former countryman who had left Caithness to work in Orkney and then Shetland. He told them Bain was married to Christian Ross, his sister, and that she had come down to the pier at Thurso in September to see the *Batchelor* leave and to have a chance to speak with her brother. He had been glad to see her. He told them he had moved to Leith some years ago as it was easier to get a berth out of Leith than out of Thurso.

His other news was that the sailors were bidden to the party on the Monday after Candlemas at Agnes Slatter's house in Stove; and, by way of response, they were asking local folk to come aboard the *Batchelor* as she was now at least safe, even if not yet seaworthy.

They wanted to share some of their provisions with Waas folk as a wee thank you for their hospitality during a hard time. Any time after kirk the next Sunday would be best as that was their only day off; and they would all be welcome. The crew would transport them from the little pier below Germatwatt. Jaanie thanked him and said she didn't think she would manage to get on board, but she was sure the younger ones would be happy to go. The McLeods thought it was just a bit too early for Katie to be out and about, and the baby might need her. Mary said she would come if her brothers and sisters were going. She hoped their parents would think it was all right on a Sunday.

'Dy faider wid laekly tink hit a spree, Mary! Wan i da eye for aald Deyell o Gröntu,' said Jaanie. 'He's sic a meesery.'

Mary soon rose to leave. Alex said he too must go, as he knew the McLeods would have a broken night ahead of them and would need some peace. Despite it being out of his way, he offered to accompany Mary a fair bit of her path home as it was slippery and dark. Jaanie and the McLeods encouraged him, so, despite Mary's protestations and assurances that she would manage fine, they headed out into the cold blast. They had to raise their voices above the wind, so most of the time there was little chance of conversation. She laughed when he asked about Jaerm and Eliza and was he right in his suspicion.

She changed the subject and told him she had heard that Balfour had ruled against the emigrants to which he just replied, 'That would be Patrick Ross's ones. I didn't sign up wi him.'

When they came as far as the gaet to Gröntu, Mary hesitated. She looked at the little croft house sitting on the brow of the hill.

She turned to Alex and said, over the noise of the wind, 'The Deyells o Gröntu dunna laek wir faemily. Der very holy – dey tink wis lasses kinda slippit! I aye feel a bit scared here; but A'll be fine noo dat I can see wir peerie licht i da Brunatwatt window.' She insisted he turn back, that she would manage easily.

He put his arm on her shoulder and bid her goodnight. Mary trudged on, pleased that he had made the kind offer and glad he did not seem to be a supporter of Patrick Ross. He was very affable and easy to talk to. And he seemed to enjoy her company. Like most of the other emigrants she knew well – especially Eliza and Willie and Katie – he seemed to fit in and was keen to work and help; and appreciated the sacrifices the local people were making. Girnals were emptying faster, butter being spread more thinly to eek it out; and portions were more meagre. They were all sharing a challenging time.

At home, they were glad to see her safe return. Mary could tell them that Erchie had seen her down the Kloss of Voe and Alex had seen her from Jaanie's as far as Gröntu. They had all been speculating on John taking over the croft from Joannie and becoming a fisherman come May. The other possibility was to ask the laird for an outset in the nearby common hill land, which would effectively give them a bit more land to croft and space to build a house; but it wouldn't make them popular with their crofter neighbours and no doubt the laird's factor would insist that both men fished for him. Joannie recounted all the miseries of being indebted to the laird; you could work and work and always you owed money; for rent, for food, for tackle. Everything. No, he wasn't going to the Far Haaf for one more season.

Mary's news of the baby lightened the conversation. She was about to mention the invitation from the crew of the *Batchelor* when Jaerm brought it up. There was some debate between Joannie and Baabie about Sunday observance but, with all the young ones keen to go, Baabie didn't feel she was going to win the argument.

'Hit'll no be a rant, Midder. Der wantin tae lat wis see da boat afore dey start serious repairs an gie wis a feed! Hit'll mak a fine change fae wis giein dem a feed.' Jaerm went on to add that there was to be a party at Agnes Slatter's house at Stove on the first Monday after Candlemas and they were all bidden.

The young folk, including Eliza, expressed delight at the thought of some music and dancing. The winter had seemed long, and spring was still a distant prospect. Mary was glad that her brother had told the family about the invitations; she did not want Jean and Christian teasing her about Alex Ross.

Saturday 29th January 1774
Happyhansel

The thaw – the tow – had come quickly on Friday and, as if miraculously, much of the snow had melted. After an earlier than usual dinner, Mary and John Jeems had taken the pony and carted a sack of oats down to the little mill in the hope that others would not have had the same idea. The burn flowing out of the Loch o Kurkigart was full and lively as it dropped quickly to the seashore. The millstones would turn effortlessly. She went on to the shop at Bayhaa and left the milling and bagging up to John Jeems. The journey back was a struggle for the laden pony, as the Kloss o Voe was still somewhat slippery.

When she eventually opened the schoolhouse door, having fed the pony and stored the oatmeal in the girnal, Mary became aware of Mr Buchan's unmistakeable voice in the parlour. It was deep and resonant, honed from years of preaching sermons. She went through the passage to the scullery at the back of the house with the remainder of the messages. Once she had regained her breath, she knocked on the parlour door and waited. Mr Greig got up and, responding to her suggestion, agreed that a pot of tea would be splendid. Erchie must have put peats on the fire, as the kettle boiled quickly. She set a tray with the best china and cut some hufsi she had baked in the morning. She spread a little fresh butter on the fruit loaf. She brought the teapot through to the parlour and set it on the hearthstone, then brought the tray through and served the two old men. She was about to retreat to the scullery when Mr Buchan called her by name. She always felt her name had a biblical ring to it when he said it; it gave her a strange feeling.

'Yes, sir.'

'Please sit down a minute, Mary. I have a message for you. Thank you for relaying the request from the McLeods about having their baby baptised and for bringing all the information that makes my job easier. Can you say to them when you see them that I will visit them and baptise their infant on Candlemas; that's next Wednesday afternoon? Candlemas seems the best day of the year for a baptism: it's the day our Lord was presented as a new baby at the temple. You can tell them that they don't need to do anything to prepare for the baptism. I'm sure they pray for their child every day. I remember they were one of the couples I couldn't really help when they arrived, as their first child had died on the journey. So many sad things happened on that voyage.'

'I'll let them know on my way home tonight, sir.'

Mr Buchan handed over the letters of recommendation to Mary, but retained her note with the details. 'You have a fine hand, Mary. I remember you were a diligent pupil.'

'She was indeed, James. I'm hoping to hire her for another year come Candlemas.' George Greig had a twinkle in his eye as he said it. 'The cake is good too?'

'It most certainly is!'

Mary felt relief and a little pride as she retreated to the scullery. She felt her work was appreciated by the Greigs, but she knew a commendation from Mr Buchan was not easily won.

She delivered her message and the letters as promised and all was set for the baptism. She said she would call along on her way home from Happyhansel around seven o'clock on Candlemas and that Eliza, who was keen to see the new baby and to meet up again with her compatriots – Willie and Katie – would drop by from Brunatwatt.

Sunday 30th January 1774
Onboard the Batchelor of Leith

Sunday dawned a cold but calm day. Baabie decided to stay at home with Joannie. She would look to the animals – that was allowed on the Sabbath. She exhorted them not to stay long onboard and to remember to look after Christian. The young ones all went to the kirk and afterwards made their way around the voe to the Germatwatt pier. Lots of others had gathered, locals and emigrants. The sailors rowed them out in groups to the ship on her temporary mooring. She still looked battered and bruised, but at least she was watertight.

There was no sight of Captain Ramage. Some of the emigrants wouldn't go below as their memories of the cramped accommodation were still too raw. Mary couldn't get the image of the McLeod child out of her mind.

The cook had laid out food for them – besides the slices of salt beef, he had made a kind of pease pudding and there was bread and hard biscuits. He had made pancakes, having bought flour and sugar and eggs. Besides a fancy urn of tea, they had gin and brandy. Glasses and cups of cheer were raised and gratitude expressed. Jean was keen to try everything the men had, but Mary, Christian and Eliza refused the offer of drink. Someone pulled out a fiddle and there was a little heuching and stamping but the space was too restricted for dancing; and anyway, it was broad daylight on the Sabbath!

They stayed an hour or two chatting and eating, pushing aside all thoughts of the horrors of the past and all thoughts of the future beyond the next few days. For the emigrants, home had become where they were at that moment. It was as much as they could bear thinking about.

The Johnson brothers and sisters, with Eliza, walked back part of the way with the young folk from Stennestwatt and their emigrants. Once the gaet forked they were on their own as they were the only folk at Brunatwatt who had billeted anyone. Sure enough, the old Deyell man was down at the lambie-hoose. John asked him if he had a sick yowe to look to. He slunk away without responding. Jean couldn't contain her laughter. Mary knew they would pay for it one way or another.

Wednesday 2nd February 1774
Stove

The Johnson family wakened to a dark, wet and windy morning on Candlemas. Their mother had seemed oddly cheered by that, reminding them of the old weather lore:

If Candlemas Day be dry an fair,
Da half o winter's ta come an mair;
If Candlemas Day be weet an foul,
Da half o winter's gien at Yöl.

Mary's day at Happyhansel went well. Though the shelves of
the larder were gradually becoming barer, there were still jars of
pickled onions and sassermaet and some dried, salted tusk and
piltocks wrapped in a bit of sacking. And there were still sacks
of oats and bere to grind in the barn. The potatoes and turnips
were getting a bit wizened, but they still tasted fine. And there
were tees of reestit mutton and bacon above the kitchen fireplace.
They had hens and fresh eggs and milk. She knew some folk were
struggling to get through the winter and that they were lucky John
Jeems and Leebie had got in all the crops before the bad gales.

She had been presented with a new contract by Mr Greig
and was relieved that her work would continue. She cleared up
quickly after tea and was on her way to Stove in good time. Not
long after she arrived, somewhat wind-battered, at Jaanie's home,
the door sneck lifted gently and Eliza popped her head in. They
had wondered if she would come, but she could tell them that
Jaerm had come with her most of the way. She was glad to take
off her wet coat and hood and sit in at the fire.

Willm was a little shy with Eliza, but keen to show off the baby
who was sleepily lying in the cradle. All had gone well with the
baptism – Jane had slept all the way through, blissfully unaware
of the drops of well-water sprinkled on her head. Jaanie had been
busy with laundry – she had a good slatted shed in the shelter
where she was able to leave clothes out to dry on days when it
wasn't damp. Wet days were ironing days.

The McLeods only knew Eliza from the voyage – they were
interested to know more about her as she was one of the few
young single women in the group.

'I just thocht tae mysel that I could do better than be a skivvy,
for that's what I was. It was hard saving up the passage money, but

I managed. Of course, noo I hiv almost naethin by way o savins; no even enough ta get mysel back tae Caithness. I feel a bitty like the prodigal son wishin he could go back tae his faither!'

Mary said, 'Maybe you could stay on here, Eliza. You feel like a sister noo an I dare say Jaerm wid be plaesed? He was just sayin da idder day that he tocht he wid laek to geng as a seaman on a packet or a sloop redder dan geng back ta da whalin. Maybe sail oot o Leith, lik Alex.'

Eliza smiled and said nothing, but turned towards the McLeods. 'What about you? You were farming folk, weren't you?'

'That we were, Eliza… tenants on the Bighouse estate in Sutherland. They pit up oor rent frae £2 to £5 sterling; an tack duty as weel. An besides that, he demanded we labour up his ground and work his peats and his hay and his corn just at the time o year when oor ain crops needed attention. It was 30 days work or mair ivery year, an mi horse an cart as weel. An no even a bit o bread. An the price o meal an corn has gone up wi the distillers bein no sae far awa. An twa bad harvests an poor prices fur oor cattle. The factor buys them aff us for 20 shilling and sells them on doon sooth for 50 shilling. That way, we poor folk end up payin the fares for a factor and his big family an aa his servants. Ach… it's an ill-pairtit wirld.'

Katie, who was rocking the cradle gently with her foot, added, 'An Willie has a brither there already… in Bladen County… that's upriver from Wilmington… he says the land is cheap and fertile. We set our heart on making a new haem there and sold up everything to pay the passage.'

Mary was thinking aloud: 'It sounds as if your lives ir muckle da sam as wir lives here. But I heard Mr Greig sayin there are a lot o slaves in the Carolinas an tinks some o da Shetland jantry wir maybe tinkin o investin.'

'Weel, at least we widna be the slaves this time. An it would be warmer!'

'Willie! We would not be wantin slaves! Dunna speak like that! But, truly, I canna see us managin to save up the fares. I would still like to go.'

'Weel, Keetie,' said Jaanie, 'you can bide on wi me, as lang as Walter is awa at sea. Your lichtsome company an wi baith o you helpin wi wark an maet, we seem ta manage fine. Maybe du could gyet mair wark, Willie, an save dat fur da passage? Or maybe dy bridder could send dee some money?'

'You're mair than kind, Jaanie. We must be the maist fortunate o aa the emigrants that landed in Waas!'

'Na billie, hadd dy wheest!' Jaanie laughed.

Monday 7th February 1774
Brunatwatt and Stove

When it came to the night of the party, they had all gone about their winter chores with a spring in their step: Joannie knowing he would not be spending any more hard days and nights at the Far Haaf, rowing thirty miles or more to reach the fishing grounds; Baabie pleased that Bella the cow was in calf; John starting to see a future here at Brunatwatt away from the whaling; Jaerm thinking of a life as a sailor and keen to help fix up the *Batchelor* now that they had got her afloat again; and the older girls looking forward to a night of merriment at Stove. They had brought in plenty well-water and several bucketfuls from Clokka Burn for getting themselves cleaned up. Only Christian was a bit despondent; she wasn't allowed to go.

After tea, there was competition for the basin and soap, the available warm water and a bit of privacy to get washed and dressed. Mary had been able to iron their sarks and blouses at Jaanie's. Jean had a blue skirt which suited her well; Mary wore a grey one which set off her neat waist. Her dark brown hair and greyish eyes gave her a solemn look at times, but they shone with excitement. Eliza, with her black hair, olive skin and dark eyes looked fine in a brown skirt. The girls brushed each other's hair and pinned it up. John and Jaerm had trimmed their beards, glad they would not need to wear collars and neckties. Baabie had cleaned all their boots and laid out their rivlins to take with them. And she had wrapped up some baking – some faerdie-maet she had joked – for the Slatters. She and Joannie were pleased to see them all looking their best.

The Candlemas gales had been replaced by quieter, colder weather. By the time they had reached the gaet leading off west to Gröntu, their eyes had grown accustomed to the dark and they could pick out the old Deyell man at his lambie-hoose door, not far from the Stove gaet.

He shouted at them, 'Whaar ir you aff tae danicht, aa riggit up?'

'Wir gyaain ta Stove, tae a foy wir bidden tae,' John answered.

The old man shook his head and made his way back to the house. The girls giggled.

Jean said, 'He's bön watchin oot fur wis. Nae doot he'll be checkin whit time we win back!'

By the time they reached the Slatters it was nearly eleven o'clock. Some local men and sailors were drinking and carousing in the narrow alleys between the houses. The big but-end had been cleared and the fire had died down. It was noisy already. Agnes had warmed whisky and it was being handed around inside – everyone drank some and passed it on. The fiddler struck up and eventually the men came in out of the cold, buoyed up with ale and spirits. The place was rather dark with just a koli-lamp in the window-sill. The sailors were keen to dance with the local girls and swung them around in great style and much hilarity. Jean, Bess o' Foratwatt and Ann o' Whitesness kept the dancing going and the men on the floor. Drink was conjured from inside pockets – it seemed an everlasting supply. Mary got caught up in the merriment, in the feeling of confidence and freedom to enjoy herself. Eliza and Jaerm danced together and she could see they were in love. Alex danced with several of the local lasses, but he seemed to favour Mary. She could sense he was noticing this different Mary, not the serious, mature-for-her-years young woman. Here she was a girl, laughing and drinking and dancing, her eyes dazzling.

Jaerm and Eliza slipped away. Some of the sailors grabbed a girl and disappeared to other rooms and recesses or out into alleyways: it was hardly noticed in the noisy throng. Some had no intention of leaving before daybreak, knowing full well that to try to find their way home in deep winter darkness when half-drunk and dead tired was a recipe for disaster. Though Jean was intent on staying on, Mary still had just enough awareness that she had work to go to the following morning and should get home. She went to find her coat and boots. Alex came to help her sort through the pile of clothes and footwear.

'A'll follow you as far as Gröntu in case that old man is out looking for you on your way haem!'

This time, she gladly accepted his offer. She joked that he could come all the way to Brunatwatt and sleep in the barn if he liked. The night was cloudy and moonless and they had to lean on one another to keep their footing.

Before Gröntu, Alex reached into his inside pocket for his whisky. 'Have a wee drap, Mary. It'll keep you warm.'

She put it to her lips and drank some, and then some more: she could feel it burning as she swallowed and then a warm glow rising in her. He put his arm around her shoulder and she didn't resist. Her body was enjoying the proximity of his. When they came to Brunatwatt all was quiet. She opened the barn door for him. He took her firmly in his arms and kissed her and she responded in a way she had never experienced before. Her legs were like jelly and her head spinning.

'Come in for a minute, Mary. It's a while till moarnin.'

She had no idea how or why her body had taken her over, but, before she knew it, she was in the straw with Alex and he was all over her and in her, moaning, with a terrible urgency. He had opened her blouse and lifted her skirt. She had lost all sense of everything and here she was lying with a man, and for all the world what was all wrong seemed wonderfully all right. All thought of work and responsibility had disappeared. There was only now.

'My God, Alex. Whit ir we dön?' As suddenly as his semen chilled on her exposed thighs, a cold awareness crept over her and, rather than curl up and sleep in his arms which a few minutes ago, unthinkingly, she would have done, she knew as if by instinct, she had to get back home, to the house, to get away from the temptation. She tried to get up, but her legs were sticky and she knew she was a dishevelled mess; her hair fallen about her and her clothes creased.

She gathered herself up and stumbled out of the barn. The cold night air hit her and she knew she was going to be sick. She groped her way round to the back of the barn and threw up. The taste of the drink was stale and rank. She was disgusted with herself. She tore some tousled grass and covered the mess on the ground and tore some more and cleaned the worst of the stickiness from her legs and off her boots.

The words of the Deyell man rang in her ear. 'You're slippit, you Brunatwatt lasses.'

Mary was shaking as she unsnecked the house door. She managed, without wakening anyone, to take a bowl of water and a cloth into the closet. She stripped off and bundled her clothes under the bed. They would need to be washed when she got a chance. Slowly, she worked out what she had to do: she washed herself, brushed her hair and put on a nightgown. She set the bowl of water safely aside and got into bed. Despite her tiredness, she knew she wouldn't be able to sleep, partly out of fear of sleeping in and being late for work, and partly with a strange mix of guilt and sweetness. The guilt won over: she had lain with a man, maybe even a married man. And had put up no resistance whatsoever. Now her mother's words were in her ears. 'Mind lasses, Alex is a mairried man.' She had broken the sixth commandment.

Tuesday 8th February 1774
Happyhansel

It was still dark when Mary heard her mother stirring in the but-end, coaxing life from the final embers of the previous evening. She managed to haul herself from bed despite a splitting headache and feeling queasy and dizzy. The walls of the closet were coming in on her. She would have to appear as if everything was normal and get on her way to Happyhansel as quickly as she could. She had a new contract and wanted it to start well. Mercifully, there wasn't much conversation. Yes, they'd had a fine time. Yes, it went on most of the night. Yes, the sailors had been there. She was relieved she was not asked who followed her home.

Normally on her morning journey to work, even in foul weather, she would be thinking of the tasks of the day ahead. But this morning all she could do was try to remember what she had done last night. She couldn't seem to think straight... what a fool, what a stupid fool... no control over what I was doing, or how I was behaving... yes, 'slippit' right enough... I encouraged him... offered him the barn... and went with him... willingly. I can't blame him... it's entirely my own doing, my own fault... Oh, but... it was wonderful, and exciting and... intimate... ah, the feeling is still there, something entirely different... But what if I end up with a bairn... surely not from such a brief coupling... I mustn't think of that... that would be the end. And did anyone see or hear us? How on earth can I face Alex now? I must apologise... I was reckless... I'm never, never going to touch a drop of drink again.

Her legs felt heavy and her muscles ached as she climbed the Kloss of Voe, but her head was starting to clear a bit by the time she reached Happyhansel. Her despair lifted a little when she saw that Erchie had, as usual, got the fires restored. She managed to smile and somehow lift the porridge pan to a crook above the kitchen fire and a kettle of water to the other. She kept her contact with the three men as brief as she could, without being unfriendly. Everything seemed like a huge effort. She knew she could not manage to do a kirnin or turn the quern. She had to stop half-way back from the well for a rest.

When she got back to Brunatwatt, she just wanted to get to bed, to get her head down. Family conversation over their eight o'clocks was animated, but the little concentration Mary could muster was elsewhere. She managed to excuse herself by saying she was tired after the late night. Which was indeed the case.

Thursday 10th February 1774
Stove and Brunatwatt

On her way home from Happyhansel, Mary dropped by Jaanie's to see how they were all getting on. She was feeling back to her old self again. Though she often caught sight of Willm during the school day, she could see that he liked having her to himself for a little while. And she too enjoyed those moments. Katie was nursing Jane, so it was easy to concentrate on Willm's world. When Katie came through to the but-end with the baby, everyone, including Willm, wanted to give Jane a cuddle before she went down for her sleep. Eventually, she became grisly and Katie tucked her in, the cradle-band looped criss-cross and Willie gave her a gentle rock. Willm wanted Mary to put him to bed. He was growing fast and she knew those days would not last.

When she came back to join the others at the fireside, Willie was recounting how he had bumped into Alex Ross who had told him that the sloop sent from Leith by Inglis, the owner of the *Batchelor,* had arrived safely. The *Mary* had tied up at the Bayhaa pier. None of them had noticed her slip into the voe, including Mary. It had been dark when she had walked to her work and also when she had returned. She had seen activity at the Bayhaa pier in the afternoon when she had gone to the well, but had not realised it was the expected boat. Alex had seemingly gone down to the pier and been on board and had seen what had been sent: two heavy new anchors, planks of solid cedar, parts for bilge pumps, some tools and new casks with provisions. Also, a master carpenter. Alex had seemingly got on well enough with him and was looking forward to getting all the repairs made. The carpenter had said that probably she would have to go into dry-dock to assess structural damage before she could tackle the Atlantic, but they could certainly get her seaworthy enough for the Sumburgh Roost and the trip to Leith. Alex had learned from the carpenter that the owner, Inglis, wanted Captain Ramage to drop the emigrants back at Thurso from which port they could be picked up at a later date and that he should give them eight weeks' provisions as an enticement.

That sparked a conversation once more about what the McLeods should do. It looked more than ever that they would either be taken back to Caithness, or perhaps to Leith rather than to North Carolina. They didn't trust Inglis and Hogg to get them to Carolina. Jaanie thought there were occasional emigrant ships that picked up folk directly from Shetland, maybe Scallowa. It seemed to Mary that the McLeods had made up their minds to stay on in Waas a bit longer till they could get a passage directly to North Carolina. They had lost their home in Caithness and Leith held out no prospect of a living for them, far less enabling them to save for a future passage. But, despite her growing fondness for the family, Mary found the mention of Alex's name had been somewhat distracting. She knew that her folk would be looking out for her as the night was dark. Jaanie offered her tengs o fire – a burning peat to hold aloft – but she said she knew the gaet well, and it was straight, with no burns to cross. She bid them all goodnight and made her way out through the alleyways of Stove.

Just before she was about to turn north, she heard her name being called out quietly. She immediately recognised that it was Alex. She didn't want to see him or speak to him so she hurried on, pretending not to hear. But he caught up with her quickly and pulled at her sleeve.

'Mary, I'm sorry to fricht you. I saw you go to Jaanie's earlier an I thocht I had to see you, just to say...'

'Der naethin ta say, Alex. What's dön is dön. I was a föl an A'm sorry. I sood nivver hae taen dat drink. Hit gud staicht tae mi head an I lost aa sense. I canna believe what I did... wi onyboady, but especially wi a man... a man wi a wife? An mi bridders' freend at dat. I dunna ken whit cam owre me. You ir married, are you no?'

'That I am, Mary, an a bairn an aa. I should no hae taen advantage: I'm the married one... I should hae had mair sense. You're just a lass. A lovely lass. I'm really sorry an aa, Mary. That's what drink does. But...'

'Let's jöst leave it dere dan, Alex. A'll gyet on mi wye.'

'Will you be aa richt findin yer wye haem? I feel I can hardly offer mi airm though I would like tae.'

'No thanks, A'll be fine. An A'm blyde ta hear da *Mary* arrived. You'll gyet aa the repairs dön an be haem shön. Dat's what's best.'

They said their farewells. Mary could feel her throat tighten and her heart pounding, but she had to concentrate on one thing only – getting home safely in the darkness. She didn't look back.

Saturday 5th March 1774
Happyhansel

It had been a busy time at Happyhansel. Tammas Duncan had been working at fixing the door of the schoolhouse which needed ventilation and he, with the help of Jeemie Ollason, the kirk officer, had lime-washed the whole building. Mary was relieved that the weather had held and that they had managed to finish up on Wednesday, after four days of having them around the place and the mess the work created. At least she had Saturday to catch up.

Mr Greig was tired too, as he had sat late on Friday writing up the kirk session minutes. The meeting had been long and complicated with many facts and figures, counting the money and accounting for all the various incomes and expenses. On one side had been collections and marriage money and fines and debt repayments. On the other side were numerous outgoings. At the end of it all, he was pleased that they had been able to find some money to give small loans to several crofters and £1/10/- apiece to four near destitute widows. There was £6 Scots for the Treasurer to disburse to poorer emigrants, and they had paid one of them, John Clerk, 11/- for taking letters to Lerwick. And there was enough to cover his school outlays and the recent work done to the schoolhouse. But he was troubled by the list of those who had not managed to pay back at least part of their borrowings. He didn't want to contemplate the trouble that might cause. He had written six pages of copperplate and managed to have no crossings out. It had been a relief to write those three brief words 'Closed with Prayer'. So today he was glad that Mary Johnsdaughter was quietly getting on with the chores, while he and Erchie saw to the boarders.

Mary was indeed quiet. Her bleeding had not started. She could not contemplate the possibility that she might be pregnant and tried to push the thought to the back of her mind. Repetitive tasks like feeding the insatiable fires with peats, kirning milk, kneading dough and turning brönnies on the hot girdle were a kind of solace. Something positive, requiring a level of care and skill that displaced darker thoughts. She was relieved Patrick Ross had moved out to be nearer his friend Alexander MacKay. He was too quick with his tongue and his hands for her liking: on several occasions when no one else was about she had tried to make it clear that she did not appreciate his advances. And that had made him more surly with her. She was relieved, too, that she had not bumped into Alex again. Jaerm had said he was busy with the repairs and that the crew hoped to be back on board within another week, so they could do the final work and get underway in April.

Sunday 10th April 1774
Brunatwatt

There was a hubbub among the congregation spilling out of the kirk: Mr Buchan's intimation had taken them all by surprise although there had been rumours after the previous Sunday's session meeting that the presbytery of Shetland was after Bain, and matters were coming to a head. Elders had gossiped, smug with their access to confidential information. It seemed that, while the parish had been difficult enough to control before the arrival of all these men from Scotland, now it seemed that the local lasses had lost their senses. But of course, David Bain was not one of the sailors, though well known to them; and Sophia Henderson was from Delting, not Waas.

One of the elders let slip that Mr Buchan had written last week to the minister of Sandsting parish, a Mr Finlayson, to tell him that his officer must cite David Bain to appear before the Waas kirk session on the 11th April at 3pm when the sailors would be due to attend also, as witnesses. Seemingly, James Hogg had been visiting Mr Buchan and had delivered the letter to the Sandsting minister on his way back to his billet there at the haa house.

Joannie Johnson had not been to the kirk, pleading rheumatics; and Mary, who had been feeling somewhat squeamish, had stayed at home, saying she had a headache. The others were full of the news when they got back to Brunatwatt.

'Faider,' said Jean, 'mind yun bairn o Sophia Henderson an Davie Bain you sponsored for baptism – weel, der a richt to-do noo. Whit wis hit Mr Buchan said?'

John picked up the thread. 'He med a inteemation dat da sailors on board da *Batchelor o Leith* sood spaek wi him an da elders afore dey left fur haem, fur da presbytery wis directit dey wid need evidence on oath aboot Bain hae'in a wife still tae da fore[5] in Caithness whin dey left last September. Sae da sailors wis still dere whin we left. I doot dey'll be telt ta turn up damoarn ta swear. Can du mind wha aa wis dere, Jaerm? Du kens dem better as me.'

'Ya, dey wir Liddle da Mate, and Alex of coorse… lat me see… John Shanks, James Bennet, an Alexander Shaw… an wha else?'

Jean added David Currie and Philip Stephenson.

'I tink dey wir anidder twartree,' said Christian.

'Oh ya,' said Jaerm, 'Charlie Jolly wis dere… an David Watters. I tink dat wid be dem aa.'

Joannie knocked his pipe against the fireplace. 'Weel, weel. Dat wisna a surprise. Dey'll be lucky if he ivver turns up.'

Baabie was bustling round getting their dinner ready.

'Why on aert did du ivver agree ta sponsor Bain if du tinks he's no a man o his wird?'

'Weel, he used ta gie me packs o bacca whin we wrocht at yun quarry soothbye.'

---

5 Well, healthy, keeping going.

'An nae doot smuggled,' quipped his wife.

'Aye tastes better whin hit's smuggled, lass!'

A cold sweat had spread over Mary as she listened. What she was hearing was sounding ever more like a premonition: adultery was nearly as bad as murder. She was pretty sure now that she was pregnant; another month had come and gone without bleeding. She was bringing dishonour on herself and her whole family. And on the Greigs, and her neighbours… and it would be another mouth to feed… and she'd lose her job… and she'd get hauled up in front of the kirk elders. And who would ever marry her? And what could she say to anyone about how it had happened? It felt as if her whole world was collapsing round her.

They sat down to their dinner. There was just some broth and brönnies and a bit of kirn-mylk, as their own produce from the previous harvest was almost done. There was little left of the fish they had salted and dried in the summer and the mutton they had reestit after hairst. The tatties and neeps were completely wizened and barely fit for the kye to eat. There weren't many sheaves of bere left and they had to save some oats to keep the hens laying. They were ever more dependent on the few shillings Mary brought home from her work and any knitting the women could sell. Jaerm was keen to get a berth on the *Batchelor* if he could, or a packet to Leith, so that he could get established there as a seaman. He would maybe be able to help the family a little. And May was coming when John would join the crew of the local sixern with his cousins from Grötquoy and go to the Far Haaf; at least they could then get errands from the laird's store, even if only on a slate.

'Ah weel,' said Joannie, 'at laest der wylks ithin da ebb an still a pock or twa o sillocks affa da craig-steyns; an we hae eggs an mylk so we'll no starve. Baabie, I tink yun black hen dat's no layin could be een fur da pot. I sall traa her neck damoarn.'

Baabie brightened. 'An hit'll shön be time ta spread da muck an stert dellin; an gyet da kye teddered apön da toonmals. Winter is shurly dön noo.'

They all agreed that it was good that the sunlight came sooner over the Gallow Hill, and there were a few indications of voar, of new life.

John and Jaerm decided that, if the weather held, the next day they would take their fishing gear to the flat rocks, the craigs, below Stapness and see if they could get a good catch of sillocks. If they got plenty, they could spare some for neighbours and maybe a few for the kye.

As they supped their broth, Jean said she had heard that there was a rumour spreading that the local lasses had been on the *Batchelor*. Every time she heard it, the tale was more embroidered and whispered more loudly.

Baabie said, 'Weel I did winder aboot da wisdom o you gyaain. Der a commandment at says "Remember da Sabbath day an keep hit holy".'

'I tocht dat wis ta stop wis haein ta dell an wirk paets; dat we needit a bit o a rest eence a week, wumman,' Joannie responded, winking as he supped.

'Ya, I agree,' added Jean. 'A day wi could pit by wir dwined makkin, Midder.'

'Weel, whitivver, I dunna laek ta tink o you gyettin inta trouble or bein taen-til. We hed a bad enyoch time last year wi dee, Jean.'

Mary felt her face reddening as her mother spoke. Jean had been caught and somehow managed to get rid of the evidence. But this was adultery. Ten times worse, and with its own special commandment. The full impact of this pregnancy was slowly dawning on her. It wasn't going to go away, but get worse. No wonder she had not been sleeping well and felt tired. Mercifully, so far it seemed that no one suspected anything, at least as far as she was aware. But for how long? She started clearing away the dishes, glad of a practical task to take her away from the table. Eliza helped her. Mary could see Eliza was also quiet.

'You'll be winderin what's best for you, Eliza. Do you think you'll geng sooth wi the *Batchelor* or wid you bide a bit langer?'

'I would like ta go if Jaerm is going. He's sort o hinted we might get married, but we would need ta get settled. If I could get a job here, I could maybe save up enough. Itherwise I would just hae ta hope I could get wark in Leith. I cannae bide on your folk like this for muckle langer. It's no fair.'

'But we laek hae'in you here, Eliza.'

The two girls smiled at each other as they washed and tidied up.

'You can come wi wis dis eftirnön, if you want. I tink wir gyaain tae Grötquoy tae veesit wir folk dere.'

Monday 11th April 1774
Happyhansel

The school children were still on holiday and the boarders had not yet returned from the break. It was a chance to give their bedrooms a good clean and airing, and deal with repairs. Two mattresses needed to be replaced. Mary had managed to buy some ticking at a shilling a yard and John Jeems had provided fresh straw and clean wool for them. He had also kindly secured some strong sacking on a few of the bed frames where it had come adrift. Mary had six bed sheets which needed to be turned sides-to-middle. Jaanie had said she would help her with the stitching.

Mr Greig returned from the session meeting just before teatime. He looked troubled. Over their meal, he was willing to disclose that Bain, who had been called three times at the kirk door, had not appeared, despite presbytery's demand.

'Hit's a sad state o affairs. Göd kens whaar he is noo an whedder da lass is bön able ta geng back haem tae her fock in Delting, wi da bairn. We nivver managed ta baptise da ting.'

Neither Erchie nor Mary felt they could comment or ask further, but Mr Greig went on to say that the sailors all swore on oath that David Bain's wife, Christian, and their little son, along with her father, John Ross, had all been to see the emigrants on the *Batchelor* before they sailed in September. It had given them a chance to see her brother, Alex Ross, the ship's carpenter.

'Sae I man write a letter ta presbytery, wi a extract fae da meenits forbye, fur der meetin on da 27th o dis mont. I dunna ken whit dey can dö if dey canna track him doon. I doot der a braa bit o bad blöd atween Bain an his bridder-in-laa, fur Alex Ross reportit him tae da kirk session awa back in January, if I mind richt.'

Mary's heart was in her mouth at this information.

'Noo, Mary, I man ax dee: I hae ta write up anidder piece o da meenits an A'm braaly afflikkit aboot hit, fur dy name wis mentioned an da Meenister is wantin dee an dy sisters and twartree idder lasses tae appear afore da session eftir da service neist Sunday. I soodna be tellin dee dis, but I canna raelly believe whit some elders wis sayin. Dat you wir dancin an takkin on apö da *Batchelor* apö da Sabbath?'

'Hit is true dat ee Sunday, a while back, whin da sailors wis first gotten da boat back apö da watter, dat dey wir bidden a lock o local fock – emigrants an aa – ta come on board an see her, an hae a coarn o maet. I suppose hit wis a wye o dem sayin "tanks" fur da help. Hit wis der only day aff. We wirna dere fur lang. An we wirna makkin a onkerry.'

'A peety hit wis apö da Sabbath fur der aye someens dat seem ta want ta mak trouble; nae doot some elders an aa,' Erchie added.

Mr Greig merely said, 'Some meenits is herder ta write dan idder eens. Maybe hit's time fur aa dis young men ta geng back haem tae der ain wives an faemlies.'

Mary was shocked by what Mr Greig had divulged. Erchie, guessing at her feelings, came through to the scullery after Mary had cleared the table and his father, having laid out his ink and pens, had started to write the minutes...

'Nivver leet, Mary. Some o yun aald men jöst seem ta enjoy a bit o scandal. An I doot dey laek ta keep da hank i der ain haands an sometimes forget wha der supposed ta be servin. Yun dusna soond laek a cardinal sin tae me... der forgotten whit hit's laek ta be young.'

Mary had to smile as Erchie laid down the plates. He always seemed so much older than his years. While she could see that it was easy now to point the finger at her sister Jean – once a transgressor, always a ready suspect – little did he know that she suspected things would get a whole lot worse for her. But his kindness touched her. She determined to say nothing of these conversations when she got back home. She could only hope that it might all blow over.

When she reached Brunatwatt, the sun was still well above Stoorburgh Hill. It was a fine evening. Birds were returning slowly to the hill and to the shore. There was an appetising smell of cooked fish. John was excitedly describing their exploits.

'We saa scarfs caain da sillocks an dookin ta catch dem; dan comin up wi a neb foo. We managed ta pock a braa twartree ivery time da fish cam near da craig-steyn. Dey wir graet shoals o dem dartin aboot.'

'Da Grötquoy fock wis blyde o a fry, an da Laings an da Musawatter fock,' added Jaerm, 'but wid you believe dat da aald Deyell wife said, "You can keep your fish! We dunna want your fish!"'

'My, my!' said Baabie, shaking her head. 'Shö's a pör sowl.'

'Mair laek a trooker!' said Joannie.

'Mind, Joannie, dey dunna hae a fine faemly laek we hae. Maybe dat's med dem kinda nipsiccar.'

Tuesday 12th April 1774
Happyhansel

In the afternoon Mr Greig went off to see James Buchan at Voe House to hand over the letter he had written to presbytery – the one with the extract of the session minute concerning David Bain. Erchie was busy in the schoolrooms. Mary had worked hard all morning and had decided to have a brief break and a cup of tea. Her eye strayed to the session minute book. She knew it was no business of hers, but she was desperate to see what Mr Greig had written. She took if down from the shelf and laid it on the table then turned the heavy pages till she came to the most recent minute.

The first bit was all about Bain and the sailors. But towards the bottom of the page, she read with increasing disquiet:

The said day the Sefsion taking to consideration that there was a Fama Clamosa through this and the Neighbouring parishes & Ministry, that several young Women in DoonaWalls, particularly Jean, Mary & Christian Johnsdaughter, daughters to John Johnson in Brunatwatt and Marg. Morison, residenter in Stove, had without their parents' knowledge, will and consent attended certain rants or Revels for whole Nights together with some Sailors aboard the Batchelor of Leith, and had behaved very indecently at these meetings in kifsing, drinking and Dancing and the like with the said Sailors, and that John Johnson's three daughters foresaid had gone aboard the sail ship in company with some of the Sailors on the Sabbath day immediately after divine service, and considering that one of these Women, viz Jean Johndghtr. had been formerly convicted of fornication and made publick repentance thereof and the Elders having reported they had been much reflected on for not bringing forward this matter sooner to the Sefsion therefore the Sefsion found themselves obliged to proceed upon the foresaid fama clamosa to enquire judicially into the Grounds and reasons of it, both that they may give opportunity to the said women for vindicating their Characters if innocent and also to inflict such Censures upon them if found Guilty as are competent to this Judicatory to inflict and in order to bring the affair to a proper Light they judged it fit to order the said Women to be cited to compear before them the next Lord's day after dismifsing the Congregation.

Before the benedictory '*Closed in Prayer*' they had finished their meeting by distributing some money to the poor of the parish.

Mary closed the book and replaced it. All sense of guilt at having read it was lost in her anger at the way she and her sisters had been portrayed... so much was misleading and wrong with it... Christian wasn't with them at Stove at Candlemas... and their folk hadn't forbidden them to go. And who had held back from bringing it to session for so long? And how unfair to have Jean's name dragged up again like that... but then... maybe Jean had been to other gatherings with the sailors... but no, Jean would have said... never any use at keeping secrets. And *'Fama Clamosa'*... what on earth could that be... a disease? But surely, surely this was just malicious gossip. Surely Mr Greig didn't believe all these things about her he'd written so carefully... how could he?

She went out to throw a basin of food scraps and vegetable peelings to the pigs. They had been let loose from their sty and were turning over the leys, the rigs left fallow last year. They came grunting when they saw her. There was a lot of rooting up going on, a lot of destruction but at least this would transform the ground and improve the chances of a good harvest at the end of it.

Somehow Mary managed to get through the meal at teatime. The frustration she felt, she turned in on herself. There was no point in hitting out and, anyway, she knew from previous conversations that Mr Greig had to write down what others had said; not necessarily his own thoughts on the matter. And she should never have read the confidential minutes. As she cleared up and made ready to leave for Brunatwatt she resolved that she would live each day as best she could for as long as that was possible. It was the only way to keep from falling apart and losing all respect for herself. And anyway, with all this anxiety, the chances of her pregnancy miscarrying were high.

On the way home she turned over in her mind who might be spreading these malicious rumours; who on the kirk session had it in for them? It must be Deyell. But perhaps there were others? She wondered, too, whether or not it was wise to warn her family that a note would be delivered before next Sunday; if that might draw the sting, or maybe it would just prolong the agony. She decided to say nothing. There was no case to answer.

Sunday 17th April 1774
Brunatwatt, Waas kirk and Stove

It was a beautiful calm spring day when they set off, somewhat in trepidation. Baabie had decided to stay away from the kirk till this affair had blown over, and Joannie had retreated to the barn. One minute he had been furious at the elders; another he had been furious with Jean and Mary, declaring them 'da spaekalation o da parish', the scandalous topic of gossip.

Mary knew that Jaerm would no doubt be meeting briefly with Alex Ross on their way out of church. The *Batchelor* was all but ready to sail south, waiting for the right wind. Already emigrants had been rounded up from all over and many were back on board. For several weeks now James Hogg and Balfour, the Vice-Admiral for Shetland, had been organising this. Their men had already spoken with the McLeods and with Eliza. Willie and Katie had opted to take some rations and stay on in Waas; Eliza had decided to take the chance of the passage in the hope she could quickly get a job in Leith and await Jaerm's arrival later. John Henry of Bayhaa had been busy transferring barrels of as yet unused provisions from his store and from the kirk. Thomas Henry of Burrastow had been helping with fresh provisions from his shop.

Mary had agonised over whether or not she should tell Alex about her state. No doubt Jaerm would be keen that his friend visit Brunatwatt at least one more time before leaving, but she knew she would not be able to face that. So she had written a brief note asking him to wait for her at Stove. She would find an excuse to visit Jaanie in the evening and could meet him briefly afterwards. He was well acquainted with the little boat and the pier, even in the dusk. Before they left for the kirk, she had managed to get Jaerm on his own and to ask him to pass the note discreetly to Alex. Jaerm had merely raised an eyebrow. He seemed to know by the look on her face that he did not need to ask.

During the service, Mary could not concentrate. She rose to mouth the psalms and sat for the rest. All she could hear were the *cullya cullya* of the seagulls around the voe as the sun streamed through the window. Eventually, they stood for the benediction before the minister walked down the aisle, followed by the beadle carrying the heavy bible. While the young women and the elders waited behind, the remainder of the congregation spilled out: Mary could hear their animated conversation – their callyshang – as they moved away from the door of the kirk. She hoped Jaerm had been able to get Alex briefly on his own.

Mr Buchan came back in and they all moved up to the front of the church, where they had to stand. One or two of the older elders shuffled along a pew. In their black suits they looked to Mary like starlings on a wall, or watchful crows. Mr Greig sat at the side with pencil and paper and merely acknowledged Mary briefly before looking down and writing.

The questions were all aimed initially at Jean, no doubt because she had fallen foul of their discipline the year before. She admitted that yes, she had attended a revel at Agnes Slatter's house in Stove on the Monday after Candlemas, but only once, acknowledging she had been in the company of the sailors and others till it was daylight. And yes, she had danced and had a drink with them, but not to excess.

Then the questions turned to whether or not her parents had consented to her attending the revel. She hesitated, answering that they had neither forbidden nor advised. She could see old Deyell's eyes light up when she was asked if she went to any bed in Stove.

Jean said, 'I was neither in any Bed nor any Room in that house but the fire house.'

The questioning did not let up. 'What about the sailors – had they stayed all the time?'

She acknowledged that they had, but denied that she was in any private room with any of them; nor did any of them offer any 'uncivility' to her.

When the questioning turned to revels at Brunatwatt, Mary realised that the minister must have had an earful from Willie Deyell: there had been that party at John Laing's house around

Yöl, the one they had not attended because their uncle had died not long before. Still Mr Buchan addressed only Jean. It didn't seem fair. But Jean was not to be broken. Asked whether the sailors had any meeting at Brunatwatt before or after Candlemas with her or other lasses there, she answered that some of the sailors came to John Laing's house in order to get music and dancing. She had heard that the sailors stayed just one night there. The minister then asked the names of the sailors. Jean said she thought it was James Bonnet, Alexander Ross, Charles Jolly and the cook. And were they all married men? Yes, except Charles Jolly. And where had they all slept the night? She stated that, to the best of her knowledge, James Bonnet, Charles Jolly and Alexander Ross lay in her family's barn and the cook lay in John Laing's house. Her brothers were friendly with the sailors.

When cross-examined about the revelry in relation to the death of her Uncle Lawrence Johnson in Grötquoy – how long it was before or after his death – she answered that he was dead and buried, but could not remember exactly how long it was after the burial. At that point old William Deyell of Gröntu, their neighbour, could contain himself no longer. He interrupted her reply stating that it was the night after the uncle's burial.

The other young women were looking more and more despondent, but Jean kept her head up and her eye steady. The questioning then turned to the party aboard the *Batchelor of Leith*. She acknowledged that yes, she had gone aboard, by invitation of the sailors, immediately after divine service. Again, she had to name the sailors. Mary was particularly sensitive to one name. Jean added that she and her sister had often been invited before, but did not go on board the ship till then and that she told the said men that she was afraid to go because they would be challenged if they went on board. But the sailors had replied by asking why should they be challenged more than other women who had already been aboard their ship? Mr Buchan looked along the line of young women and asked if she knew who those women were, and whether it was on the Sabbath day? Jean answered that the women were Margaret

Irvineson of Stennestwatt, Agnes Sletter of Stove, Bess Sletter of Foratwatt, Christian Morison of Stove and Helen Fullertoun and Ann Johnsdaughter of Whiteness. And all those had been aboard the *Batchelor* on the Sabbath day before them.

Mr Buchan then turned to the other young women present and put the same questions to them. Almost without variation they gave similar responses to Jean. Only Margaret Morison, whose name Jean had not mentioned, said that she had not attended the Yöl party at Brunatwatt and therefore could tell nothing about it and also that she was never on board the ship, though she had often been invited.

There was foot shuffling and restlessness among the elders. Mr Buchan decided that as the Sabbath afternoon was far spent, they would need to defer any further questioning and consideration of the affair until the following Sunday. He appointed the officer to summon Margaret Irvineson, above mentioned, and the women present, to attend the session next Sabbath day. He then said a prayer and closed the meeting.

Mary felt relief that she had not been interrogated, as she knew she could never have held up against the barrage of questions. But why had Jean been picked on and made to bear the heaviest burden of interrogation? She was proud of the way her elder sister had remained calm, despite provocation.

They walked up the brae to Stove with Agnes and Christian, hungry, half-stunned and angry. Why was it that women were always the targets? Old men – she found herself despising them. It seemed they wanted to control young women, their every movement. Jean could see the funny side and at times was quite a mimic. She recounted an old neighbour woman warning her against Willie Deyell – 'du sood keep dy haand apö dy ha'penny[6] when he's aroond.' She had mistakenly thought the old woman had meant that he was apt to steal if he got the chance; but no, that was not the meaning at all! They all laughed at the grotesque thought. After all, you could only laugh or cry. So, they could all

_____

6 Beware of wandering hands (lit. keep your hand on your halfpenny).

expect a summons for next Sunday.

When they got home, there was much de-briefing. John, Jaerm and Eliza were shocked, but Baabie and Joannie were unusually quiet.

'Du sood watch dy step, Jean,' her mother warned.

'Deil tak dem aa,' was Joannie's only comment.

Baabie had kept them a bit of the cold salt pork their Grötquoy cousins had kindly given them, and some soup which she put back on the crook. Mary tried to eat, but felt nauseous and made an excuse that she was tired so she could get away to the closet on her own. She managed to get a signal from Jaerm that her note had been safely delivered. She needed to think of an excuse for visiting her friends on a Sunday night – and she needed to think what she would say to Alex.

Presently she fell asleep, wakening when Eliza opened the closet door. Mary sat up and Eliza put an arm around her shoulder.

'A'll truly miss you, Eliza. I canna believe you'll be gyaain sae shön.'

'It'll be hard ta leave you aa, Mary. An even mair sae noo, wi aa this trouble. It seems unfair.'

'Nivver you leet, lass. We'll manage. I hoop Jaerm 'll win ta Leith shön an gyet a berth. A'll no be sae vexed aboot him gyaain, kennin he can meet up wi you. Tink-you, will you mairry shön?'

'As soon as we can get some pennies thagither!'

Jaanie knew about the summons. Everyone in the parish knew. So Mary decided that would be her excuse – she would say that Jaanie had asked her to come along in the evening to tell her how it had all gone. As for what she might say to Alex, she had no idea.

Jaanie's fireside at Stove was warm and welcoming as usual and before long the kettle lid was rattling and a pot of tea brewing. Katie, who was looking really well, cut a few slices of a gingerbread she had baked. Both Willm and Jane were already asleep. There was news of work for Willie: John Henry of Bayhaa needed a man to work land and to cart. He could have a job at least for voar through to summer and into hairst if he wanted.

'That should be enough for our passage to North Carolina,

if we can get a berth frae Shetland afore it's owre late i the year.'

Mary was delighted to hear their good news. The baby would be more robust by then, and probably young enough not to be charged.

'Noo, lass, foo got you on?' Jaanie looked kindly at her.

Mary recounted the questions and the way Jean had been treated. And how the old Gröntu man had tried to make trouble.

'Weel, at least these days they don't declare you aa to be witches an drag you aff tae the Gallow Hill!'

'Willie! Don't speak like that tae Mary. It's no funny,' Katie remonstrated. 'It's the sam whaar we come frae – the kirk is run by auld men, for auld men.'

'I tink Mester Buchan is gyettin tired o hae'in ta uphowld da aald rules dat keeps draggin weemen doon. Hit shurley canna geng on laek dis muckle langer.'

'I hoop you're richt, Jaanie,' said Mary, mustering a smile.

They all commiserated and, for a little while, Mary felt some of her anxiety lift. But time was moving on relentlessly and she had to excuse herself. She was probably a little late.

He was there. She could see him in the shadowy alley. She checked over her shoulder, before moving nearer.

'Mary.'

Hearing Alex say her name so quietly cut through her. Something about him still made her heart sing.

'Is everything all right?' Mary's face, even in the gloom, was serious.

'I dunna ken whit I sood say, Alex. A'll be sad to see you aa go, but I ken hit's fur da best.'

'I hear there's been trouble wi tha kirk... they didna like us invitin folk aboard on Sundays.'

'A lock o trouble, but hit wunna lest forivver. But I... I tink I micht be gyaain ta hae a bairn. I dunna ken fur sure... hit's aerly yet... but...'

'O my God, Mary. Surely no.'

'Weel, time 'll tell. An even if I am, hit micht miskerry.'

Alex looked down, stunned.

'Hae you telt anybody?'

'No… I dunna ken whit I sood do. Maybe wait a bit to see if dis bairn growes or comes awa…'

'What about your job?'

'I could probably go on for a mont or twa yet. Hit'll no shaa fur a while an A'm stertin ta feel better. But hit's no aesy, whit wi Mr Greig bein da session clerk an awaar o aa da clash i da parish, an him hae'in ta write doon dis deevilry i da meenits. Maist o hit isna true. But I canna hoid a bairn… an fornication is ee thing, but adultery is dealt wi severely. Weel, you ken dat fae Bain's case gyaain tae presbytery.'

The irony of the situation now must have hit Alex.

'It'll look as if I'm runnin awa. A'm nae better than Davie Bain. It'll look like I dunna care what happens to you or the bairn.'

'But you hae your ain faemly, Alex. An hit's göd dat you're gyaain back haem. You hae ta pit dis ahint you. I mean dat, truly I do.'

'But when folk ask wha the faither is…?'

'Whit sood I say?'

'Tell the truth, Mary. Lies just mak it aa worse an, anywye, it's more serious if you don't name the faither, is it no? An I'm no ashamed to faither a bairn ta you. I'm mad at mysel, but A'm no ashamed.'

'An if dey ax if I kent you wir a mairried man?'

'Say "no". Oh heevens, that would be a lie – what an awful muddle. Just do what's best for you, Mary.'

'Weel, I wisna raelly sure dat you wir, though Midder aye warned wis. Sic a peerie meenit o maddrim hit wis…'

'Maddrim? Ya, that's what is was.'

'Fock here say a bairn boarn laek yun is "mirry-begyit"! I felt so different. Hit wisna aa bad shurly…'

'No, Mary… whit can I say? I cannae turn back time an mak different decisions. I didna mean tae cause hurt or trouble. But I hiv, I truly hiv… an it'll rest on my conscience. An Jaerm 'll never speak to me again. Just when I thocht we micht see een anither in Leith, maybe sail thagither.'

'A'll deal wi Jaerm. Dunna worry aboot him.'

'That's good. I dinnae think I could face coming to say cheerio tae your faemly; they've been that kind.'

'A'll hae ta gyet on mi wye haem, Alex. Da Gröntu spies 'll be luikin fur me!'

'I'm worried for you.'

'Dunna wirry. A'll manage, somehoo. A'll tink it trowe. Fin a wye.'

'You're good wi bairns, Mary.'

Mary could feel tears behind her eyes and wanted to go before she did anything stupid. She turned away. Alex suddenly fumbled in his pocket and pressed a note into her hand. She couldn't see what it was, but she took it.

She smiled as best she could an said, 'Cheerio, an Göd bi wi dee, Alex Ross.'

He just replied 'Mary…'

Monday 18th April 1774
Happyhansel and Brunatwatt

The fine weather continued. Mary would normally have enjoyed her morning walk to school, with the sun well up over the Gallow Hill and the Hill o Foratwatt. The thought of the children returning would have pleased her; their shirts, blouses and pinafores all freshly washed and their boots mended; and soon they would throw off their heavy footwear in favour of bare feet. They would be glad to see her with her trays of sweet milk and brönnies and kirn-mylk. But she felt uneasy… why had Alex given her 10/-? It was a lot of money, many week's wages… it didn't feel right… but maybe it made him feel better… What to do with it… keep it… spend it… hold on to it? Perhaps she'd be glad of it later, might need it. And what would Mr Greig say to her today? She had undermined his trust in her… but then, he hadn't helped her when she needed it… could he not have said something at the session meeting in her defence… in defence of all of them? He'd taught most of them after all, at least from time to time... Maybe it was to show other lasses in the parish what happens... if you dare step out of line, transgress... and to remember who draws the lines. And Erchie... oh dear... he would have heard by now... dear, kind Erchie... it would be difficult for him. Maybe his father would have warned him to keep his distance... And for how much longer could she expect to keep her job? It would be easier if she lost this thing growing inside her, as Jean had done... but then Jean had hinted it hadn't happened spontaneously... And who would she tell... who must she tell... and when? Perhaps Jaerm and Eliza... and offer them the money to help them be together... if they would take it.

When she arrived, she quickly got into the swing of the kitchen and breakfast preparations. There was no fresh bread, but she had baked plenty oatcakes before the term ended and Leebie had provided some fresh butter and kirn-mylk. After the boarders were fed and the table set in the parlour for the Greigs, she slipped back to the kitchen, saying she wanted to get on with the baking while the fire was right for it. Come tea-time, she knew she couldn't make a similar excuse.

Mr Greig said, 'Come an set dee in, Mary. I hoop du'll aet wi wis as usual.'

'I wid understaand if you preferred ta be on your ain,' she replied, 'eftir aa da onkerry o yesterday.'

'My dear, du's no da first lass an du'll no be da last dat's faa'n foul o da kirk session. Hit's a institution dat's meant ta be ordained bi da Göd-Man himsel, an we can try wir best, but sometimes I tink we faa weel short; aye luikin backlins redder as forwirds.'

'I ken you dö a lock o göd wark an aa,' she replied.

'We try, but wir aa gyettin owre aald. An hit's bön a aafil upheaval lately. I hae ta say I tak nae pleasure in writin up dis meenits. I tink ill apön a lass whin shö's fae Dale o Waas or fae Foula, een dat I dunna raelly ken; but whin I ken someen laek dee, hit grieves me mair ta be pairt o hit.'

'Hit aa needs ta be changed, Faider. Hit jöst encourages fock ta clipe on een anidder an mak trouble. Da kirk sud nivver be involved wi dis kinda thing.'

'I doot, at times laek dis, da meenister tinks laek dee, Erchie. He's no a favourite o da presbytery. But he has ta try an toe da line, or he'll be in trouble wi da kirk authorities!'

'Foo will onythin ivver change dan? Maybe you sood resign?'

'Na, boy, da money I gyet paid fur hit helps pay Mary's wages an a bit towards John Jeems an Leebie an aa; an onywye, wir ordained fur life. Hit's dead men's shön.'

'Aa men?' his son replied.

Erchie's pun relieved the tension and the conversation turned to school and schoolhouse matters. Mary could almost have confessed everything there and then; got it off her heart and taken the consequences. She hoped there might still be a manageable way forward. While she felt the immediate burden lift a little, she knew this reprieve from her employer was unlikely to last.

***

As she approached the croft-house she realised she had the perfect opportunity to see Jaerm and Eliza on their own. They had been working late in the rigs having carted tang from the ebb during the day. They had gone to stow away their forks and kishies in the barn.

'A'm managed ta gyet a berth on da *Batchelor,* Mary! Dey'll tak me as a deck-haand. A'll wirk mi passage.'

Mary, who could see how pleased they both were, said, 'I im da blyde fur you baith.'

There was a pause till Jaerm asked, 'Is somethin wrang, Mary?'

'Ya, I tink you could say der micht jöst be a clood apö mi horizon. I needit dee ta gie yun nott tae Alex on Sunday fur I hed ta see him afore he sailed; an I didna want ta see him here.'

'Why fur no?'

'Weel, I tink I micht be gyaain tae hae a bairn; his bairn.'

'Whit?' The blood drained from her brother's cheeks. 'Does du mean...'

'Ya, Candlemas. I wis stupeed an sae wis he. We'd baith hed

owre muckle ta drink an I didna raelly ken jöst whit cam owre me.'

'Oh Mary, this is serious. Really serious, what wi him married in Leith.'

'I ken, Eliza. I dunna raelly blame him – I sood a hed mair control o mysel… I want him ta geng back ta his wife an bairn an pick up his life as if dis isna happened.'

'Does onyboady else ken?'

'Na, Jaerm, only you twa an Alex an me. I felt he needit ta ken.'

'Maybe you'll miscarry, Mary. No that I wid want that for you, but it wid mak life easier?' Eliza said.

'Maybe. A'll jöst hae ta wait an see. A'll keep mi job as lang as I can an A'll try ta gyet wark whaar I can eftir dat. But A'm no luikin forward ta tellin wir fock.'

Jaerm thought for a minute. 'I tink du sood keep hit quiet eenoo, Mary, an see foo du gyets on. I ken du'll fin a wye; an someen 'll be blyde o dee as a wife, even wi a bairn.'

'Time 'll tell, Jaerm. But I doot A'll hae me a trysht wi da kirk, wan wye or tidder. Noo, Alex gied me a bill for 10/- an truly I tink you twa sood tak hit wi you ta Leith. Hit micht help you gyet settled, an… mairried!'

'That's really kind o you, Mary, but…' and here Eliza waited till she could see agreement on Jaerm's face, '… but we couldn't tak it. You'll need it. Keep it safe for noo.'

'A'm gyaain ta miss da pair o you. An A'll hae ta gyet mi spade oot!'

'We can write twartree lines, Mary, even if it taks a age ta win tae dee,' said her brother. 'Dey'll aye be boats gyaain nort fae Leith.'

'I dunna want dis ta come atween dee an Alex.' Jaerm looked broken by the news.

They embraced briefly and Mary went into the house while they picked up the forks and kishies lying about. The family were all talking about the imminent departure of Eliza and Jaerm, and his lucky opportunity to sail as deck-hand on the *Batchelor*.

'I jöst hoop dis fair wadder hadds an der nae mair gales,' said Mary. 'Shö's maybe mendit up, but shö's no ready fur deep sea.'

Thursday 21st April 1774
Happyhansel

A kind of calm settled over Happyhansel. The bustle of recent days had subsided. Final repairs to the *Batchelor of Leith* had been completed and checked and the crew had managed to bring on board the last of the emigrants. They were packed in, but not quite so cramped as they had been on the initial journey: eleven had died and twenty-eight had opted to stay on in Shetland rather than return to Thurso or to Leith. Those families staying on had each received their share of food: eight weeks of provisions per head. The remaining barrels had all been stowed and lashed down. The squabble between some of the emigrants and Balfour over court costs had somehow been resolved. The rumour was that Patrick Ross's followers had withdrawn their appeal.

The crew had been keen to get underway while the weather was favourable. Some local people had stayed away, glad to see the back of the emigrants. Mary knew that John, Jean and Christian as well as Willie and Katie had been among the throng gathered at the shore to see them off. Many emigrants were still angry that their hopes of a new life and a new home in America had been dashed. But yesterday's sun had shone on them and a good breeze had rattled the yards and promised to fill the sails. While in some ways it had been reminiscent of their arrival, it was very different. Local men had helped tow them into Vaila Sound, past the Baa o Saatness, and out through the narrow Aester Soond till they were able to unfurl their sails within sight of the open ocean and, at last, the horizon. There had been sadness as well as relief etched on the faces of the Waas folk as they saw the masts disappear.

The immediate concern for the Greigs was that there were several of the remaining families in Waas hoping to settle permanently, and thus a sizeable influx of schoolchildren to seek out and integrate into classes at Happyhansel. At least the provisions would mean that families would not starve at that time of year when the meal-chest is emptying fast and the summer fishing has yet to get underway.

Despite the huge gap left in Brunatwatt with Jaerm and Eliza leaving, and the dreadful thought they might never see each other again, Mary had felt a sense of relief knowing the ship had sailed. Yes, she had been fond of Alex Ross, and knew she could have grown fonder had it been permissible. She knew that she was now, more than ever, on her own; author of her own destiny. However, as long as she could stay healthy and strong, there was a chance she could manage. She could only hope for the best. She had laid by the 10/- bill where no one would find it.

Sunday 15th May 1774
Waas kirk

Sunday 24th April had come and gone. None of the young women had received a letter summoning them to appear as had been expected. The rumour was that the officer had reported that he had not known he was to cite the women: no one had told him while he had been busy clearing up after the service. There was irritation that it would now be a whole month since the session had questioned them, that their memories would be taxed. Some wondered if Buchan had got cold feet or whether the kirk officer had sabotaged their plan deliberately. But the Brunatwatt folk knew that the officer would not risk his job: he would need the little money he earned from his various kirk tasks.

As before, the young women stayed behind after the service. All but Margaret Irvineson from Stennestwatt had turned up: Mary and her sisters, Margaret and Christian Morison from Stove, Agnes and Bess Slatter as well as Ann Johnsdaughter and Helen Fullertown from Whitesness. Mr Buchan looked somewhat gaunt and in need of his dinner. It had been a particularly demanding time with all the arrangements for the emigrants to leave or, in some cases, to help them stay. The officer, when asked about Margaret Irvineson, reported that she was indisposed in bed, and unable to be at the kirk.

Having concentrated on Jean at the last interrogation, the minister turned to Christian Morison, the older of the two sisters from Stove. Had she been on board the ship on the Sabbath day? She admitted that she had, but had been there with their brother Andrew 'upon no bad design' and that one of the emigrant women accompanied them.

Her sister Margaret, who had said before that she hadn't been on board, denied that any of the sailors had ever been in their house at Stove. She worked to Mr Henry of Bayhaa and, when not working there, she worked for Agnes Sletter and had been in her house. One of the elders at this point slipped Mr Buchan a note. He read it quickly then asked Margaret what seemed like a pointed question. Who gave you half a guinea which you got rid of recently? Margaret quickly responded that she got that coin 'about a dozen of years ago from her brother Gilbert Morison in Lunnasting parish.' There was some incredulity on the faces of the old men.

The minister then turned to Agnes Slatter who said she had indeed gone onboard, accompanied by her brother Robert and also William Monroe and his wife, two of the emigrants. However, she now realised this was wrong, it being the Sabbath, confessing she was very sorry. Mary wondered if, by saying that, they might forgive her for hosting the Candlemas rant.

Ann Johnsdaughter from Whitesness answered that she and Helen Fullertoun were returning from kirk with their fathers when they were all invited very innocently to dinner onboard. One by one, the young women recanted or found ways of emphasising the innocence of their behaviour. Jean's boldness under cross-examination had left her and Mary somewhat exposed.

All eyes then fell on Mary as Mr Buchan turned to her, asking whether or not she had received a bill for ten shillings Sterling from Alexander Ross, one of the sailors on board the *Batchelor*. Mary, completely floored by this question, wondered how on earth such information had become public. But she was determined she was not going to be made out to be a harlot.

She could hear herself answer firmly, 'Yes.'

'So what had she given him for that sum?'

'I gave him nothing for it, nor was I desiring any neat thing from him; he insisted I take it.' Alex was, after all, a friend of the family and had received hospitality and help on numerous occasions. 'I still have the money,' she said. Again, the old elders shook their heads and looked at one another in disbelief.

'Well, you must produce it before the session at the next meeting,' said the minister. 'We will hear your confession and those of your sisters and Margaret Morison next Lord's Day. It will be *ad avizandum.*'

During the closing prayer, Mary's heart was racing. This was intolerable and if they knew about the money did they know more? Had someone at Stove seen them that night? Had Alex said anything? Or Jaerm or Eliza? But they were all well away by now and beyond asking.

On their way up the brae to Stove, there was no hilarity this time. Mary wasn't far from tears.

Jean said, 'You'd tink we wir aa hussies or hooers. An whitna bloddy cheek o dem axin aboot da money? I wis gien twartree pennies an aa – da sailors kent dat we nivver see money; dat wir lives is jöst varg an mair varg. I didna feel bad aboot takkin hit. We'd brichtened up der winter a coarn. Weel, dat's whit dey said. I feel laek ballin hit i da faces o yun elders. Dey mind me o aald fozie neeps!'

Jean's outburst made them laugh. Christian, however, was serious. 'Whit on aert is ad avizandum?' Up until now she had not been upset by being part of the group, but it was maybe time for her to remove herself even if she was about to leave school.

'Wha kens?' said Jean. 'An wha cares?'

A depression settled over the Brunatwatt family. Mary could no longer hide the fact that she had received the money from Alex. At least she could say truthfully that she had wanted to give it to Jaerm and Eliza; that she did not mean to keep it for herself. Her mother looked at her rather too knowingly for comfort. The more she thought about it, the more she decided that Alex must have let something slip, perhaps to a sailor friend; perhaps someone who had lent him money. She was pretty sure that no one had seen their brief encounter that night. She suddenly felt furious at the thought that he could sail away with no repercussions while she was left with the full price to pay.

They were all feeling the loss of Jaerm and Eliza. At least when he was at the whaling there was the prospect of him coming home over the winter. John was busy with his preparations for the fishing. He would be staying over at a summer böd between Littlure and Burrastow where there was a beach for the catches of cod and ling to be landed, weighed, salted and dried. And all within sight of the laird's watch tower on Vaila, overlooking the Waster Soond. He would be leaving the next day.

Monday 16th May 1774
Happyhansel and Brunatwatt

Mary was up early to say cheerio to John. She suspected he had guessed her condition but had said nothing. She walked with him as far as Happyhansel.

'Mary, A'm kinda wirried aboot dee. Some fock hae evil tongues. I ken du's sensible an göd-haertit an foo o courage, but hit can be a herd rodd fur a wumman ta traivel on her ain. A'll be tinkin aboot dee. Takk care, an A'll be haem as aften as I can.'

Mary struggled to keep back a tear: her brothers were well-thought of and could always be depended on to give their support.

They said their goodbyes and he got on his way west. Mary caught sight of John Jeems checking a new born lamb. The mother was tethered nearby.

'Fine day, Mary. Foo's du?'

'A'm fine, tanks. An aa you?'

'Tae da fore. Wir boys is managed ta gyet da paet banks aa flaed an cleaned wi dis fine spell o voar wadder; an der awa dis moarnin wi der tushkers. I daar say dey'll be kyempin… come haem dug-tired!'

'Weel, hit's a göd day fur da hill. No owre waarm, an nae mudjicks! Is yun peerie lamb kinda pör aamos?'

'Ya. Da midder hed a wrastle wi her. Cam oot da wrang wye. But shö's kyuckerin up an I tink shö'll be spricklin aboot nae budder afore lang. I jöst wantit ta mak sure shö wis sookin. Noo lass, I hear du's no hed dy soarros ta seek an aa. Whit wye da kirk is makkin a wark o a bit o fun, I raelly dunna understaand. Wir aa bön young. I canna ken why Mr Buchan is taen up in hit. He's a göd sowl. But wir aa vexed fur dee fur we ken du's a acht ta aan.'

Mary was somewhat taken aback at his directness. She had unconsciously developed a tough layer around her feelings, but genuine kindness cut through. 'Bliss dee, John Jeems. He's a queer onkerry an no laek ta end. I suppose Mr Buchan is reffelled up in rules: kirk session an presbytery an general assembly an aa. I doot he dusna mak da rules but haes ta apply dem.'

'Aye aye. Du's laekly richt, hinny. Dey hae ta keep some oarder ithin da parish. But jöst du keep dy head up. An mind, "Ivery een has der ain grey yowe."'[7]

Mary found the old man's understanding touching. 'A'll hae ta try,' she responded.

'I traad da neck o a hen fur you owre da helly. Leebie is pluckit an draain her, sae A'll be alang as shön as A'm dön wi dis lamb.'

The conversation helped Mary feel a little less apprehensive and lighter in her step as she entered the schoolhouse. It was still going to be a difficult day. Little was said as she served their breakfast. She mentioned John Jeems's progress with the schoolhouse peats. Erchie tried to keep the exchange going, but it was a struggle. Mr Greig said little, but thanked her and smiled as he always did. Afterwards, Erchie brought dishes through to the scullery.

'Nivver leet, Mary. Mi faider is kinda upset aboot aathin eenoo.'

'I sood maybe gie up mi job, Erchie? A'm makkin hit dat aakwird fur you baith.'

---

7 Everyone has their own skeleton in the cupboard (lit. everyone has their own grey sheep, with fleece of little value).

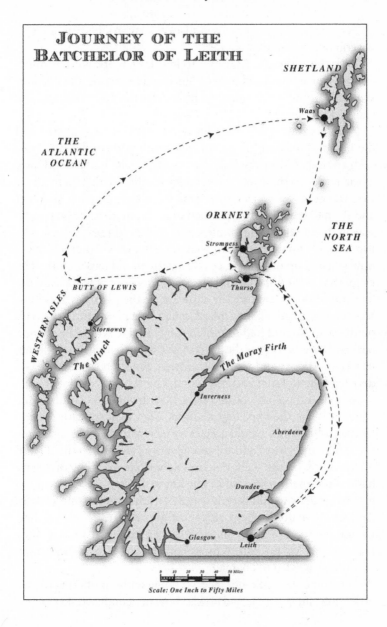

JOURNEY OF THE
BATCHELOR OF LEITH

'Na, na, lass. I tink someens jöst laek ta mak trouble. An onywye, we couldna manage ithoot dee.'

With that thought, Mary set to her day's work with as much enthusiasm as she could muster. She loved her work: the freedom she had to make decisions; to look after the two men and the children.

John Jeems was as good as his word and Mary was able to boil the hen and make a big pot of rich broth with barley and peas with enough left for the boarders' tea later. She had a good look at the larder to think what she might be able to feed them all on over the next few weeks: there was still some salt pork and beef and she had managed to get a load of fresh piltocks, the first of the season, from one of the families who had children at school. The fish, though small, had dried well in the good weather and were now stacked up on a shelf, covered with an old cheesecloth. The rhubarb was shooting up and blackcurrants setting. In the yard the first tiny shoots were already showing on the potatoes and John Jeems had carried a kishie full of young kale plants from the crub on the scattald and had got them safely in. He would be sowing oats and bere as soon as the ground was damp enough. Meantime, it was good peat and lambing weather. So often the voar was a disaster, but, so far, it had been conducive to croft-work.

At dinner time she busied herself with the new children for whom this was their first day at school. They looked a little unsure. Erchie had said they would need extra help with their lessons. Later, she tidied and swept and dusted. Her eyes strayed to the session minute book on the shelf, but she knew what would be there and had no temptation to read it. She knew she was not the woman it portrayed, or would portray once her situation became known. And surely many in the parish must know that. People she had met on the road or at the shop had said as much. Mr Greig must know it, and Mr Buchan. Why were they not brave enough to say that things needed to change?

At teatime she could not face Mr Greig without offering to give up her job, although she had no idea how her family would manage without her wages. She could not go on sitting at his table in this awkward situation.

'I wis winderin, Mr Greig, if hit wid be better fur aaboady if I gied up mi job here aside you an Erchie. I love wirkin tae you, but I dunna feel hit's richt wi you bein on da kirk session an hae'in ta dael wi…'

'Mary, I dunna want dee ta tink dat wye. Hit is difficult, A'll admit dat; an nae doot tongues is waggin, but I canna faat dy wark ava. Lat's jöst see foo we gyet on. An onywye, wha could we gyet ta dö aa da wark du does? We'd need twa lasses!'

Mary managed to keep her outer persona calm and smiled in response. She knew it was a privilege for a servant to be treated as one of the family; somehow that made her treachery seem worse. But for now, she felt the air a little clearer.

It was still a fine day when she reached Brunatwatt. She could see her mother out flitting the kye. She would have to know sooner rather than later, and anyway Mary had a feeling that her mother suspected something.

'Foo got du on daday, Mary?'

'Fine, Midder. We hed eicht new bairns – emigrants – ta settle in. Pör tings, maist o dem is nivver bön tae a scöl afore, sae dey wir braaly faert. But Erchie is göd wi da young eens an da aalder lasses kinda cöllied aboot dem an aa. Dey'll be fine damoarn. Dey fairly supped up da maet I gied dem.'

'I doot dat.'

'I could set twartree kale plants afore wir eicht o'clocks. Hit's sic a fine nicht.'

'Na lass, Jean an Christian is gotten hit dön. Hit's a blisseen wir boys laabored wir rigs afore dey set aff. Anidder voar, hit'll be mair o a ontak ithoot Jaerm.'

'But A'll maybe be here ta help instead. I tink I micht no hae a job bi dan.'

Baabie, who had been driving in a peg to secure the tether, looked up and her face darkened.

'Weel, mi jewel, A'm bön kinda winderin if somethin wis up wi dee, du wis dat quiet. Is hit whit I tink hit is?'

'I'm lippenin a bairn, Midder. A'm jöst afflikkit ta tink A'm browt distress on you an da faemly. I canna tink whit cam owre me... drink, hit's deveelry, but nae excuse.'

'Candlemas?'

'Ya.'

'Alex?'

'Ya.'

'I could see you laekit een anidder.'

'You warned wis weel, Midder. An if I hedna taen drink hit wid nivver a happened. I ken dat.'

'Weel, mi joy, der a dose o bairns dat's mirry-begyit an dis 'll no be da hidmist ting. But I doot... I doot he's maerried, an dat maks hit a aafil onkerry wi da kirk. We'll jöst hae ta manage somewye.'

'I kinda hoopit at da stert dat hit wid jöst come awa. But I ken noo dat's less laekly.'

'Does Alex ken?'

'I telt him jöst afore dey sailed... I felt he needit ta ken. A'm blyde he's gien, Midder. He gied me yun 10/- bill... I sood nivver a taen it fae him... but Göd kens foo dat cam oot i da parish.'

'Der naethin secret here, lass. Naethin ava.'

'I tink you're richt dere. I doot Alex manna telt een o his freends, no tinkin he wid spread hit.'

'Maybe dat.'

'Whit sall I tell Faider?'

'I sall tell dy faider an da lasses whin I see a chance. Nae doot he'll geng up laek a blue lowe.[8] But he'll gyet owre hit. We'll wadder hit tagidder whin da news gyets oot. Nae doot du'll hae dee a time o hit wi some o yun elders... but dat passes.'

They fell silent. Mary stroked the cows' flanks and went inside, following her mother.

---

8 To explode, lose one's temper (lit. to ignite quickly, with a blue flame).

Sunday 22nd May 1774
Waas kirk

Buoyed up by their payment of a crown to Dodie o Watness for teaching poor children and half-a-crown to Lowrie o Braebister who was in dire straits having recently lost a cow, the old elders turned their attention to the young flesh in front of them. There was no doubt that this was why they had been content to stay behind after the service: their dinner could wait. The young women, now whittled down to five, had been called in by the officer. The others, given that they had confessed their guilt, had been dismissed from discipline. The three Johnson sisters and Margaret Morison from Stove were kept standing while everyone waited to see if Margaret Irvineson of Stennestwatt would appear. But there was no sight of her. No doubt she would be cited to appear yet again.

Immediately, Mr Buchan turned to Mary and asked if she had brought with her the 10/- bill given her by Alexander Ross, the one she had promised to deliver to the session at this meeting. Mary said she had mislaid it, but that she should seek for it yet and, if she found it, would deliver it afterwards. She had not been able to bring herself to take the bill with her, but did not really know why she felt that way.

Turning to Margaret Morison, who denied receiving a half-guinea from a sailor, he deferred passing sentence until 'Providence gives further light.' Given the splutters into moustaches and clearing of throats, it was easy to see that the elders were hoping that her belly would swell and give her away. The minister seemed keen not to prolong the meeting any further. He stated that the Johnson sisters should see him, privately – *ad avizandum* – before the next Sabbath with a view to repenting before the congregation.

'A'm no turnin up ony mair,' said Christian, on their way home. 'Why sood I confess? I wisna allooed ta geng.'

Jean said, 'Maybe if we see Buchan privately, ithoot da laeks o Deyell oglin wis, we'll be able ta explain an no hae ta staand up in front o aaboody.'

Monday 13th June 1774
Brunatwatt

On the way home down the Kloss of Voe, Mary's mind turned to her recent visit to Voe House; how the three of them, waiting in trepidation for Mr Buchan to appear, had been shown into a small, gloomy room with not much of a fire, and with stern-looking portraits on the walls.

He had greeted them pleasantly enough and shuffled through his papers. He had then asked Jean what she had to say by way of explanation of their behaviour. She had started by saying that Christian had not been to any entertainment and had been wrongly accused all along.

Mr Buchan may have taken that into account, or perhaps he was just tired of the whole business, as it had not been long before he said, 'I've discussed this matter at some length with my session clerk and we are both of the opinion that you have all learned your lesson and that the matter can be dropped.' Before dismissing them, he had said, 'I'm off to Foula soon and trust that you will all calm down now that the *Batchelor of Leith* and her sailors are away south. It has been a very unsettling time for everyone.'

They had thanked him and were shown out. It had been a big relief, at least for the time being.

Mary had heard from Erchie that the minister was just back from one of his very occasional short trips to Foula to take holy communion and to meet with some local islanders who had grievances or who had been called as witnesses. He had said his father was busy deciphering all the notes Mr Buchan had made while in Foula and recording them in the minute book. There had been so much rumour and gossip lately coming out of Foula that it had entirely eclipsed the Waas tittle-tattle. And there had been talk of leprosy in Mid Waas. The kirk session had agreed with the ranselman that a spilt-house should be provided for an old woman showing signs of leprosy, but there was some dispute among local folk as to where it should be built. Everyone would be glad that the Waas kirk session was now in summer recess.

Crossing the burn at the head of the voe, Mary was suddenly gripped by what felt like indigestion, almost under her ribs. Just as it eased, it gripped her again. Slowly it dawned on her what it was; most probably, the baby quickening. Part of her was pleased with this sign that all was as it should be; that the baby was thriving.

She was relieved that her family now knew about the pregnancy, as the deceit had been difficult to bear. Her mother had first told her father and, by the time he had spoken with Mary, he had calmed down. She knew he had depended on her to set a good example to Christian. Jean had always been more headstrong, more difficult to bridle. He'd merely said to her, 'Dat bloody *Batchelor* is left a wake as shö disappeared oot da Aester Soond.' Jean, when she was told, had said she suspected as much and Christian had been upset at the news. Mary could visualise their faces as her mother told them. Baabie had sworn them all to secrecy in the meantime. It would no doubt become obvious before the summer was out.

Mary had decided that this week, sometime, she would have to tell Mr Greig; that she would offer to stay on until the end of the school term so that he had all summer to find a suitable replacement. It would allow her to help her family with the croft work and the peats at that time of year when everything clamours for attention.

People were out in their rigs after their tea heaping early potatoes and singling turnips. So often the wind fell in the evening and, with the long light nights, it was the best part of the day. Lambs were already starting to nibble occasional tufts of grass and caper around in groups, ignoring the ewes. She almost felt light-hearted; that is, until it all came in on her again. Approaching home, she could see their cows out on the toonmals – the pasture near the house – gently chewing the cud; and Bella getting heavier. This would be her second calf.

The five of them were all glad to sit down to their eicht o'clocks. Jean had been to the shop and was bursting with the Foula news.

'Dey wir seeminly a lock o bad blöd atween faemlies, fur Elspet

Magnusdochter wis refused ta mairry dis man an he "took grief an deed" – dat's whit dey said – an his midder wis up in airms aboot hit. An fock said dey wir awfil tongues apö da weemen... biddin Elspet "kiss her erse"... caain her a "damned bitch"... an a "midden mare"; an dan... yun sam Elspet hed ta appear afore da elders aboot anidder case – a neebor lass, at Quhinster. Dat lass wis accused o gyettin rid o a bairn... an aaboady kent dat hit wis a Vaila man at wis da faider... but Elspet seeminly swör shö wis bön sent fur ee nicht, to come and see da lass when shö wis laek ta faa by an could hardly spaek... shö said just laek a wumman in travail... but Elspet mindit dem dat a lass or virgin can gyet pains laek dat. Dey wir a braa argie-bargie aboot wha said whit. An hit wis gien on dat lang dat hit wis hed ta be left tae da neist time da meenister could win ta Foula!... An...'

'White yun, Jean!' said Baabie.

'Heth, hit maks Waas seem laek da Holy o Holies!' said Joannie.

Mary filled up their cups. 'I doot maist o hit's a lock o bruck. Jöst neebers makkin trouble. Hit's no aesy livin in a peerie place.'

Jean was pleased she was the news-bearer. 'An a man fae here wis in trouble in Foula an aa. Dey wir seeminly a Umphray man dat swör dat da ranselman – a elder in Waas – wis no coontit his sheep richtly while Umphray wis at da haaf... dat'll be a tricky een fur Buchan! Een o his ain elders!'...

Baabie raised her voice once again, interrupting the flow, 'I said "white yun, Jean!" an I meant it.'

So chatter turned safely to peats, lambs, crops and plans for the next day, should it be fair.

Tuesday 14th June 1774
Happyhansel

Mary could see tiredness written all over Mr Greig's face. After their tea, he moved to the fireside and, once she had cleared away their dishes, she brought through the teapot and cups for the two men. She stood for a minute, before saying, 'Mr Greig, I hae somethin I need ta tell you.'

'Is du aaricht, Mary? Set dee doon, lass. Du luiks as if du's seen a ghost!'

'A'm fine, tanks. Hit's jöst dat I hae a confession ta mak; an ta you… although nae doot A'll hae ta mak hit ta da meenister afore lang. A'm lippenin a bairn i da late hairst, maybe November, an A'll hae ta gie up mi job here. If hit suitit you, I could wirk till da end o dis term, an dat wid lat you hae time ta fin someen else.'

She could hear the tick of the clock as the news sunk in.

'Or, of coorse, if you wid redder I left noo, dat wid be entirely raisonable.'

'Mary, I canna richtly tak dis in. Aa da ramifications…' said Mr Greig.

'Drink you your tae, sir. Hit's aa mi ain faat. I took drink an I didna ken whit I wis döin… his wis eftir da Candlemas spree an…'

'An can I ax wha da faider is?'

At this point Mary could see Erchie put his head in his hands.

'Hit wis Alex Ross, da ship's carpenter.'

'But he's a mairried man, is he no, Mary?'

Mary was silent for a moment. 'Ya, I hear dat is da case. An I realise dat maks hit far waar, accordin tae da kirk.'

'An accordin tae da bible, Mary.'

'I hae nae doot dat you're richt, Mr Greig. I feel A'm lat aaboady doon, especially mi ain fock an… an baith o you, fur you're aye bön dat kind ta me. I canna believe wan stupeed mistak can laand me in sic a mess. A'm nivver gyaain ta preeve a drink again…'

'Wir you pushed ta drink an…'

'Na, I canna say I wis. A'm entirely da caase o mi ain haertbrack.'

'Weel, my dear, whit can I say? A'm haert-sair. I can see dat du canna wirk on here dat muckle langer. Laekly da end o da term wid be da ill-best time an, as du says, wid gie wis time ta fin someen. But of coorse du can bide on as lang as du feels du can manage. I canna tink wha could dö da job here as weel as du's dön.'

'A'm truly grateful fur your wirds, Mr Greig. I dunna deserve dem. Do you tink I sood tell Mr Buchan or jöst wait eenoo.'

'I wid say jöst wait eenoo, Mary. He's braally daeved wi aa da onkerry among da Foula fock. I doot he'll hae ta geng dere again ere lang.'

'A'll hae ta tell Leebie an John Jeems afore muckle langer, an Jaanie Jeromson. I dunna want dem finnin oot fae idder fock. But dat can wait an aa.'

'Ya, hit can wait.'

'Tanks tae you. A'll wash up da lem an gyet on mi wye haem shön.'

Mary left the two men by the parlour fire and escaped to the kitchen. She was shaking, but relieved to have told them the truth; well almost the whole truth. How many more difficult days lay ahead? Presently, Erchie came through to the scullery. He took the food scraps out to the pigs for her and helped lift heavy pots on to shelves.

Suddenly he turned to face her, 'Mary, I canna bear dis. I wid mairry dee if I tocht hit wid help!'

Mary smiled and shook her head.

'Wirkin tagidder here i da scöl is wan thing, Erchie. I doot bein man an wife is braaly different. An we'd be da spaekalation! Du's da dearest freend I could hae, but I widna draem o ruinin dy life as weel as mi ain. I doot du's better lang lowse as ill-teddered![9]… Na, I jöst hae ta gyet on wi hit as best I can. Adultery is a serious business – da sixth commandment, if I mind richt.'

'Ya, but A'm sure der a bit i da bible… ya, somethin Jesus wis supposed tae a said… aboot da wumman taen in adultery… hadd on… A'm gyaain trowe ta da scölroom ta gyet a copy. A'm sure hit's in wan o da gospels; maybe St John.'

Mary was partly humbled and partly amused by Erchie's response. He was indeed the kindest and most thoughtful young man she knew; she loved him like a brother and appreciated that he would say such a thing. But she knew he had a good life ahead of him. He

---

9 Better to wait to find the right partner (lit. better free to roam than tethered in poor grazing).

would take over the schoolmaster's role when his father needed to give it up. He could marry well and be happy with his own family around him.

He wasn't long in finding it. 'Tak it haem wi dee, Mary. Du can bring hit back damoarn. St John, chapter eicht, verses tree ta eleeven.' He set the testament down and Mary could see he had left a piece of paper to mark the passage.

'Tanks, Erchie. A'll nivver foryat dy kindness.'

There was still just enough daylight to read by when Mary eventually got to bed. She opened the testament and found the passage Erchie had marked:

3 And the scribes and Pharisees brought unto him a woman taken in adultery; and when they had set her in the midst,
4 They say unto him, Master, this woman was taken in adultery, in the very act.
5 Now Moses in the law commanded us, that such should be stoned: but what sayest thou?
6 This they said, tempting him, that they might have to accuse him. But Jesus stooped down, and with his finger wrote on the ground, as though he heard them not.
7 So when they continued asking him, he lifted up himself, and said unto them, He that is without sin among you, let him first cast a stone at her.
8 And again he stooped down, and wrote on the ground.
9 And they which heard it, being convicted by their own conscience, went out one by one, beginning at the eldest, even unto the last: and Jesus was left alone, and the woman standing in the midst.
10 When Jesus had lifted up himself, and saw none but the woman, he said unto her, Woman, where are those thine accusers? hath no man condemned thee?
11 She said, No man, Lord. And Jesus said unto her, Neither do I condemn thee: go, and sin no more.

She closed the book and carefully laid it with her clothes so she would remember to bring it back. The course of the day's conversations and Erchie's selflessness had taken her by surprise. While she tried to sleep, the text went round and round in her head, 'He that is without sin, let him first cast a stone…' The kirk certainly didn't see things that way: there would be stones coming her way before long.

Friday 17th June 1774
Happyhansel

When Mary got to Happyhansel, Erchie could tell her that his father was staying in bed, nursing a bad summer cold. The old man had wanted to get up, but his son had forbidden him meantime, making it clear that he could cope. Mary served their porridge and Erchie took a bowl through to his father who managed to sup it.

'Der plenty o soup for wir denner an I can waarm up yesterday's bannocks i da Dutch oven… an, if we hae somethin aesy laek bacon an eggs fur wir tae, dan I could come trowe an help dee a coarn wi da peerie tings. Du'll hae dy haands foo wi da muckle eens an da boarders an aa. Dat is, if du tinks I can be o ony help.'

'Weel I did winder aboot axin Mr Buchan ta lend a haand, but I ken he's braaly trang eenoo… sae, if du dusna mind, Mary, dat wid be a help, fur A'm still hae'in ta dael wi some o da new bairns – maistlins boys. Wi aa da croft wark eenoo der affen a braa twartree bairns keepit fae scöl sae dey can help der fock. An dat means der aa at sixes an seevens whin hit comes tae der lessons.'

Erchie went through to settle the children while Mary cleared up quickly and fetched water from the well. John Jeems had already brought fresh milk and eggs. She then went through to the classroom where the younger children were sitting at their desks. Erchie had taken them through the Lord's Prayer and laid out slates, chalk, dusters and some books. The youngest children had been learning words that had a 'ch' in them so, once they had told Mary all the words they had learned (churn, church, chop, chance, choose), she got the older ones to add some more and help spell them. Then they each wrote down on their slates one word with an 'O' sound: they got boat, coat, goat, load, moan, road, toad, bore, core, more, hole, coal, cole... they kept them coming. Sometimes she pretended she could not remember how words were spelled and they enjoyed keeping her right. Suddenly, she became aware that the children were not looking at her, but over her shoulder. When she turned round, Erchie was standing in the doorway. He said 'Whoa!' while pretending he was pulling on reins, and she – pretending to be frightened of the horse – said 'Oh, no!' and the children smiled and looked at one another, wondering if they could laugh. She was suddenly embarrassed at the thought that he had been watching her and had joined in. However, he seemed happy and she commented that they were very good at spelling. He looked at Mary as if to ask if he could leave her to get on with it and she indicated all was well. She was just hoping she could hold their interest, neither boring the older children nor leaving the little ones floundering. She had kept an eye open for Willm's response as an indicator. He seemed content.

The younger children were eager to impress Mary with the rhymes they had learned, so, one by one, they stood up and recited a nursery rhyme. Some were keen to come out to the front of the little classroom and say it out more loudly; some were shyer. The morning ended with reading from *Gulliver's Travels*. The older children read a paragraph each and everyone followed along on their own copy. It was one of those stories that appealed to a wide range of ages. Mary kept a note of the tricky words and went over them later.

There was just time to get them to clean their slates, tidy away their books and to learn a scripture verse before they broke at dinner time. She chose an easy text from St Matthew's Gospel which neither she nor they needed to look up: *'Blessed are the peacemakers: for they shall be called...* (what?) *the children of God'*. Then she left them to finish tidying away their books while she quickly made her way to the kitchen. She hooked up a pan of soup to heat and set a few bannocks to warm.

The children knew the drill: most had brought some bread or a brönnie wrapped in a cloth and a drink of milk or blaand in an old medicine bottle, while those who otherwise would go hungry quickly helped themselves to the sweet milk, bannocks and kirn-mylk she brought for them. They were all keen to get out to play for a while before being called back in.

Mr Greig was sitting by the parlour fire, well happed up.

'Jöst a aetmel brönnie, if du haes een, an a peerie aer o soup, Mary. Du'll hae ta come an tell me foo du got on.'

Arithmetic in the afternoon was easier for Mary, and by now the children had lost their shyness and seemed to respond well to her requests and suggestions.

The older children were using the textbook she remembered well – *Hodders's Arithmetic* – with its many tables involving money, time, weights and measures.

They worked on exercises using their slates and, once correct, they carefully copied them into their ciphering book, cleaned their slate, and went on to the next set of sums. Erchie had made a list of correct answers and Mary had to select one of the children to be the checker, a role they seemed to relish. That left her free to listen to the younger children recite their tables together.

She made up little questions for them: 'a sheep-dog manages to drive eight sheep into the pen, dat's inta da crö, but two are left running away. How many sheep was he meant to pen? Another day the crofter looks over his wall and sees that half his flock has lambed. He has twenty-two sheep. How many have lambed? And if five of those sheep have had twins, how many lambs are there so far?' And so on, with mental arithmetic involving croft animals with which they would be familiar. Eventually, she gave them simple sums to set out on their slates and to answer with or without the help of Erchie's store of grottie-buckies. They loved the little shells, turning them over in their hands and comparing them for size and colour. Some of them were starting to set out the sums in their notebooks, too.

By the end of the school-day, she was glad to see them safely on their way home. She wondered what they might tell their folk. It had all been a bit of an unknown, feeling her way along and having to remember to speak in English to the children as Mr Greig and Erchie always did. But there had been no tears, and no fighting or swearing; no wet trousers or torn pinafores; no disasters of which she was aware.

Erchie tidied and swept both classrooms so that Mary could return to the schoolhouse and her familiar role. She sliced the bacon she had bought from the shop as thinly as she could manage and fried it. She beat the eggs and scrambled them up ready to serve. By now, the boarders had smelt the bacon and were ravenous. She had meant to make a bread and butter pudding for them all with rhubarb in it, one of their favourites, but that would have to wait for another day.

Mr Greig and Erchie both thanked her for helping out; she felt relieved that perhaps she had managed to overwrite something of the upset and embarrassment she had caused them. She knew tongues would wag as soon as the news got out and folk would speculate how much the Greigs had known. The tale would no doubt be embroidered.

She left for Brunatwatt a little lighter in her spirits, glad that Mr Greig looked somewhat better and would probably manage on Saturday, always a less arduous school day. She felt a kind of poignancy, knowing these days were numbered.

On her way, Mary dropped along to see Jaanie briefly. Willm was having a cup of milk before bedtime. He was a little shy of her now, but eventually came over to give her a hug.

'Du's braaly göd at dy sums, Willm, an dy readin an aa!'

He beamed. 'I laek coontin an döin sums. An dy sums wis funny sums, Mary! Will du be dere on Monday?'

'I tink A'll be back i da keetchen on Monday, mi jewel. An blyde o da paes; an kennin you're aa laernin whit you're meant ta be laernin.' Then, turning to Jaanie, she said, 'You'll be missin Katie an Willie I doot.'

'Ya, dey wir göd company an a help an aa; an Jane – sic a peerie moot – but I am da blyde der gotten awa ta Nort Carolina dis time. Weel, der on der wye, an we hae ta hoop hit aa gengs fine fur dem. I tink Willie haes a bridder dere, sae he'll shurly see dem safely settled. Fine fock dey wir.'

Willm went off to bed happily. Jaanie set up the fire, adding a few peats to the outside to keep it going till she too would turn in. She took a letter from her apron pocket and handed it to Mary.

'A'm hed dis letter fae Walter, Mary, an windered if du wid read him ta me. I jöst hoop he's weel an micht even be comin haem afore lang.'

The writing wasn't quite the copperplate Mary was used to, but she managed to decipher it in the evening light coming in the western window.

Liverpool, 20th May, 1774

My dearest Mother,

I am writing this quickly at Liverpool docks where we are unloading a cargo of tea from India. I've lately bumped into a sailor from Unst, a Hughson man, and his next berth is Leith from where he then hopes to take a turn home. So he said he would take this and find a way of getting it to you in Waas.

I hope you are well and Willm too. I miss you both and long to get home to see you. I think sailing to the Far East is fine, but we have to be careful we do not catch the fevers they suffer from. I think I will stick with home trade after one or two more long voyages. The cotton trade is picking up, so there is plenty cargo between Liverpool and India. Flax too.

I hope that you are managing. No doubt the money I was able to leave last time will be running out and I need to be home before long.

I'm used to sailing as Mate now and I'll tell you, the navigation I learned at Waas has helped me. There's one

*more Shetlander joined wir crew as bosun. He comes fae
Skeld. We enjoy a yarn tagidder.*

*I cannot express how grateful I am to you for looking after
Willm. He will be at school now and growing into a big lad.
I try to imagine him. Tell him I miss him and hope to be
home before too long. He'll soon be able to read my letters
to you. Meanwhile, I hope you can find someone who will
do that.*

Ever your affectionate son,
Walter

'My, dat is da fine ta hear fae him. A'll try an read hit tae Willm
noo dat I ken whit hit says.'

'Hit'll no be lang till Willm can read hit, Jaanie.'

'I wirry dat Willm 'll hardly mind his faider whin he sees him.
Noo, lass, will du tak a coarn o eicht o'clocks? Du's hed dee a
day o 'im bi da soond o hit!'

But Mary's errand was just to ask if it was all right to come
along the next evening as she wanted some advice. She might be
a little later.

On her way home, she wondered if Jaanie had suspected
anything. Normally she wouldn't ask if she could come along:
that door was always open.

Saturday 18th June 1774
Stove

Mary had told her mother she would be at Jaanie's and wouldn't be
home at her usual time. She didn't rush away from Happyhansel,
glad of a bit of extra time to bake brönnies and a bit of fruit loaf
for the week ahead. At least these would keep. They were now
at the stage of buying bolls of oatmeal and flour from the shop,
waiting for their crops of grain to swell and ripen. They all prayed
for a good hairst. So many folk were finding this a hungry time.

John Jeems and one of his sons had been carting the Happyhansel peats home and, in the evening before leaving, she gave him a help with building the big stack. You had to take advantage of a fine summer evening whenever possible. She knew he would work at it till late. He had carefully set the steid, the foundation layer, and laid aside the big mossy straight peats that would form a good wall. There was something satisfying about building a sturdy stack that would stay dry and see them through the year. But then she remembered she would not be there to keep the fires in. Eventually, she got on her way to Stove thinking that, by now, Willm would have gone to bed.

Jaanie looked tired. Her day with laundry-work and mending had been harassing and she was ready for her cup of tea. Mary offered to fold some sheets and blankets with her.

'Mary, mi jewel, du luiks as if der somethin budderin dee.'

'You're richt, Jaanie. I hae somethin ta tell you dat, wi wan braeth bracks mi haert, but wi da neist braeth kinda maks me happy.' She made the final fold in a sheet and smoothed it carefully on the table before picking up the next one. 'A'm lippenin a bairn come November.'

Jaanie sat down, obviously stunned at Mary's news.

'Fadder o mercy![10] Du's shurly flyin me!'[11] But Mary shook her head. 'Weel, A'm stumsed, Mary. But Göd bliss dee, lass, foo is du? I wid nivver a jaloused; an I hae a göd eye fur dat kinda thing. Minds du, I wid say du haes a kinda bloom apö dee dat's a göd sign.'

'A'm feelin fine noo. I wis kinda seek aff an on fur a bit, an most awfil annoyed wi mysel fur bein sae stupeed... hit wis Candlemas... an drink... I sood nivver a preeved hit. Jöst knockit da sense richt oot o me.'

'Dat's no laek dee, ta be aesy led I wid say. Du's een o da canniest I ken. Can I ax if der ta be a weddin?'

'Nae weddin. An, nae doot, nivver laekly ta be een noo, Jaanie. Dis da awfil bit: hit's Alex Ross – mind, da carpenter aboard da *Batchelor*.'

---

10 Mild version of 'Good God!'.

11 You're telling me a tall story, to shock me.

'An he's awa sooth noo an dusna ken?'

'He's awa sooth, but he kens. I tocht hit only richt ta tell him afore he gud. Da trouble is, he's a mairried man, Jaanie, an… I kinda jaloused he wis. Dat's whit's sae aafil: hit's a lock waar as fornication, or gyettin rid o a bairn, or a infant comin owre shön eftir a couple is mairried; at laest i da kirk's reckonin.'

'I daar say du's richt, jewel. Though dey aye say "der lifeless dat's faatless"[12] an der nae end o fock bein disciplined fur aa yun things. Hit's stupeed. But… a baby is a blisseen.'

Mary filled the kettle from the pail and hooked it over the crook. While she brewed the tea and set out cups and milk, Jaanie buttered oatcakes. Mary disclosed that, so far, she had only told her immediate family and the Greigs.

'I felt I hed ta lat dem ken sae dey can fin someen else ta stert owre da simmer. An I dunna want tae embarrass dem. Redder dat dan me hingin on till dey tell me A'm a disgrace an hae ta laeve!'

'Dey wid nivver dö dat,' replied Jaanie. 'Mr Greig is a jantleman an hit luiks as if young Erchie is cut fae da sam cloot.'

'He is indeed.'

Though Mary was relieved to tell Jaanie of her pregnancy, and knew her friend would be supportive, she was starting to feel as if she would have to keep confessing possibly for the rest of her life. There would be no end to it. It was an indelible stain on her character.

'Sae, whit tinks-du micht du dö?'

'Weel, A'll jöst bide wi mi fock an help wi da croft as best I can. An mak. Wir Jean is coortin… wi een o da Laing boys fae Brunatwatt, sae I tink shö micht gyet mairried at Yöl. I tink wir John is coortin an aa, wi a lass fae Brouster… but I doot he'll want ta hae anidder saeson at da Far Haaf afore dey gyet mairried. Sae until he brings a wife in, I tink A'll be owre wylcom at haem. Midder still manages ta wirk wi da kye an Faider wi da sheep, but der aye gyettin aalder. Haem is changin. Weel, naethin ivver bides da sam I suppose.'

---

12 Making mistakes is a necessary part of a full life.

'Whit aboot if du baed dere owre da simmer an hairst, an helpit dem, till jöst afore du wis due, an dan du could möv here fur a while owre da winter? Du could hae mi closet. An I could luik eftir dee at dat time an, eftir dat, du could help me? I hae owre muckle wark ta dö an could dö wi dee helpin me, an I could shaa dee foo ta starch a collar or iron yun frilly keps an blooses. An shew claes an mend. If du wantit. Tink aboot hit, Mary, an I can speak tae dy midder if du laeks. Wir bön göd freends fur a lang time.'

Mary felt tearful as Jaanie made her generous offer. It could solve a lot of problems.

'Dat wid mak life a lock less wirryin fur me, Jaanie. An I wid love ta laern, an ta help wi Willm an da cookin an aa.'

'Weel, dat's nearly settled dan. Noo, drink up dy tae. Neist week du man come alang an A'll hae a göd luik at dee an see if aathin is as hit sood be. Du'll be blyde ta ken dy midder hed nae budder hae'in aa her bairns, sae I tink hit soodna be dat bad fur dee.'

Mary got up to go. 'Hit wis göd dat Willie wis able to taek your röf afore dey gud.'

'Ya, dat hit wis. Dey wir da fine, dat pair. I jöst hoop dey settle weel in Carolina.'

Monday 22nd August 1774
Brunatwatt

Mary had collected Willm from Stove on Wednesday as Jaanie had been suddenly summoned to Mid Waas to look after her older sister who had taken a turn for the worse and was dying. Jaanie was hoping to be back for Willm's first day of the new school term, but had said that, if she wasn't, he was to walk on to Brunatwatt and Mary would keep an eye out for him. With Mary being at home, there was no problem and, anyway, Baabie was happy to keep the little boy a few extra days.

The weather had been mixed, sometimes sunny in the morning, then rainy by dinnertime, then fine in the evening. Daylight hours were still long and every dry one was a prisoner. It seemed summer was a constant battle against clock and calendar, with the peat hill, the animals and the crops all impatiently competing for attention. And housework was a constant, with knitting filling up any spare daylight moment.

It was all somewhat novel to Willm as, besides a few hens, Jaanie had no animals or land. He happily tagged along after Mary and they made up games and competitions as they piled up the peats into roogs at the hill, rooed the soft wool from the sheep before it fell off and even lifted a few early potatoes. The only task she had given up, on her mother's advice, was fetching water from the well. Christian and Jean were used to that. They were kind to their prodigal sister who had come home, contrite. Even Joannie had bridled his tongue.

Mary was feeling the weight of the now fast-growing baby, but still enjoyed the physical work of lifting and stacking, of digging and raking and dealing with the wily sheep. Her body was a joyous thing and beyond her control. She wondered what Willm was thinking. He would sometimes look at her side on when she stretched and held her back after stooping for a while, but so far he had not commented on her changed shape. For him, the highlight had been the previous evening's fishing trip, at the invitation of neighbours who had a rowing boat.

Mary walked him as far as Stove, till he was able to catch up with the other children on their way to Happyhansel, all tidily washed and dressed with fresh shirts and pinnies. They were still in bare feet, enjoying the freedom. She had carefully wrapped up some food for him.

'I wid laek ta geng tae da eela again, Mary. I laekit catchin yun piltocks. Dey fairly sprickled on da dorro.'

'Weel, I hoop we can afore lang. Hit wis göd fun. An der sookin up fine apö da sooth gavel o da barn. A'll bring twartree alang whin dy granny wins haem een o dis days.'

'Foo mony did du catch?'

'I doot no as mony as dee, jewel!'

'I catched ivver sae mony.'

'An du can fairly row noo an aa. Dy faider 'll be prood o dee.'

'I hoop Faider comes haem an bides haem.'

By now they were nearing Stove and Mary knew that Jaanie would be keen to be back if at all possible. But she reminded Willm about the arrangement and that she would check after school. He ran off happily to join the other pupils, a new term facing them. Mary had heard that a girl from Stapness had replaced her. She felt a pang of sadness as the school-children ran down the brae.

She knew that her condition was no longer a secret in the parish and that gossip was rife. Some of the Stennestwatt folk – even her friend Margaret Irvineson – seemed to have taken against her and had spoken harshly to her cousins there. No doubt that was old Deyell's influence: he had relations who lived there too. She was expecting a summons from the kirk any day now. The kirk session would be meeting again shortly after the summer break and would be keen to knock a wayward parish into shape. It was painful for her to imagine Mr Greig having to write up the minute when her condition was brought to the attention of the kirk session.

She stayed away from the shop as she could see people looking at her sideways. Her near neighbours were less judgemental, treating her like one of their own, and she was relieved that the Brunatwatt rigs, though visible, were not too close to the Gröntu rigs.

Sunday 4th September 1774
Waas kirk

The summons had indeed arrived. Seemingly one of the elders had reported that Mary was 'with child by uncleanness' and that it needed to be investigated. She had little doubt which elder had brought this to the attention of the session clerk and minister. She had been at church most Sundays over the summer but lately, being less able to hide her condition, had not been attending. Now, she had to choose how to present herself. She had respect for Mr Buchan and Mr Greig and several other elders she knew, but some she suspected of enjoying the humiliation of young women and she was not going to let them shame her. She knew one elder had stolen sheep, another was cruel to his wife and young women of the parish had reason not to trust several of the others: age, it seemed, had not diminished their sense of divine right to young flesh. The difference was, so many girls kept their secrets in case it made matters worse, hoping against hope there would be no child. But today, it was as if she was the chosen scapegoat sent out into a harsh desert to carry the transgressions of others – an Old Testament story vivid in her imagination.

When called, she walked in alone, blooming, her hair and skin never bonnier. She knew to her cost that she had tarnished her own reputation and that of her family. But though it grieved her that she had somewhat undermined Mr Greig's authority, she did not see that she should forever apologise for one irresponsible moment. The sixth commandment was one thing, the gospel was another and it sustained her. Who would have the nerve to throw the first stone?

The meeting was mercifully short. She could see old Deyell's eyes fixed on her every word. 'Was she with child by uncleanness, as stated?' She replied she was with child. 'And to whom?'

'To Alexander Ross, sailor on board the *Batchelor of Leith* which lay in the harbour last winter'. At this response, there was a noticeable intake of breath, a looking round from one to the other, bushy eyebrows lifting, eyes widening.

'Did she know him to be a married man?'

She lied more easily and convincingly than she ever thought she could. 'He did not make that known to me.' Well, he had never directly told her, but of course she had suspected that he was.

There was silence for quite some time. Then Mr Buchan reminded her that adultery was a serious sin and, given that the man involved was no longer in the parish and thus beyond their interrogation, she would have to appear before the Shetland presbytery in Lerwick. She would be told when and where. The minister then bid them all pray and closed the meeting. This had been the sole item on their agenda.

Mary walked home despondently. She had managed to hold it together in front of this court of old men, but the presbytery was an unknown quantity... never for a moment had she thought it would go so far... that meant she was in the same predicament as Sophia Henderson and Davie Bain... would they chase after Alex... and make things difficult for his family?... That was the last thing she wanted... better they never knew... And Lerrick... she had never been there... had heard it was a long and difficult journey by land... and on her own... maybe someone would come with her... but that would cost more... they would need lodgings for the night, maybe two nights... and the season was already turning... and she was getting heavier and less comfortable... But... maybe folk would soon tire from gossiping about her... there was always a thirst for new scandal. And everyone seemed to be complaining about the way the same houses got burdened with the Quarter-poors in DoonaWaas... five poor old destitute women this time round... she could picture their haggard faces... Baabie Jeemsdochter, Babsie Smith, that Sinclair woman, Jaanie Andrewsdochter and Margaret Willmsdochter from Vaila... some of them doitin, lost their wits... no wonder... Maybe this time their family would be asked to take someone in for a season... oh, surely not now...

Monday 31st October 1774
Brunatwatt and Stove

The day came that Baabie and Jaanie had agreed on for Mary to move to Stove to await the arrival of her infant. Jaanie thought that the baby would probably come by the middle of November and, given the short daylight and wild weather, the sooner she was safely in Stove the better.

James Ollason, the kirk officer, had already visited, telling her that she was cited to appear at the November presbytery meeting in Lerwick. He could see that she was in no fit state to undertake such a journey and, when Mary asked him to report back to Mr Buchan that she was unable to attend, he agreed quickly to her request. She knew that would not be the end of it. It would merely postpone the inevitable.

Mary put all the belongings she thought she would need in her kishie, including clothing and bedding for the baby, and was ready to set off after dinner. Willm would still be at school and she and Jaanie would be able to speak freely. She embraced her anxious mother, assuring her she would be fine; that she would probably see them before the baby was due. The first fine day, she would come home for a visit. And they could always come along Stove if they were going to the shop or the kirk.

Her father was emphatic. 'I'll no be darkenin dat kirk door, lass. No till dis onkerry der caased is feenished. A'm no hae'in wir faemly dinged doon ony mair bi yun bunch o aald föls wi naethin better ta dö dan point a finger at aaboady else. Der no gyettin a black ha'penny fae me edder. Nor even a benkled een!'

Mary wrapped her hap around her. Her father lifted her kishie for her and she looped the band over her head and round her shoulders.

'Göd bi wi dee, lass,' said Baabie.

'Cats i dy böddie!'[13] said her father, with a twinkle in his eye.

Mary laughed at the old fishing imprecation, her father's way of dealing with awkward moments, and waved to her family. She ran the gauntlet of the old Gröntu folk. Luckily, they were nowhere to be seen. She thought they generally had a snooze after their dinner.

Jaanie was waiting for her. She had moved Willm through to the closet as it lacked the space for a birth or a cradle. She had tidied the ben-end and made up a fresh bed for Mary. Mary had no words she could think of to express her gratitude, but was determined she

---

13 Fishing involved a lot of taboo words and sayings. Cats were bad news, so this saying was a way of wishing poor fishing success. (In the story, Mary's father, given to a pauky, ironic humour, says this to her as she places her böddie on her back, but meaning quite the opposite.)

would repay the kindness. Jaanie wanted to examine Mary while Willm was still at school: to feel her belly and check whether or not the head was engaged. She thought Mary's pulse and colour were good, she had no swelling in the legs and the baby seemed to be lying comfortably. To Mary, it seemed strange having her intimacy invaded, but she knew it was necessary and was glad it was by someone she trusted and loved.

After a cup of tea, she set about helping with ironing. She fetched the clothes in from Jaanie's drying shed – her skeo as it was known locally – and made a start. Although she had never done ironing at home or at Happyhansel, she realised that her practice at getting the heat of the fire just right for cooking and baking made it a bit easier to learn where to place the iron to heat up and when to swap them. But it proved more difficult than she had imagined. The main thing was not to scorch the clothes and to keep the irons spotlessly clean. When it came to the tricky garments, she was content to stand back and watch as Jaanie coaxed the frills and tucks around her goffering iron. The finished ironing was aired in the ben-end during the daytime, and then folded carefully away before bedtime. Most people collected their laundry; often it was a servant who came. Mary would no doubt have some explaining to do.

It was not long before Willm arrived back from school. His granny had told him about Mary and the baby. He seemed pleased to see her and told them both about his reading and his sums. Mary could picture him in the classroom, head down, concentrating on forming his letters and numbers. Her mind strayed to the parlour, the kitchen, the yard and well; someone else no doubt doing a good job and life moving on. She remembered her final Saturday when Erchie had said, 'A'll dance at dy wedding, Mary!' the humour somehow lessening the discomfiture felt by both of them. She had appreciated Leebie's comment that she would be missed and her kind concern about the baby. It had all been lightsome, even if frantically busy at times.

Mary had brought Willm two gifts: a little book all about animals which she had been given as a child as a prize for her handwriting; and a pocky, which she handed him. Willm opened it carefully and burst out laughing.

'See, Granny. Saat piltocks… da eens we catched an saatit!'

'My dear, dat is da fine! We can hae some o dem on Setterday fur wir denner.'

'Maybe neist simmer du'll be able ta fish affa da craig-steyn an catch sillocks, Willm.'

'Will du come wi me, Mary.'

'I wid laek ta dö dat. But we'll hae ta see whit neist simmer brings.'

'Will dy bairn be here bi dan?'

'Hit sood be comin shön. Weel afore Yöl.'

A serious look came over Willm. 'Mary hed da baby Jesus at Yöl.'

It was all Mary and Jaanie could do to keep a straight face.

His granny responded, 'Dat's true, jewel, but I doot dat wis a coarn different. He wis a very special peerie ting. At laest dat's whit a lock o wis tink. Noo, lat me rowe up da rest o da saat piltocks.'

After Willm had settled for bed, Mary went through to the ben-room to lay out her things. She refolded the little gowns she had sewn and the vests and socks she had knitted. She was proud of the hap she had made in the softest wool she had rooed from the summer fleeces; that warm creamy-colour. She glanced at the bed and it was as if Katie were still there sweating and straining, looking apprehensive – as if the baby would never come. But Jaanie's presence had been calming, had got her through. Mary felt her belly. There had been less kicking for some time, which had worried her, but Jaanie had assured her that was normal. A strange calm came over her.

She brought the 10/- bill through to the but-end. 'Jaanie, mind aboot da money dat Alex Ross gied me afore he left fur sooth? Dat first got me inta trouble wi da kirk? I want you to hae hit. Hit'll maybe pay for a coarn o da maet I aet.'

Jaanie looked as if she would refuse, but Mary insisted and Jaanie gave in. Money was a necessary commodity when you were a cotter, and generally in short supply.

Sunday 6th November 1774
Stove and Brunatwatt

Mary was delighted when Christian came along briefly on her way to the kirk to tell her that, at long last, there was a letter from Jaerm and Eliza and that their mother was wondering if she would come home for the afternoon and maybe stay on till teatime. Jaanie and Willm were welcome too. It was agreed that Willm would go with Mary and that would allow Jaanie some time to rest.

Mary was pleased to be with her family again. Jean took one look at Mary and said, 'Lass, du's gyaain in staavs!'[14] Mary laughed at the comparison to a barrel, but took the insult in good part.

'Maybe no lang afore I can gaff at dee, Jean!' She was keen to hear about the preparations for the Brunatwatt wedding. It would be a quiet marriage at Yöl, with the minister coming to the house to perform the ceremony and then a party in the Laing's barn for family and a few friends. Just one fiddler. After all the recent troubles, no one had the stomach for anything which might raise an eyebrow. Jean had borrowed a lace collar from one of the Stennestwatt cousins.

Willm was keen to explore the barn and the byre. Mary had told him that Bella was going to have a calf soon. She had been moved into the barn, where she was lying on a pile of fresh straw. When she heard Mary's voice, she struggled to her feet and came towards them. She was loosely tethered to a veggel, a wooden stake fixed in the wall. Mary spoke soothingly to her and stroked her neck.

'I winder if du'll calve afore me, Bella?'

'Du's no gyaain ta hae a calf, Mary!' Willm said, in some consternation.

'Dat's true, but me an Bella is baith aboot ta gie birt. Hit's no dat different.'

By the time they returned to the but-end, Baabie had brewed a pot of tea and was sitting looking at the letter. Though it had been read out to her more than once, she was keen for Mary, the best scholar in the family, to read it for her. Mary was happy to oblige.

---

14 Expression for heavily pregnant (lit. like the curved construction of barrel staves).

Sunday 18th September 1774
High Street, Prestonpans, Haddingtonshire

Dearest Mother and Father,
  *We have been waiting for some time to find a way of getting
a letter north to you – and can only hope this reaches you
safely. We hope too that you are both well and that John,
Jean, Mary and Christian are all in good spirits and that you
have had a fine hairst. We miss colin da hay an ripin da tatties.*
  *You will see from the address that we are living in
Prestonpans, about eight miles east of Leith and Edinburgh.
We got married soon after we landed in late April and have
been a bit on the move since, trying to get settled. At first, we
were in Leith, near the docks and got some work, but now we
are settled in a smaller place. Morison's Haven here is almost
as busy as Leith and there are cargo boats coming and going
all the time. I have sailed on several ships, as an Able Seaman
now. There's no difficulty getting a berth and I can be home
regularly. We bring in clay from Cornwall for the potteries
here and take coal, salt and beer south to London and
Southampton. Eliza is working in the kitchen of a big house
nearby. But she is going to have a baby in Spring time, so we
will see how that works out. We are managing fine and I think
her notion to go to the Carolinas has faded. She seems happy
here, as I am. And we get fine fresh fish, just like at home!*
  *The journey south was hard on everybody, bringing back
many bad memories. Ramage and Hogg wanted to drop all
the emigrants off in Thurso but not one person was willing, so
they had to take us on to Leith. The Batchelor needed some
serious repairs to her hull. Everybody was struggling to get
work and somewhere cheap to live. The kirks in Leith kept
us all from starvation and managed to persuade some of the
local merchants to give some money to help too.*
  *Edinburgh is growing fast – they call the new bit the New
Town. It is very grand – big houses, four storeys high, and*

basements. The windows are huge. And water laid on and drains. So some of us worked on that for a while, carting stone from a big quarry to the west. Some emigrants moved from Leith to settle in the old part of Edinburgh. It's very cramped and dirty. One poor family lodged in a part called the Pleasance. As the rooms had no grates, they were obliged to light their fires upon the hearths. But one of the chimneys in a room was blocked and the smoke scomfished them. The mother and servant were found dead in the morning, and the father and son were in a state of stupefaction and died the next day. They were buried in the kirkyard at Chapel Street and a large crowd attended the funeral. We saw a lot of the emigrants there.

So we have been fortunate to escape the city and all the dirt and smell, and get down to the sea! Mind you, coal burning fairly makes reek. They heat huge pans of brine with it here to evaporate and leave the salt.

By the time you receive this we wonder if Mary's baby will have arrived. We hope she keeps well and that the kirk doesn't give her a terrible hard time. We think of her every time we think of our expected baby. Eliza is keeping well.

We miss you all and just wish we were some nearer so we could see you. Write a few lines if you can. It would be good to get news of you all. How did John's first season at the Far Haaf go?

We send our deepest affection to you all,
Jaerm and Eliza

Mary managed to hold herself together as she read their news and their kind mention of her situation. Thankfully, there was no mention of Alex Ross. She didn't want to hear anything about him. She had decided on that the moment the ill-named and ill-fated *Batchelor* disappeared through the Aester Soond. Christian was to write back for them all and they would try to find someone who was travelling south to Leith who could take it for them.

They teased John about his intentions. He seemed in a good mood and was looking forward to being a married man and bringing a wife to Brunatwatt after another year. She would be Betty o' Brunatwatt instead of Betty o' Brouster! Her folk kept a fine croft there and she was well versed in looking after crops and animals.

They were all solicitous about Mary, but aware that she was in good hands.

'Du'll be a help tae Jaanie,' said Baabie. 'Laek wis twa here, shö's feelin her age I doot.'

Mary had a request for her brother John. She wanted to ask him if he would be willing to be a sponsor for the baby's baptism, given that their father had shown his unwillingness to give in to the kirk rules and disciplines. Despite the problems with the kirk, and the likelihood that they would get worse before they got better, Mary still wanted the baby baptised. After all, it hadn't done anything wrong.

She was relieved at his immediate response. 'Dat I wid, Mary, if dey'll dö hit.'

At teatime, they all enjoyed Jean's beremel bannocks with kirn-mylk before Mary set off to Stove with Willm. Though she missed her home and her family, she was content. As she walked back, she could feel the baby low in her belly; lower than of late. She knew her time was coming closer.

Monday 14th November 1774
Stove

As the afternoon wore on, Mary became aware that her pains had started. At first, they were no more than occasional tightenings across her belly and they did not get in the way of her baking. Willm had arrived home and was hungry for his tea. She helped Jaanie with that and, later, with Willm's lessons. He had taken down some multiplication sums on a piece of paper and was keen to have Mary check that he had done them correctly. She was able to concentrate on his various requests, gathering the pain into herself as it intensified and then lessened. She had let Jaanie know early on and Jaanie had quickly transformed into howdie mode, busily preparing the ben-room for the delivery. Before Willm went to bed, Mary told him that she hoped there might be a baby by the morning, but they would all have to wait and see. He seemed excited at the prospect.

'Mind whin peerie Jane cam, Mary. Dat wis queer. Shö used to screw up her face whin shö gret, did'n shö?'

'I bet we aa did da sam whin we wir peerie mootie. Hit's da only wye a bairn can tell wis whit ails dem. Noo, aff ta bed, an we'll see whit damoarn brings wis!'

Mary sat up till late with Jaanie, occasionally sipping a little water or a drop of tea. But she had no appetite. In between the pains she was fine; but then they would grip her, ever tighter, fiercer and more painfully, like a serpent coiled around her middle. She gripped the chair arms and tried to breathe deeply when Jaanie told her to. Soon, her waters broke and Jaanie suggested she should go to bed, propped up, and try to get a bit of rest; it was promising to be a long night and she would need all the energy she could muster. Jaanie examined her from time to time to check just how much or how little her cervix had dilated.

'I dunna want dee pushin dis bairn oot afore dy boady is ready. Jöst tak hit aesy, Mary, an we'll gyet dere. Du's half-gaets dere noo.'

'Only half-gaets? A'm pooskered already!'

'Na, lass, du haes plenty stimna ta see dis trowe. Du's young an healty. Jöst try to tink o da waves as if der bringin dee nearer an nearer tae da shore. Du comes a bit closser wi ivery wan.'

Mary gritted her teeth and screwed up her face through the pangs; the harder she tried see them as friendly waves, the more the image of a serpent's grip seemed to assail her. She would flop back between each wave, exhausted and sweating. Jaanie held her hand, massaged her aching back and wiped her brow.

Suddenly, Mary realised what a toll this was taking on the older woman and she mustered a smile and said how glad she was to have her help.

'Lass, someens curse me an swear at me whin der pains gyet

sore! Hit's a joy ta help dee, except mi aald back is mindin me o mi age…'

But her words were stopped by a sudden exhalation and 'Ah, ah, oh…' from Mary.

Tuesday 15th November 1774
Stove

Eventually, about two in the morning, the pains eased, giving a moment for Jaanie to build up the fire again and Mary to gather her strength for the final onslaught. It seemed quite amazing to her how her body knew exactly when to push and when to stop pushing. The snake was still there, contracting her muscles, but it was no longer biting her. When Jaanie gave the command, she pushed as hard as she could, trying to obey the older woman's instructions: 'jöst blaa as if du wis snuffin oot a candle, Mary. Du haes ta keep blaain, but jöst peerie wyes. Dat's da wye! Noo, lie back an tak paes til na neist wave.'

Several times, Mary thought she could take no more; that she had nothing more to give, that the baby would never come, that it was stuck. But Jaanie kept encouraging her. 'Birze du, lass. Push herder. Noo, I can see da head comin. Peerie wyes noo, sae du dusna tear. Jöst peerie breaths as du strains. Weel dön! Weel dön!' At last, Mary felt the relief of the head emerging and, almost before she knew it, the shoulders and rest of the body just slipped into the world with one final push. Tears of relief and joy ran down her cheeks. The pain had disappeared as miraculously as it had arrived and suddenly she felt fit and well, even if exhausted. Baabie held up the child, declaring her a fine peerie lass before clamping and cutting the cord. The baby cried immediately. Baabie gave her a perfunctory wipe before wrapping her up and handing her to Mary while she checked the afterbirth and washed the wearied mother. The warm water was soothing.

Mary couldn't believe it – this little person in her arms was hers;

this beautiful child. Exhausted and exhilarated in equal measure, she was engulfed in a tide of inexplicable love, more powerful than the waves which had almost overwhelmed her in bringing the infant into the world.

Jaanie tried to clean up as best she could so that Mary could rest undisturbed. She insisted the child, for this one night, would sleep in the but-end, next to her box bed, and that she would bring the baby through to Mary when she woke for a feed. She was already sleeping in Mary's arms, no doubt fatigued by the rigours of her own mysterious journey.

Mary gave in for, although she wanted to watch over the child, she knew Jaanie was right.

'A'm gyaain ta christen her Janet Barbara Johnson. Dat's eftir you, Jaanie, an my midder... I tink dat's soonds better as Barbara Janet? Whit tink you?'

'I tink dat's lovely, but maybe du could caa her Babsie? I tink shö luiks braaly laek dy midder.'

'Babsie hit is dan.'

Sometime well before daylight, Jaanie came through to the ben-end with Babsie swaddled in the new hap Mary had knitted. She was crying. Jaanie handed her to Mary.

'Pit her tae da briest an see if shö'll sook a coarn.' Jaanie sat down on the bed and waited to see what would happen. The baby was like a new lamb, unsure which part of the anatomy to aim for. Mary tried to help, but after some minutes the crying got worse. Jaanie showed her how to make it easier for Babsie to clamp on to the nipple, to grab it all in her little mouth.

'Der no muckle mylk at dis stage, but whitivver shö gyets is speeshil. Jöst laek baess-mylk.'

'I wonder foo wir Bella is gyettin on? At laest shö's dön hit afore!'

By now the baby was sucking and then refusing to suck and crying in frustration. The process had to be repeated several times before she seemed satisfied.

'Noo we'll need ta see aboot hippens an clean cloots fur dee an aa. Du'll blöd fur a braa twartree days so dunna wirry aboot dat.'

'Jaanie, whit wid I dö ithoot you? A'll be apö mi fit shön.'

'Tak du dy time, jewel. Maybe danicht du can come tae da but-end fire fur a peerie little eence Willm is in bed. A'm gyaain ta pit a fire on here fur hit's no waarm an dan A'll bring da cradle trowe fur dee.'

With the fire lit and Babsie safely in her cradle, Jaanie proceeded to clean the bed for Mary and provide napkins for both her and the child. Although wobbly on her feet, Mary was glad of a chance to wash herself.

Soon, Willm got up and Jaanie brought him through to see Mary and the baby, who was still asleep.

'Dis is Babsie, Willm,' said Mary. 'Whit tinks du o mi peerie lass?'

Willm didn't know what to say, but Mary held out her arms and he had a cuddle.

'Wis du maybe hoopin hit wid be a peerie boy?'

There was no reply for quite some time, then he asked tentatively, 'Will dee an Babsie bide wi wis?'

'Na, mi jewel, eence I gyet apö mi fit an manage ta luik eftir Babsie dan I doot we'll hae ta geng back ta Brunatwatt. But hit's no far, an du can come ony time du laeks ta see wis. We'd love dat.'

'An da calf?'

'Ya, da calf an aa… whin hit comes.'

By now Willm was gently rocking the cradle and looking carefully at Babsie.

Jaanie encouraged him ta get washed and dressed and have some breakfast before leaving for school. 'Du'll gyet ta hadd her afore lang.'

Once Willm was off to school, Mary insisted Jaanie should rest. It had been a hard night for both of them. Luckily, Jean came by on her way to the shop and was able to keep Mary company. She placed a silver sixpence on the cradle to hansel the baby. She had also brought some fresh butter and some beest from Bella's calving, which they had baked and sliced.

'Midder said hit wid be göd an strentnin.'

In the afternoon, Baabie, only partially relieved by the news from Jean, came along to see them all. She had made two little knitted vests and a gown. The baby was awake, Mary struggling to give her a feed.

'Shö'll be sookin awa nae budder in twartree days' time, mi jewel.'

'Whit if shö wunna?'

'Dunna tink laek dat, lass. Da peerie moot is döin fine,' said Jaanie.

Eventually, Mary was able to hand her over to her mother.

'Babsie, du is a lovely peerie ting. Foo's du feelin, Mary? Wis hit a braa strug?'

'A'm fine, Midder. Hit wis a strug at da time, but dat's aa by wi. An Jaanie did half o hit fur me!'

Baabie eventually laid the baby in the cradle and tucked her in.

'Jean wis sayin dat Bella is calved.'

'Dat shö is – shö hed a peerie bull-calf dastreen. No sae muckle budder dis time.'

'Willm will be da plaesed.'

'He'll hae ta come an see wis shön.'

They sat around the bed talking till Mary suddenly dropped off to sleep.

'Shö's pyaagit, Jaanie. A'll awa haem. I canna tank dee enyoch fur luikin eftir her sae weel. I hoop we can mak hit up ta dee.'

'A'm jöst blyde I could help her – for shö's hed a herd time.'

'Ya, an hit's no feenished yet. Yun presbytery thing 'll nae doot no geng awa. Minds-du, Jaanie, whit hit wis laek whin we wir her age; whin da lass hed ta wear yun aafil coat o sackcloot afore da congregation?'

'Dat I dö! An staandin apön yun step sae as iveryeen could see you. An bein marched in an dan oot again wi da fock aa luikin at you. At laest Mr Buchan is med things a coarn less difficult to bear.'

'Ya, but I doot he can only geng sae far.'

Jaanie put her feet up till she heard Willm arrive home from school, more animated than usual. Although Mary was stiff and sore and her breasts painful, she was determined to get up and not be a complete burden on Jaanie. She wasn't able to do much, but at least she could keep Willm company while Jaanie got on with the work. By now, she could bear the thought of Babsie being in the other room. She told him about the calf arriving on the same day as Babsie. He seemed pleased that it was a bull-calf.

'Dey'll hae da sam birthday dan?'

'Ya. An Midder says you man come nort ta Brunatwatt ta see him shön.'

'I telt wir teacher dat you wir hed a peerie lass.'

'An whit did he say?'

'He said dat wis lovely news… an… an he hoopit he wid see baith o you afore lang.'

Poor Erchie. What could he say in response to the enthusiasm of a little boy? But not for a moment did Mary consider it was anything other than genuine.

Wednesday 16th November 1774
Stove

Mary was still dog-tired and a bit tender but gradually getting to grips with her new role; sole responsibility for another life, and a fragile one at that. Babsie seemed a strong enough baby, with good lungs and a voracious appetite. She sucked and slept and did little else. When she opened her blue eyes, Mary could indeed catch a glimpse of her mother. Mercifully, there was nothing about the infant that brought back a memory of Alex Ross, though she had thought him a fine-looking man. That painful memory was fading fast, which Mary could only consider a good thing. She had virtually no recollection of the Candlemas coupling, except that she had felt sick as a dog and exceedingly stupid. No, this little baby cancelled all that out.

Christian dropped by just to see them. She had brought some baking from home and a bag of potatoes and turnips. Babsie had just had a feed and was already half asleep but happy to be held.

For Christian, being the youngest of the family, it was a more novel feeling and Mary could see she was very taken with her little niece. There would be no lack of nursemaids for Babsie when she returned to Brunatwatt. She too dropped a little silver coin – a groat – as a hansel on Babsie's cradle.

Meanwhile, Mary wrote a note for Mr Buchan, the minister, regarding Babsie's birth and desiring baptism for her. As well as her own name, she wrote Babsie's full name and date and place of birth. And that she was staying at Stove in the meantime.

'Tink you sood I say dat I ken I still hae ta appear afore presbytery an da congregation. An dat I hoop dat wunna gyet i da wye o her baptism... her bein ithoot faat?'

Jaanie thought for a moment. 'I tink dat micht be wise, jewel. Idderwise hit'll pit Mr Buchan ithin a bit o a paes-weesp. I tink da kirk generally pits aff baptism till da penance is owre an dön wi an, i dis case, du kens du's in for a braa coarn eence presbytery gyets der say.'

Mary nodded and kept writing: that she was willing to confess her guilt; that she trusted the unfortunate circumstances surrounding the affair, and the fact that she was not able to attend presbytery when called, would not be held against the child, who was entirely innocent. She hoped her words sounded suitably contrite, though in her heart she did not feel she had committed a punishable sin. And when her eye fell on Babsie, she was sure the kirk had got it wrong. She knew, however, she had little choice but to work within the accepted rules if Babsie was to be baptised and if she herself was to be deemed respectable and accepted back into the community. She added that her brother John was willing to be sponsor or witness and asked if that was sufficient. He was available any day as the Far Haaf season was finished. Mary read it over to herself before folding it up and addressing it to the Rev James Buchan, Voe House. Christian agreed to deliver it right away and, if necessary, wait for a reply.

Christian was back within the hour. She could report that Mr Buchan had been most civil and had written a reply to Mary's request. Mary tore it open. It was brief and said that, given her willingness to confess and repent, he would baptise Babsie privately at the home of Jaanie Jeromson at Stove on Friday 25th November, at 2pm. He wrote that she would need two witnesses and that perhaps she could ask a Grötquoy cousin.

Christian was bidden to let the family know, especially John, and to ask him to persuade one of their cousins to attend with him. Mary read between the lines that the minister had worked out that her father was unlikely to defer to the kirk's rulings.

Friday 25th November 1774
Stove

The day dawned late, with heavy clouds. As it progressed, the wind rose and the rain became persistent. Mary had fetched water and brought in peats. It was her first outing since the birth and she was anxious to relieve Jaanie of these burdens. Between dealing with her baby, she had taken care of the washing while Jaanie had spent the morning ironing. Thankfully, her energy had returned. By dinner-time, they put all signs of work away. Mary set some broth to heat for their meal and laid out, on the dresser, the fruit loaf she had baked the previous day just in case any could stay on after the baptism. While Jaanie cleared up, Mary got washed and dressed. She would feed Babsie so that, with luck, the baby would most likely sleep her way through the baptism. They were into a good routine now, with regular feeds and much sleeping.

John and their cousin Jeems o' Grötquoy arrived in good time, and Jaanie insisted they dry off near the fire. Mary was pleased to see her big brother and hear his news. She was grateful that both of them were willing to act as witnesses.

'No a second tocht, Mary,' said Jeems. 'Du's mi favourite cousin, an onywye, hit's shurly no da warst sin i da book!'

Before long, there was a knock at the door and the minister came in. He seemed a big presence in the small cottage. He took off his hat and tweedy Inverness cape and Mary hung them up for him.

'Come awa in trowe, Mester Buchan. You're gotten sokkit.'

'Yes, Jaanie, it's not a day to be furt.' He acknowledged the young men, '… John… Jeems…' and then, turning towards her, 'You look well, Mary… I can see Jaanie has been looking after you.'

'She has indeed, Mister Buchan… and I'm very grateful that you're willing to baptise Babsie when I still have to appear before presbytery. It was impossible for me to make the journey at the time.'

'The main thing, Mary, is that you've stated you are contrite. Bringing forth a child out of adultery is a serious sin, even if you didn't know Ross was married; and the kirk looks on it gravely. There's likely little we can do about the father in this case. But the child is here and, as you say, is an innocent; and the kirk has to be here for us all. I am not one for sticking with all the old ways, but it will no doubt still be a hard time for you, Mary. Now, Jaanie, would you be as good as to put a little water in this font? And maybe a drop from the kettle to take the chill off it?' At this point, he took a small wooden box from his pocket, opened the lid and gave the simple pewter bowl to Jaanie, who was quick to oblige.

'You know the promises, Mary?'

'Yes, sir.'

'Well, I want you to think about each one of them seriously when I ask you and before you respond with "I do". Now, can I hold the child… and can we all please stand?'

Mary lifted Babsie from the cradle, tucked her hap about her and gently placed her in the old man's arms. She hardly stirred. He looked at the infant as a father might; this man whose own infant had lived but one day, and yet had baptised hundreds.

'She's a lovely bairn, Mary, and I know you will care for her. Now, you're naming her Janet Barbara?'

'Yes, sir. I've named her after Jaanie here, and my mother Baabie. I'll call her Babsie.'

'Peerie Babsie. That's a fine name… now, I need to ask you… Do you believe in God, the Father Almighty, in Jesus Christ his only Son, and in the comfort of the Holy Spirit; one God, three in One?'

'... I do.'

'Do you promise to bring up this child in the teachings of the Church?'

'... I do.'

'And do you promise not to do anything that might cause this little one to stumble?'

Mary took a deep breath.

'... I do.'

'May God give you the strength to fulfil these vows.'

He then turned to the witnesses and asked them to pledge support to Mary in this 'arduous undertaking'. That being affirmed, it was time to baptise Babsie by sprinkling a little water on her head. His voice was noticeably gentler in tone:

'Janet Barbara Johnson, I baptise you in the name of the Father, of the Son and of the Holy Spirit. May the grace of the Father, Son and Holy Spirit bless you and keep you always. Amen.'

Mr Buchan then sat down, still holding the sleeping infant: it was as if he wanted to hold on to the moment of grace. Eventually, with the emotion of the moment subsiding, he passed Babsie back to her mother who placed her in the cradle. It had all gone remarkably smoothly and although Mary had felt somewhat exposed, she had no argument with God, or indeed with Mr Buchan; just with some self-righteous lay elders and their apparent appetite for casting stones.

Jaanie put the kettle on to boil and offered tea, but Mr Buchan said he really should get away before it grew any darker in the sky. However, he was prevailed upon, and they all relaxed. Mr Buchan was keen to catch up with everyone; to hear how they were getting on and whether they had heard from Jaerm and Eliza or the McLeods. Eventually, he rose to go. Mary went to get his coat.

He said, in a low voice, 'I don't know when we will hear from the presbytery again; it may be a while, but I would advise you to admit adultery, whether or not you were aware, and do the confession which they demand. It's easier that way, Mary, although it will feel harsh. But you are a strong young woman and I know, too, that you are a good woman. I hear they are missing you very much at Happyhansel! May God go with you.'

'Thank you, sir.' She wondered what the church register of births would record, since normally only the father's name was entered. But she did not ask. She was relieved that Babsie had been baptised.

It was time for Willm to get home from school. He would be full of his own news which she always loved to hear.

Thursday 5th January 1775 – Old Christmas Eve
Stove and Brunatwatt

January would be a month of two new moons. Aald Yöl Ee'n, Jean's wedding day, with its moon only four days into waxing, was an auspicious day for a marriage. A waning moon for a wedding was sure to bring bad luck. The various traditions had been upheld: the spörin, when the permission of the bride's parents was sought, and the biddin – the inviting – and the avoidance of a Friday. How often had they heard the sayin 'Friday's flittin is short sittin'?[15] Baabie had insisted Jean get married in the legal way, so the banns had been duly called in the kirk.

The morning dawned bright and cold. Snowfalls from earlier in the week still happed the land: the Hill of Foratwatt, the Hill of Voe, the Hill of Elvister – with the heights of Stoorburgh beyond – held Waas in a glistening bowl, while the islands of Linga and Vaila seemed closer, completing the circle. There was a strange stillness: everywhere reflections gleamed on water; on the voe and on the lochs. Bayhaa and Foratwatt House, purple-tinged in the low sun, sank deeper into the sea than they were high.

Jaanie had prevailed upon Mary to stay at Stove over the winter. She had decided to give up her work as a howdie. The last birth, at Mid Waas, had been a difficult one, and the journey hard in poor

---

15 Best to avoid moving home or getting married on a Friday; possibly a reference to the pre-Reformation influences and the importance of Good Friday in the Christian calendar.

weather. Nor had she had the heart to take her full fee from the couple. The other local howdie was younger and no doubt would be happy to expand her work and reputation.

The two women enjoyed each other's company and Willm seemed every day more intrigued with Babsie, who could now respond with smiles and kicks. Her fair hair was growing and her eyes were becoming bluer by the day. He had been off school for the holiday, enjoying the snow with other local children. Mary tried to do the heavier work to relieve Jaanie, but otherwise they shared the tasks.

Although Jaanie and Willm were bidden to Jean's wedding, she had said to Mary that she would rather stay in and look after the children. So Mary would be going alone. She did, however, have the perfect excuse to return to Stove after the ceremony; Babsie would need to be fed. It was to be a quiet marriage ceremony, at home rather than at the kirk. There was more than one reason for that decision, but trudging to the kirk and back on a cold, snowy morning was a considerable undertaking for a wedding party, especially for older guests.

Mary went to Brunatwatt a little early to help with final preparations and to get changed for the wedding. Jean had slept her last night at home and had already moved her things to her in-law's house. There had been a frantic relay race to get washed and dressed. The washstand had been moved to the ben-end and the fire lit there to warm water. The men went first, as they knew they would be quicker. Baabie had ensured that they had trimmed their beards in advance. Then Baabie had her turn at the washstand, followed by the girls.

Jean had a beautiful blouse to wear with her blue skirt: it had belonged to their mother, one of the only pretty things she possessed. With the fine lace collar she had borrowed, she looked lovely. Mary brushed her hair for her and twisted it up, pinning it securely. All of them had colour in their cheeks after walking in the cold air and fetching and carrying. Mary felt like the older sister: she had known in her head for almost a year that her life was changed for ever, that she was not just 'wan o da Brunatwatt lasses', and that somehow the simple communal act of getting ready for a special occasion, which they had always relished, had changed. She was the outsider. But she wanted Jean to look her best, and Christian too. They helped each other with pins and combs and checking hems. Jean started reciting the traditional rhyme which they would have chanted had they walked back from the kirk:

> *Noo man I laeve Faider an Midder*
> *Noo man I laeve sister an bridder*
> *Noo man I laeve kith an kin*
> *An follow da back o a fremd man's son.*

'Jean, dunna say dat! Du's no laevin wis aa,' Christian pleaded.

Mary agreed and added, 'an du can hardly caa da Laing's fremd, lass. Der da freendliest neebirs we could hae!'

Eventually, they emerged into the but-end, ready for the arrival of the women guests who would come with gifts of food.

'My dear, hit is true indeed dat a boannie bride is aesy buskit!'[16]

'Tanks fur lattin me borrow your bloose, Midder. I winder whit een o mi sisters 'll wear hit neist?' Mary was very aware of her swollen breasts; not only would she not fit the blouse now, but the prospect of marriage now seemed like an improbability.

Mary was glad that their father had seemed in an hospitable mood which made it easier for everyone. Visited by visions of Jaanie trying to placate a hungry Babsie, she was relieved that it was not long before the menfolk arrived, as well as Mr Buchan. The minister shook hands with both sets of parents. He seemed pleased that Jean was settling down and he, like Baabie, fervently hoped that there would be no sign of pre-nuptial congress; that any baby would arrive no sooner than the presbyterian calendar deemed appropriate. The Johnson family needed no more scandals.

The ceremony in the ben-end went well and then they all moved through to the but-end where planks of wood on trestles had been quickly transformed into tables, now laden with boiled mutton,

---

16 A pretty bride is easily dressed up.

freshly killed roasted lamb and pork, kirn-mylk, bannocks, brönnies and hufsi. The Laings and the Stennestwatt cousins had brought assorted crockery, cutlery and glassware to augment the Johnson's sparse tableware. With a grace from the minister and a toast to the bride and groom, they all started on the wedding breakfast. Despite a January wind at the door and the snow lying outside, the room was aglow with conviviality. The merriment had to be contained as they could barely budge an inch on the various chests, borrowed chairs and creepies crammed into the room. They would move to the Laing's barn later for the music and dancing. It was bigger than the Johnson's barn and had been cleared and swept.

Mary slipped away at this point, anxious that her child would have been aware of her absence. It had been the longest she had been away from her since she was born. Her mother managed to catch her before she left. 'My dear, du haes ta geng, I ken. We miss dee here, an will dö even mair noo dat Jean is möved across ta da Laings.'

'But you'll see her ivery day, Midder. Shö's nae distance awa, an nedder am I. Jaanie fins da winter herd noo but whin he comes voar A'll win haem ta help you. Onywye, you'll aye be alang Stove, an whin da better wadder comes A'll bring Babsie ta see Bella an da calf. Foo's he comin alang?'

'He's a fine calf, Mary; a hairst calf but growin fast. We sood hae enyoch fodder ta see wis trowe da winter.'

Mary quickly changed back into her working clothes, said her goodbyes to the young couple and set off for Stove. There would be singing and dancing and drinking and more eating. She was glad to be giving it a miss.

Saturday 22nd April 1775
Stove and Brunatwatt

It had been a long, hard winter. Snow had been blown into deep drifts along croft dykes and filled in dips and hollows on the scattald. Young men had gone with their fathers, uncles and neighbours to where the older men knew from experience they were likely to find sheep snowed in. Lambs would be coming before long and it was essential to get the ewes to safety. There was little enough hay left to spare for them and a few wizened turnips and bare kale stocks.

During the week, there had at last been signs that winter was relenting and Mary was keen to get back to Brunatwatt where she would be needed for the spring work and on into summer and hairst. She had left Jaanie with plenty water and peats brought in and promised she would spend two mornings a week helping at Stove. Jaanie had a neighbour who worked her peats for her for a modest charge. There was no doubt that her strength was failing, though she would not admit it. Willm now was able to help and was an amenable and friendly child.

She had brought her things home the previous night. Willm had gone off to school looking a bit despondent, but Mary had reassured him that, once the evenings lengthened, he would be old enough to come to Brunatwatt, 'in aboot da nicht' with Jaanie. It was not far. And he could come in the school holidays too.

Mary had packed Babsie's things in her kishie and, having got that safely on her back, Jaanie handed her the baby, now five months old, showing off her teeth and babbling her own conversation. Mary felt very torn: she loved staying with Jaanie and Willm and felt she could be a help to them, but she knew that her folk could do with another pair of hands on the croft, especially on those days when John would be at the fishing. The sooner he got married, the better. She realised how lucky she had been to get the chance to work for Mr Greig. It felt like a world away now.

The two women were tearful as they bade farewell. Mary tried to lighten the moment by saying she would be down along Stove on Tuesday morning. By then, Babsie should have settled and would be familiar with the new arrangements.

As Mary walked along the gaet, she stopped to show Babsie the occasional hill lamb busily nudging milk out of its mother. Babsie responded with her full array of pleasure, with her little plump arms and legs and her burbles. There were northern divers – rain geese – flying overhead, heading homeward from a fishing trip to their nests on some little lochan away to the north. The Brunatwatt sheepdog was out pacing his policies, waiting for action, and just beyond her home she could see the white wings of black-headed gulls on the marsh surrounding Smalla Waters. Perhaps they would be nesting there. It was good to be back home. The only dark spectre was Gröntu.

Tuesday 25th April 1775
Stove

Mary set off from Brunatwatt early with Babsie to catch Willm briefly before he left for school. When he was gone, Jaanie took Babsie and sat with her on her knee for some time, chatting to her. She was holding herself up well with a bit of help and was fascinated by everything she saw and could touch or put in her mouth.

'Shö's a peerie doll, Mary.'

'Weel, sae far, shö's bön nae budder. Shö's gyettin teeth an can be a bit girny noo an dan, but generally shö's no bad ava. I took your advice an tried her wi a coarn o gruel an shö fairly suppit hit up! An Midder gied her a peerie crust o toast ta showe apön. A'll maybe try her wi a coarn o soup ere lang. Noo, Jaanie, ir dey muckle ta wysh come in owre da helly?'

'No dat muckle, jewel. Twartree sarks an collars an a couple o blooses fae Bayhaa. And der a peerie parcel fae da Kurkigart fock – der wantin some things starched.'

'Weel, A'll fetch watter an set some on ta haet an A'll bring in plenty paets.'

'Bliss dee, Mary. I miss dy cheery wyes an da strent i dy back! While da watter is haetin up A'll gyet dee ta read a letter fae Walter dat a sailor fae Seafield haandit in dastreen. He said he wis gotten hit fae a sailor fae Reawick wha wis spokken wi Walter in Liverpool, an Walter wis axed him ta tak da letter nort wi him whin he gud haem.'

Liverpool
Sunday 26th March 1775

My dearest Mother,
  I hope you are keeping well and Willm getting on fine at
school. I'll not recognise my peerie boy when I eventually win
home. At this time of year, I start to miss Waas – the thought
of voar and the sudden activity after a hard winter.
  I am back in Liverpool docks after a long trip out to Africa
and India. I could fairly do with a cool breeze! Though this
dock is full of ships on the Atlantic trade, we have been
bringing cotton as the spinning industry is growing fast in
this area. We picked up the cargo in Madras and Bombay.
Liverpool is a very well organised dock by comparison with
others, even with London.
  I'm always on the look-out for a Shetlander who might
carry mails home – I think I've been very lucky to meet a
sailor from Reawick and he is hoping to make a trip north
soon. He was telling me he had heard there had been a big
upheaval in Waas with the stranding of an emigrant ship
bound for the Carolinas. That must have been a ontak for
everybody. I hope you weren't badly affected.
  I think I've just about decided to come back to Shetland by
this time next year. Much as I love the sea, it's dangerous work
and I never get to be with you and Willm. So I have decided
I'll settle back home, if I can get employment. Maybe I'll get
a job with one of the gentry folk – some of them have boats
and may need a man to look after their business. If I can't
get a job, I can always sail out of Leith. My wages must be
mounting up. If you need money, I hope you can get it from
the shipping company. It's not easy getting hold of it!
  I hope that you are managing.
  Tell Willm I will see him before the tirricks arrive next year!
  Ever your affectionate son,
  Walter

Sunday 14th May 1775
Brunatwatt

Voar was well through and Mary was back into the rhythm of
croft life at Brunatwatt. She, along with Baabie and Christian, had
finished digging the rigs. They worked together in a row and kept
a regular rhythm. Baabie thought she would never be able to keep
up with her daughters, but she was still a force of nature with her
little Shetland spade – light, but perfectly made to match her height
and give good purchase. Earlier they had spread tang from the ebb
and muck from the midden, so the rigs were almost ready now
for planting potatoes and turnips and for sowing oats and bere.
Many of the lambs had arrived and John had managed to prepare
the banks and cut the peats before setting off for the böd and the
summer fishing. This was his final weekend at home meantime.
It was a sunny morning with not too much chill in the air and Mary
had decided she would leave Babsie with her grandparents and
brave the kirk with Christian. She had not attended since the final
time she had been cited to appear and answer charges. At home she
could escape the kirk, but continuing to stay away from it meant
losing her community. She would have the support of both her
sisters: Jean would be there with the Brunatwatt Laings. She was
expecting a baby, but only just, much to her family's relief. It was
baby news all round, as they had recently had a letter from Jaerm
and Eliza in Prestonpans, telling them of the birth of their baby
boy. They had named him Donald John, after his two grandfathers.

The sound of the birds on the moorland encouraged her to relax
from the toil and enjoy the spaciousness of the landscape: larks,
so high as to be barely visible, filled the air with unceasing song;
curlews and lapwings – whaaps and peewits – lifted from their
nesting sites and flummoxed off nervously; oyster catchers, the
tjaldurs in their black and white livery, attempted to divert passing
groups of kirk-goers with their excitable peep-peeping call. The
cows were out of their winter byres; and sheep, already shedding
a veil of finest fleece, mostly had lambs with them. The heather

was dotted with their tufts of wool, wispiest hentilagets, marking where they had grazed.

They walked down past Stove and Mary slipped in to see Jaanie and deliver a bottle of sweet milk. Since Mary had come back home for voar, she had returned at least twice a week to give the older woman a hand with the heavier tasks. She hoped that the fine morning might have tempted Jaanie to join them at the kirk, even if now it was a bit of struggle to walk home up the Stove brae. But Jaanie declined; and anyway, Willm was still a little young to be expected to sit through what could be a long service.

At the kirk door they were welcomed by one of the kindlier elders who shook Mary's hand and said it was good to see her. They sat in the family pew as usual, Mary wishing it were a little further back so she could slip out quickly at the end. She had felt the eyes of the gathered congregation following her into the pew. Mr Greig and Erchie, who were sitting a few pews in front and across the aisle, did not see her enter. Erchie looked older. It was strange seeing them again after so long; she had not been up at Happyhansel, although many times she had longed to go, especially to hear how they were feeling now that, at long last, presbytery had agreed to the legal status of the school which was so dear to their hearts. Indeed, other than visiting Stove and her Brunatwatt neighbours, she had hardly seen anyone for many months. When Jaanie needed errands from the shop, Mary enlisted Christian's help.

Being at the kirk elicited a strange mix of feelings for Mary – happiness to be out in the community again with her family, but nervousness about what people might be saying behind her back; what looks they might be passing along the pews. And the memory of the interrogation she had endured at the hands of the kirk session was still raw. She tried not to imagine what she might yet have to endure by way of penance.

The service eventually drew to a close and they rose to leave. Some of the congregation seemed in a hurry to disappear. Erchie and Mr Greig then caught sight of her. They were friendly in their concern for her and for Babsie. Erchie said she must bring the baby up to see Leebie and John Jeems, who were always asking for her.

The family did not linger long, but Jean had just enough time to pick up the gossip. One of the Voe House maids was full of the news that Mr Buchan was thinking to marry again! Several times recently he had seemingly been to Garderhouse, home of the widow of Cumming, the local merchant. Though she herself was ages with James Buchan, and particularly well connected – being a daughter of Sir John Mitchell of Scalloway and Sand – his matrimonial interest lay instead with one of her youngest daughters, Miss Agatha Cumming. Agatha had several older unmarried sisters, but, at twenty-five, she was the one who had sparked his interest. He had already enjoyed a biblical span of years, more than half of it married to Margaret. However, he had also known her paternal grandfather, the Rev John Cumming who, as the older man, had mentored him as a young cleric. No one could doubt the young lady's credentials, but eyebrows were raised at the age gap. And she was said to be a headstrong young woman.

'Gadge! He's aald enyoch ta be her graandfaider!' was Christian's judgement on the matter.

'Der nae föls laek aald föls,' was Baabie's comment. 'I winder if he's telt da midder dat he's made owre his property tae Tammie Henry o Burrastow. He jöst haes life-rent noo, sae shö'll be oot afore his corpse is caald.'

Jean's mother-in-law was equally dismissive, 'Ya, whitna spaekalation! I wid say he haes wan fit i da grave an da tidder on a bar o sopp![17] But nae doot shö'll laekly inherit aa da plenishins – I daar say der wirt twartree guineas.'

'Maybe der jöst göd freends.'

'Na, Mary,' said Jean. 'He'll be tinkin he's gotten da richt soo bi da lugs.'[18]

Though Mary could not imagine being married to such an old man, she sensed that he must feel lonely in that big house. And she

---

17 A somewhat precarious existence (lit. one foot in the grave and the other on a bar of soap).

18 He has made an advantageous marriage.

was sure he would not wish to compromise any lady he was seen with frequently; that he would feel he should offer her marriage. Perhaps he was surprised when she accepted. No doubt it would be a very quiet wedding.

Monday 15th May 1775
Brunnatwatt

Mary was on her own at the croft. Baabie and Joannie had gone to check for lambs on the hill and Christian was well on her way to the shop, her kishie holding socks and spencers which she hoped to exchange for tea, some nails for her father and threads for Jaanie. Babsie was having a nap, so Mary had peace to get on with a churning. Even the dog, usually around, was away to the hill.

Out of the corner of her eye, she became aware of a slight movement at the barn door. She hesitated momentarily, thinking she must have imagined it, before picking up the rhythm of the churning again. But then the door creaked loudly and who was standing there in the sudden light but Deyell. She felt herself go rigid. Her arms refused to turn the handle of the churn. His face was one of fury.

'Mi faider's awa oot eenoo. He'll no be back fur a ooer or dat.'

'Hit's no dy faider A'm luikin fur; hit's dee, du lipper! I saa dee gyaain tae da kirk yesterday as if naethin wis amiss. Has du nae shame ava? An dy fock, der nae better! An I hear dat hooer o a sister o dine is gotten a belly foo an aa, an her new merried. You're a damned disgrace tae da parish! A'll tell dee dat, if du's sae free wi dy favours, A'll bloddy weel no be missin oot!'

And with that he made towards Mary, his foul mouth full of threat. His face was red and eyes flaming. She screamed, but he didn't stop. She ran towards the back of the barn where the implements were kept and grabbed a flail. She brandished it and swung it round in the small space sending kishies flying off their hooks and spades tumbling to the ground.

'Gyet oot o here, du dirty pictir! Dunna du dare lay a finger apön me or da meenister an aa dy bridder-elders 'll hear o hit!'

The mention of the kirk session seemed to stop him in his tracks and he kicked the churn, almost knocking it over. By now Mary was standing her ground. She grabbed a hold of him and somehow managed to shove him out the door.

'Dunna dare darken dis door again!'

She watched him slink off towards Gröntu.

She leaned herself against the doorpost, suddenly aware that she was trembling violently. Gradually, she got her breath back and returned to her task. There was no way the incident was going to frighten her. She'd never threatened anyone before – had barely raised her voice in anger. But her rage had been cathartic, and the barn – which had been a constant reminder of her weakness – was now a symbol of something very different. She knew Deyell would not bother her again.

She brought the butter through to the but-end, then tidied the barn and washed out the churn. This was a moment of triumph she would savour alone. She had dealt with Deyell, without the support of her father or brothers. If things got difficult with the kirk, she would bring it up. But meanwhile, she had lost any sense of fear or shame.

Sunday 22nd October 1775
Stove

Jaanie was keen to see Babsie again. It had been hard for Mary over the spring, summer and hairst to have time to take the child to Stove and, as she was becoming ever more mobile, somewhat more difficult to be a real help to Jaanie when she did. There was no doubt that Jaanie was barely managing and yet she needed to keep taking in the laundry and mending. Mary tried to do most of the washing so that Jaanie could do the tasks which allowed her to sit most of the time.

There was still no sign of Deyell, not even at the kirk, for which Mary was grateful. The memory of the encounter in the barn still left her with a feeling of disgust. Though her fear had been replaced with a calm self-assurance, she preferred to avoid him. She had been to the kirk service and, since the afternoon was dry, had decided to take Babsie to see the Stove folk. She had parcelled up a bottle of sweet milk, some fresh butter and kirn-mylk, some potatoes and a jar of rhubarb and ginger jam; with them safely stowed in her kishie, she took Babsie – now toddling proudly in her first little boots – all the way to Stove. At times, she had to lift her on her back and struggle with the kishie under her arm. But the skirls of the child made the journey lightsome. She could not imagine life without Babsie now, however hard the start of that fateful journey had been or however distressing it might yet become. Mary preferred not being apart from her, although the little girl was sociable and would happily stay with her grandparents or with Christian.

Willm was more than willing to entertain the child, hiding objects in his closed palm or behind his back or up his sleeve, allowing Mary to fold clothes for Jaanie and tidy up.

'Mi jewel, will du be comin ta bide wi wis again afore lang? Dee an Babsie?'

'I tink we could come shön noo, fur da hairst is weel trowe. We got da hidmist paets haem an biggit, an aa da tatties ripit. I can aye dö mi makkin here.'

'Dat wid truly be a blisseen, lass. Noo whit uncans heard-du at da kirk daday?'

Willm had taken Babsie out to the peat-stack to collect fuel, so Mary was free to talk.

'Weel, dey wir bön da usual accusations at da kirk session… antenuptial fornication… a Duncan wife fae Elvister. Shö wis denied hit and seeminly da elders decidit tae "refer hit til Providence gave further Light"! I hoop shö's proved richt. An Jeems Umphray an Katherine Petersdochter, dey wir dismissed fae ony mair rebuke – dat's twice I tink der hed ta appear afore da congregation. An dey wir a charge o fornication – Jean Irvine fae Scarvister. Shö's gyaain tae hae a bairn. But nae adultery!'

'Weel, da aald elders 'll nae doot be up i der cuddie[19] aboot aa dat!' said Jaanie.

'Some o dem at laest. But der göd eens among dem an aa. Nae doot A'll be hearin fae da presbytery shön. I tink Mr Buchan said dat dey meet in November. Tae be honest, luikin at mi peerie lass, der naethin dey can say or dö dat'll tak awa da plaisure o her. But hit's sic a nuisance especially at dis time o da year.'

'Dat's true, mi joy. Dey canna tak dat awa ava.'

Wednesday 8th November 1775
Stove and Voe House

When she and Babsie moved back to Stove, Mary insisted that Willm should no longer give up his bed in the ben-end – she and Babsie could manage fine in the closet. They had slipped back easily into the old pattern of life, of working together. Willm was more self-reliant and was doing well at school. Mary was more confident now about being seen: she had even taken Babsie to the shop several times and, being a bonnie little blond child with a happy nature, most folk seemed to have forgotten the past.
It was a fair day for early November, with a thin sun and not too much wind. Mary had wrapped Babsie up well and had set off for Voe House to be there by 11am, the appointed time.

The previous afternoon, just as Mary was finishing a baking, one of the servants from Voe House had knocked and entered. She had handed Mary a letter from Mr Buchan and, although the girl was in a hurry to get to the shop, she sat down long enough for Mary to write a short reply as was requested.

The minister's note was brief, merely stating that notice from presbytery about her case had been received and he would be informing the kirk session about it on Thursday 9th. He asked if

---

19 Pleased with themselves (lit. like being up in a salt basket hanging on the wall).

she would come along to Voe House on Wednesday at 11am, as he wanted to discuss it with her. He added – in brackets – that if Babsie were likely to be awake at that time, and if it was not too cold a day for the baby, he would be happy to see her too.

She knocked on the door and was shown into the dark parlour by Annie, the same maid who had delivered the note. It was a relief not to be in the room where she had been interrogated along with her sisters. Mr Buchan was seated at a table spread with papers, near the window.

'Come away in, Mary. Let me take your coat. Annie, could you fetch us some tea, please?'

He indicated a chair for Mary to sit down with her child.

'So, this is Babsie! Well, she's certainly grown a lot since I baptised her. She's a lovely little girl, Mary, and a credit to you. I'm vexed about the way all this happened and the ensuing trouble. I want to help you as best I can. But please understand, there's only so much I can do: the kirk's view of adultery is very severe and you have a long road ahead of you, for the Shetland presbytery is not given to much compassion. But before we get on to that, tell me first, how are you, and how is Jaanie? It's good that you can help her through the winter. We have so many ageing people in the parish facing winter hardships. I hear her son is thinking to give up the deep sea.'

Their conversation was pleasant and he seemed genuinely interested in their lives. Annie brought in the tea and served it just as Babsie was trying to shift the papers on the desk. Mr Buchan offered her an oatcake and the little girl took it eagerly in her fat little hands.

'Well, Babsie, I see you don't much care for these papers. No wonder. You know, Mary, Mrs Buchan and I had a little infant, Elizabeth; but she only lived for one day on this earth. I think that experience has marked me for life.'

'I can't imagine how tragic that must have been for you.'

'Well, poor Mrs Buchan never quite got over it. I think seeing wee Babsie brings it back. Now, let me see… where were we?'

Mary retrieved the papers and Mr Buchan pulled out a letter.

'I take it you are willing to confess adultery, Mary, even if you were at the time unaware that the father of your child was a married man?'

'Yes, Mr Buchan.' Mary, who was not given to crying – and particularly as she had heard that a few tears did not go amiss at such times – had a lump in her throat.

'Well, that should make the process a little less arduous in terms of questioning, but the rebuke will be no less easy to bear. The reason it has gone to presbytery is because it is beyond the resources of this kirk session to trace the man and call him to account. You will have to attend the presbytery meeting in the South Kirk, in Lerwick, on the 22nd of this month; that's a Wednesday. I'm afraid I will not be attending… there's too much needing my attention in the parish. At this time of year it's held in the afternoon, so I would advise you travel on the Monday and return on the Thursday. Do you have any relations you could stay with in Lerwick?'

'No, I'm afraid not. But I've saved up some money and will be able to pay.'

'I've been thinking about what you might be able to do. But first of all, I will tell you what will happen. You should be at the kirk in good time for two o'clock. I don't know when you will be called to appear, but you may well be the first on the list once they do their initial business. They will no doubt ask you why you were not able to attend this time last year when you were first called and details about the case, but nothing that you haven't been asked before. You will also need to confirm that you have confessed and are ready to receive your discipline. Is that… clear now, Mary?'

'Yes, sir.'

'And you will have to take this letter with you and present it to the presbytery clerk at the meeting. He will be sitting at the front with the moderator; that's the minister chairing the meeting. Best stand unless you're asked to sit.'

Babsie was gradually demolishing the oatcake and Mary trying to retrieve bits before they fell to the floor.

'Don't worry about the floor, Mary. Now, let me see. First of all, your journey. It's a long way to Lerwick and difficult at this time of year. I dare say you will get advice about the best way. I'm not aware of any boats going to Scalloway on that Monday or Tuesday before presbytery meets on the Wednesday... pity, as that would be much easier. I was just thinking... our kirk officer, James Ollason, will be delivering a letter from me to the minister at Garderhouse on the Monday. If it would be a help to you, I could ask him if he would accompany you as far as the Effirth junction. There, you would be in sight of the Scord at Weisdale, almost your half-way mark. From there, you would drop down to Sound where you would get a boat across to Kalliness to save you miles of walking round Weisdale voe. You could get lodgings there for the night with the ferry-man's family... he would point you to his house. It's not a place I can easily recommend... and if it's busy you might have to make do in the barn...' He looked up to gauge Mary's reaction.

'That would be all right, I'm sure. But I'd hoped I might make the journey in one day...'

'Not at this time of year, Mary, when the days are so short. Now, I'll ask James to be at the Brouster junction about nine o'clock on the Monday morning. It should be light enough by then. How does that sound?'

'That would be a great help to me, Mr Buchan. But the kirk officer...'

'No need to worry, Mary. James Ollason is a good man and will take care of you. Young women are often in need of protection...'

He looked out of the window and nothing was said for a moment.

'You may have already heard that I am to be married next spring to Miss Agatha Cumming of Garderhouse. She is young like you, Mary...'

Mary did not know how to respond, but merely said, 'Yes, I had indeed heard. And I hope it will be a happy union.'

'There may well be others at Weisdale who will be on their

way to Lerwick but, whatever, the people there will make sure you know the way.'

'Thank you, sir.'

'Now, as to your return journey, I know that the *Hawk* is making a trip to Scallowa on the Wednesday with wool and the plan is to return on the Thursday, leaving for Waas at ten o'clock so, if you could get to Scallawa by that time, it would save you a lot of walking in wintry weather. They would probably reach Waas just as it was darkening; as long as the weather was suitable. If it was bad weather, you might be stuck in Scallowa for the night and need accommodation there. I think I should give you a crown, just in case.'

He stood up and reached into an inside pocket for his wallet. 'You can return it to me if all goes well. And here's a groat[20] for the ferry and bed at Weisdale.'

'That's very kind, sir. I would endeavour to pay it back to you if I need to use it.'

'Now, as to accommodation in Lerwick, Mary. I suggest a place in Bakers' Kloss... a Mistress Anderson. Here, I've written a note for you to give to her. She's one of the few I've found who can read! She runs a very respectable, modest house where a young woman can rest assured she will not be troubled. I think she charges a shilling a night; perhaps 1/6 if she provides food for you. You can reach the lane either from the top at the High Street end or at the foot of the lane from the street along the shore.'

'I can only thank you, Mr Buchan, for all this help. I would have been very anxious otherwise.'

'I think before I seal up the letter to presbytery and give it to you, I should let you see what it says, Mary.' She took it from his hand and read it slowly, trying to concentrate as Babsie beat her hands on the table, as if in protest.

'RDBB is a mode of address. It means 'Reverend and Dear Brethren."

---

20 A crown is a silver coin worth 5 shillings; a groat is a small silver coin worth fourpence (4d).

Mary nodded.

Slowly, she read the words. It was not like Mr Greig's copperplate.

Voe in Walls Novr 10th 1775
RDBB

The Bearer hereof Mary Johnsdr. guilty of Adultery with
a Sailor on board the Batchelor of Leith *(Captain Ramage*
Commander) gave in her confefsion before this Sefsion,
which was transmitted to the Pby by a reference, but as the
woman did not attend the Pby as ordered by the Sefsion,
we could not enter her on the Profefsion of her Repentence
hitherto. It is hoped the Pby, now that she is to compear
personally before them, will give Orders concerning the
proper discipline according to the Rules of the Church.
The woman seems much more concerned for her Sin than
heretofore and is very willing to satisfy as the Pby shall order.
The Man's name whom she gave in as the Father of her child
is Alexander Rofs, who was a Residenter in Leith, and lived
there with his wife. The woman indeed did not give in any
Confefsion till the man and the Ship he belonged to were
gone off the country, but there is no ground to doubt of his
having been guilty with her, and the Father of her child. The
Pby Clerk no doubt having the Reference in his custody,
which the Pby will please to cause be read, and send their
Deliverance upon it by the bearer.
Wishing you the Divine Direction and blefsing on all your
proceedings and determinations, I am

                    RDBB
                    Your affec Brother
                    & most humble Ser.t
                         James Buchan
*   PS The Bearer will Acquaint the Pby of the reasons &*
causes of her not attending them sooner.

'Thank you for letting me read it, sir.'

Mr Buchan folded the letter carefully, tucked it in and sealed it. He wrote on the outside:

Letter addressed (& sealed) 8th Novem.r 1775
To
The very Reverend
The Moderator of the Pby
of Zetland, to be communicate

Then he handed it to Mary, reminding her to give it to the presbytery clerk. Mary was keen to get on her way back to Stove, as Babsie was becoming ever more restless.

'I hope this will not be too much of an ordeal for you; that God will give you strength. As I've said, I'm afraid this presbytery is not a lenient one. But you will get through it, Mary.'

'I hope so, Mr Buchan. I find the story in St John's gospel of Jesus and the woman taken in adultery to be very comforting. I try to bring that to mind when I feel upset.'

'Yes, that is a very interesting story. The Pharisees were trying to trick Jesus into renouncing the Old Testament commandments; but he didn't. Instead, he challenged her accusers to admit their own sins first and... he encouraged the woman to live circumspectly... a good story for all of us to bear in mind.'

Mary thanked him and got on her way. The mention of Alex Ross's name troubled her. She hoped presbytery would not be successful in finding him: one life turned upside-down was more than enough. As she walked down towards the sea, she could visualise Mr Greig's copperplate minutes of the next day's kirk session meeting:

Thursday 9th November, 1775

The Minister states that he had told Mary Johnsdaughter
to appear before Presbytery at its meeting on Wed 22nd

November 1775 to which she had been appointed to wait upon... and that he had written a line to the Presbytery along with her (letter dated 8th/10th November 1775, transcribed below)...

Monday 20th November 1775
Waas to Kalliness, Weisdale

Mary had slept the night at Brunatwatt and had arranged to leave Babsie there as it would be too much for Jaanie to manage the children on her own. As a mother, Mary knew in her heart that she would miss Babsie more than the child would miss her; that her little girl would be content, and no doubt somewhat indulged. She had delivered a note to Voe House to confirm that she would be at Brouster at 9am. She was up early and had packed a small kishie: the letter and money safely in the bottom, then rivlins in case her feet got sore, some extra hose and undergarments and a thick gansey. On top, she packed faerdie-maet: bannocks spread with butter and rhubarb jam, brönnies, kirn-mylk, two bottles of blaand and a knife. Her mother had insisted on wrapping up some boiled chicken for her to take too.

The wind was light but, being out of the east, was cold. She laced up her strong boots and dressed as warmly as she could, her hap round her head and shoulders. She was off before the family stirred, skirting the Gallow Hill. Beyond lay *terra incognita*.

She arrived at the Brouster junction, the agreed meeting point, in good time and mercifully did not have to wait long for James Ollason. Though she did not know him personally, she remembered he had helped with lime-washing the schoolhouse more than a year previously. And he had delivered the notices to Brunatwatt regarding the various hearings. She thought he came from Mid Waas. He was a quiet man in his early middle years. Although initially he seemed a little taciturn, he offered to carry the kishie for Mary.

'Du'll hae ta kerry hit up owre da Scord an nae doot owre Wormadale an aa… sae lat me kerry hit eenoo.'

There was a slight awkwardness between them which made conversation difficult. Mary was aware that he would know her business and possibly harbour a low opinion of her; or maybe he was a man of few words, given the nature of his work and the fact that he often had to deliver unwanted news, which rendered him unpopular.

The gaet was rough and boggy in places, but as the track followed relatively level land it eased the journey. As the sky brightened, Mary was able to enjoy the ever-changing vistas in their muted autumnal colours even though the cold wind sneaked around her legs. Gradually, her companion seemed to forget his official role. He asked her about her little girl and her family, and whether she missed her job at Happyhansel. He told her that his sweetheart had died from tuberculosis some years before and that he was keen to marry and settle down with a family. As time went on, they relaxed and chatted in each other's company. He seemed to know everyone. She had never had reason to venture beyond Elvister and knew the Mid Waas folk mainly through their children coming to school.

The track wound along the gentle slopes above Hulmawatter, through the peaty mires at Wallacetoon from where the well-worked slopes of Twatt came into view, before reaching the head of Effirth Voe where James would turn southwards towards Garderhouse. He lifted her kishie for her and she settled it comfortably over her shoulders.

'Noo dan, dat's six mile dön an gotten dee weel apön dy wye, Mary; an at laest he's no rained. Du has da letter safe?' She nodded, and he continued, 'I hoop hit'll no be owre muckle o a ordeal fur dee. I canna say I agree wi aa dis discipline. Fock is braaly weary o hit.'

Mary was surprised that he, the kirk officer, should express this view.

'Weel, Jeems, I doot A'll gyet mi pexins fae presbytery!'

'I hoop hit'll no be owre herd fur dee, lass. Hit dusna seem fair.'

'An I hoop a fine lass 'll faa inta dy lap whin du's laest lippenin hit, Jeems!'

'Noo dat wid be a miracle!'

She smiled and thanked him for accompanying her.

He pointed on past Bixter to where they could see the top of the Scord of Weisdale, that landmark dip between the hills. 'Noo, du has as far again ta traivel daday, but he's no sae flat as du can see, sae hit'll laekly be tree ooer or dat afore du wins tae da ferry. Eence owre da Scord, du sood be able ta drap doon da steepie ta Soond an fae dere der aye someen ta tak fock across da voe to Kalliness.'

Mary thanked him again and they bade farewell. He was lucky – he would have the wind behind him for the next part of his journey.

By now the weak sun was almost at its zenith and Mary felt she must speed on rather than linger for something to eat. She had a quick drink of blaand and a bit of bannock and got on her way. The land soon started to rise and her kishie felt more burdensome. Low cloud had gathered along the far ridge and, as she bent into the wind, she could feel spots of drushy rain settling on her hap and overcoat. At the top of the Scord, gusts of wind lifted her hem and sneaked up her sleeves. She gathered her outer clothing as tightly around her as she could. Soon, she was descending the steep slope to the jetty: it was slippery and rocky in places and she had to grab hold of the tussocky grass. When at last she got out of the teeth of the wind and below the cloud, she started to enjoy the view, so different from Waas. The long valley was deep and already losing the sun. Little crofts were strung out along both sides of the narrow voe, and on the far side a large loch left Kalliness almost stranded. The islands in the outer voe stretched on and on to the far south.

A couple of men with a sheepdog were waiting at the jetty and they hailed the boatman as he approached. It was good to feel the thwart under her and the gentle movement of the rowing. At Kalliness, Mary paid the boatman the groat and he pointed to a small, thatched cottage where she would find his wife and family and her lodging for the night. It was a relief to reach her destination while there was still light in the late afternoon sky. She was welcomed warmly enough by a big woman and several small children whose pinafores Mary sensed had not been acquainted with the wash tub for some time. But then she checked herself, knowing well enough how difficult it was to keep everything clean, especially in winter. The low but-end was dark and chilly, with only the smallest of fires burning in the centre of the room. There was no glass in the tiny windows; instead they were covered by stretched lambskin. What little light the room had to offer entered mainly through a hole in the thatch that served as a chimney. The loft area was open with a laim at each end, a deep shelf supported by joists. A ladder balanced against one of them and it looked, from the straw poking out, as if the children probably slept there among the various items stored. Legs of reestit mutton hung from the rafters. Mary was familiar with the old style of croft houses. She realised her family was relatively fortunate that her brothers, who had been to the whaling in good years when the season had ended with money in their pockets, had been able to help with some improvements to their home.

The mother told the oldest girl to show Mary to the barn and to make sure she had straw for bedding, a blanket and some water. Meanwhile, she would roast some mussels and make a pot of tea for Mary to share.

Mary made her corner of the barn as comfortable as she could. As she retraced her steps to the but-end through the narrow passageway that divided the house from the byre, she caught sight of the animals tethered in their stalls: two cows and a quaig turned their heads to look at her, with their big, soft eyes and dribbling muzzles. She resisted the desire to stroke them; the byre floor had not been mucked out recently and she did not want sharn all over her boots. However, there was something curiously comforting having the cows so near, even if the stench was strong. She could hear their shifting and occasional lowing.

She was keen not to engage much with the family, as no doubt they would want to know her business. They would probably already be speculating as to why a young woman would make a trip, unaccompanied, all the way from Waas to Lerwick, and in winter-time. Some might go with their mother or aunt to buy wedding clothes for a Yöl ceremony, or perhaps as a group with knitwear to sell, but generally not on their own.

Mary finished the mussels and tea as fast as she could, giving the excuse that she was tired and would prefer to rest; and that she had enough food with her for the morning, so there was no need for anyone to be up early to serve her. She planned to leave at first light, as it would be as far again, if not a little further, to Lerwick. She had rehearsed the route in her mind; south along Weisdale Voe, round the end of the ribbon of Stromness Voe and across the causeway at the Loch of Strom. Then, keeping the sun on her right side, she would have to snake up and around Wormadale Hill at the head of Whiteness Voe, before at last reaching the broad, fertile Tingwall Valley and a sight of the east coast. From there, it should be easier, even if hilly, as the track from Tingwall to Lerwick was reputedly better and there was a likelihood of others on the road.

In the darkening, Mary cut some kirn-mylk and spread it on a brönnie she had brought. Instantly she felt herself back at Brunatwatt with all the comfort of family around her. She was missing them all, especially her little girl. Then, as no one had indicated a dry closet, she relieved herself round the back of the barn. Back inside, it was a relief to take off her boots and ease her wet feet. She was, however, reluctant to take off her overcoat and hap, although she knew they would be more effective as coverings. She had the briefest of washes and lay down in her clothes, tired from her long day. She knew she would sleep soundly.

Tuesday 21st November 1775
Kalliness to Lerwick

Although the barn was windowless and dark, Mary was wakened early by the persistent bellowing of the cows in the adjoining byre.

It started with one cow, until the three became an unstoppable cacophony. They needed to be milked. It was all Mary could do to ignore them when her hands were itching to make them more comfortable. As she got up, she suddenly became aware of the heavy breathing of a man sleeping a few feet away from where she had lain. It startled her and, for a moment, brought back the grim memory of Deyell. Strangely, the heavy breathing also thrust Alex Ross into her mind – the mad passion of the moment she thought she had forgotten – and her feelings almost took her over. Thankfully the noises from the byre distracted her and, quickly realising it was just another innocent lodger, calmed her enough to take a swig of blaand, pack her things and set off before either he or the family would stir. The sun was still well below the ranging hills to the east and the morning air held intimations of winter. However, it was dry and cloudless, the wind had eased and, as the sky lightened, she could pick out the path to the south without too much difficulty.

An hour took her from Kalliness to the Strom causeway and soon she was trudging up the steep slope of Wormadale. Her spirits were bright: she thought of this time the previous year when she should have made the journey; that she would now be asked to explain why she had not attended presbytery when called. She remembered coming to Jaanie's to be in good time for the birth. How different life was then and how fearful she had been. No, there was nothing they could say or do now which would reach her inner soul; nothing that would diminish or destroy her. The child was her unalloyed joy.

As she reached the dip between the hills, the morning sun was lighting what could only be the Bressa Wart. She had heard of that hill, with its cone shape dominating Lerwick harbour. From there, she turned south-eastwards towards the Tingwall valley and the green parks of Veensgart.

Kishie somehow feeling lighter, Mary followed the path down the long slope, sensing an easing of the anxiety she had unwittingly felt as she made her lonely way across an unfamiliar landscape. Her mind was free to wander. She mused on how the kirk might read the facts of this part of her story: that she had taken advantage of the company of James Ollason, a man she barely knew but who was looking for a wife... that she had accepted a crown from another man, one about to be married. The inquisitional words, '*So what had you given him for that sum?*' came back to her... She remembered saying, '*I gave him nothing for it, nor was I desiring any neat thing from him; he insisted I take it.*' ... Not only that, she had now lain in a barn overnight with yet another man... one she had never set eyes on before. Was there no room for human kindness in the kirk's interpretation of regulations? Did proximity between men and women always hold seeds of shame?

Away to the south, she could pick out Tingwall Kirk, with its distinctive round tower to the west, and the hills closing in above the lochs there. She knew that valley led to Scallowa. But she must bear east and climb to the Windy Grind before dropping down the slope to Dales Voe and again up the steep brae on the other side, past Frakkafield. She had been told there was more of a road there, which could be followed easily.

Before she tackled the slope up to the Windy Grind, she looked for a big boulder near the track where she could find a bit of shelter to have a brief rest and something to eat. A bannock with rhubarb jam and kirn-mylk had never tasted so good and the few mouthfuls of blaand were just what she needed: clean, cold and sustaining. Although she was tired, she was on her feet again quickly, being anxious not to linger long: daylight was short and, having heard of the notorious Black Gaet between Lerwick and Scallowa, she did not wish to get lost in the mirk.

From the top, the view of Dales Voe – though not as stunning as Whiteness – was still dramatic, with steep hills closing in on either side. The rough road was clearly visible, leading up and over the Staney Hill. She knew that Lerwick was not so very much further on. She could see several groups of people on the way ahead of her.

As she trudged on, she became aware of people filling kishies of peats from stacks near the roadside and setting off towards Lerwick. She immediately felt more at ease at the familiar sight and the comfort and warmth it signified. The ground levelled off and the road was easier under her feet. When the island of Bressay came into view and the land started its descent to the sea, even though the little town of Lerwick was still out of sight, she felt hugely relieved that she had found her way safely.

Light was fading fast now, but she pressed on, ever more aware of the weight of the kishie on her back and the biting easterly wind. The track gradually widened into a road which followed the harbour with its jetties and little docks. Occasional low houses had their doors almost on the road. Smoke rose silently from their chimneys. Mary noticed that they had tiny stacks of peats, barely a week's fuel. She hoped she would be able to work out which road was the High Street just from looking at the lie of the land. Mr Buchan had said that Bakers' Kloss was quite far along. A road soon branched off to the right and she thought that was her best chance. She asked a passer-by if Bakers' Kloss was near and the woman indicated she should keep going. It wasn't long before she found it and the door the minister had described. She knocked and waited. By now it was getting quite dark and she hoped she would be able to get lodgings.

A little woman, not unlike her own mother in age, opened the door and greeted her. It was Mistress Anderson, as Mister Buchan had explained.

'I wid laek a room, or a bed, for a couple o nichts, please.'

'A'm sorry, jewel, I dunna hae ony space left. I winder if Mistress Jamieson in Da Steep Kloss…'

Mary's face no doubt showed her disquiet and disappointment. She handed the woman the letter from Mr Buchan, which she opened and read.

'So, Mr Buchan is sent you? An you hae ta geng ta presbytery damoarn? Oh dear, dear. I winder… aa I hae is a peerie closet but truly hit's hardly kirsen…'

Mary brightened immediately. 'A'm sleepit ithin a closet maist o mi life. Hit wid jöst be splendid!'

'Weel dan, come dy wys in trowe an A'll shaa dee. Hit is da peerie!'

Mary stepped inside the low door, met by the familiar smells of koli lamp, peat fire and cooking. The closet was tucked under the stair, but at least had a window, if only into another room at the back. There was a small bed, a shelf, a hook on the door and little else. But to Mary, it was home, secure in the knowledge that Mr Buchan had recommended it. As it was so cramped, the landlady insisted on giving her food as well as the bed for 1/- a night; she was to come through to the kitchen and have some soup when she was ready. This simple act of kindness had Mary close to tears. She took off her outer clothes and boots and lay on the bed for quite some time, allowing the fatigue to sweep over her. Eventually, she brought her own food through to the kitchen where she shared it with the landlady who served them both a bowl of thick, hot broth. Mary learned that she was a widow and her only son was a bosun who used to sail from Liverpool to Boston, Massachusetts, but lately war with the American colonies was killing that commerce and he was back to the home trade. And there was talk of strengthening the old fort in Lerwick; maybe garrisoning troops. It sounded a world away from Waas.

Wednesday 22nd November 1775
Lerwick

Mary took her time in the morning, glad of some gruel and hot tea from Mistress Anderson. She was aware of other lodgers, but kept herself to herself. She ascertained that the building where the presbytery meeting would be held was further south in the town at Sooth Kirk Kloss.

She paid her landlady for the two nights she would spend there and, with the letter from Mr Buchan safely in one pocket and a small pack of food in the other, she set off by mid-morning to be in good time. But not without advice to turn up Bakers' Kloss rather than down; 'Tak care noo if du gengs doon da wye fur sometimes da street floods at dis time o year.'

She was glad to reach the top of the kloss as it was so cramped and crumbling, with sewage running in open drains and seagulls swooping for leftover food and fish entrails.

Mary skirted along the Hillhead, crossing a burn as she stepped. The small town, happed in peat-reek, huddled down the steep slope to the sea. Beyond it, Bressa Soond was busy with sloops coming and going. She could see what could only be Gairdie House on the island of Bressa; the heritor there had housed several of the emigrants in what she thought must be Shetland's most imposing residence. She wondered where they all were now. Eliza and Jaerm suddenly came to mind; and the *Batchelor of Leith* and, unexpectedly, Alexander Ross. It was as if those thoughts were from a different life.

She was looking out for the new Tolbooth; she had heard it was a useful landmark, not far from the kirk where presbytery would meet. There was no mistaking it – the most impressive building in the town, reminding her of Bayhaa, but with the addition of a steeple and weather-cock on the ridge of the steep roof, and an imposing entrance with steps. It had its back to the harbour, unlike the stone houses which clung to the foreshore, their gable ends to the sea for a bit of shelter. Those belonging to merchants had jetties and stores. She had heard of these lodberries, well-known as places where smuggling was still rife. They had their foundations in the sea and boats could tie up and unload relatively unseen from the landward side, and without the need to tranship goods. It was all so novel, each corner she turned offering another kloss up the slope or a narrow trenkie down to a jetty. There were several little booths where traders were selling meat, fish and bread and flinging offal and scraps to the seagulls down on the beach. The street along the shore twisted away in both directions, its flagstones wet, but not enough to ruin boots or soak the hems of clothing.

Mary doubled back towards the kirk and found a suitable

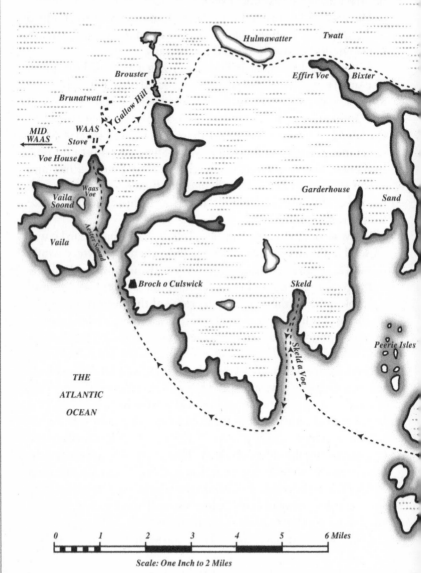

MARY JOHNSDAUGHTER'S JOURNEY FROM WAAS TO LERWICK AND RETURN

Hulmawatter

Twatt

Brouster

Effirt Voe

Bixter

Brunatwatt

Gallow Hill

MID WAAS

WAAS

Stove

Voe House

Garderhouse

Sand

Waas Voe

Vaila Soond

Aester Soond

Vaila

Broch o Culswick

Skeld

Peerie Isles

Skeld a Voe

THE
ATLANTIC
OCEAN

| 0 | 1 | 2 | 3 | 4 | 5 | 6 Miles |

Scale: One Inch to 2 Miles

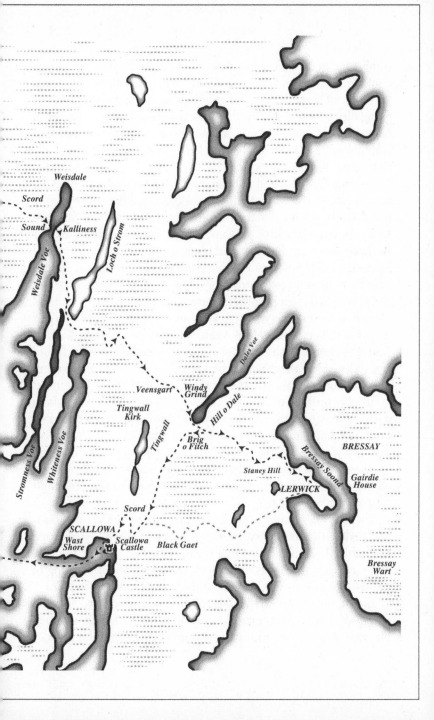

tombstone in the kirk-yard, sheltered by some bushes, where she could sit quietly, confident she would be in time. She ate a brönnie and a bit of the chicken brought from home. It would keep her going till her ordeal was over and she could escape to her lodgings. Mistress Anderson had guessed what her business was and had commiserated. 'Du soodna hae ta kerry aa da blame, Mary. I aye tink he's a ill-pairtit wirld.'

Eventually, she could see men gathering around and entering the church, so she waited until it was quiet and then approached the door. It wasn't much of a building compared to Tingwall Kirk, or even to the kirk in Waas. The presbytery officer took Mr Buchan's letter for the clerk and made a note of her name. He led her into a chilly anteroom with a dank smell and said she should wait there; that it would probably be at least half an hour before she was called. Several others were soon brought in. She could guess that most of the young women and couples were in a similar situation to herself: they looked anxious and no one talked. Mary found herself reprising that sense of self-confidence which had emboldened her after the ugly barn incident. She tried not to think about the interrogation that lay before her. Instead, she kept in her mind's eye the beautiful child. The warm softness of her, the skirls and liveliness. She was worth every cold mile, every bitter question, every piece of penance that would be exacted.

Mary was first on the list of miscreants. The place seemed full of heavily-whiskered old men in dark suits. To her, they looked for all the world like hoodie crows with their sharp beaks; even their voices were raw and edgy.

They kept her waiting, standing in the front pew. The moderator and clerk to the presbytery, robed in long black gowns, were seated at a table. The officer, also in a gown, flapped round with notes and messages; there was mumbling, muttering and a shuffling of papers. But at least this time she did not recognise any of them.

At last, the old minister, in his role as moderator, lifted his head and looked at her with piercing eyes that seemed to bore into her. He cleared his throat and spoke formally in the southern manner which always seemed to embody authority.

'You are Mary Johnsdaughter of Brunatwatt, in the parish of Walls and Sandness?'

'Yes, sir.'

'You were called to appear before this presbytery in November of last year, but failed to appear. What was the reason?'

'I was heavy with child, about to give birth any day, and could not travel such a distance.' Mary could see the clerk scribbling furiously.

'Was the child conceived in uncleanness, as stated?'

'Yes, sir.'

'And to whom?'

'To Alexander Ross, a sailor on board the *Batchelor of Leith* which was stranded in Waas... I mean in Walls... for most of six months.'

'This Alexander Ross was a married man?'

'He did not make that known to me at that time.'

'Mary Johnsdaughter, do you admit committing adultery and breaking the sixth commandment?'

'I do, sir.'

'There is no hiding this sin, confessing in some dark corner. You have transgressed against your community and brought the parish into disrepute. By confessing openly to this sin and repenting publicly, you will be one step nearer to a clean heart, to forgiveness and to reinstatement within your community. So, do you repent of that sin?'

'I do. I am sad that it happened that way.'

'And are you ready to receive your discipline so that you can return to the communion of the faithful?'

'Yes, I am.'

'In that case, I will order the kirk session and congregation of Walls to hear your profession of repentance as adulterer seventeen times, generally weekly, starting next month on 3rd December. That will be all.'

Mary left the room as quickly as she had entered it. The

questions had not distressed her the way they had when first she was interrogated in her own church and among people who knew her. Surely a letter of confession could have sufficed to save the upheaval of travelling all that distance and delaying a year. It slowly dawned on her that part of the power-play was the demand that you appear; the trappings of a court of law. She briefly wondered to herself how many of those butchers and bakers and ministers were blemish-free? How many had put an unwanted hand up a girl's skirt? But for now, this particular ordeal was over. Already, she could visualise Mr Greig sitting at the table she had so often laid for meals, writing up the session minute for November:

This day the Moderator reported that Mary Johnsdaughter ordered to wait on the Presbytery had done so, and was appointed by them to enter on her profefsion of repentance before the Congregation of Walls as adulterer till further order.

She wondered what he truly thought of her. No doubt there would be other names of girls in trouble further down the minute. She determined to put the experience, the attempt at humiliation, behind her.

As she walked back up to the Hillhead to her lodgings, her main regret of the day was that she had not been able to go with Mistress Anderson to collect peats. Her stack was a good mile or more from her home; to relieve her of some of the burden would at least have been purposeful, and the clean, fresh, cold air would have wiped away the sense of wrongdoing which these old men had tried so hard to drum into her, and which was difficult to banish completely.

Thursday 23rd November 1775
Scallowa

Mary was up and dressed well before the light came in, as she wanted to be on her way as quickly as possible. She was grateful for a little warm water for washing and some gruel and tea. Mistress Anderson had wrapped up a few oatcakes for her and refilled her bottle, but with sweet milk. She urged Mary to go by the Staney Hill and Brig o Fitch rather than the south road and Black Gaet. There might be Hollanders about, and it could be boggy in wintertime. And, as the wind had veered to the south-east, the route along Dales Voe might also offer a bit more shelter.

'Ir you sure A'm gien you enyoch fur luikin eftir me?'

'Dat du is, hinny. Hit wis da fine ta hae dee bidin an I wiss dee an dy peerie ting healt an strent. If ivver du needs a bed in Lerrick, A'm here. But I hoop hit wid be fur something mair lichtsome! Noo, Göd geng wi dee, lass, an pit aa yun ahint dee.'

Mary waved and set off up Bakers' Kloss. Her kishie and her heart felt lighter. She was on the homeward path; the wind – though cold and threatening sleety showers – was behind her and Mistress Anderson had warmed her boots and overcoat for her. She headed along the High Street and North Road, cutting up over the Staney Hill at its lowest point. Although the gaet was rough in places, it was at least clearly visible. It was a relief to drop down the slope, along the Hill o Dale to where she could cross the Burn o Fitch and turn towards the south. The sun was still to rise above the ridge, but the sky was lightening with every stride. It was only about six miles, so she was sure she would be in good time to find the *Hawk*, wherever it was berthed. She kept one eye on where she put her feet and the other ahead of her, on the notch in the hills which she had to reach. Looking back, she could see several small groups of people making the same journey. As she climbed to the Scallowa Scord the wind hit her again, but was still behind her: Mistress Anderson had given good advice. To her left, she could see the Black Gaet going off over the hills in the other direction. It looked altogether more threatening: narrower, steeper, lonelier and more winding.

As she rounded the corner at the top, she was met by a view she had never imagined and the joyful realisation that it would remain uninterrupted all the way down the slope to the jetty.

Scallowa was spread around the inlet below, and beyond it there were low islands, not blocking the voe as in Waas, but stretching away into the distance and hovering near the horizon. Scuds of sleet would suddenly obscure the vision, whipping down over the slope and then, just as quickly, the veil would be lifted to reveal the panorama. She had heard of Earl Patrick Stewart's castle at Scallowa, but had not realised just how imposing it looked with its fancy turrets, perched on the promontory. No wonder 'Black Patie' was hated, living in such style and extorting money from poor people. She had heard stories of his harsh dealings and those of the Scots lairds he had brought in. But he was long gone and the castle looked dilapidated. She could see what appeared to be a few fine houses, much grander than she had seen in Lerwick.

As she approached the shore, she passed a huge haa house, bigger and grander than Bayhaa with three storeys and a steep slated roof. It was set above the bay, looking towards the west, with an imposing gateway in a high wall to the front and a garden wrapping it round. The upper floors had five windows. There was something oddly foreign about these houses; Shetland houses were low, almost apologetic by comparison, and generally tucked in wherever shelter allowed, not standing boldly in the face of a westerly gale. Mary imagined there would be maids scurrying up and down stairs already, with ewers of water and peats for bedroom fires. Above the door was a coat of arms with a shield sculpted on it, but she had no idea who owned it. She had heard of Mitchell o Wastshore, but knew this could not be his house as it was on the east shore of the inlet. Far to the right, along the bay, she could see what looked like a new residence set in a walled garden: perhaps that was Mitchell's. Just below that house, several sloops were anchored close in to shore and small boats were plying back and fore with bales and sacks and tea-chests. One of the bigger sloops, with a distinctive white strip painted along its black hull, she recognised as John T Henry's *Hawk*. Relief flooded through her.

At last, she recognised a Waas man and asked if it would be

possible to get a passage to Waas.

'I wid tink dat wid be nae budder. Ah, noo I recognise dee, Mary. Whaar's du bön stravaigin?'

'A'm bön ta Lerrick.'

'My mercy. Dat's no a place fur a fine lass laek dee!'

'I managed, but I widna laek ta bide dere. Hit's dirty an croodit, an der a braa niff i da air.'

'Weel, du'll certainly gyet rid o dat apön da trip haem! We sood be blaan dere wi dis fine stoor o wind.'

'Whaa dö I gie da fare tae?'

'Da mate acts as purser sae he'll tak dy penga, dunna wirry. If du laeks, I can ship dee oot noo. A'm no awaar o ony idder passengers.'

Mary climbed into the flit-boat which, already loaded with several tea-chests and sacks, was rowed out to the vessel. Another sailor onboard the sloop leaned over and offered a hand to take her kishie and help her up. His face was familiar, too – she thought he was maybe from Skeotaing or da Brunthill.

'Yun's Lowrie; he's da mate an da man ta see aboot dy fare.' Mary thanked him and smoothed down her coat and tucked in her hap. Lowrie indicated where on deck she could find a place to sit, relatively out of the way of the rigging and offering a little shelter. The fare would be a shilling. She was relieved to know that she would get home with a little of her savings intact and Mr Buchan's crown still untouched: she had sewn the coin carefully into the lining of her coat-pocket and could feel it when she wanted to check it was safe.

Now, at last, she felt she could relax a little, even if all her energy would be needed to keep warm. She had time to look back at Scallowa and admire its houses and the way it nestled neatly along the shore. She knew that the local people resented the fact that Lerwick had gradually usurped the role of capital. The fishing on the east coast and all the summer trade with the Dutchies and the Low Countries had eclipsed that of Scallowa; and the law courts too had moved from Tingwall.

Just as the sun rose above the Clift hills, the crew raised the fore-sail and the *Hawk* nudged slowly round by the Wastshore. As soon as the channel widened, the main-sail was hoisted. The young deck-hand she had first met introduced himself as Mathou o' Riskaness. He pointed out the various skerries as the sloop made her way westwards.

'We'll keep bi nort o da Green Holm an dan head oot atween Papa Skerry an Langa. Der a lock o baas here aboot. But aald Tammie o Germatwatt is a safe skipper.'

The skies had lost all the excited bird sounds associated with summer breeding, but the occasional shag sped by, its wing beat mesmerising as it skimmed the waves; or a cormorant silently dipped under the surface and popped up further on. The wind picked up as they left the lea of the land and headed out into the Atlantic, bearing south of the island of Hildasay.

'Dis da Middle Channel, Mary. Hit'll shön be 50 faddom deep!' Mathou fell into easy conversation with her, saying how different Da Peerie Isles looked when you were near them, compared to when you saw them from the Scord at Weisdale. Mary could see several small houses on the isles and wondered how the folk managed to keep body and soul together. There was so little land to cultivate or pasture a cow. But they would no doubt have plenty fish.

'Whaa aans yun muckle haa-hoose near da castle, Mathou?'

'Yun's Jeems Scott. I tink his midder was a Scott fae Melby, Sannis… an Vaila… an his faider maybe a Scallowa Scott. But der laekly aa relatit! Onyway, yun Jeems, he mairried wi a Katherine Sinclair – shö hed forbears fae da Houss estate an Bruce o Sumburgh, an some Scott forbears an aa, sae nae doot da pair o dem is come inta money. Saa du yun fancy coat o airms abön der door?'

'Dat I did. Is hit da Scott een?'

'Ya, I tink sae,' he replied.

'I warn da Mitchells o Wastshore 'll be feelin kinda owreshadowed bi yun haa, wid du say, Mathou?'

'Na, na. Nae shöner wis Jeems Scott gotten his haa biggit here dan didna Sir Andrew Mitchell bigg a even graander-laek een at

Saand, whaar he shippit oot his faemly i da simmer time – hit wis his "simmer residence" I hear tell! Hit's Sir John Mitchell's noo, fur da aald man is dead.'

'Oh, noo du says dat, A'm heard dat afore. Dat's da haa wi steyn ta'en fae da castle here… an fancy wid-wark… an wan o yun armorial panels an aa! Dat's whaar Hogg an his faemly wis billeted yun time.'

'Dat's da very wan! Noo, I better geng below an check da cargo for Skeld. We'll be gyaain in dere ta unlodd some tae an mel an saat. Hit'll tak a ooer or sae ta win in an oot o Skelda Voe an da brucks o anidder ooer tae unlodd. Da wind is steady, no richt ahint wis, sae we sood hae a fine trip as lang as we dunna end up apö da Braga Skerry!'

Mary stood up to stretch her legs and pull her hap closer. She had put on an extra gansey before they set off from Scallowa and was glad that she had brought it as there was little shelter. She nibbled an oatcake and had a drink of the milk Mistress Anderson had given her. The open ocean was an unknown quantity and yet another novel experience for her. Eventually, the sleety showers cleared and she could see Foula crisply contoured on the horizon. It was not an identical profile to the one she could see from Waas, but she thought it just as lovely.

The crew were kept busy as the *Hawk* was suddenly on a run into Skelda Voe, bucking and heaving. By the time they reached the jetty, the sun was at its zenith and the sailors keen to unload quickly and be underway as the second half of the journey would be slightly longer. Mary tried to keep out of the way. She was amazed how they all seemed to know exactly what they had to do, whether dealing with ropes or sails or cargo.

They cast off again within the hour, tacking to the open ocean and, once they had rounded Skelda Ness, they headed north-west to Vaila Soond. The wind was fresh, having veered more to the west: however, despite the sounds of ropes being let out or pulled in, or the boom passing overhead, or water slapping on the hull, she drifted off to sleep. She was eventually wakened with a sudden movement of the boom. The cliffs were nearer now, and she could see the occasional kittiwake sheltering.

Mathou came over again and chatted. 'Noo dan. Dat wis a fine rest fur dee! Sees du yun rain-gös near in tae da banks, Mary?'

'Oh, I didna recognise him in his winter plumage; nae red neck. Oh, he's disappeared... I winder whaar he'll come up again? Is yun... da back o Vaila comin up... an da Broch o Culswick? A'm nivver seen hit fae da sea afore.'

'Dat hit is. We'll no be lang noo.'

He went on to tell her a bit about his family at Riskaness. They were all a bit older than Mary, so she had never really known them although she knew of the family name.

'Whit browt dee ta Lerrick, Mary?' She had been waiting for that question to surface and had decided she would tell the truth. After all, everyone would know soon enough, so why not let this friendly, helpful lad be the bearer of the news.

'I towt dat wis aa blown owre last year,' he said.

'Naethin is dat aesy, Mathou. Da kirk seems ta hadd da reins, an... I med a silly mistak. But I hae a lovely peerie lass caa'd Babsie an I widna pairt wi her, no even fur da finest haa hoose.'

'Göd fur dee, lass. Hit's no aesy bein young. A'm coortin wi a lass fae Houll, sae I better no gyet her inta trouble or shö could be settin aff fur Lerrick an aa!'

They both laughed at that and the conversation turned to the coastline which was now close. Light was fading, the sky gold and dark grey ripped apart here and there by strips of salmon pink; and Foula black on the skyline. With the wind behind them as they negotiated the Aester Soond, they reduced sail and Mary was excited to see all the well-known sights of Waas Voe, albeit from a different angle. Her eyes had become accustomed to the dusk. They were soon tying up at the Bayhaa jetty and the crew fell to unloading and shifting the goods to the nearby store. Mary was helped off the sloop, got her kishie on her back, thanked them and set off for Brunatwatt, her torment at presbytery all but behind her. She was well aware there would be more obstacles ahead and that, unlike Mathou, marriage for her was more than likely completely out of the question. But at least she would soon be reunited with her loved ones and she could not get up the Stove trenkie quickly enough.

Babsie was still up, on Christian's lap, as Mary lifted the sneck. Immediately, her little arms and legs started to wave wildly. She reached out to Mary who threw down her kishie and took the child in her arms and danced her round and round to the child's skirls of delight. For Mary, everything that meant home and comfort was here in this small, sparsely plenished room with its winter fire of summer toil, its steady koli lamp, its earthen floor polished by the footfall of her family.

Baabie was the one to break the spell, 'Du's won haem, jewel. We ir da blyde ta see dee safe an soond. Come du inta da fire an waarm dee.'

Sunday 3rd December 1775
Stove and Waas kirk

The first fine day after returning from Lerwick, Mary had delivered the crown to Mr Buchan with a note of thanks. She was now more determined than ever that she was not going to be worn down by the ignominy of appearing, in repentance mode, seventeen times before the congregation. She would be contrite, as was required of her, but not abased. Somehow, she would get through it. She knew that many in the parish had fornicated or indulged in ante-nuptial relations, had brought children into the world outwith the official married state, or had even committed adultery. The sexual improprieties of some sitting in the pews would be well-known, some unknown; there would be some who had paid a price and some who had gone undetected and unpunished. And there would be the self-righteous and the proud. And the envious, too. She knew also that there would be some who still believed the old superstitions that an individual's fall from grace put the whole community at risk, causing storms or crop failures or bouts of illness. But that there were many others who were good-hearted and just wanted her back into full communion with them.

Jaanie was glad to have Mary and Babsie back staying at Stove. She was able to cope with looking after the little girl, with Willm's help, for the time Mary would be at the kirk. In her simple dark overcoat and freshly dressed hap, Mary was ready for the toll of the bell summoning the congregation for the noon service. Over their eleven o'clocks, Jaanie could tell her there was general contempt these days in Stove for kirk elders who paraded their disapproval of the minister seen to be going soft on people, especially miscreant men: whether it was interrogating them privately in the vestry rather than before the whole session, or baptising infants before the offending parents' discipline was completed.

'I dunna tink da Stove fock is aa dat buddered noo-a-days, Mary. I canna understaand why elders wid tink laek yun onywye: shurly a infant is entirely blameless.'

Before the service began, Mary had spoken briefly with her mother and Christian in the family pew. Jean, who was at home still nursing her baby boy – born just as the last corn screw was weighted down in hairst – had sent her love. As Mary moved forward to sit alone at the front, on the seat of repentance, she saw Erchie turn his head and acknowledge her. Others looked understandably awkward. They had all seen many young women sit there, with bowed heads, looking ill at ease. Many parishioners were uncomfortable with the practice, the ritual humiliation, but some still took pleasure in the power accrued to the kirk session over centuries.

Mary let the service wash over her, keeping in her mind's eye the day Erchie had rushed to find his bible to show her the passage about the ritual stoning of the woman taken in adultery and how Jesus had challenged the men – the Deyells of this world – with their hypocrisy and their barbaric practice. It made her feel stronger each time she thought of it. While she was willing to thole the imposition of public repentance – and was genuinely sorry for what she realised was rash and thoughtless behaviour – in her heart she felt no real gutting sense of guilt. Babsie would never be allowed to feel the sting of illegitimacy; she would know she was deeply loved and wanted.

Towards the end of the service, Mr Buchan told Mary to stand. Her seat being at right angles to the congregation, and to the side, meant that she was seen by both the minister and congregation. The parishioners were well used to the performance: some particularly enjoyed the vicarious pleasure of a sexual misdemeanour; others wished the minister would not prolong the proceedings so they could get home to their dinners; some felt sorry for the penitent and could imagine the humiliation.

From the pulpit, Mr Buchan turned slightly to face her and intoned slowly: 'Mary Johnsdaughter, do you confess your sin of adultery before this congregation?'

'I do.' She kept her head steady.

'And do you repent of this sin and beseech the congregation to accept you back into its fellowship, notwithstanding the former offence?'

'I do'. She dropped her gaze a little.

'To fulfil the church's discipline, you will be required to attend Divine worship each Sunday it is held here, on sixteen more occasions. You may be seated. Let us all confess our sins... let us pray...'

Many of the congregation were quick to leave after the service, no doubt embarrassed for Mary or unsure what they might say to her. Her family waited in their pew and walked out with her. She could see Robbie Henry o Breck skulking in the porch, waiting to be called to appear before the session which was about to meet. There was no shortage of parishioners to summon. Tongues would no doubt be wagging on the gaet to Stove.

That was it; the first of seventeen such Sunday mornings. And she had survived. Agnes Slatter walked up the brae with them.

'Lass, du did weel, sittin dere sae prunk an boannie! I canna ken whit why da session dusna gie up on dis kind o thing. Wis weemen is sittin targets; da men can möv aroond, or disappear! ... An saa du Robbie o Breck yundroo daday? Seeminly he wunna admit he's da faider o da Irvine lass's bairn; her dat's servant at Scarvister. I hear shö's due ony day noo. He admits he's lain wi her, but da bugger is tryin ta mak oot dat he maybe wisna da only een. I tink hit's terrible ta traet a lass laek dat.'

'Less a less,' said Baabie. 'For siccan a onkerry. I heard dat someen wis reportit da Elvister lass dat mairried wi Joannie Jamieson. But der baith denyin der bairn is due afore da nine mont is up. Da elders is seeminly referred hit till Providence sheds some licht apön hit! Wid you believe hit? Hit's jöst stupeed aald men watchin da bellies o young weemen, mairried or no mairried. I heard da couple hed ta pay der fine jöst in case. I hoop dey gyet hit back, even if da Poor Box could dö wi da money!'

Thursday 4th January 1776
Brunatwatt

By now Mary had appeared before the congregation five times. She was glad that Stove was near the kirk so that even when it was a gale or heavy rain or snow she was still able to get there. Some who were now joining her on the repentance bench as penitents had longer journeys and often arrived soaked through and shivering. The kirk was a cold hole in winter when the sun hardly rose in the sky and the draughts sneaked in. Jean Irvine, the servant girl from Scarvister, had appeared as demanded on the first Sunday of the New Year, despite still nursing her baby. And Robbie o Breck, who continued to deny fathering her bairn, appeared for his third censure. He had paid £3 Scots by way of fornication fine and once he had coughed up another crown he would be absolved. The girl would get nothing but a bad name. Mary had thought that the way they were sitting, not looking at one another, seemed to suggest an icy blast had swept over the Hill o Scarvister. Others had shared the bench too, but the Elvister couple, who were adamant they had not had antenuptial relations, had recently got their consignation money back from the treasurer. Providence had spoken and come down on their side!

Mary was forced to acknowledge she had a long way to go to put this whole business behind her; but today was her brother John's wedding day and a time for a happy celebration. She, Babsie and Willm were all going to Brouster for the marriage and the party. His bride, Betty, and her Brouster folk were known as kindly and sociable. Jaanie had been invited too, but did not feel she was able to make the journey, especially since it would be late by the time she got home.

Mary had arranged that she and the children would be at Brunatwatt overnight as the bride and groom were going to stay at Brouster after their wedding, which would go on till the small hours, arriving at Brunatwatt the next day in time for a second night of celebration with more friends and family. Baabie, Joannie and Christian had said they would help Mary return with the children and they could have the ben-end before it was made ready for the new couple.

She had worked hard at Stove to finish the week's laundry and had laid in enough food, fuel and water for Jaanie for the weekend. Jaanie had made a jacket for Willm which made him look so much older and a neighbour had handed in a little pinafore dress that could fit Babsie. Jaanie had overseen Mary ironing all its tucks and frills. They both knew from experience that it would be dribbled on and crushed before the afternoon was over, but they took delight in dressing up the little toddler, camouflaging her warm woollen clothing. All their clothes were ready and folded; they would drop along Brunatwatt as early as possible so that Mary could help with any last minute preparation before they left for the wedding. She packed her kishie with everything they would need, as well as food she had prepared as gifts for the wedding table, and set off with the two children. It was a cold, crisp day, but luckily without a threat of snow. Getting home in the dark was difficult enough without all the gaets being masked. The sky should remain clear and the almost full moon would help light their paths.

Brunatwatt was already a busy place, with a tee of reesit mutton being sliced, fresh butter packed up and bannocks baked. Soup was also being simmered for the next day when they expected family and friends to join them for a second night of jollification.

It was Jean's turn to miss out on the first night of a family wedding as her baby was still very young, but she planned to be there for part of the second night. She was also keen to help with preparations. The three sisters took turns looking after the two little children. Willm did jobs to help Joannie: feeding the hens and scaring off the flock of linties which descended on the seed; chopping kindling with a steady hand and occasionally entertaining Babsie when she became fretful.

By now it was time to get ready, with the usual pressure on the washstand. But they helped one another, and all were declared smart enough to be on their way. Thoughts strayed to Jaerm and Eliza; at family occasions like a wedding, they were particularly missed. Jean waved as she returned to her own home, happy with her new life as wife and mother, but glad to have spent time with her own folk.

It was just a mile to Brouster. They called along their Musawatter neighbours on the way and by the time they reached their destination they were a happy band, glad to be indoors, their heavy garments cast aside.

Betty had on a lovely dress specially made for the occasion: it was of blue and white floral cotton, flowing down from the waist and with a neat bodice. A loose white muslin stole lay around her shoulders. John had on his best shirt and collar to set off his suit. They were a handsome pair.

Mr Buchan had already arrived and soon had the marriage ceremony underway. Mary felt a strange combination of happiness and sadness. It would be good to have Betty at Brunatwatt, but family life would change as they settled into the croft there and, by the time she would return for voar, Mary knew that, however well everyone got on and worked together, things would be different. Betty would need to be given her place as the wife of the tenant-crofter; Baabie and Joannie would be the old folk, and it would be time for Mary and Christian to be moving on with their own lives. Christian would no doubt marry and leave home, and she would be left, the maiden aunt, unmarriageable. Erchie's kind offer came back to her. She tried to ignore all these conflicting thoughts: after all, this was a day for everyone to be happy for the bride and groom.

After the short ceremony, they all transferred to the big barn where trestle tables had been set and food laid out. There had been many gifts of meat, baking, kirn-mylk and butter and the usual sharing of tableware. There was home-brewed ale, a little whisky and what seemed like gallons of tea. The bride and groom were duly toasted, and food and drink passed around. The hours slipped past, everyone seeming to enjoy the chance to celebrate, to have a little excess, and to share it. They had all known lean times.

Once the tables were moved back to clear the floor, Mr Buchan – who was about to leave – came over to speak to Mary and to see Babsie and Willm. He commented on what a fine child Babsie was and asked after Jaanie. Before slipping away, he commended Mary for her diligence in attending the services, acknowledging that it was difficult for her on her own.

The Brig o Waas fiddler struck up and the dancing started. He played for *Da Aald Reel* an for *Da Muckle Reel o Finnigart* and several other Shetland reels. Babsie was dancing in Mary's arms, enjoying the excitement. Baabie held her for a little while to allow Mary to show Willm how to do a Foula Reel, her favourite dance. He was enjoying meeting up with some of his friends from school: together and emboldened, they sneaked around the dark perimeter of the adult company for food or simple pranks. Both the Brouster and Brunatwatt families seemed pleased with the union and the young couple did indeed appear well-matched.

Eventually Mary could sense both Willm and Babsie were tiring and she too felt the need to get home. She was vexed she would miss the special bride's reels and the bridegroom's reels towards the end of the evening: the ones where first all the women danced together, the men sweeping the bride with brushes of gloy, of finest straw, each brush decorated with a ribbon; and then followed by the men dancing together and the woman wielding the brushes. It was always a merry finale with coy kisses. Christian was happy to leave as well, knowing she would have another chance to enjoy herself on the second night. They thanked their hosts, said goodnight to the wedding party and invited everyone to Brunatwatt the next evening.

Dressed for the cold, they stepped out into the bright moonlight. Willm had never seen such a huge moon with its beaming face so clearly delineated. Mary remembered that the next day would be Aald Yöl Ee'n and she reminded him that Santy Claas might come. She had already prepared an old woollen sock, with a cup and ball toy she had from her own childhood and some sweet buns she had baked. Jaanie had added a few pennies. In her mind's eye she could see herself as a child catching the ball with Christian watching spell-bound, and could imagine Willm similarly demonstrating how it worked to a delighted Babsie.

Friday 5th January 1776 – Old Christmas Eve
Brunatwatt and Stove

It was well past nine o'clock on Aald Yöl Ee'n before the first light lifted over the Gallow Hill and the family gradually awoke to a fine, still, wintry morning with the lightest dusting of snow.

It was to be another busy day making preparations to welcome the young bride to Brunatwatt and all the guests who might come for the second night of the wedding. The barn had to be cleared, the cows fed and mucked out, a baking and a kirnin done as well as getting ready for the evening. The Grötquoy cousins and the Laings would be bringing reestit mutton, salt beef and bannocks. The Brouster folk had killed a pig in preparation for the wedding and had promised a bit of fresh pork. The adults took turns keeping an eye on Babsie who was tottering around behind them, grabbing at skirts and furniture. Willm helped Mary and Joannie sweep and prepare the barn, gather eggs, feed the hens and tend the cows. He

THE TRIALS OF MARY JOHNSDAUGHTER

missed the calf: the young stot had been sold some months earlier, but Bessie, the other cow, was due to calve in the spring.

While Babsie had a nap, Mary did the churning. Christian and her mother baked and cleaned and prepared the ben-end for the bride and groom. Jean and her baby joined them for dinner, after which Mary felt it was time to take the children back to Stove. The sun would dip over the Hill o' Voe by three o'clock and it would soon darken. Jean offered to follow her part of the way as her baby was sleeping.

Willm was keen to lead the way, which gave the sisters a chance to chat. Mary had Babsie bound close to her chest, wrapped around with her hap, her little feet poking out towards the kishie. She was playing a game with her mother: every time Mary opened her mouth she would push her hand over it and skirl and bounce with delight. Jean carried her for a bit and the game continued till she tired of it.

'Shö is da boanniest ting o bairn, Mary… kinda laek Christian is shö no?'

'Ya, I wid say so… der baith laek Midder. Shö's bön nae budder raelly. I jöst hoop we can aa steer clear o scarlet fever. I hear hit's gyaain aroond.'

'Dat's a horrid thing. At laest at dis time o year we hae plenty maet laid in an dunna need ta geng ta da shop muckle.'

'But I hae ta geng tae da kirk!'

'Whitna strug dat man be, especially trowe da winter. Wis hit seeventeen times? I tink der a braa twartree fock a coarn surprised at da severity o da decision. I tocht tree was bad enyoch!'

'But we hae wir peerie bairns, Jean.'

'Dat we dö. I can hardly mind whit wir aald life wis laek, Mary. Da days o da *Batchelor o Leith* seem laek a lifetime awa.'

'Nivver spaek,[21] lass. A'm owre blyde hit feels laek dat. But I dö miss Jaerm an Eliza.'

'Ya, I tink wir fock misses dem awfil. But dey'll hae Betty noo, an shö's lichtsome an göd-naitired.'

---

21 Oh dear, don't even mention it.

'An a herd-wirkin lass an aa, an a fine makker. Whin John's at da Far Haaf, shö'll help keep aathin gyaain. I winder whit wir Christian 'll dö, Jean? Shö's nearly sixteen noo an luikin dat grown up.'

'Shö's a göd lass, Mary.'

'Weel I hoop shö's laerned fae wir mistaks! Shö's a boannie lass an I hae nae doot da laads 'll be eftir her.'

'Sniffin aroond nae doot!'

'Jean! Dunna say dat. Noo, du sood gyet on dy wye back ta Brunatwatt. I hoop you aa hae a fine time danicht an nae sair heads come damoarn. I can tak paes dis helly fur der nae service, sae I hae a Sunday aff!'

'Tell Jaanie I wis axin fur her.'

'Dat I will.'

Sunday 4th February 1776
Waas kirk

Candlemas had come and gone, and despite Mary being aware of some partying in the vicinity of Jaanie's on Friday evening, she had kept a low profile. She had returned from the kirk service, her third since New Year, and was now almost half-way through her penance. Jean Irvine, the lass who had been a maid at Scarvister, had shared the seat of repentance with her along with Robbie o' Breck. Still denying paternity, he had handed in the final crown of his penalty for fornication and had been absolved. It was wonderful what a coin could do in the laundry of the soul.

Mr Buchan had intimated that the communion season had started and that he would be visiting families in Mid Waas. He would cover the west side of the Burn o Setter on Monday and as many as he could manage on the east side of the burn on Tuesday. No doubt catechisms would be dusted off. In his pocket he would have communion tokens for those deemed worthy of the Lord's Table; those little oval disks with their cautionary text from 1st

Corinthians chapter 11 stamped on the grey pewter – 'Let a man examine himself'. Mary knew that this year there would be no token for her, or for Jean Sinclair. No sooner had she joined the kirk, but she had been swept aside in a wave of moral indignation. She could see the elders seated round the tables with the white cloths, the pewter flagon and cup to hand, and the broken loaf. There would be special services of preparation. They would partake, and she would miss them all. Many a time her mother, following a visit from the minister, had pointed out to her father the wording on the token. It was her opinion that the parish would be a much better place if men were less in control of things and more aware of their short-comings. But Baabie, along with her daughters, had to admit that Mr Buchan was diligent despite his advancing years: he put the parish and the school ahead of himself, and had even been up to Scord several times to visit old Archibald Henry, father of Thomas, who was known to be dying. They wondered when he would manage to fit in his own wedding. It was rumoured that he was going to attend the General Assembly of the Church of Scotland in Edinburgh in May and that he might be planning to get married down south.

As they were the last to leave the kirk, save the minister and beadle who were in the vestry, Mary had a chance to speak to Jean Irvine.

'Foo's dy baby gyettin on? Hit most be herd hae'in ta laeve him sae young, an come a fair piece.'

'He's fine, Mary, tanks. A'm back wi mi ain fock eenoo, but Göd kens whit'll happen later. I wid need ta be wirkin again. I hae ta pay in tree an fowrpence neist mont afore I can gyet dis discipline dismissed.'

'Hit seems hit's wis dat hae ta pay da price, wan wye or tidder.'

'Du's richt dere. Dat lipper – hit maks me mad ta tink he disowns his ain flesh an blöd, an me an aa. Feth, I tink da bairn is da very face o him, sae he'll no be able ta deny hit furivver.'

'Dat wis raelly a horrible thing ta dö ta dee.'

'An dis elders here… der een or twa o dem I can tell dee dat wid grab you as quick as luik at you, if dey tocht dey could gyet awa wi hit.'

'Du's richt dere, Jean. A'm already fun dat oot! Some men luik at me differently noo. But der no aa laek dat!'

'I man say, Mary, I admire da wye du jöst sits dere, sae calm. Hit kinda gies me courage.'

'A'm still barely half-gaets trowe hit, but I hoop I can hadd hit tagidder. Maybe A'll skyip doon da aisle apö da hidmist Sunday!'

'We could hae a peerie bonfire o da sackcloot! Weel, I ken we dunna hae ta wear hit noo, but hit kinda feels laek hit's hingin aboot wis.'

They laughed as they went off in opposite directions, hoping they had not been overheard.

When she got back from the service, Mary could see Jaanie was noticeably struggling to look after Babsie; she determined that she would ask Christian to come along Stove on Sunday mornings rather than accompany her to the kirk. She would miss knowing Christian was in the family pew, but Jean and her man were back at the kirk now and John and Betty, so there would be plenty of family support.

'A'm sorry, Mary, A'm no managed to get da tatties on ta boil or cut up a bit o kale.'

'Nivver leet dat, Jaanie. We'll hae hit raedy in nae time ava.'

Mary set to getting their dinner ready. Before leaving for church, she had put a hen on to simmer which a neighbour had killed for them, so it was at the stage of falling apart. It wasn't long before they were all tucking into tasty platefuls with plenty left for tomorrow and good stock for broth.

'A'm hoopin Walter 'll be haem afore voar, Mary, fur I dunna tink I can kerry on muckle langer wi takkin in wyshin if du's no aroond ta dö da haevy wark.'

'Eence I möv back ta Brunatwatt, I could try an come here ivery moarnin if da fock can manage ithoot me. But A'm sure Walter 'll be haem shön an dat'll mak a differ.'

Monday 22nd April 1776
Stove

Mary was apprehensive as she approached Jaanie's house. She was back home at Brunatwatt with Babsie but still helping Jaanie every morning except Sunday. When she left on Saturday, she knew that the long-awaited Walter would probably be home the following day. She had carried extra water and peats in and prepared some food that would keep. Something in her bones nagged at her – how would she manage to step back from her close relationship with Jaanie and Willm without hurting the little boy?

She had waited until she knew Willm would be well on his way to school. Jaanie was sitting by the fire with Walter when she entered. He seemed somewhat older than she had remembered – his hair was greying at the temples – but he smiled and got up to shake her hand.

'Fine ta see dee, Mary. I hear du's bön helpin Midder.'

'Göd ta see you, safe an soond, Walter. You man be blyde tae a won haem at last.'

'Weel A'm certainly blyde ta see him,' said Jaanie. 'Hit's bön sic a age.'

'Ya, A'm tinkin ta bide haem aboot noo, if I can fin a job dat suits me. I tink A'm hed enyoch time awa an need ta be here fur Midder an fur Willm. He hardly kent me!'

Mary, who was already hanging up her outer clothes and putting on her apron added, 'I doot dat. He's fairly grown lately – an sic a fine ting he is. Noo, you'll hae ta mak on dat A'm no here: A'll jöst dö whit needs ta be dön an gyet oot o da wye sae you can catch up. He's a fine sook daday sae A'll gyet da wyshin oot an A'll iron hit damoarn.'

'I wis tinkin, Midder, dat if I can gyet a job, dan maybe you could gie up takkin in wyshin.'

'A'm no dat pör aamos yet, Walter!'

'Weel, der nae hurry. As lang as Mary is willin ta help. Noo tell me, Mary, afore du sterts plottin claes, foo's dy fock? A'm luikin forward ta seein dem again. Midder wis tellin me dat Jaerm is awa sailin, an dat John is taen owre as tenant an is gyaain tae da Far Haaf.'

'Wir aa tae da fore, tanks. John is mairried noo – wi Betty o Brouster – sae dey bide wi wis, an Jean is married wi een o da Laing boys neist door, sae shö's fine an clos. Dey hae a peerie boy. An Jaerm does an aa… dey bide in a place caa'd Prestonpans, near Leith. Christian's still at haem of coorse… shö's left scöl noo, jöst helpin da fock.'

'An does Baabie still hae her kye?'

'Dat shö does. I canna see her ithoot dem.'

Mary extricated herself at that point in the conversation, lifting the big kettle of hot water and going through to the back-house, where the wash-tub, soap and laundry were kept. From there she could get out to the drying shed. She suspected that Jaanie had not yet told Walter about Babsie and all the trouble with the kirk. Nor did she know what she felt about the possibility of Jaanie giving up the work. It was hard, especially in cold weather, but they split the money between them and Mary did most of the work. The arrangement worked well and it also meant that Mary was there for Willm too, especially on a Saturday morning when there was no school. That was her favourite day of the week. She always brought Babsie with her, as the little girl loved Willm and, when she wasn't having a nap, Willm often entertained her. On fine days, she would climb into his little wheelbarrow, and he would hurl her around all the alleyways of Stove, much to her delight.

Jaanie called her through for eleven o'clocks, but Mary did not sit down; she put more water on to heat, built up the fire, and drank her tea quickly. Walter was telling his mother about his sailing trips; the ports, the people, the goods transported. And the occasional fever caught.

'Lass, tak paes. Dip dee a meenit.'

'Na, Jaanie, A'll gyet aa da wyshin dön an oot an dan A'll gyet on mi wye. Maybe Walter could tak hit in fur you later? Wid you laek me ta come damoarn or will you manage?'

'Maybe hit wid mak sense ta keep gyaain eenoo, Midder, till I fin wark?'

'Ya, Mary, come du.'

'A'm gyaain alang Bayhaa damoarn ta see if John Henry could dö wi a bit o help. I hear dat da skipper apö da *Hawk* is comin braaly aald an tinkin ta gie up. But of coorse, Henry maybe haes someen idder in mind.'

Mary's thoughts turned to her winter trip from Scallowa on the *Hawk* – the sense of purpose the men displayed. She could see the attraction. Better than the drudgery of a croft, or labouring on someone's else's rig, or enduring the dangers of the Far Haaf.

She finished her rinsing and starching and hanging it all out over slats so that it would dry and not blow away in a gust. Jaanie tried to insist that she stay for a bite of dinner, but she wanted to get home. There would be plenty work to be done at Brunatwatt. And she thought she should be well away before Willm got home from school.

Tuesday 23rd April 1776
Stove

Mary again arrived after Willm had gone off to school.
She set to work while Jaanie managed the heating of the irons. As the fire went down, she took the kishie and went out to the peat stack to load up. Walter took his coat and followed her out, telling his mother he was off to Bayhaa to see if he could speak with John Henry.

'A'll gie dee a haand wi yun, Mary.'

He started filling two kishies before he turned towards her. 'Midder was tellin me dastreen dat du haes a peerie lass noo.'

'Dat I dö, Walter. Some folk micht say "a peerie misanter" but I canna tink o Babsie laek dat ava.'

'An dat du's hed dee a time wi da kirk.'

'Weel, rules is rules, an I brook dem. Sae, what can I lippen?'

'Dat is a peety though.'

'Ee half o me tinks laek dat an da tidder half is very blyde. A'm braaly muddled shurly.'

'Dat ship seems tae a left a braa coarn o flotsam ahint her... hit man a bön a awfil upheaval aroond here.'

'Hit wis a strange time fur aaboady, Walter; but, fur da life o me, fooivver muckle I wiss hit wisna happened laek yun, I canna see mi peerie lass as a trysht. Shö's mi life noo an I jöst hae ta wirk hit oot somewye.'

'I... I didna mean hit dat wye...'

'Mi big regret is haein ta gie up mi job at Happyhansel. I loved wirkin tae da Greigs. But of coorse I laek wirkin wi your midder an aa. Shö's bön dat göd an kind ta me. Noo, I man gyet dat fire med up. I hoop you fin Mr Henry.'

'A'll see foo hit gengs.'

He carried in the peats for her. Mary, while glad to have Babsie's existence no longer a secret between them, felt that burden of shame, the stigma, sneak up on her again, just as she expected it might.

There was no doubt that Walter being at home had eased Jaanie's mind. Mary was pleased to see her old friend move about the house without the usual sighs. They worked all morning, stopping only briefly for their cup of tea. Jaanie still liked to iron the frilly edges and, however hard Mary tried, she never felt she got as perfect a finish as Jaanie.

'I tink dat if Walter does manage ta gyet a job aroond here, he wid laek me ta gie up dis wark, Mary. He says we widna need hit an why sood I be vargin on wi hit.'

'I tink he's richt, Jaanie. An hit is difficult in a peerie hoose tryin ta keep hit oot o da wye, an gyet it aa dried an aired. Especially wi a muckle man aboot!'

'But I love hae'in dee comin here owre da simmer an bidin wi wis i da winter. An Willm, he's da sam.'

'I love hit an aa, but wir no far awa. An Willm is aye comin aalder an he'll shön no be wantin ta be buddered wi me an Babsie. He'll be aff wi da tidder bairns.'

'Weel dat's true, mi joy. But he aye laeks Brunatwatt an da animals; an dy fock is dat göd wi him. Wid du miss da aer o money?

I dunna laek ta tink o dat.'

'But I wid hae mair time ta mak... an help on da croft... sae hit's kinda six o wan an half-dizzen o da tidder. Sae dunna you wirry aboot dat.'

'Weel, dat's a blisseen. I widna laek ta mak dat decision ithoot dee feelin hit wis richt.'

They worked quietly for a bit as they concentrated on the garments. 'You wir sayin aerlier on dat Walter wis hed a nairrow escape fae da Press Gang. Dat man a bön terrifyin.'

'Ya, he telt me dat, wi da war on wi America, da navy is braaly keen ta gyet a hadd o sailors, an der aye smootin aboot ports laek Bristol an London an Liverpool. Seeminly Liverpool can be a violent place... da navy officers is aften in cahoots wi da toon cooncils; but da local folk come oot in thoosands, an riot ta mak hit aakwird fur da Press Gang. Nae doot der money in hit.'

'An some fock dö volunteer, an laekly gyet a bounty fur dat. But I tocht dat captains an mates wis exempt.'

'Weel Mary, dat micht be, but Shetland sailors is laek gowld. He wis sayin if you wir kerryin whale oil or coal – dat muckle in demand – you wir generally safe, but no wi cotton.'

'Nae winder you're blyde he's haem, Jaanie. We jöst hae ta hoop noo dey dunna come seekin seamen roond da back o Vaila!'

Walter returned just as Mary was getting ready to leave for Brunatwatt. She could tell he had been successful from the look on his face.

'Göd news, Midder. John Henry wants me ta stert at da Bayhaa store neist week, jöst general wark an gyaain on some trips wi da *Hawk* sae I gyet ta ken da sloop an da crew an da boats dat wirk tae her. He'll see foo hit gengs, but hit luiks laek aald Tammie o Germatwatt is no wantin ta sail anidder winter. I reckon he man be weel owre seeventy bi noo. An der naeboady aroond eenoo wi muckle navigation experience forbye him.'

'Dat's winderfil, Walter! An du'd be haem maist nichts.'

'Ya, A'm plaised. Hit maybe wunna be as excitin as roondin da Cape o Good Hope, or seein da Suddern Cross or... feelin a waarm air comin affa da sails, but I can live ithoot aa dat!'

'A'm very blyde fur you, Walter,' said Mary. 'An hit'll be göd fur Willm ta hae you aroond an aa. Jaanie an me… we wir jöst spaekin aboot… weel, maybe no wirkin wi dis laundry muckle langer eence you got a job. Sae dunna lat me gyet i da wye o you makkin decisions dat suit your faemily.'

'Tanks, Mary. I tink if you're baith agreeable, we sood white takkin in ony mair… less fur Mistress Henry's fancy collars an cuffs an da laek.'

'An John Tammas Henry's sarks, nae doot!' said his mother. 'Maybe, Mary, du could still come apön a Monday moarnin an we could gyet da Bayhaa laundry wöshen, an wir ain an aa, fur I dunna tink dat I could manage dat noo ithoot dee ta help.'

'Dat wid be nae budder, Jaanie. A'm sure Jean wid luik eftir Babsie if wir fock wis owre trang.'

'But du'll hae ta come alang fur dy tree o'clocks apö Setterday etfirnöns sae we can see peerie Babsie.'

With that agreed, Mary excused herself as quickly as she could, getting on her way home. She knew that the Brunatwatt folk would be stopping soon for their dinner before an afternoon of digging. She would get her spade out.

Saturday 27th April 1776
Brunatwatt and Stove

Saturday morning was busy at Brunatwatt. Mary had been up early to do a churning and then joined Christian, John and Betty planting potatoes. Babsie came for a little while with Mary and took a delight in removing seed potatoes from the kishie and then putting them back in. Betty, in the early stages of pregnancy and feeling a bit tired, was happy to look after Babsie and let Mary get on with the work untrammelled.

After their dinner, Mary cleaned herself up, changed Babsie and set off for Stove with the child who, more and more, was keen to toddle rather than be carried. There were so many distractions for her: a bird, a lamb, a stone, a clump of heath rush. Mary would pull out a stem, a burrie, and let her suck on the end. Eventually, she picked Babsie up, the child wriggling and objecting but easily placated by the promise that Willm would be waiting for her. Suddenly, she saw Willm a few hundred yards from Stove. Mary waved and hurried on, Babsie's legs dancing on her hips. As soon as they met, he went shy as they hadn't seen each other since before his father had arrived. He ran on ahead to announce their arrival, holding the pack of fresh butter Mary had handed him for his granny.

Walter was working dubbin into the household's boots when they came in.

Jaanie reached out to the child. 'Come awa in trowe, bairns. Come du ta me, Babsie, while dy midder taks aff o her. My, my, peerie moot, du's fairly grown.' It was as much as Jaanie could manage to hold the lively child. Meanwhile, the toddler looked at Mary and at Jaanie and then at Walter... and then back to Mary again; suddenly, she went quiet.

'A'm shurly gluffed dee, Babsie!' said Walter.

'Dis is Walter, Babsie. Can du say Walter? He's Willm's faider.' Mary reached over to relieve Jaanie.

The child turned away, but was soon diverted by Willm who had fetched his cup and ball to play with her.

'Tanks fur da butter, Mary. Hit's aye a treat. A'll spread a brönnie fur wis.'

'A'll mak da tae, Jaanie.' Mary propped up Babsie in a chair and Willm sat on the edge to keep her from falling.

Walter put away the boots and dubbin and washed his hands. 'So, foo is aa da Brunatwatt fock daday?'

'Oh, der aa taatie-hael, tanks Walter. Spaekin o taaties, we wir settin dem dis moarnin. You'll gyet some whin we ripe dem.'

'A fresh taatie, lovely. I missed aa dat kind o thing whin I wis sailin. Last nicht I gud doon wi a pock an managed ta come haem wi a dose o sillocks fur wir supper. A'm fairly luikin forward ta gyaain tae da eela come May – da Sletters is said I can geng wi dem.'

'You'll be luikin forward tae your job. Da *Hawk* aye seems ta be on da go. Der shurly nae want o wark fur her.'

'Ya, A'm keen ta gyet stertit.'

They settled to their tea, Mary taking Babsie on her knee. 'Foo got du on at scöl dis week, Willm? Ony new sums?'

'We wir döin lang multiplication dis week. I laek big sums. But if you dunna set dem oot richt, you get da wrang answer!'

'I doot dat. Du's lucky fur du's aye at da scöl. A lock o da bairns is laekly aff noo ta help wi voar.'

'Ya, der no sae mony eenoo.'

By now, Babsie was reaching over to Walter and pulling his sleeve.

'Wid du come ta me dan?' But she backed off as soon as he spoke in his deep voice.

'Shö'll shön come roond, Walter,' said Jaanie. 'Shö's jöst no wint wi dee yet.'

'A'll need ta come alang an see dy fock, Mary.'

'Come you alang aboot da nicht ony time dat suits you. An of coorse you're aa wylcom. Wir kinda prammed in eenoo, whit wi John an Betty hae'in da ben-end. Christian is bön awfil göd an löt me an Babsie hae da closet – shö's up i da laft whaar da boys used ta be!'

'A'll come shön afore John gengs ta da Far Haaf.'

'He says he's no gyaain ta da lodges da year… he wants ta come haem as muckle as he can, although hit's a braa stramp ta win haem.'

'Dat soonds göd. Maybe he'll bring some cod livers or raans wi him!' Walter replied.

It was not long before Babsie wanted down on to the floor where she could move around between Jaanie, Willm and Mary. Soon, she ventured towards Walter. He had picked up the snorie-ben, a toy made of bone that he had made for Willm, and she was fascinated enough by its whirr and spin to forget she was unsure of this new person and came to him, laughing and reaching out to grab the toy. Willm was amused by her antics.

'Faider is tinkin we micht gyet a boat, Mary.'

'Dat soonds awfil fine, Willm. I nivver hed onythin mair is a peerie seggy-boat: a richt boat wid be speeshil.' But she looked a little anxiously at Walter in case the child had meant the *Hawk*.

'We'll hae ta see, Willm. Richt enyoch, I wis tinkin hit wid be göd ta hae a fowrareen, wi a sail an aa, an we could geng ta da eela or maybe catch a olick. A'm gyaain ta hae a luik aroond ta see if onyboady haes een ta sell.'

Eventually, it was time to set off for home and Mary promised she would be back on Monday morning to help Jaanie with the Henrys' washing, which their maid usually brought early.

'Is du still hae'in ta sit at da front o da kirk, Mary?'

'Ya, Jaanie, but no fur muckle langer... I tink damoarn 'll be my... sixteent time! Sae hit's jöst wan mair eftir dat afore I can sit wi da fock again.'

'A'll laekly hae ta shaa mi face at da kirk afore lang,' said Walter. 'Willm, will du come wi me or bide wi granny?'

'I tink... I tink... A'll bide wi granny.'

'Oh weel dan, I tink we'll leave hit dis Sunday.'

Sunday 12th May 1776
Waas kirk

It was Mary's final Sunday: her seventeenth appearance before the congregation to repent of her adulterous relationship with Alexander Ross. His name no longer unsettled her; no longer conjured up those mixed emotions. It was more than two years since the *Batchelor* had sailed out the voe. She thought of that day only in terms of her brother who had befriended him; of Jaerm leaving, and now of his little family settled so far away in Prestonpans. She hoped she might be able to ask Mr Buchan if he could take a letter south for Jaerm and Eliza when he went. Mary had dressed herself doucely and Christian had fixed her hair for her, before covering it with a light scarf. Joannie, who had no intention of going to the kirk while Mary was still under discipline, had opted to look after Babsie to allow all the others to accompany her.

The day was calm and sunny, and there was a goodly number at church. Walter had brought Willm for the first time. Everyone was fascinated by the news that Mr Buchan would soon leave for Edinburgh where he would marry Miss Agatha Cumming of Garderhouse on the next sabbath day, which just happened to be Ascension Sunday. There was still a degree of disbelief in the parish. How could a young woman of twenty-five marry an old man of seventy? And he looked his years. The minister's pew would soon be occupied again. There were those who had laughed that she might wear a stylish hat in summer weather – something wide-brimmed and decorated with flowers and feathers held in place in the Shetland wind by a ribbon or scarf. There were those who, knowing she would expect the best of everything, including china, said, 'Dat een 'll no hae morroless trunshers!'[22] It was thought she had insisted she bring her own lady's maid to Voe House. Some said he was taking an extended tour and would not be back till later in the year; that the Northmavine minister was coming instead. Some said Buchan would live to regret it. Some shook their heads and muttered, 'der nae föls laek aald föls!'

Mary, illuminated by the noon sun streaming through the kirk window, sat alone on the seat of repentance. She was enjoying the peace and warmth of the beams playing on her through the dimpled glass. Though her face was inscrutable, her heart was singing. She was determined to keep her composure for this last test of her resolve. So many girls had been broken by this process.

Towards the end of the service, Mr Buchan turned to Mary and asked her to stand. His voice was strong and steady. 'Mary Johnsdaughter, do you confess before this congregation your guilt of adultery?'

'I do.'

'And do you believe in the forgiveness of transgressions and our need, as sinners, to put ourselves right with God?'

'I do.'

'I now turn to the congregation. Do you agree that Mary

---

22 She will expect, and have the best (lit. 'She'll not have unmatched plates').

Johnsdaughter has now fulfilled all the obligations as directed by presbytery and that she be accepted back into full communion with you, as her brothers and sisters in God?'

There was a general ripple of approval. They knew the drill from years of practice.

'I ask ten of our elders to represent you in extending the right hand of fellowship to our sister and to welcome her back into the community of the godly.'

As Mary looked at each one in turn as they shook her hand, it seemed to her that the elders, though grave in expression, genuinely had accepted her confession. Mr Buchan kissed her lightly on the cheek, a brotherly kiss, and put his hand on her head in blessing. Deyell was nowhere to be seen, for which she was thankful. It was over.

Mr Greig waited for her at the end of the Happyhansel pew. 'Bliss dee, Mary, du's gotten trowe wi dis at last! I hoop du can pit hit aa ahint dee. A'm bön instructit ta write ta presbytery ta say da Waas kirk session is willing tae absolve dee. Mr Buchan was keen ta gyet hit dön afore he gengs awa an afore da neist communion season sterts. Nae doot he haes a braa lock on his mind eenoo!' He smiled and walked up the aisle with her, Erchie just behind. 'Noo, Erchie and me… we wir jöst winderin if du tocht dat Christian micht laek ta wirk ta wis. Or if dat micht be aakwird. No in charge laek du wis, but helpin wi da wark. Naeboady seems ta be able ta dö as muckle as du wis able tae!'

'Tanks, Mr Greig. A'm sure shö wid, but A'll ax her an… wir fock… an see whit shö says. Wid dat be eftir da simmer?'

'I wid say edder Whitsun or Lammas wid be fine, if dat suitit her.'

By now Mary was able to join her family and move towards the door with them. She could see Walter and Willm a little ahead of them.

Mr Buchan was at the door to shake hands, but the worshippers were a bit unsure what to say and could only nod by way of acknowledgement.

'Ah, Mary! You've done well. I know it's been hard on you. I've written many testimonials in my time and I would have no difficulty in writing one for you, should you ever need one. I trust little Babsie is well? I hope to be visiting in Brunatwatt before too long… and will look forward to seeing her again.'

'Thank you, sir. I was wondering if it might be possible for you to take a letter to Edinburgh for Jerome and Eliza; and if it might be possible to get it to Prestonpans?'

'That would be a pleasure, Mary. There are lots of church officers at the General Assembly and messages being taken all over, so I can include that one.'

'Thank you so much, sir. And can I wish you and Miss Cumming a very happy marriage.'

He smiled and acknowledged her good wishes.

The family soon caught up with the Stove folk and Willm sought out Mary.

'Why wis du sittin on dy ain, Mary?'

'I brook een o da rules, sae I wis taen oot tae da front; jöst laek at scöl sometimes. But du's nivver bön taen oot tae da front is du, Willm?' He laughed, and somehow seemed content with that answer.

Walter congratulated her on her composure. 'Yun wis aafil, Mary. I canna believe whit du's hed ta geng trowe. Yun wid brack mony a boady.' She shook her head and said she did not really know how she had found the strength to get through it, but she was determined to put it behind her.

As they came to the brow of the Stove brae, suddenly there was a commotion on the skerry, the scolding cry of arctic terns returning.

Walter was first to say, 'Da tirricks is here! Mind I said, Willm, dat I'd be back haem afore dem!'

Everyone stopped and watched the excitement, the diving and lifting; the pairs, already reunited, arguing with others over nesting sites; the solitary ones, still waiting in hope that their mate would arrive shortly, despite an incredible journey endured.

Gradually, folk peeled off and went home for their dinner. Babsie was happy to see them all return. Joannie had his own way of celebrating Mary's release from discipline. 'Noo dan, Mary Johnsdochter, du luiks muckle da sam as whin du gud oot dis moarnin.'

'Ya, Faider, A'm still med o clay, da sam as you. But A'll watch mi step. Naeboady 'll mak a föl o me again.'

With that, she lifted her child, hugged her and then, on request, swung her around till she laughed and laughed.

After dinner, she said, 'I wis tinkin ta tak Babsie oot for a turn i da sunsheen; maybe doon tae da mill an up owre da Scord o Brouster an haem bi Musawatter. Wid ony o you want ta come an aa?' All except Christian agreed that they needed a day of rest after their week's work. She was keen to accompany her older sister. They set off, Babsie alternately around Mary's waist or up on her shoulders, with Christian taking the child from time to time. One or other occasionally made 'clip-clop' sounds with their tongue, which amused the toddler.

'Hit'll no be lang afore du's owre heavy fur dis, Babsie!' But Babsie was enjoying the moment. Mary felt lighter in heart than she had for a long time.

They stopped at their mill which lay to the east of their rigs, where Clokka Burn flowed out of the Loch of Brunatwatt. The mill lade was shut off, so most of the water was in the burn. They sat and watched its movement: dancing over and between stones, lingering where it flowed more slowly, the brown-tinged foam forming and swirling silently. It gave Mary an opportunity to tell Christian of Mr Greig's suggestion; his offer of a job at Happyhansel.

'Dat wid be graet, Mary. But tinks-du, wid da fock manage ithoot me, noo dat Betty is gyaain tae hae a bairn an John awa at da Far Haaf fur a braa twartree days ivery week i da simmer, jöst whin aathin needs dön.'

'I wis winderin aboot dat an aa. But A'll be aroond maist o da time, an John can win haem mair as we lippened; an Betty 'll be apön her fit again afore lang. I tink hit wid be a fine thing fur dee. A'll try an help persuade Midder an Faider, an if du can gie dem some o da money du wid be gyettin, dey could pay someen ta help wi da laand. Der aye fock keen on a antrin day's wark at da paets or maain coarn or turnin hay.'

They turned over the arguments and decided that Christian should accept the offer, even if she met with some opposition from family at the start.

'Come on dan. Lat's clim up dis brae.'

Mary led the way. At the top of the Gallow Hill, she was pensive.

'Christian, I aften winder aboot foo, no dat awfil lang ago, dey laekly hanged fock here or med bonfires an brunt dem: maybe doitin fock laek da aald weemen wi naethin noo but da Poor Box, an kindly neebirs ta tak dem in fur a bit. Or lasses laek me dat fell foul o da rules: dey say dat some o dem killed der new-boarn infants redder as face public penance. An if dey wir fun oot, of coorse dat wis murder.'

'Dat's a horrible tocht, Mary. Lat's gyet apön wir wye while da sun is still waarm.'

When they got home, Betty was making some three o'clocks. They fell to conversation quickly, Mary raising the offer which Mr Greig had made. Joannie wis just getting up from his afternoon nap on the resting-chair.

'Weel, whit wid we dö ithoot dee here, Christian. Mary is no aye aroond, Jean is trang wi da Laings, John is awa a braa bit o da week, an Betty 'll shön hae a infant ta luik tae… an, wis twa, wir comin aald!'

The younger members of the family were generally in favour, Joannie sceptical and Baabie wanting Christian to have the opportunity, but anxious whether they would all manage to look after the crops and animals, the peat-working and the home. Christian said she would want to hand over part of her wages and Mary suggested that the family could save up the money and use it to hire help at busy times. Betty was the one who finally won the day, speaking up strongly in favour of Christian having the chance of employment. Mary and Christian were warming daily to their sister-in-law. It was agreed that Lammas would be the better time to start and that she should deliver a note to Mr Greig to that effect.

Sunday 28th July 1776
Stove

Mary had been too busy heaping potatoes and building the peat stack to visit Stove on Saturdays for a few weeks, so Jaanie had suggested she bring Babsie on Sunday afternoon instead. She had missed seeing the child, who was by now saying quite a few words and moving around more confidently.

Mary had baked some hufsi and brought fresh butter, kirn-mylk and blaand with her as she knew Jaanie was now finding baking a struggle. The ironing too was proving tiring and often Mary had to return on a Tuesday or Wednesday to help.

While Wilm and Walter kept an eye on Babsie, Mary made tea for them and spread butter on the fruit loaf. 'Dat is da fine, lass,' Jaanie said appreciatively. 'Back in dy kert[23] noo an aet du up!'

Mary, who had given Babsie a bit of hufsi and was holding a small cup of blaand for her, turned to Walter. 'Did you see da new Mrs Buchan i da meenister's pew dis moarnin?'

'Dat I did. I man say der a ill-matched pair. I canna raelly understaand whit wye der gotten tagidder.'

'Shö seems fine enyoch. Shö man a kent he jöst has life-rent o da Voe property noo dat Henry o Burrastow aans hit.'

Jaanie shook her head. 'My dear, du needna wirry fur her – shö comes o money. Da Mitchells o Saand wirna short o a penny.'

'Weel, dat's true. But I wid say he's a gödly man… an maybe… shö jöst wants ta help him wi his wark an luik eftir him in his aald age.'

Walter looked a little disbelieving. 'Weel, maybe so. But he nivver seems ta lat up wi keepin aathin gyaain. Da tidder day Mrs Henry o Bayhaa got a oarder fur sixteen barrels o lime an her man got me ta bring dat owre tae da kirk, fur der gyaain ta limewash hit; alang wi a "dooble deal" – dat's planks o pine – an some nails. Dat cam ta be weel owre ten pound; sae whin you add in labour, hit's a braa cost.'

'Dat's true, but da communion saeson 'll shön bi underwye an

---

23 Pull in your chair to the table (lit. back in your cart).

I mind Mr Greig sayin dat whin you add up da fowr collections – dat's fast day, preparation day, action day an tanksgivin day – dey aften tak in mair as a hunder pound.'

'Dat's a lok o money. Fock is shurly generous.'

'I tink dey dö der best. An dey ken hit's da only wye dat da pör aamos 'll gyet lookit til whedder here aboot, or in Sannis or Papa… Foula an aa.' Then, turning to Jaanie, she said, 'Someen said dat Jeems Umphray couldna afford a doctor, sae da kirk paid da £3. I winder if dat wis fur der infant.'

Willm, who was tiring of this conversation, said, 'Faider is gotten a boat, Mary!'

'Weel, dat's da best news A'm heard in a graet while, Willm!'

'Ya, I boucht her fae da Pointataing fock – dey wir come owre aald ta dael wi her. Boannie boat… isna shö, Willm?'

'Shö's paintit black, Mary, wi a peerie line o red aroond da gunwales. An shö haes a sail! Wir bön oot in her twartree times.'

'Du'll fairly be rowin noo?'

'He's göd at da rowin an helpin wi da sail an aa,' said his father, 'an can catch piltocks wi a dorro!'

'Mary, wid du laek ta come tae da eela wi me an Faider?'

She looked at Walter to see if this would be in order. He just smiled.

'I wid love ta dö dat. Maybe ee nicht whin A'm gotten Babsie ta bed aerly.'

The little boy turned solemn eyes on the toddler who was asking for more fruit loaf. 'Does Babsie hae a faider?'

Mary looked at Jaanie and took her time to answer.

'Shö did hae een… but he gied awa ta sea an didna come back.'

'Why no?'

'I dunna raelly ken, Willm.'

'Maybe he'll come back yet.'

'I dunna tink sae. An, I dunna raelly mind. An nedder does Babsie!'

'Is du gotten dy dismissal fae presbytery yet, Mary?'

'Ya, Jaanie. Mr Greig gied me a peerie nott dis moarnin ta sae I wis "dismissed from discipline." I didna ken whedder ta gaff or greet!'

'Dat's göd news, jewel.'

Walter managed to navigate the conversation round to Brunatwatt and Bayhaa. Mary told them about Christian's good fortune. She was due to start her work at Happyhansel in the middle of August, just before the pupils returned to school. He told them about the store and the trips with the *Hawk;* and how he had fallen in with her brother John when picking up a load of salt fish from the laird's beach. John had helped ferry it out to the sloop.

By now, Babsie was demanding more attention. 'We'll need to gyet on wir wye an lat you hae a rest, Jaanie. A'll be along damoarn's moarn, usual time, ta gie you a haand.'

'Bliss dee, lass. I couldna dö ithoot dy help. I hoop dey'll no be dat muckle damoarn. But you ken whit Mistress Henry is laek – shö laeks iverythin jöst so.'

'Dat shö does, Midder. But dey pay me a fair wage! Noo, Mary, I winder if hit micht be a idea ta see if Christian wid laek tae geng tae da eela wi wis an aa. We dunna want tongues waggin!'

Mary could feel her face reddening slightly. 'Dat's a göd plan. A'm sure shö wid love tae. Maybe afore shö sterts her job… sometime neist week if hit cam awa a fine nicht?'

Thursday 1st August 1776
Stove

Willm had run along to Brunatwatt after teatime to say that he and his father were thinking to go to the eela and would be leaving by eight o'clock. Mary and Christian were to meet them at the Bayhaa pier, where they would have the boat ready. And they were bidden to bring a böddie – a straw kishie – to carry fish home.

The weather had held all week and the Brunatwatt family had been busy with sheep and hay, so a fishing trip on such a fine evening was the best possible start to the weekend for Mary and Christian. Betty was happy to stay at home with the old folk and finish a hap she had been knitting. Mary got Babsie to bed in good time and they set off, enjoying being sisters together on a trip with no responsibilities.

They took the shortcut through Stove, down the trenkie to the bridge and along by Seafield to the jetty where the boat was ready. Walter took the böddie Mary had brought and gave them a hand to step onboard, the boat tilting as they put a foot down.

'If du sits yundroo, Mary, wi Willm, an Christian comes apö da middle taft wi me, dat micht balance wis.' They sat as advised and he pushed off. Once safely free of the jetty, and heading out past the skerry, they started to row. The tirricks on the skerry created their usual commotion at the disturbance, dive-bombing and screaming. Their young were well fledged and starting to fish for themselves. It would not be long before they set off on their intercontinental journey. Walter told them how he had often seen them off the coast of Africa.

It took a little time to adjust their rowing so that they all pulled together, but soon they were in rhythm and making swift progress out the voe. The houses were all reflected perfectly in the stillness.

'Shö's a fine, trim boat, Walter,' said Mary.

'A'm braaly plaesed wi her, I man say. Wir no gien her a name yet. Whit tink you?'

'Whit aboot... lat me tink... *Da Tirrick*? Der sic boannie birds an möv laek hit's nae budder.'

'Dat's maybe a fine name. Whit tinks du, Willm?'

'Ya, I laek dat. Hit minds me dat you wan haem, Faider.'

'Richt, *Da Tirrick* hit is!'

'Jöst as weel hit's no a Friday or dat wid maybe bring ill luck... namin da boat I mean.'

'Ach, dat's aald supersteetion, Mary.'

'I ken, Walter, but somehoo hit seems ta stick.'

They rowed out past Pointataing and the Holm of Stapness towards the Wester Sound. As they neared the Holm of Burrastow, Mary said, 'Yun man be Tammas Henry's fine new hoose. See's du yun, Christian! Twa storeys, an muckle lums an a slatit röf, an a stair up tae da front door!'

'Ya, an hit's luikin owre da soond tae Vaila Haa… dat's some place da laird aans apö da isle,' her sister replied. 'An sees-du, da luik-oot too'er up abön Burrier Geo.'

'Dey'll be checkin up apön wir John,' said Mary, 'makkin sure he laands aa da fish apö da laird's beach.'

Walter chipped in: 'I mind whin I wis dy age, Willm, I used ta geng wi mi uncle awa oot bi Burrastow ta seek birds' eggs. We'd clim doon da banks an tak dem haem i wir keps!'

'Gadge! I tink A'm blyde we hae twartree hens!'

It was time to ship their oars and start fishing. Mary offered to keep the boat in position, only the slightest motion being required.

'A'll aandoo if you laek, Walter.'

'Dat wid be great. Noo dere's a dorro fur dee, Willm. Christian, wid du tak a waand?'

The three of them set to trying their luck and, in no time, Willm said, 'I feel a nyig apö mi line, Faider.'

'Weel, wind him in dan! Tak care wi da heuks. My, sees-du yun, du's gotten twartree fine piltocks already!'

Walter helped the boy lift the fish over the gunwale and remove the hooks from the mouths of the piltocks. The fish were coming thick and fast and, once off the hooks, were lying all around their feet, gasping their last. Christian was swinging the rod in over the gunwale in great style, catching the line as it came over and steadying the lively fish.

'Mary, wid du laek a shot?'

'Na, Walter, A'm happy jöst aandooin. You're aa döin dat weel.' They went several times slowly around the holm before thinking it was time to return.

'I foryat ta tell dee dat John T, da boss, is ta'en on a new factor, a Alex Irvine fae Mid Yell. Seems a moaderate fellow.'

'Will dat affect you muckle?'

'I dunna tink sae. He'll maistlins be i da shop, maybe mak up da wages; but I tink he's mair interestit in da laand dan in da *Hawk*. At laest, A'm hoopin sae.'

By now, Mary had turned the boat around. Walter, who had tidied up the handlines and made safe the rod, suggested that the two women row while he and Willm dealt with the fish. He had a sharp knife for slitting them open. Willm was to collect the livers in a little bucket and the guts would go over the side. They rowed more gently on the way back. In front of them the sky was a palette of colour with the various points of land – Vaila, Burrastow, Riskaness, Linga, Pointataing, Saatness – slowly coming into view, all fretted bold and black. The water looked like molten gold with darkening shadows shimmering down into it. The oars, rising from the calm, lifted threads of glinting drops. Behind them Walter worked deftly, the guts bringing a flurry of seagulls, excitedly fighting over the spoils.

'A'm bön across da Atlantic an da Indian Ocean, but der naewye boannier tae me is da Waster Soond i da hömin.'

'You're richt dere, Walter.' Mary wanted to keep that image of the voe intact and eradicate all images of the *Batchelor:* battered, broken, beached.

By the time they had reached Bayhaa jetty, they had a kishie and a böddie full of fish and half a bucket of livers. Walter anchored the boat off and they made their way up the trenkie with their various loads, calling along a few neighbours on the way – the ones with no access to boats and for whom fresh fish was always a treat. Jaanie insisted they stay for a bit of supper. While Walter and Mary, with Willm's help, salted down most of their catch, Christian helped Jaanie fry the livers and simmer a few fresh piltocks till they were ready to fall apart. They crumbled the fish flesh into the liver and mixed it to make stap.

Jaanie, connoisseur of the dish, said, 'Lat me taste hit, Christian... I tink a coarn mair saat an pepper... oh nyim, nyim, dat is da göd noo!'

The sea air and the rowing had given them all a good appetite, so plates were cleaned in no time. Walter went out to fill up the Brunatwatt böddie and a bowl with some livers. 'I tink I ken whit you'll be aetin fur your denner damoarn!'

It was well past eleven o'clock when Mary and Christian thanked them all for their kindness and said their goodbyes. They would drop some fish and livers off at the Laings – no doubt Jean or one of the others would decide on a very late supper. As they were salting down the last few piltocks, Christian remarked that she thought Walter was showing more than a little interest in Mary.

'Whit maks dee tink dat?'

'Jöst da wye he luiks at dee.'

'I tink du's imaginin hit, Christian. He's fine enoch, but I doot he fins da fact dat I hae a peerie lass kinda aakwird ta dael wi.'

Christian looked up quizzically, 'We'll see!'

Saturday 22nd September 1776
Happyhansel

The Brunatwatt rigs were by now well gleaned, the corn and bere stooked and most of the potatoes lifted and stored. Mr Greig had asked Christian to pass on an invitation to Mary to visit them, with Babsie, some late Saturday afternoon when the harvest work was all but through. She knew the times of classes well and arrived with Babsie just as the boarders were finishing their Latin class and would have free time before their meal. Christian was in charge on Saturdays, a lighter day without the day-school pupils.

As Mary entered the schoolhouse she had a stab of memory, half painful, half pleasant. So little had changed. Erchie was in the parlour to greet her.

'Come awa in trowe, Mary. An Babsie – dis is a treat ta hae dee an aa!' He had an instant rapport with little children and she went to him immediately. He lifted her up and took her to the window. She was keen to point out 'kye' and 'yowe' and gauge his reaction. But it was soon 'doon' and 'Midder' and 'Kistan'. She was in command of all she wanted.

'Whittan a lovely peerie lass shö is, Mary! Du man be prood o her.'

'Dat I im, Erchie. An hit'll be nae time afore shö's comin tae Happyhansel tae dy class! Shö'll be twa year aald shön.'

Soon Mr Greig came in and Christian served tea and a bit of cake she'd baked. Babsie was a little hesitant coming forward to meet him and clung to her mother's skirt.

'Set dee in, Mary. Noo, Babsie, I winder if I can fin a book fur dee? Wid du laek dat?' Immediately, the little girl lost her initial reserve. He brought one with pictures of farm animals for her to look at. She sat on the floor happily trying to turn the pages and saying the names of animals she recognised: grice, hen, chicken, yowe, lamb… and making the appropriate sounds which amused the adults who encouraged her efforts.

'Christian is döin nearly as weel as du did, Mary!' Mr Greig laughed and looked at Christian who accepted the joke. 'Dat lamb stew I can smell is… ya… I wid say… jöst as göd!'

Mary was pleased that Christian had fitted in so well and was managing what she knew was quite a demanding job.

'Wir aa laerners here,' said Erchie. 'Faider is hae'in ta tak da Latin class, fur Mr Buchan is no bön sae weel. I doot aa da stramash lately is bön owre muckle fur him.'

'Der nane o wis gyettin ony younger, Erchie. James Buchan an me, wir ages, baith inta wir seeventies. We canna geng on furivver. Sae, du better stert learnin da Latin shön!'

'You'll keep gyaain a while yet, Mr Greig. Der nae sign o you tirin,' said Mary. 'I wis gyaain ta ax you wha yun Reverend Jack wis dat took tree o da services owre Communion time?'

'He's da Nortmaven meenister. A William Jack bi name, cam originally fae Inverness but he merried wi a Bruce wife fae Symbister. I tink shö's maybe a relation o da late Mrs Buchan… shö wis a Bruce originally… I doot der aa linkit… But, ya, Erchie, I tink du's maybe richt. Wir meenister nivver lats up wirkin, but he's said he's no gyaain ta hae ony mair session meetings eenoo – ony business can wait till December whin we'll hae ta mak da neist arrangements fur da Quarter Poors. Der eicht needin lodgin dis time, at da hidmist coont, sae ivery bit o da parish 'll be affectit, wan wye or da tidder.'

'Hit's no laek Mr Buchan ta cancel kirk session meetings… I doot hae'in tae geng sooth in May wis a burdeen on him,' said Erchie.

'An gyettin used ta a new wife… weel… I canna imagine takkin aa dat on at wir age!'

'A'm blyde ta hear dat, Faider!' And they all laughed, with Babsie joining in.

Mary felt at ease with the Greigs, father and son. She was able to express that she missed Happyhansel, but that she was happy that Christian had replaced her. And they could see that she was happy in her role as mother.

On her way back to Brunatwatt, she slipped along John Jeems and Leebie to let them see how much Babsie had grown. They were a warm family and glad to see her and the little girl. She didn't linger as Babsie was tiring and it would be a slow journey back home to Brunatwatt.

Friday 25th and Saturday 26th October 1776
Brunatwatt and Stove

There was a full harvest moon shining in the closet window as Mary had retired to bed. Gently, she moved her child, who was deeply asleep, just enough to make room. Saturday would be her 20th birthday and she would have a lighter than usual day's work ahead. In the afternoon, she and Babsie were bidden to Stove. She had not brought her along for some time as it was difficult to work steadily amid kettles of boiling water, tubs of washing and hot irons with a small child to keep an eye on.

She was just drifting off to sleep when she felt a hand move over the bedding and a deep voice say, 'A very happy birthday tae dee, lass!' She just managed to stifle a scream. She recognised the voice, though a little disguised, as Walter's and, though the terror subsided, her heart was thumping. She could see that he had raised the window sash just enough to put his arm through.

'Whitna gluff! I nearly jimpit oot o mi skyin!' Her voice was almost whispered. 'Jöst as weel hit wis me in here an no onyboady idder!'

'I tocht I wid gie dee a peerie surprise apö dy birthday.'

'Weel, du certainly did dat!' Mary suddenly realised she had used the more intimate form of address for the first time.

She was about to retrieve the situation when Walter added, 'A'm blyde du's managed at last ta drap da "you". Hit med me feel laek dy uncle!'

Mary was embarrassed and quickly pulled a shawl around her. Walter said he should be on his way home; he had been along seeing the Laings and Jean had mentioned the birthday.

They whispered their goodnights, but Mary was now wide awake. She sat up in bed for quite some time watching clouds drift across the moon. It seemed so near and huge. Maybe… just maybe her life was changing again; maybe there was the possibility of love. She had accepted that having a young child – especially one from an adulterous union – made her a much less attractive prospect in everyone's eyes. She was damaged goods and had been publicly shamed and rebuked for two years. Eventually, she drifted off to sleep, feeling somewhat unsure whether the moment had really happened, or she had imagined it.

Jaanie seemed more tired than usual and Mary did not feel she should stay long despite Willm's protests that she should wait until his father got home from work. She had brought a piece of fresh hill lamb and a bag of new potatoes, some of which she had washed and set ready for Jaanie to cook for Walter coming home from Bayhaa.

Other than on Sundays, Mary had been spending most mornings at Stove helping the old woman with the chores and the laundry. Occasionally, if the weather was dry and the ironing finished, she would take Babsie with her. The child enjoyed accompanying her to fetch water from the well or peats from the stack. Walter brought home the messages they needed from the Bayhaa shop, so that saved time and effort. When not following her mother around, Babsie was easily amused: Jaanie could work the snorie-ben that Walter had made for her from a chicken bone and a piece of string. And on Saturdays Willm was around and often played with her.

As Mary left for home, she caught sight of Walter coming through the alley near the peat-stack. For a moment she had almost thought it was Alex Ross. But Walter was taller. She hesitated for a moment before deciding to wait. He had a broad smile on his face. Babsie ran to meet him and he picked her up.

'Ay ay! Babsie! My, du's a heavy weicht!' He pretended not to manage to lift the little girl. 'I hoop I didna gluff dee owre muckle dis moarnin, Mary – hit wis jöst a mad idea dat cam ta me as I passed your hoose. I mind dee sayin du hed da closet. I wid a felt a föl if hit hed a bön dy fock, or John an Betty, or Christian!'

Mary smiled. 'I got owre da shock quick enyoch!'

'Is du hed a fine birthday?'

'Ya, hit… got aff tae a göd stert!' She could see he caught her meaning. 'Is du hed a herd day?'

'He's bön no sae ill. I spent maist o hit clearin up da store – der dat muckle timber an fish oil an oo an da laek: eftir a week or twa o collectin an deliverin you need a bit o a redd up… noo, while du's here… I managed ta gyet dee a peerie present. Hit's naethin, raelly. Tak hit eenoo an du can oppen hit whin du wins haem.'

Walter pulled a little parcel from his jacket pocket and Babsie immediately tried to snatch it, saying 'book, book.'

'Can du gie dat tae dy midder, Babsie?' Immediately, the child held out the parcel to Mary.

'Hit does feel laek a book, Walter?'

'I hoop he's aaricht an dat du fins time ta read him.'

'Hae'in a book is speeshil. Du's richt dere though: finnin time ta read is nearly impossible. But I can read an mak at da sam time, sae I dunna feel owre guilty. Tanks very much. I dunna even ken whin dy birthday is.'

'Dat's a secret, fur A'm already hed far owre mony!'

She laughed. 'A'll maybe fin oot!'

When at last she managed to get a moment on her own, she untied the package. Inside was an edition of Allan Ramsay's *Poems*. Mary turned the book over in her hands, admiring its boards of tan linen with dark brown leather. Inside there were beautiful illustrations with decorative capital letters at the start of each poem. She read:

When genial Beams wade thro the dewy Morn,
And from the Clod invite the fprouting Corn;
When chequer'd Green, wing'd Mufick, new blown Scents,
Confpired to footh the Mind, and pleafe each Senfe:
Then down a fhady Haugh I took my Way
Delighted with each Flower and budding Spray;

It was a summer scene she recognised: the first shoots of green in the rigs – the breer – birds singing, and the scent of meadow flowers. At the front, she saw he had written, '*for M, 26th October, 1776*'. The 'M' was as beautifully decorated as the initial capitals of the poems. She read a few more, slowly, then kissed it and placed it under her pillow.

Saturday 23rd November 1776
Stove

Willm had been coughing for two days, so Mary had left Babsie behind at Brunatwatt, anxious that whatever might ail Willm should not be transmitted to Betty's baby, which was due any day. Mary had heard from Christian that there had been an outbreak of measles among the school children and many had been off.
As soon as she came in, she could hear the rasping cough; it sounded worse. Willm was still in bed, in the closet. She quickly hung up her things and went to see him. He tried to smile, but she could see that he was poorly: his eyes were bloodshot and he was running a temperature. There was no sign of a rash, but she was fairly certain it was measles. She remembered when she and her sisters had all had measles at the same time, and how miserable they had felt. Willm had thrown back the blankets, but she tucked him in again saying he must keep warm. She brought some water for him to sip and a cloth to bathe his eyes. She knew Walter had some handkerchiefs which she had laundered and asked Jaanie if

she could let Willm use them.

'Of coorse, jewel. Onythin he needs.' She could see Jaanie was anxious.

In between looking after Willm and keeping Jaanie company, fetching water and emptying chamber-pots, Mary made some chicken broth on the hen Walter had killed. She also made some bannocks on the braand-iron. Willm tried a few spoonfuls of soup, but had little appetite. He was hardly even interested in a story. At least with the closet door open he was able to hear the familiar voices of the two women in the but-end and Mary could keep an eye on him.

She was keen to get back to Brunatwatt before the light faded completely, but torn at the thought of leaving Willm feeling so miserable. He took a little more soup and, with encouragement, a cup of milk.

'Du man keep drinkin, Willm. Dat'll help dee gyet better. Noo, A'll need ta be aff ta Brunatwatt, but dy faider 'll be haem shön, so dunna wirry. Damoarn's Sunday sae A'll no be here, but A'll slip by on mi gaet haem fae da kirk jöst ta see foo du's gyettin on, an dan A'll be back on Monday moarnin, fur du'll no be gyaain tae da scöl fur a while yet.' She tucked him in again and kissed his warm brow.

Friday 29th November 1776
Stove and Brunatwatt

Snow had laid on soon after Mary arrived at Stove in the morning. It had been cold all week and it looked as if it would settle. Willm was sitting up in bed, his itchy rash fading and his throat less painful. He was annoyed to be missing the snow, which Mary took as a sure sign that he was on the mend. Two days before, she had left a note for Walter to bring some white flour and sugar so that she could make pancakes to tempt Willm to eat.

She insisted Willm stay in bed to rest, but allowed him to the fireside for a little dinner. Jaanie had lain late as it was such a cold, dark morning. Mary had helped her up for her eleven o'clocks.

'Still naethin happenin wi Betty?'

'Na, Jaanie, I tink maybe anidder week.'

'I jöst wiss I hed da strent ta be dere ta help her.'

'I tink we aa wiss dat. But da Stapness howdie is bön ta see her an shö said aathin was fine.'

'A'm blyde ta hear hit. Du'll be a help an aa – a calm head.'

'Poor John, he's on a amp. Wirried seek.'

'Der maistlins aa laek dat. I canna say I blame dem fur things can geng wrang. A'm bön braaly lucky aa mi time. But if a midder isna healty hersel... but dan Betty is a strong young wumman. Shö'll be fine.' She paused briefly. 'I mind whin shö wis boarn, an John an aa! Fine fock, da Brouster fock.'

'Dey ir dat. You man a helpit maist o wis inta da wirld aroond here.'

'Whin I wan dere in time!'

Mary lowered her voice. 'Does Walter ivver spaek aboot da loss o Etta, Jaanie? Hit man a markit him.'

'No raelly. I tink hit gluffed him an med hit difficult ta tink o ivver pittin anidder wife trowe da sufferin.'

'A'm no surprised at dat.'

'But kens-du, Mary, I see a odds on him since he cam haem. He seems happy. An I wid say he spaeks aboot dee an peerie Babsie a braa lock! I wis jöst winderin...'

Mary just smiled and got back to her work.

In the afternoon, Mary made the pancakes on the girdle and Willm had two, his appetite slowly returning. He didn't want to go back to bed, so she propped him up on the resting-chair and put a blanket around him. She had thought to leave for home in the middle of the afternoon while there was light in the sky, but the snow was still coming down thickly.

Walter arrived early from Bayhaa as some of the workers had a distance to go to get home. She was cutting slices of bacon and beating eggs for their tea when he came in.

'Du's still here, Mary.'

'Ya, I wis gyaain, but I tocht I wid wait a bit ta see if da moorie aesed.'

'Dat wis a göd idea. Weel, Willm, du's shurly feelin a coarn better?'

'A'm hed twa pancakes!'

'Mary, du could bide an hae a coarn o maet an dan A'll follow dee ta Brunatwatt. Dy fock 'll ken why du's a peerie bit later as usual.'

'Babsie 'll be luikin fur me.'

'Shö'll be fine fur a extry ooer. I winder if shö wan ootside i da snaa. Dat wid a bön a fun fur her.'

'I canna wait ta gyet oot i da snaa, Faider!'

'I doot hit'll be twartree days yet afore du can win ootside, Willm. But no owre lang. I man mak dee a sledge.'

Willm's eyes lit up. 'Dan I can sledge doon da Stove brae!'

'An laand ithin da ebb if du gengs owre fast!'

Mary soon had the food on the table and the plate of fresh pancakes. Willm took some scrambled egg and a drink of milk and two more pancakes.

'I am da blyde ta see dee aetin, Willm,' said Jaanie.

Mary cleared up as quickly as she could, being anxious to be on her way home. She changed into her boots, heavy overcoat and hap.

'A'll see you damoarn, Jaanie… maybe a peerie bit later seein hit's Setterday an Willm is kinda come at. Maybe aboot 10? But A'll no bring Babsie eenoo wi da maesles aboot, wi Betty as shö is. An onywye hit wid be a braa buks trowe da snaa wi her!'

They set off with a little light in the far western sky, enough – once their eyes had adjusted – to see landmarks and where the track should be. The snow was still coming down, but more lightly. In some places Mary had to walk behind Walter where he pushed the snow aside.

'Mary, A'm truly in dy debt fur bidin wi Midder an Willm, while der baith bön sae poorly. Hit's most horrid göd o dee.'

'Dat's nae budder at dis time o year, Walter. I dö winder though whedder dy midder 'll be able ta manage muckle owre da winter. Even winnin furt tae da closet is mair as shö's able fur noo, an shö neebs aff trowe da day a braa lock an aa.'

'Du's richt. A'm bön pitten aff acceptin dat her haert is failin. I doot der naethin muckle a doctor could dö fur her.'

'I doot du's richt dere. Shö's jöst kinda fadin awa.'

'I wis winderin if du wid come an bide da winter laek du used ta dö afore I cam haem? Wi Babsie of coorse. Du could hae da ben-end an I could share da closet wi Willm.'

'Na, Walter, I dunna tink dat's a göd idea ava. Fock wid spaek, even if dey wir naethin ta spaek aboot. An A'm hed mi fingers brunt afore.'

'My mercy! I nivver tocht o dat. Hit's jöst dat fine kennin du's dere...'

'Kennin someen's dere...?'

'Kennin du's dere.'

They trudged on in silence, the snow falling round them in large, light flakes, until they finally reached the path that led to Brunatwatt.

'A'll manage fine noo, Walter. Hit's jöst flukra; but bliss dee fur comin. Noo, tell me afore I geng... I meant ta ax... whaar got du yun boannie book?'

'I bowt him ee time I wis in Leith an I traivelled up ta Edinburgh jöst ta see whit hit wis laek. Aathin wis braaly prammed in alang a rodd dat rins fae da castle at da tap tae da palace at da boddom an da High Kirk i da middle... an hooses wi maybe six or seeven storeys piled up an clos tagidder raikin doon da brae apö baith sides, wi trenkies aawye. Dey wir men wi wigs waanderin aboot an fishwives an traders an aa kind o things. But dey wir twartree bookshops – een wis caa'd John Bell. I towt hit wis a boannie book an I wis heard o Allan Ramsay... but... I nivver tocht I wid fin a boannie lass dat micht read him.'

Mary just looked at him but said nothing. As she turned to go, Walter said, 'Da moarn, if da snaa is da sam or maybe waar, A'll be haem i da late eftirnön fur we'll be shut aerly. An A'll follow dee haem ta mak sure du dusna smore apö da gaet!'

They bade farewell and Mary was left wondering about all her attachments: Babsie, her family, Jaanie, Willm and now Walter. She was being pulled in several directions. But she hoped the snow would stay for one more day at least.

Saturday 30th November 1776
Stove and Brunatwatt

Mary arrived without Babsie, having beaten a path through the snow. It was a cold crisp day with little wind, so at least it was not drifting. She quickly roused the fire which had gone down and re-heated the gruel. Jaanie needed her assistance to get up and wash and dress. Willm was happy to rest as long as the closet door was open and he could hear the conversation. He had asked for salt piltocks for their tea – there were still some left, stored carefully from their fishing trips. They had been soaking overnight. He shouted through for Mary to come and see the drawing of *Da Tirrick* he was making.

'Dat raelly luiks laek her, Willm. Weel dön dee! Du'll hae ta draa een o da *Hawk* fur dy faider.'

'Faider wis axin me last nicht if I towt dat dee an him sood maybe gyet mairried.'

'Did he raelly? Weel, he's no mentioned hit ta me!'

'I tink he wis faert ta ax dee in case du didna agree.'

'An whit did du say ta him, Willm?'

'I said I wid laek dat. I wid gyet a midder an Babsie wid gyet a faider. An du widna hae ta traivel back an fore sae muckle edder.'

It was all Mary could do to keep a straight face. The child's simple honesty was disarming.

'Weel, I tink gyettin sic a lovely son wid maybe mak me tink hit wis a göd idea.'

She wondered if Jaanie had overheard either this conversation or the one between father and son.

The day wore on and Mary's resolve not to make things quite so easy for Walter started to fray. She realised how much she enjoyed trying to make a home for him and his ailing mother and his son. She was already thinking what they might have for their meals on Sunday – when she wouldn't be around – and making preparations.

Walter was home in time for their three o'clocks. Willm was up and dressed; he looked and sounded much more like himself. Walter told them he had sailed the *Hawk* to Skeld and back again as they had not managed to go into Skelda Voe to drop off goods on their last trip from Scalloway. The good news for Mary was that he had been given a letter for the Brunatwatt family from Jaerm, which had been carried north from Leith by a sailor home to Skeld between trips. Mary was delighted. She opened it quickly, but merely scanned it to see that was all well with the family and, having confirmed that, put it in her pocket. She did not want to rush away from what was a happy time with the family at Stove: tea and fresh pancakes around the fire, with Willm at last able to enjoy the experience, rather than be cajoled to eat.

'Will du mak pancakes ivery day, Mary?'

'Weel, we hae plenty butter and mylk an you hae eggs, but we canna growe wheat or sugar at Brunatwatt! Dat haes ta be boucht.'

'Maybe ivery noo an again dan?'

'A'll teach dee foo ta mak dem whin du's better.' Then, turning to Walter and Jaanie, she said, 'I dunna ken whit you tink, but my feelin is dat Willm sood hae twartree mair days keepin waarm an restin afore gyaain back tae da scöl… but of coorse dat's fur you ta decide. Noo, while I mind, I sood be able ta be here as usual, but if ee day I dunna turn up hit wid be becaase o Betty's baby comin. A'm sure a neebor boady wid gie you a haand, Jaanie.'

Mary was more than a little apprehensive about the journey home, still musing on her conversation with Willm. She and Walter set off in the darkening with snow falling very lightly. The moon – barely on the wane – was already rising, helping them find their way more easily than the previous evening.

'Will du manage aaricht damoarn, Walter?'

'Weel, A'll hae tae. Willm is fine noo, but hit's no very aesy wi mi Midder bein sae pör aamos. Hit's jöst as weel I cam haem fae da sea whin I did.'

'Ya, du's richt dere. Hit wid a bön awfil herd on Willm.'

'Spaekin aboot Willm... I wis axin him yesterday whedder he tocht dee an me micht a med a göd pair.'

'Twa morroless sowls?... I soodna provoke dee, Walter! Willm did mention hit ta me.'

'An whit did du tink, Mary?'

At this point he stopped and faced her. The snow, sticking to the edges of the hap around her head and shoulders was like a veil framing her brown hair. Her eyes looked bigger than usual and serious in the low light.

'Weel, I tocht hit soondit laek a göd idea as lang as hit wisna jöst a convenience or a wye o avoidin a spaekalation!'

'Oh, Mary, du man ken bi noo whit I tink o dee! A'm faert even ta gie dee a peerie smoorikin in case du took hit da wrang wye. Du's bön ill dön bi an I dunna want ta tak advantage o dee, but I wid laek hit if du wid mairry me.'

'Weel i dat case, Walter Jarmson, mi answer is "yes"!' And she reached up to kiss him, the snow falling on their faces.

'Dat's jöst winderfil, Mary. Why do we no gyet da banns up an see if Mr Buchan 'll mairry wis at Yöl whin I hae time aff wark, an while Midder is still tae da fore.'

'Dat soonds fine ta me as lang as he's no a waanin mön! I tink hit wid need ta be a quiet affair eftir da upheaval A'm caased, an wi dy midder as shö is. An we wid be a peerie faemly richt awa.'

'An A'll raise da aeshins neist simmer if dy fock could spare some strae. We micht jöst need some extry room afore lang... but mairriage first!'

'Wid du come in alang eenoo an see mi fock an tell dem, Walter? I can aye help dem whin der trang, an dat wye we can hae sweet mylk, an butter... an kirn-mylk... an strae an maybe some taaties an aa!'

'Ya, fine dat. An damoarn, whin du comes fae da kirk, drap in alang an we'll tell Midder an Willm.'

Walking along the path to Brunatwatt, Walter put his arm around Mary's waist. 'Dey say "A lang airm in a gansey sleeve aye maks a boannie belt!"'[24]

'Dan A'll need ta lay dee up a boannie gansey.'

He embraced her briefly as she lifted the sneck of her childhood days, crossing the threshold, the treshel-tree, into a new world; already on her way home.

---

24 The best (knitted) belt is an arm around the waist.

Postscript

Almost all of the characters in this story are real and snippets of their personal histories can be gleaned from a range of sources. So what eventually happened to them?

Mary Johnsdaughter – her sisters and friends: sadly, there is no trace of them in official church registers. In those years – before the state assumed responsibility for registration, and before censuses – it appears that the only remaining record of their existence is through the minutes of meetings of the Church of Scotland Kirk Session. (Her mother has a fictional name and, while siblings John, Jean Mary and Christian existed, Jaerm is fictional.)

Alexander Ross – he returned home to Leith on the *Batchelor*.

Sophia Henderson – she was born in Delting, had a son, Henderson Bain (b1773), to David Bain, a married man. She later moved back to Delting and eventually settled with Francis Yates in Hillswick, Northmavine. They had seven children between 1778 and 1793. There is no record of a marriage. There is no trace of **David Bain**.

The Emigrants
Of the 280 original emigrants (including 90 children under 8 years) who left Caithness on the ill-fated *Batchelor of Leith*, it is estimated that there were 11 deaths, either en route or while billeted. Twenty-eight stayed on in Shetland – they were given 8 weeks' provisions. Some surnames still traditionally associated with the *Batchelor* are Reid, Fraser and Balfour. Two-hundred-and-forty-one were taken back to Leith (including Hogg's family, plus servants). Of them:

James Hogg's party later sailed from Greenock at the end of June 1774, arriving in August. He was a natural entrepreneur and quickly became a prosperous landowner and merchant of Hillsboro and Cross Creek, North Carolina. Eventually, he rose to prominence in the state as a political and civic leader and promoter of the University of North Carolina. He was on the side of Revolution in the American War of Independence, unlike his prosperous brother who had settled there earlier.

The remaining 226 emigrants, having refused the chance to disembark at Thurso, were all put ashore at Leith. Few would have had any money left. They became a charge on the authorities in the City of Edinburgh.

Initially churches in Leith (three Leith ministers, Rev Scot, Rev Johnston and Rev Logan) and an Edinburgh merchant, Mr William Taylor from the Luckenbooths in the Lawnmarket, helped them and raised 'fuch charity as any well-difpofed person may chufe to give on this occafion.' Twenty-nine pounds, two shillings and sixpence (£29/2/6) was raised in South Leith. Some managed to get work building the New Town. One family suffocated in a room in the Pleasance, due to a blocked chimney. There was a huge turnout for the funeral at the Chapel-of-Ease churchyard.

Of those who survived, presumably over 200: some stayed on in the lowlands; some tried to reach Caithness; some tried to get to the Carolinas – possibly 22 sailed from Kirkcaldy in 1775.

The *Batchelor of Leith*
Once in Leith, the owner – James Inglis – declared the contract at an end and refused to refund the fares to James Hogg. He did not accept responsibility for further re-provisioning of the ship and transport of the emigrants under the original contract.

In Leith, Hogg acquired Power of Attorney for the emigrants, went to court and won some redress: Inglis was found liable to pay £684/10/-. In response, Inglis had the *Batchelor* repaired, declared seaworthy and ordered the emigrants aboard so that he could be seen to discharge his responsibility to them. By this time, however, the emigrants had dispersed, seeking employment, and Hogg was on his way to America.

There followed many claims and counter claims.

James Inglis put the *Batchelor* up for auction in September 1774, with a quantity of provisions (beef, biscuit, meal, barley, pease and molasses). He died at home in Edinburgh on 6 November 1775.

Rev James Buchan
James Buchan had worked tirelessly to build Happyhansel school, establish it as a legal school and ensure there were SSPCK charity schools in Sandness, Papa and Foula. The kirk also paid fees to teachers, eg in Dale of Waas. He died on 5th October 1778, just two years after marrying his second wife, Miss Agatha Cumming. He has a headstone, in disrepair, in Waas kirkyard. In 2018 the Waas history group erected a plaque in his memory on the occasion of the 250th anniversary of the founding of Happyhansel School.

Mrs Agatha (Cumming) Buchan
James Buchan and Agatha Cumming had no family. She possibly stayed on for some time at Voe House after he died as she had two court cases in

1779, both relating to local property. At some point she may have moved back to the Cumming home at Garderhouse in the parish of Sandsting and Aithsting, as it was from there she married a second time, on 23rd December 1794, aged 45. Her second husband was George Barron, c 60. They had no family. She died on 10th November 1810, aged 60.

George Greig (c1705–1779), schoolmaster at Happyhansel and session clerk, died in 1779. By then, Happyhansel school had become an educational beacon for Shetland. Besides providing a good basic education free for local children, sons of lairds and merchants boarded at Happyhansel where they received an advanced education to take them to higher education or the professions. The old school building remains (now a house); the schoolhouse, still standing to the gables in the 1950s, has been subsequently knocked down and a house built on its foundations. The croft, though still there, sadly bears little resemblance to what the author remembers in the 1950s and 60s. It must be the only school in Scotland with a croft. The equally unique name 'Happyhansel' has been attached to the two subsequent school buildings in DoonaWaas: the 1872 building at the head of the voe and the current building (opened November 1982) which lies between the voe and Loch of Kurkigart. Happyhansel School celebrated its 250th anniversary in 2018.

Archibald Greig (1757–1831) – Erchie in the text – succeeded his father as schoolmaster at Happyhansel. He married a second cousin, Christian Greig (1752–1818), in Waas and they had six children: two boys and four girls. Two of their girls died in infancy or early childhood and one son died as a young man. Their oldest son, James, became Procurator-Fiscal of Shetland and one daughter married a Capt George Cheyne. Archibald petitioned the presbytery of Zetland in 1784 concerning his salary. (CH2/1071/43/24). As an older man, Archibald, along with many others in Waas, joined the Wesleyan Society (1824). At this time, the Rev John Lewis – a young itinerant Methodist preacher from Wales – was a popular, tireless and effective proselytiser. By then, there was a chapel established at Bayhall and the Lewis family made it their base.

John T Henry (c1738 – before Nov 1791) and Mistress Margaret (Scott) Henry (1740 – before 1784) had three daughters, Johanna Elizabeth aka Betty (1767–1847), Margaret (1768 but predeceased her father), and Lilias (1772–1820). Lilias married Thomas Henry of Burrastow (see below).

John T Henry's wife, Margaret, must have died before 9th September 1784, as Shetland Archives holds a Bond of Provision and Disposition (SC12/53/6/folio 182v) to his (second) wife Katherine Nicolson (Henry) in liferent, and to his daughters Betty and Lilias of land in Copister and Houlland, Yell. Presumably there were no children of the second marriage. Betty, the older sibling, appears to have moved away from Bayhaa on her marriage to Andrew Irvine of Lerwick. (Bayhaa was acquired by the local authority in 1978 and converted into flats.)

Thomas Henry of Burrastow (1746–1845), was the son of Archibald Henry of Scord who, as a successful landed proprietor and local merchant, built Burrastow House nearby in 1759. Around 1793, after the death of both her parents, Thomas married Lilias Henry (see above). So, the two Henry families were thus joined again in marriage. He was 47 and she was 21. Although the younger of the two surviving Bayhaa Henry daughters, it would appear that she may have had some ownership of or interest in Bayhaa. Her third child and second son, Archibald (b 1800), was born in Bayhaa. Thomas and Lilias had four children, three of whom stayed at Burrastow and never married.
Archibald (1800–1837), through marriage to Jane Scott of Melby, his second cousin and daughter of the 'boy' laird, bound the two Henry families even more closely; the Vaila estate thus eventually included not just Bayhaa but also Burrastow. He became a sea captain. They had four children. Sadly, Archibald died relatively young.

Though considerably older than his wife, Thomas outlived Lilias by 25 years, dying at the ripe old age of 99. In his later years, he often provided bed and board for Rev John Lewis and use of 'the large parlour and barn' at Burrastow for preaching. Some of his family became Methodists in 1824. A Methodist chapel was built at Bayhaa.

Burrastow House was eventually sold by the Vaila estate and is still a private hotel.

Glossary of Shetland dialect (Shetlandic) words and phrases

Some general points – mainly spelling and pronunciation:
'th' is often replaced by 't', eg: *tree* for three; *tresh* for thresh; *trist* for thirst; *tink* for think; *aert* for earth; *birt* for birth; *strent* for strength; *healty* for healthy

More generally, 'th' is replaced with 'd' eg: *dem* for them (and those); *dat* for that; der for their, there, they're; *dey* for they; *dis* for this; *wadder* for weather; *midder* for mother; *whedder* for whether; *gadder* for gather

Vowel pronunciation varies across Shetland but on the west side where this story is set there is a long **aa** sound, a pronounced ö (similar to French 'tu') and an **ae** dipthong with an 'aye-ee' sound. Some typical sounds are **ky** as in kyittle – tickle, kyemp – compete 'Wh' (west side of Shetland) is generally sounded as 'quw'

The familiar, singular 'du' is prevalent and used by adults to children, among children and among adult friends. In some cases children use it to very familiar adults; (du ('you', subject), dee ('you', object), and, in the possessive, it is dy (your) and dine (yours)

Past tense of verbs ending in 'ed' is usually replaced with 'it' (eg 'parted' would be 'pairtit'); and 'ing' endings are usually 'in' eg 'singin'

The auxiliary verb 'to have' takes the form 'a' when used with could, should, would, might, must ie could a, sood a, wid a, micht a, man a
Verbs in the negative take the form: canna – cannot, didna – did not, dunna – do not, manna – must not, soodna – should not, widna – would not, wirna – were not/ had not, wunna – will not

Plural subjects frequently have a singular verb

aa	all
aafil	awful(ly)
aakwird	awkward
Aald Yöl Ee'n	Old Christmas Eve
aan	own
aandoo	to row gently to maintain a boat's position
abön	above
acht (ta aan)	a valuable possession; good to have around
aer	small amount
aeshins	top of side wall of house
aetmel	oatmeal
affa	off
afflikkit	afflicted, mortified
amp	state of anxiety, watchfulness

an aa	as well, also
antrin	occasional
apö(n)	on
argie-bargie	dispute
arl	crawl
arles	down-payment by way of promise to provide a service
ava	at all
ax(in)	ask(ing)
Ay! Ay!	form of greeting
baa	submerged rocks
bacca	tobacco
backlins	backwards
baed	stayed (also 'bidden')
baess-mylk	first (rich) milk from a newly-calved cow
baith	both
ball	throw
banks	cliffs
bassel	struggle
beest	cooked baess-mylk (see above)
ben-end	'ben' room is a 'best room' but in old croft-houses with just two main rooms, it was generally a bedroom
benkled	dented
bere	a primitive form of barley which ripens in high latitudes
beremel	dark-coloured meal ground from bere
bidden	stayed (also 'baed'); invited
bide	stay
bigg	build (biggins – buildings)
billie	lad, fellow
birze	squeeze
blaa	blow
blaand	sour whey
blöd	blood (n), bleed (v)
blyde	happy, content
booce	work energetically, bustle
bosie	bosom
böd	booth, bothy
böddie	small basket for the back, generally made of straw
böl	bed down
bön	been
böries	buries
braa	considerable, grand
braaly	considerably, fairly, pretty (adverb)
braand-iron	grid-iron
breer	first green shoots of a crop, generally grain
bridder	brother
briggisteyns	footpath of flagstones laid in front of house
broo	brow
brook	broke
brose	communal dish of uncooked oatmeal, eaten hot with

	dripping
brönnie	round, thick oatmeal scone
bruck	rubbish, refuse
brucks o (a ooer)	most of (an hour)
brunt	burned
buckle	tangle, muddle
budder	bother
buks	trudge heavily
burrie	stalk of the heath rush with seed head
but-end	living area in small cottage
caa	call; drive eg sheep; turn the wheel (da tirl) of a mill or spinning-wheel
caerd	wooden board with prongs for carding wool
caerdin	women's gathering to card wool with neighbours
callyshang	uproar, noisy dispute
clash	gossip
clew	ball of wound wool which has been spun
clim	climb
cloot	cloth
coarn	oats; small quantity
cöllie	appease
come at	start to feel better
come dy wys	come away (in)
coo /kye	cow/ cattle
coortin	courting
coupit owre	capsized, tilted over
craig-steyn	flat rock along foreshore from which fish could be caught
creepie	small wooden stool
creeshy	greasy, particularly lanolin feel and smell of sheep's fleece
crö	sheep-fold
croft	small holding rented from laird, with arable, pasture and common grazing rights
crook	hook from which pots were hung over open fire
crub	small, circular drystone enclosure for raising cabbage plants
curny puddeens	currant puddings/ dumplings (savoury) cooked in cleaned intestine
daal	valley
daar	dare
daeved	overcome (lit. deafened)
damoarn's moarn	tomorrow morning
danicht	tonight
dastreen	last night
datn	so very, such a
da year	this year
Deil	Devil
dell	dig
dess	large stack of hay
dey wir	there was, there were, they were, there had
dey'll	they will/ there will
ding doon	knock down

dip	sit down
dochter	daughter
doitin	mentally confused
dook	dip in the water
doot	doubt (in negative sense as in 'no doubt'; also affirmingly as in 'I warrant')
dorro	handline with several hooks attached for fishing
dose	a large quantity
döl	grief
dön	done, finished
drushy (rain)	fine rain
dwined	bothersome
ebb	foreshore
edder	either
eela	fishing from small boats, using rod or handline, usually for saithe
een	one
eenoo	at the moment
eicht o'clocks	evening snack with tea
enyoch	enough
erse	backside
faa by	collapse, faint
faa	fall
faat	fault
fael	a sod or turf
faerdie-maet	food for a journey
faert	frightened
faider	father
fann	snowdrift
fantin	famished
farder	further
Far Haaf	deep sea fishing, 30–40 miles offshore in open boats
feth	like English 'faith'; (bi mi feth: indeed)
fiery-braand	tongs with lit peat (for light when walking at night)
fin/ fun (pt)	find/ found
flae	remove turves from surface of peat-bank to prepare it for cutting
flan	sudden squall of wind
flit	move (eg tethered animals; households)
flukra	snow in large flakes falling gently
fock	folk, relations
follow dee haem	accompany you home, often romantically
foo	how; full
forbye	as well, besides
foryat	forget
fowrareen	four-oared wooden boat
foy	celebratory party
fozie	wizened
föl	fool
fremd	stranger

froad	foam, froth
frushin	frothing, spluttering
fry (n)	enough fish for a meal
furt	outside
gadge	exclamation of disgust at something unpleasant
gaet	track, path
gaff	laugh
gavel	gable
geng (v)	go
gie	give
girnal	chest for oatmeal
glansin	sparkling
glooral	faint trace of light
gloy	clean straight straw used for making kishies, thatching
gluff	fright(en)
göd	good
grain	small quantity
greet	cry
gret	cried
grice	pig(s)
grind	gate
grottie-buckie	cowrie shell
gud	went (pt of verb 'to go')
gyaain	going
haa	large house of land-owner (laird)
hadd	hold
hadd dy sheeks!	shut up!
hadd dy wheest!	shush! no need to say that!
hael	whole
haem	home
haet	hot
hairst	harvest
half-gaets	half-way
hansel	gift to commemorate an inaugural occasion
hap	shawl
harned	hardened
hattered	roughly treated, worn
helly	weekend
hentilagets	tufts of wool, lost from sheep's fleece, often caught on heather or on a fence
heth	mild oath
heuch	communal cheers at certain parts of a traditional dance
heuk	hook
hidmist	last, final
hinny	term of endearment
hippens	nappies
hoid	hide
hoodie craw	hooded crow

hooer	whore
horrid (eg fine)	very (adding emphasis of approval)
howdie	midwife
hömin	twilight
hufsi	home-baked fruit loaf
hüld	held
idder	other
ill-best	the best of a poor choice, 'least worst'
in aboot da nicht	social visiting in evening
jalouse	guess, suspect
jantry	gentry
jewel	term of endearment
kep	cap
kirk	church
kirn	churn
kirn-mylk	soft curd cheese
kirsen	decent, proper, fit to eat or wear
kishie	straw or cane basket to carry on back
kloss	steep path, often narrow
knap	to speak (English) with affectation, attempting to impress
koli-lamp	open, iron lamp with wick in fish-oil
kyempin	competing
kyucker up	revive
laaber	work; often used re digging and manuring (lit. to thrash)
laek	like
laevrik	lark
laft	loft
laim	wide shelf in roof space of croft house stretching across room, generally used for storage
lambie-hoose	small, thatched outbuilding for sickly animals on croft
langbed	improvised bed, usually of straw, made up on the floor for several people staying overnight
lay up	cast on stitches in knitting
lee	tell a lie
leet	heed (used in the negative 'nivver leet')
lem	earthenware; crockery
less a less	alas
leys	fallow ground
lichtsome	cheerful, light-hearted
lintie	twite
lippen	expect
lipper	derogatory term for a person
lock	lot, much, many
lodberrie	18th century house in Lerwick incorporating pier, courtyard,
store	and dwelling built with foundations in the sea
lodge	fisherman's bothy at haaf-fishing station

löt	let (past tense)
luik	look
luik til	look after
maa	to mow
maddrim	fun, hilarity
maeshie	net constructed for carrying load of hay or oats on the back
maet	food
maistlins	mostly
mak, makkin	make, knit; knitting
mak a wark o	make a fuss about
mak on	pretend
man (v)	must
midder	mother
mind	remember
mirry-begyit	illegitimate child (lit. conceived in merriment)
misanter	mishap, accident
moch	moth
moorie	blizzard
moot	mite; very small creature (term of endearment)
morroless	not matching, as of a pair
mödow	meadow
möv	move
muckle	big, much
mudjick	midge
My mercy!	Goodness me! (exclamation)
neb	beak
neeb	nod off to sleep
neebir	neighbour
neep	turnip
neist	next
nev	fist
nevfoo	fistful
New'r Day	New Year's Day
nipsiccar	caustic in manner
noo	now
nyig	tug
nyim	expression of pleasure on tasting food
olick	young ling
onkerry	carry-on, disturbance
ontak	heavy undertaking
oo	wool
ooer	hour
ootset	a piece of common grazing rented to a tenant who had to build a house on it, bring it under cultivation and generally fish for the laird
ös	use

paap	breast
paes	peace (also Easter); tak paes – be at peace
paes-weesp	tangled mass of lines or threads
paets	peats
peerie	small
peerie little	short time, small amount
peerie wyes	gently, cautiously
peewit	lapwing
penga	money
pexins	punishment
pheesic	medicine
piltock	saithe (mature)
pleepsin	whining, complaining
plenishins	internal finishing and furnishings of house
plot	wash, soak
pock	a net on a pole for catching fish, usually off the rocks
pocky	pouch, small bag
poo'd	pulled
pooskered	exhausted
pör aamos	frail
pram	squeeze together
preeve	taste, generally in context of small amount; often used negatively
press	cupboard built into a wall
prood	exposed
prunk	poised, proud
prunkit up	smartly finished, firmed
puckle	seed of grain
pyaagit	exhausted from hard work
quaig	heifer
Quarter-poors	people in parish with no home or means of sustenance; the church organised their upkeep, moving them on Quarter Days
raan	fish roe
raep	line stretched between two fixed points for the purpose of hanging things to dry
raik	aimless roving
rain-gös/goose	red-throated diver
ranselman	constable with authority to search for stolen or smuggled goods, apprehend thieves and keep order in local parish
rant (n)	wild party
redd (up)	tidy up, sort
reek	smoke
reestit mutton	salted, smoked-dried mutton
reffel	tangle
resting-chair	long wooden bench with back and arms
rig (n)	small field (run-rig system whereby a crofter might be allocated several small fields, not adjacent; and each year this

	was varied, for fairness)
rig (v)	to dress
ripe	to harvest
rivlins	homemade shoes of untanned hide, with hair outermost
roo	pluck the fleece off sheep
roog	heap, pile (eg when turning half-dry peats)
rowe	roll up; row a boat
rowers	rolls of clean, carded wool prepared for spinning
röf	roof
saat piltocks	saithe, salted and wind-dried and capable of storage
Santy Claas	Santa Claus
sark	shirt
sassermaet	minced pork, well spiced
scarf	cormorant
scattald	common hill land, with pasturing and peat-cutting rights for adjoining crofts
scomfished	choked by smoke
scöl	school
scrit	hurry
scunner	scoundrel (n); to be fed up with (v)
seggy	wild iris
shaest	chase
shew	sew
showe	chew
shö	she
shön	soon; shoes
sic, siccan	such
sillock	saithe (immature)
simmins	ropes made of straw, floss or heather
skeo	hut for drying salted fish, constructed to allow wind through
skirl	shrill laugh
skrew	large stack of corn (oats)
skyimp	ironic praise (n); to praise ironically (v)
sleekit	sly
slippit	lacking self-discipline; unchaste
smeeg	smirk (n) to smirk (v)
smoorikin	kiss
smoot	slink, move furtively
smore	smother, drown
snaa	snow
sneck	latch
snorie-ben	child's toy made from a piece of bone or wood which, when spun on a doubled string, then pulled, makes a snoring noise
sokkit	soaked
solemn	almost unbelievable; dreadful; strange
somewye	somehow
sood	should
sook	suck (v); drying quality (n)

sookit piltocks	saithe, salted overnight and wind-dried
sooth	on the UK mainland
spaek	speak
spaekalation	scandalous talking-point
sparl	anus of animal, cleaned and prepared for cooking
spilt	leprous
spörin	proposing marriage, often accompanied by the gift of a bottle of whisky for father of the bride
spree	jollification
sprickle	wriggle
staavs	barrel-staves
stank	deep ditch
stap	mix of cooked fish with fish livers, seasoned
steid	foundation of building; base of corn stack or peat stack
steyn	stone
stimna	stamina, strength
stook	to stack (v); stack (n) of a few sheaves
stoor	strong breeze; dust
stooshie	fracas
stot	young castrated ox
strae	straw
stramp	walk firmly
stravaigin	wandering aimlessly
strug	toil, labours
stumsed	bewildered, bemused
sweet milk	fresh milk
swör	swore
tae da fore	very well (health-wise)
taek	thatch
taen-til	having a bad reputation
taft	thwart in a boat
tagidder	together
tattie-hael	in good health (lit. 'potato-whole' – well-fed)
teddisome	tedious
tee	leg of smoke-dried lamb
tengs	tongs
tengs o fire	a lit peat held in tongs to light the way
tidder	other
ting	a young child, term of endearment
tipperin	tip-toeing
tirrick	arctic tern
tjaldur	oystercatcher
tocht	thought
toonmals	permanent grazing near croft-house
toons	arable fields
tow	thaw
towe(s)	rope; baited lines
tö	too
traa	to twist

traik	aimless walk
traivel	walk
trang	busy
trave	thrave ie 24 sheaves of oats
trenkie	narrow path or passage
treshel-tree	threshold
tristy	thirsty
trooker	disreputable person
trowe	through
trysht	difficulty, trouble
tumpit	thumped
tushker	peat-cutting spade
tusk	fish of the cod family
twartree	a few
tyoch	tough
uncans	news
varg	heavy, dirty work
veggel	wooden stake in byre wall to which a cow is tied
voar	spring planting time
voe	inlet of sea, generally narrow
waal	well
waand	fishing-rod
waanin	waning
waar	worse; also seaweed
wadder	weather
wan	one; reached (pt of verb)
warn	warrant
wast-owre	to the west
whaap	curlew
whiss	interrogate, question
white	stop
whitna	what a
win	reach
wint wi	accustomed to
wippit	wound round, bound
wiss	wish
wöshen	washed
wrastle	struggle
wrocht	worked
wylk	whelk
wysh	wash
yerd	area enclosed by stone wall, either (croft) arable, or graveyard
yield (yowe)	barren female (sheep)
Yöl	Christmas
yun	that
yundroo	there

Sources

Specific sources

Kirk Session minutes
National Records of Scotland – Ref CH2/380/3 (Walls & Sandness Kirk Session minutes, 1771–1857). These hand-written minutes provide much rich social detail of the era: the poverty, the moral strictures, the power of the kirk and landowners. In particular, sexual behaviour was strictly monitored and public rebuke meted out regularly. I had suspected that the appearance in their midst of a large number of impoverished, disappointed and scared emigrants, not to mention several sailors, would spark some discussion at the kirk session, and they did not disappoint. While initial concern was for the welfare of the emigrants, the focus soon turned to the moral sphere.

Title deed relating to the croft land associated with Happyhansel School, transferring ownership and burdens from the deceased Archibald Henry of Scord and Burrastow to his son Thomas Henry. It was registered in 1780. (The original agreement with Rev James Buchan had been with Archibald Henry.) This somewhat convoluted deed was transcribed some years ago by Iris Sandison and Drewy Georgeson, both of Waas. I am very grateful to them. In short, it ensured the schoolmaster had full use of the croft and was paid a small annual income.

Shetland Archives – letters and references to court proceedings
D56/2/14 notes by R Stuart Bruce, Some Old Shetland Wrecks: The '*Batchelor*'.
SC12/53/4/folio 107r (contract between James Inglis and James Hogg) dated 24 August 1773.
CH2/1071/34/6 Letter from Rev James Buchan to Presbytery of Zetland concerning Mary Johnsdaughter, alleged adulterer with Alexander Ross, Leith, sailor on the *Batchelor* – dated 18 November 1775.
GD144/11/57 Letter from Arthur Nicolson dated 15 November 1773.
D25/112 (typescript – unfinished – of lecture by Tom Henderson on the topic of the *Batchelor* (c 1978).
SC 12 /6/1779/8 Agatha Cumming defended herself against Robert Jeffrys in Voe, Walls, of whom no trace found. Title: Petition for return of writ concerning steelbow tack – 18 March 1779 – 6 items [Steelbow tack was an agricultural term used to describe a system whereby the tenant 'rented' livestock from the landowner and, at end of the tenancy, had to return to the owner livestock of similar value or pay for any deficiency].
SC 12 /6/1779/31 – Agatha Cumming raised a Summons as Pursuer against James Henry, tenant in Watsness – 22 November 1779.

Bayanne genealogical website has been invaluable:
www.bayanne.co.uk

The Scotland's People genealogical website:
www.scotlandspeople.gov.uk
It contains a record of the marriage between James Buchan and Agatha Cumming in Edinburgh.

Graham, J, *A Vehement Thirst after Knowledge*, The Shetland Times Ltd, Lerwick, 1998.

Leet, G, 'A Tacksman at Borlum, 1765', *Caithness Field Club Annual Bulletin*, 1997. (This includes a letter written by James Hogg while staying at Garderhouse, Sand, dated 29th March 1774, as printed in *The Scots Magazine*, July 1774, pp 345–6).

Newsome, AR, (ed) 'Records of emigrants from England and Scotland to North Carolina, 1774–1775', *North Carolina Historical Review*, Raleigh, North Carolina, 1989.

Newspapers and magazines (also useful for contextual information – there were no local Shetland newspapers at the time): *The Edinburgh Evening Courant*, 16 May 1774; *The Scots Magazine*, February 1774.

Other printed and manuscript sources

Bailyn, B, *Voyagers to the West*, Random House, New York, 1988.
Beach, K, 'From Caledonia to Carolina: The Highland Scots', *Tar Heel Junior Historian*, no. 45.2, North Carolina Museum of History Office of Archives and History, 2006.
Bowes, HR (ed), *Two Calves in the House: Being the Shetland Journal of the Reverend John Lewis 1823–1825*, Shetland Amenity Trust, Lerwick, 2005.
Finnie, M, *Shetland: An Illustrated Architectural Guide*, Mainstream Publications (Scotland) Ltd, Edinburgh, 1990.
Flett, JP & TM Flett, *Traditional Dancing in Scotland*, Routledge & Keegan Paul, Abingdon, 1964.
Hibbert, S, *A Description of the Shetland Islands*, Archibald, Constable & Co, Edinburgh, 1822.
Knox, SA, *The Making of the Shetland Landscape*, John Donald Publishers Ltd, Edinburgh, 1985.
Macdonald, NM, *Reconciling Performance: the drama of discipline in early modern Scotland, 1560–1610*, Thesis for PhD in Ecclesiastical History, University of Edinburgh, 2013.
Mill, Rev J, 'Diary of the Reverend John Mill, Minister of the Parishes of Dunrossness, Sandwick and Cunningsburg in Shetland, 1740–1803', *Scottish History Society Journal*, vol v, Edinburgh, 1889.
Nicolson, JR, *Traditional Life in Shetland*, The Shetland Times Ltd, Lerwick, 1978.
Schaw, Janet, *Journal of a Lady of Quality; Being the Narrative of a Journey from Scotland to the West Indies, North Carolina and Portugal in the Years 1774 to 1776*, EW Andrews and CM Andrews (eds), Yale University Press, Newhaven, 1921.
Smith, B, *Toons and Tenants*, The Shetland Times Ltd, Lerwick, 2000.
Smith, HD, *Shetland Life and Trade 1550–1914*, John Donald Publishers Ltd, Edinburgh, 1984.

For those interested in James Hogg more broadly, the University of North Carolina holds his extensive papers including details of his various legal battles. finding-aids.lib.unc.edu/00341

Images and Photographs

Church of Scotland records for parish of Walls and Sandness

Kirk Session minutes, 17th October 1773

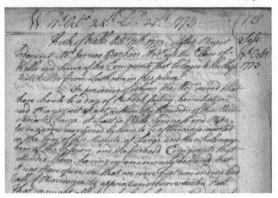

Two weeks following the arrival of the ship – the crew of the *Batchelor* (labelled 'Emigrants') meet with the Kirk Session and arrangements are made to raise money for them.

Kirk Session minutes, 11th April 1774

David Bain fails to appear to answer the adultery charge. His adultery is then attested by all the sailors on the *Batchelor*, including Alexander Ross, Bain's brother-in-law. The sailors who are witnesses are all named, including

Alexander Ross. The minute then goes on to record that some young women of the parish, including Mary Johnsdaughter and her two sisters, had gone aboard the *Batchelor*, with sailors, on the sabbath.

Kirk Session minutes, 4th Sept 1774

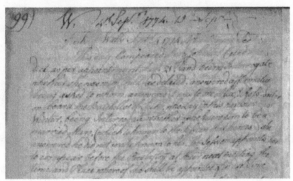

Mary admits the charge of fornication with Alexander Ross, but not – knowingly – the much more serious charge of adultery. Her case will be passed to Presbytery.

Letter from Rev James Buchan to Presbytery 10th November 1775 concerning Mary Johnsdaughter's case.

Waas in the late 19th century. The buildings (top right), dating from 1768, are Happyhansel: the smaller building was the school; the larger building was the schoolhouse, home of the teacher George Greig. The schoolhouse also accommodated boarders. Voe House, centre right (above the church), was the home of the Rev James Buchan. Bayhaa, home of John T Henry and his wife Margaret, is the large house in the centre of the photograph. (Photographer unknown.)

Happyhansel schoolhouse – the ruin (on the right) – as it was in the 1960s. The school, a smaller building (out of sight) was attached. It is still occupied, but as a house. (Photographer Alexander Pearson.)

Bayhaa – centre of photograph, home of John Thomas Henry of Foratwatt and his wife, Margaret (née Scott) – local heritor and owner of trading sloop. (Photographer HF Anderton, late 19th century, reproduced with permission of Shetland Museum and Archives.)

Voe House – home of Rev James Buchan. (Photographer unknown, c 1940s, printed with permission of Leanne Johnson.)

Burrastow – home of Thomas Henry, local heritor and merchant.
(Photographer unknown, late 19th century. Reproduced with permission of
Shetland Museum and Archives.)

Plaque unveiled in 2018, on the 250th anniversary of Happyhansel school.
(Photographer Barry Broadbent)

Acknowledgements

Many people have kindly offered their skills, knowledge and support, for which I am indebted:

My lifelong friend, Iris Sandison, read the manuscript meticulously as it unfolded. I knew I could always rely on her good judgement, particularly in relation to dialect phrasing. Other friends of mine, Diana Hendry and Ruth Jonathan, read it as a semi-complete manuscript and offered both constructive criticism and, that vital ingredient, encouragement. I was heartened by the fact that, although both were born and brought up in England, they did not find the dialect dialogue to be a barrier.

I consulted other friends of mine, Jack Goodlad and Laughton Johnston, particularly on matters maritime, my *terra incognita*. This was most helpful. Gratitude is also extended to other writer friends, Jenni Daiches and Mandy Haggith for reading the novel and for their generous comments. Jenni, though she was unaware, played a part in my fascination with the story of the *Batchelor of Leith*. I first came across a reference to its storm-stay in Waas Voe in her book *Scots in the USA*, Luath Press, 2006.

I have had my many requests met with interest as well as with professional skill by archivists and historians, in particular at the Shetland Archives and the National Records of Scotland (NRS). Permission from NRS and the Church of Scotland to use images from Walls & Sandness Kirk Session Minutes 1771–1857 (Catalogue Reference CH2/380/3) is gratefully acknowledged.

Professor Stewart J Brown and Dr Nikki Macdonald of the University of Edinburgh, School of Divinity, were more than helpful in filling in gaps in my knowledge of ecclesiastical history, in particular, 18th century Church of Scotland discipline.

The book is much enhanced by the maps and for that I thank Robert Wishart for his skill and flair. I have to thank Leanne Johnson for permission to use her photo of Voe House and Barry Broadbent for his photograph of the anniversary plaque in memory of the Rev. James Buchan. The photographs of Bayhaa and Burrastow are with kind permission of Shetland Museum and Archives.

I am particularly grateful to Gavin MacDougall of Luath Press Ltd, for his continuing support of poetry and prose written partly in Shetlandic. When many publishers concentrate on work which is easier to market, he has shown commitment to minority voices within Scotland. His staff too have been most helpful and efficient. Rachael Murray has been a meticulous editor. Finally, perhaps I have to thank 'lockdown' 2020 for giving me, after seven years of dithering, the motivation and time to write this story.

Luath Press Limited

committed to publishing well written books worth reading

LUATH PRESS takes its name from Robert Burns, whose little collie Luath (*Gael.*, swift or nimble) tripped up Jean Armour at a wedding and gave him the chance to speak to the woman who was to be his wife and the abiding love of his life. Burns called one of the 'Twa Dogs' Luath after Cuchullin's hunting dog in Ossian's *Fingal*. Luath Press was established in 1981 in the heart of Burns country, and is now based a few steps up the road from Burns' first lodgings on Edinburgh's Royal Mile. Luath offers you distinctive writing with a hint of unexpected pleasures.

Most bookshops in the UK, the US, Canada, Australia, New Zealand and parts of Europe, either carry our books in stock or can order them for you. To order direct from us, please send a £sterling cheque, postal order, international money order or your credit card details (number, address of cardholder and expiry date) to us at the address below. Please add post and packing as follows: UK – £1.00 per delivery address; overseas surface mail – £2.50 per delivery address; overseas airmail – £3.50 for the first book to each delivery address, plus £1.00 for each additional book by airmail to the same address. If your order is a gift, we will happily enclose your card or message at no extra charge.

Luath Press Limited
543/2 Castlehill
The Royal Mile
Edinburgh EH1 2ND
Scotland
Telephone: +44 (0)131 225 4326 (24 hours)
Email: sales@luath.co.uk
Website: www.luath.co.uk